THE EYRIE

THE BAERSLADEN

VIL-ROSSENGARD

VIL-KEVI

THE WOLLIN

THE MIRIEN

RUMA

ZARADONA

SCARLIGHT

CASTLES OF THE EYRIE BOOK ONE

EVIE MARCEAU

THE BEGINNING...A BLACK FAWN...RUNAWAY GIRL...WOLVES IN A SAINT'S GLEN...SCARS... TEN YEARS LATER

TEN YEARS AGO

"A black fawn was seen in the forest."
"Black? Are you certain?"
"Black as night."

Eight-year-old Bryn sat beneath the banquet hall's giant oak table, hidden by a velvet tablecloth, eavesdropping on two of her father's guards. Her hands were sticky from the half-devoured honey cake in her lap. Mam Delice had slipped her the treat along with the last of the winter strawberries after the feast, the only person in Castle Mir who recalled—or cared—that it was the youngest princess's birthday.

"The sighting of a black fawn is one of the war omens," the first man said darkly.

The second, her father's captain of the guard, replied, "It's been spotted three times. Twice by my men and once by a journeyman from the south of Eyrie. A team of my huntsmen is preparing to set out at first light. They'll slay it and throw the carcass in the ravine. No one will know."

"And the journeyman?"

"Who will he tell? The wastrels at the tavern? No one will take it as more than a drunkard's rumors."

"It's a risk to let this man live."

"It's a greater risk to order the murder of a man during the Low Sun Gathering. You saw the families who arrived this afternoon. The Hytooths. The Surins. The Baer king and his three half-wild sons—they're hungry for a fight, even at their young ages. If murder were discovered, it would break whatever tentative peace there is."

Bryn frowned. The honey cake sat heavy in her stomach. *The poor fawn. I must try to scare it away before they kill it.* She lifted the tablecloth an inch with the tip of her spoon and crawled out, only to immediately collide with a pair of shoes she recognized all too well.

"Bryn!" Her mother frowned downward with her hands resting on her hips. Her cheeks were dusted with rust like a dawnsong angel, and her golden hair was woven into its crown braid. Mama's lips pressed together. "Up."

Bryn clamored to her feet.

"Why must you crawl on the floor like a dog, my child? And during the Gathering! The other royal families are going to think I raise heathens like those Baer princes."

Curious about this wild, disreputable family she kept hearing about, Bryn scanned the crowd until she found a family dressed in bearskin cloaks. A great grisly man wearing a carved oak crown, sullen and serious, and three boys a few years older than Bryn.

The Baer king and his sons.

In their heavy fur cloaks, Bryn thought of them more as *Bears*.

Mama cupped Bryn's chin. "Go on. Upstairs to change your dirty clothes and wash the honey from your hands. Tell Nan you're excused from the festivities."

Bryn didn't need to be told twice. She wanted nothing more than to escape the party, and besides, there was the black fawn to rescue. She snuck away in the opposite direction, throwing a look over her shoulder. Her brother, Mars, wouldn't tattle on her, but her sister, Elysander, might. She spotted Elysander perched by the roaring hearth with her ladies-in-waiting: hands clasped, blonde hair perfectly in place, eyes lowered demurely.

Bryn darted behind a maid carrying an empty tray down the stairs to the kitchen, where she traded her party shoes for a pair of muck boots, grabbed a lantern, and escaped the castle.

It was black out, a moonless summer night. She hesitated, looking out over the dark forest. Even at eight years old, she knew better than to go into the woods at night. But if she ever had a chance of rescuing the black fawn, it was now.

Her lantern shone over a path through the trees to a Saint's glen with a water shrine. It looked different at night. The water was so black that she couldn't see the fish in the shallows.

The grass crunched a few feet away, and she sucked in a breath.

Footsteps.

The forest suddenly went quiet. Bryn could hear her heart beating. An owl hooted, and she got spooked. She grabbed the lantern, started to run back to the castle. Then, she stopped. The path ahead was marked with wet red spots and downy fuzz.

Blood and fur that was black as night.

She'd found the fawn, but so had something else. A branch snapped behind her. A growl came from the shadows. All she saw of the first wolf were two yellow eyes. The second wolf was on her before she could scream.

Their claws found her ribs, tearing through her dress, slicing her flesh like knives. Then, out of nowhere, someone else was in the glen. Someone who didn't scream as the wolves turned on him, too, who bore their sharp claws with nothing but grunts as he continued to fight until wolf blood mixed with her own.

A boy in a bearskin cloak.

One of the Baer princes—the youngest. He must have seen her lantern's light at the edge of the forest.

A Bear.

Her Bear.

* * *

TEN YEARS LATER

BRYN STOOD HALF-NAKED in the royal dressmaker's chambers, surrounded by seamstresses, being squeezed and tucked into a gown for the night's ball. But the worst of the process was listening to yet another lecture from her mother, the queen, as she tightened the bodice of Bryn's gown.

"At the feast, Baron Marmose will ask you to dance. Accept, but don't appear too eager." Her mother caught her finger on a pin and gasped. She dropped the pin, and the dress fabric fell away from Bryn's torso. Before Bryn could grab it, her rib cage was bare. One of the maids made a small, surprised sound to see the scars.

Turning red, Bryn quickly scrambled to cover herself. Few people knew about the jagged, ugly lines that ran from her left rib cage and curved around her waist to the base of her spine: only the dressmaker, the physician, her brother and sister, and her parents.

"Cover yourself," her mother hissed. "Quickly."

Bryn hurried to do so. It wouldn't do if rumors spread that a Mir princess was disfigured. Especially not tonight. Her mother had arranged for a Ruma baron to be in attendance for the ten days of the Low Sun Gathering. He was thirty years of age to Bryn's eighteen, but her mother promised he had a pleasant face and was an excellent huntsman—not that Bryn had any choice about the matter.

Mama clapped her hands. "That's enough fitting. You can finish on your own, can't you, Mam Nelle?"

"Of course, my lady," the dressmaker said, and directed the assistants to leave with a flick of her hand.

Once they were gone, Bryn bit the inside of her lip and faced her mother. "What if the baron doesn't ask me to dance?"

Queen Helena frowned down at Bryn's neckline and then whispered something to the dressmaker, who lowered the neckline three inches. Her mother gave a wry smile. "He will *now.*"

The entire castle was busy preparing for the feast of First Night, so once Bryn was free, she climbed the long stairs to the castle's watch room. It wasn't much to speak of—an empty stone chamber with open windows that offered little protection from the wind—but she dragged over a wooden stool and flopped down, waiting for guests to arrive. It wasn't long before the first carriages came. She watched as the Mirien's oldest families arrived one by one. There were a few girls her same age, dressed too lightly for the cold—it wasn't only Bryn who was supposed to catch a husband tonight. Eventually, a carriage pulled up, drawn by four black horses with coarse manes. The driver wore a bearskin cloak and a carved oak crown.

Her mouth fell open. *The Baer king! And he is driving his own carriage!*

Her heart began to pound in loud thumping beats. It had

5

been ten years since anyone from the Baersladen had stepped foot in the Mirien, and for good reason. Her hand went to the scars on her ribs, hidden beneath her dress.

The Baer royal family climbed out one by one. The king, then his white-haired sister, Mage Marna, who was rumored to be a witch.

Then the sons.

Bryn had learned about them in her studies. Trei was the eldest and the future Baersladen king, just as Mars would one day rule the Mirien. He was the fairest of the brothers, but that wasn't saying much. Their hair was black as ink, and his was chestnut brown, cut to fall just above his brow.

Next came the middle son, Valenden, who was taller than his brother but held none of Trei's regal bearing. His hair was pulled into a knot at the base of his skull, though strands had come loose, and he brushed it back with a practiced flick that implied disarray wasn't an unfamiliar concept to his dark locks.

Then the third brother stepped out of the carriage, and she forgot about the others.

It was *him*.

She sucked in a breath. Suddenly it was ten years ago, and she was waking up in the great hall covered in blood. She'd just been attacked by wolves. Her mother and siblings huddled around her, but her father and the "Bear" King were by the fireplace, hurling accusations at each other in two different tongues, with Mage Marna using the magic from the hexmarks carved into her forearms to translate. The youngest Baer prince, the one who had saved her, sat by the fire. His face was destroyed—deep gashes ran over his brow and temple: scars he'd carry for the rest of his life.

"We won't let them take you, mouse," her brother had insisted.

Bryn had blinked in confusion. *"The wolves?"*

"No, the Baers, of course. The Baersladen has different laws from us. In the Outlands, if you save someone's life, that person belongs to you. That's what their king is arguing. Young Prince Rangar saw you leave the castle and followed your lantern into the forest. He killed the wolves and brought you back here. Now his father claims you belong to them. A life saved is a soul owned."

Bryn had started crying. "I don't want to go to the Bear Lands!"

"The Bear...? Ah. No, you won't go. You won't ever see that prince again, I swear it. Nor any of them."

Now, in the castle tower, Bryn touched her own scars beneath her dress with a shaking hand. Her mother's promise ten years ago hadn't meant anything. Bryn was staring at "that prince" right now.

2

THE LOW SUN GATHERING...RANGAR
BARENDUR...A LOT OF WINE...A BALCONY AT
NIGHT...BEARSKIN CLOAKS

*B*ryn watched as, in the courtyard below, Rangar Barendur adjusted his bearskin cloak before entering the castle.

He was a head shorter than his brothers, but part of that was how he held himself: low, guarded, head lowered. His dark hair was shoulder-length, as wild as his aunt's, not pulled back like Valenden's. He rubbed his hands together and breathed into them for warmth. Beside him, Valenden reached into his cloak, took out a flask, and took a deep drink of something that Bryn guessed—by Trei's disapproving slap on his shoulder— was not water.

The Bear King said something to his sons, and Rangar turned toward the light of the castle.

Bryn swallowed a gasp. Even from a distance, she could make out the four scars marring his face. In the ten years since he had saved her life, she'd wondered about him often: Was he shunned because of the scars? After all, he couldn't hide them as she could. Did he think about her? Did he fear wolves to this day, as she did? Did he possibly still believe that ridiculous old rule that she belonged to him because he saved her life? She'd lain awake in bed countless nights wondering if the three Baer brothers were going to come to steal her away in the night and take her back to their distant seaside kingdom. The idea had terrified her and thrilled her in equal measure.

But in her mind, Rangar had still been that young boy just a few years older than her. Now, he was a man. She wasn't prepared to see him fully grown. If he would only stand up straight and raise his chin, he'd look just as formidable as his brothers. If it weren't for the scars, he'd be devastatingly handsome. A chiseled jaw, a wide, straight nose, and sensuous lips that had been almost spared the scars.

She drew back from the window sharply, filled with worry. Was this it? Had they come to take her according to their decade-old claim that a life saved was a soul owned? Before she knew it, she was pacing. After the incident when Rangar had saved her life and his father had tried to claim her as their own, Bryn had believed that her family banned them from setting foot in the Mirien. They'd never come to a Low Sun Gathering before. By law, they were part of the Eyrie alliance, but in name only.

Her anxious pacing took her right back to the window, searching the front lawn for a glimpse of Rangar again. The family members were approaching the castle gates. For a moment, Bryn felt certain that they would be turned away. Maybe even threatened at arrow point. But to her shock, after a brief few words she couldn't make out, the guards at the castle gate opened the doors for them.

She stared down in utter shock. *The Baers are in Castle Mir!*

Was it possible that they'd been invited? She couldn't imagine that was so. Still, why hadn't anyone warned her they were coming?

She pressed her back against the tower wall, telling herself to breathe. A bell chimed to signal the start of the candle lighting for First Night. Lords and ladies, how had it gotten so late? Dazed, she stumbled down the winding stairs into the castle, where a frantic maid found her and took her to where the royal dressmaker was pacing anxiously.

"Ah!" Mam Nelle cried. "Bryn, where have you been? Your mother will be looking for you! We must get you dressed. Hurry, the bell for first candle has already rung…"

"I heard it. I'm sorry." The arrival of the Baer royal family still consumed Bryn's mind, her every thought spinning.

Mam Nelle helped her into the many-buttoned rose gown as maids tamed her hair into a crown braid and dusted rust on her cheeks and down the length of her nose. Then they herded her out and toward the ballroom. She nearly tripped as she struggled to get her feet in her dancing shoes. The candlelight and music of the party radiated throughout the castle. She stumbled into the ballroom, heart pounding as fast as a bird's. She felt herself sweating despite the cold. Her eyes went to every corner, looking for Rangar and his brothers—

"Ah, mouse, there you are. Isn't that the baron you're supposed to be romancing?" Mars appeared at her side, looking dashing as always in his gold-trimmed tunic, as he motioned toward someone in the crowd.

In another few years, Mars would sit on the throne once Father retired from his reign. All his childhood, Mars had been groomed in the ways of politics and law. If he wasn't up late studying with tutors, he was away with Father inspecting crops and managing the Mirien's army. But he'd still found time to tease his youngest sister, chase her around the castle and play hide-and-seek with her and Elysander in the miles of hidden passages.

Bryn grabbed his arm hard. "Mars," she gasped. "The Bears...I mean, the Baers are here!"

His smile faltered. He nodded, more serious now. "I know. It caused a stir when they arrived. We didn't expect them. In ten years, they've never accepted an invitation to a Gathering."

"Invitation? I thought they were forbidden from coming!"

He explained, "They're one of the royal families of the Eyrie, even if they are savages. They can't be banned. They had an agreement with Father...but don't worry, mouse. It was so long ago. You and that Rangar boy were both so young—Father sorted it out back then. I'm sure no one remembers what happened."

Bryn started to contradict him. *She* remembered. And she would wager that Rangar, face permanently marred, also remembered. Her eyes hunted through the crowd for the fur-clad warriors. She must look obsessed, maybe even a little mad, but so be it. There was something about them that captivated her. There were stories that the Baer people slept in the straw with their horses and flea-ridden dogs, that they fed their children raw venison to toughen their guts, that they didn't learn to speak Mir on purpose. Too arrogant to learn another language, especially when their mage could translate with her hexmarks, those mysterious emblems of magic that both frightened and intrigued Bryn. Magic was forbidden in the Mirien. *Magic is the old way. Backward.* The Mirien was all about science, and the Mir people rarely spoke of what magic still existed in the Outlands, those distant kingdoms on the edge of the Eyrie where soil met the sea.

But Mage Marna was *here*. A real witch. Practicing actual magic to translate languages. And no one was stopping them! With a gasp, Bryn found the Baer royal family amid the crowd at last. The older two brothers stood by the ballroom's fireplace. They, too, had grown from boys to men. Trei, the eldest and the future king of the Baersladen, was everything you'd expect from an heir: the body of a warrior but the countenance of a natural leader. He held himself much like Mars did: straight spine, an air of confidence. Next to Trei, Valenden sneered at Mam Delice's tarts, swaying like he was already drunk.

But where was her prince? She caught herself. Why had she thought of Rangar as *her* prince?

Mars nudged her. "That's your baron, isn't it?"

Lords and ladies, she'd completely forgotten about Baron Marmose from Ruma. In a daze, Bryn turned toward the man who might be her future husband, identifying him in the crowd from the burgundy crest on his chest. He had warm brown skin, striking blue eyes, and a good head of curly hair, though it was graying at the temples.

She grabbed the glass of wine from his hand and downed it in a few long sips. Their mother had warned her to stay away from wine, to keep her wits about her. But she reached for another glass.

Mars laughed at the look on her face. "Careful," he teased.

She finished off the second glass with a gasp. "I need some air." She stumbled for the door to the courtyard. When she'd been a little girl, she used to sneak off and hide among the tombs in the courtyard's remembrance garden, inventing ghostly playmates. She pushed open the glass door and dashed out, gripping the stone railing of the balcony that overlooked the garden. Cold air burned against her cheeks. She closed her eyes and drew in crisp breaths.

Suddenly, a voice came out of the shadows. "Tonight, it is cold."

Her eyes shot open. *I'm not alone.*

The voice was male and deep, the words spoken inexpertly

in Mir in an accent she couldn't place. The flames of the balcony lamps caught on a face that any woman inside would have taken a long, appreciative look at—if not for the four hideous scars carved across it. Scars Rangar Barendur had gotten for the unforgivable sin of saving her life.

3

A FORBIDDEN TOUCH...MEMORY OF
WOLVES...STUBBORN AS AN OX...SPARKS AND
SMOKE...PROTECTIVE BIG BROTHER

*B*ryn touched the scars across her ribcage before she realized what she was doing. She stepped backward, but the balcony edge was at her back. Her eyes darted through the glass window to the feast. If she screamed, someone would come.

Rangar was holding an unlit *statua* pipe. He traced a hex shape in the air and whispered a spell, and the herb sparked and caught fire. Bryn tried not to gawk at the brazen use of magic. He took a long inhale, blew smoke into the air, and then came forward slowly, shrugging out of his black fur cloak. "Take my coat. For you to be warm."

She stared at him with a mix of fascination and terror. It had been ten years since he'd saved her life. She felt that she was back there in the forest, in a pool of blood that was half-animal and half-human, with the wolves tearing at her, and him tearing at the wolves.

She whispered, "It's you."

He didn't answer. He only held out the bearskin cloak. She was suddenly very aware that they were alone on a balcony. Should she scream for Mars? Rangar could do anything to her here. For years, she'd had dreams that the "Bears" had come and stolen her away in the night. Half of the dreams had been nightmares. The other half…

"It is cold," Rangar said again. He spoke strangely, and something about this shook her out of her stupor.

"You speak Mir," she realized.

He nodded.

She blinked. "No Baer people speak Mir. Father says you're stubborn as oxen. That you don't learn it out of spite."

Something wavered in his eyes. "*I* learned." He came toward her and, before she knew how to react, draped his cloak around her shoulders. It smelled like the forest and like the castle cellars in midwinter, dark and deep. It was so heavy on her shoulders that she stumbled in her high shoes.

"No. This is…no." She pressed a hand to her forehead. She was quite sure she was supposed to be running away to Mars or her father. Lords and ladies, wasn't there a baron from Ruma she was supposed to be seducing? And yet, she stood above the dead in the remembrance garden with the prince who had saved her from being buried along with them.

She shrugged out of the cloak as she glanced toward the door. "I should go back inside."

Rangar took a step to his left, blocking her path. "Wait." He was close enough that his voice whispered along her neck. She closed her eyes. Squeezed her hands into fists to remind herself this was real. "Do you fear that I will throw you over my shoulder? Steal you away?"

Her eyes snapped open. No one in the Mirien spoke so plainly. Then his dark eyes sparked, and she realized he was mocking her. She took a tight step to her left. "Move aside, please."

He did, but only a hair. "You are frightened of me."

She breathed hard, her cheeks warming. "I'm not." When he only smirked, she insisted, "I'm not! I owe you my gratitude."

He raised an eyebrow, not expecting this.

She suddenly regretted her words but stammered nevertheless, "I never had a chance to thank you all those years ago. For what you did. My father said that I should never thank you because your people have some tradition, some notion that I...that I belonged to you. That I was yours." She forced a laugh, but any laughter was gone from his own eyes now.

"You *are* mine," he said.

She felt a creep of panic spread up her bare arms. She could scream. Mars would come running. He'd run Rangar through with his sword. And yet this Baer prince hadn't done anything but give her his cloak—that was hardly a crime. She looked at his thin woven shirt and realized he must be freezing, though the cold didn't seem to bother him.

"Don't say that," she ordered sharply.

"My people have a belief. If you save a life, that life is yours."

"That's called *slavery*."

"No. It is not the same." He seemed to search for the word. "It is more like...a ward. A responsibility. Ten years ago, you became my responsibility." The lights from the great hall shone on his face. His scars ran from forehead to chin. He was lucky not to have lost an eye. Then, on impulse, she asked, "Is that why you learned Mir? Because of me?"

The smirk returned to his face. He stepped forward faster than she could react, and then his hand slipped beneath his cloak over her shoulders, his palm pressed to her left side. His fingers knew exactly where her scars were.

"Do you not feel it?" he whispered.

She could smell him, could practically taste him. Her head was light from the wine and the late night and his touch. Lord, if her mother saw her now... She forced herself to meet his eyes. "I have no idea what you mean."

"You and I are connected. Our lands do not have the same laws, but we have the same souls. You live today because I followed you ten years ago. Because I kept you safe when your father and brother could not. And so your life is mine. We are supposed to be together. Do you not feel it?"

His fingers slid to the base of her spine, where the scars ended.

All she could smell was the musk of his cloak, the warmth of it—of him—and she thought she must look like a savage dressed in his fur cloak. What would Mars think if he saw them? Rangar's breath carried notes of pipe smoke. She balled and unballed her hands. Her palms had developed a sudden urge to touch his face. Those scars that she might as well have clawed into his flesh with her own fingernails. A face that would be as devastatingly handsome as his older brothers if it wasn't for her. She'd cost him his beauty. Nearly cost him his life. And she'd never given him a thing in return.

She could feel the tips of his fingers pressing through her dress, straight to the scars beneath, practically to the bone. She'd never been this close to a man before—but no, that was wrong. These very same hands had been on her already, ten years ago when he'd carried her home from the Saints Forest.

But neither of them were children anymore.

A crazy impulse filled her, and before she realized what she was doing, she lifted her hand to his face, but she didn't touch him. Not yet. The pads of her fingers hovered over each scar. She slowly curled her nails, imagining the wolf that did this to him.

He closed his eyes. "Touch me," he ordered.

Bryn's hand was shaking. She felt like she was walking in a dream. That the balcony overlooking the tombs was in some other world, far from her brother and father and mother on the other side of the glass door. One by one, she placed her fingers on his scars. Traced her fingers down his forehead and over his eyes, against the sharp edges of his cheekbones, and down to his jawline. His hand tightened on her hip. He closed his eyes and leaned into her hand. He let out a breath like a soft growl.

She whispered in understanding, "No one has ever wanted to touch my scars, either." She brushed her thumb over a mass of scar tissue on his cheek. "Do you promise you haven't come to steal me away?"

He turned his head so that his lips brushed her palm. He didn't open his eyes. "Do you want me to?"

Her childhood dreams rushed back to her. For a fleeting moment, she thought of what it would mean. The cold castle of Barendur Hold, villagers sleeping on the floor, bodies thrown together for warmth, everything reeking of woodsmoke, a barren land, windswept by the sea, a land just as scarred as he was, tainted through and through with magic.

The balcony door flung open.

Bryn flinched, letting her hand fall. Rangar's eyes snapped open. Mars was there, his eyes flashing between them, his glare shooting arrows at the prince. He snatched Bryn's hand and pulled her back into the warm safety of First Night.

Into Castle Mir. Where she belonged.

4

THE INSUFFERABLE SUITOR...COOKIES...A RIDE THROUGH SAINTS FOREST...THE PRIDE OF THE EYRIE

"*I*t looks like rain," Bryn observed, peering out her bedroom window at the overcast sky. "Does that mean we can cancel the tour?" It was nearly midday, and not a moment had passed that she hadn't thought about last night: Rangar on the balcony, his hand slipped under her cloak. Mars had given her an earful about staying away from the Baer princes—using more black words than she'd ever heard—but at least he hadn't told their mother.

Elysander joined Bryn at the window and peered upward. "A few clouds don't make a storm. You'd best accept that you're not getting out of this. Mama's been planning it for months. There, look. The baron's carriage is pulling up now. That's his, with the burgundy banners, isn't it?"

Bryn groaned. "Yes."

Elysander went to the mirror to make sure her hair was tucked beneath her hat and then turned around and frowned at Bryn's rumpled clothes. She picked up Bryn's hat from the dresser and smooshed it down over her sister's hair. "Come on. We can't keep him waiting."

"The last thing I want to do is take a tour of the Mirien with a man twice my age," Bryn lamented.

Elysander rolled her eyes. "Really, Bryn, you're impossible. Do you think *I* want to be chaperoning my baby sister and her suitor all day? I'm supposed to sing at Second Night, and I can't practice with the song master because I'll be traipsing around the countryside all day making sure Baron Marmose doesn't stick anything where it doesn't belong. Yet."

Bryn gasped, then once the shock of her sister's scandalous words faded, she shook her head. "You're lucky that you've been betrothed since birth. You don't have to perform like a well-trained pony." Elysander had been betrothed to a duke from Dresel practically since birth, so she'd never had to undergo the torture of courtship.

"No one would mistake you for being well trained, Bryn, even if you were a pony."

The castle hallways were quiet, except for the maids cleaning up from First Night. On the second day of the Low Sun Gathering, it was tradition for young and old—especially those seeking betrothals—to pile into carriages with a tray of orange-glazed biscuits and tour Saints Forest and the Mirien countryside.

Baron Marmose was waiting beside his open-top carriage, holding the requisite tray of biscuits. When he saw the sisters, he gave a polite bow. To his credit, his gaze remained fixed on Bryn instead of at the far more elegant Elysander. He offered Bryn a kind smile. His teeth were uneven, but she'd seen much worse.

"Lady Bryn. Lady Elysander. You look like summer visions," he said.

Don't roll your eyes, Bryn told herself.

Elysander beamed at the baron. "We can't thank you

enough for your offer to take us out. On such a beautiful day, we'd hate to be stuck in the castle."

"Beautiful?" Bryn squinted up at the gray sky. Elysander nudged her in the ribs.

Baron Marmose helped them into the carriage. Bryn sat next to Elysander, the tray of biscuits balanced on her knees, but Elysander switched to the opposite-facing seat so that the baron would be able to sit next to Bryn. Bryn narrowed her eyes at her sister, who smiled back sweetly.

The driver signaled to the horses, and the carriage lurched forward. Bryn clutched the biscuits and looked over her shoulder at the castle's dark windows and couldn't help but wonder about their guests from the north.

Where are the Baer princes staying?

Which rooms?

Is Rangar looking out his window now, watching? What does he think to see me with another royal suitor?

The driver led them down the stone-paved drive to the stables, the gardens, and through the Saints' glens, where Elysander gave a detailed history of the Saints' numerous good deeds. "Saints Forest is protected by eighteen glens, in all," Elysander explained as the carriage rolled onto the dirt path through the forest, bumping over roots. Bryn clasped the biscuits to keep them from falling off her lap. "It is our gift to the commonfolk of the Mirien. A place for them to find respite."

"Forest" was a loose term, given that a fleet of gardeners manicured every branch. Besides, Bryn had *never* seen any commonfolk in Saints Forest. If the commonfolk sought respite from difficult lives, they seemed to prefer the taverns— but she kept that observation to herself.

"It's so important to take respite," the baron said. "When I take a bride, I shall build gardens for her to ruminate in and endless libraries for her studies."

Bryn was busying herself by picking at the orange glaze on a biscuit. She stuck her finger in her mouth when she realized the baron was looking at her expectantly. She pulled her finger out and wiped it on her skirt guiltily. "That sounds, ah, lovely."

At last, the carriage left the forest and emerged back onto the road. Bryn sighed with relief. The village of Tureen was just ahead. That would provide a distraction, at the least.

Elysander nudged Bryn's foot. "Sister, why don't you tell Baron Marmose about the Mirien's yields?"

Bryn shot daggers at her sister. "Oh. Right. The yields. The yields…um…"

Elysander groaned, closed her eyes briefly, and when she opened them, smiled sweetly. She was the daughter who had been trained in decorum, not Bryn. "Tureen grows most of the Mirien's summer grain and corn," Elysander explained. "Later in the year, they produce winter gourds. Our soil in the Mirien is the best in the Eyrie, though I'm sure I don't have to tell you that, Baron. We send produce to the Outlands during the harsh months. Nothing grows in the Outlands in winter, as you know."

Bryn sat up, toying with her top button. "Come to think of it," she mused, "what do you think they eat in the Outlands in winter? Besides our gourds, I mean. They must hunt and fish for a good portion of their diet. But in the Baersladen, for example, do you think they—"

Elysander kicked her harder. Bryn shut her mouth. The baron was looking at her oddly. "Do you have a particular interest in the Baersladen, Miss Bryn?"

"Um," she said haltingly. "No. Of course not. I don't know what made me think of the Baersladen."

The baron patted her knee. "I can tell you are always thinking of others. A generous spirit."

Bryn fought to keep a straight face. Well, she hadn't exactly been wondering after Rangar's diet. More like *everything* about his land. She sat back in the carriage, letting her mind wander. All she really knew about the Outlands was from the bedtime stories Nan told her. In stories, the Outlands were the place of creatures that crawled out of the deepest sea. Of mages who could summon rain with wicked dances. Of warriors who cut each other to pieces for sport. What did they eat in winter? Raw venison? Still-squirming salmon? Could their mages summon sweet cocoa?

"We have the finest army in the Eyrie," Elysander was explaining when Bryn tuned back in, pointing to the soldiers posted at every corner of the market square of Tureen. "Our father, the king, ensures that our people are protected."

"Mirien is indeed a jewel," the baron said, though something had shifted in his tone. His eyes met Bryn's, but she wasn't sure what she saw there. A flash of danger? "The pride of the Eyrie."

By the time the carriage pulled back to the castle courtyard, rain had come. Despite Baron Marmose's attempts to shelter Bryn with his cloak, she was soaked through and all too happy to blame the weather for why she had to bid him an early farewell and flee upstairs to her room. But a second before she escaped, Elysander cornered her in the foyer and dragged her through a faux painting into one of the castle's many hidden passages the servants used to move throughout the building without being seen. In the faint light, Elysander prodded her. "What are you, obsessed with the Baer royal family? You couldn't stop talking about those wild princes in front of your suitor!"

Warmth spread to Bryn's cheeks. "Was it that obvious?"

Since Elysander was already betrothed, she had never questioned her own romantic future. She didn't know how awful it was to have to be paraded around like a prize sow.

Elysander sighed, giving her sister some sympathy. "Mars told me that you spoke privately to Rangar Barendur last night. You could get in serious trouble if you're caught speaking to him again." Despite her warning, curiosity danced in her sister's eyes. "What did you two speak of?"

Bryn thought of the fact that Rangar had learned Mir the old-fashioned way, not taking the quick route of hexmarks and spells. *Just for me.* So that he could steal a few moments alone with her and remind her of their connection. She could still feel the weight of his hand pressed against her waist, and it left her breathless. Bryn swallowed. "We spoke of nothing. It was an accident. I needed air, and I didn't know he was out there."

Elysander folded her arms tightly, giving her sister a doubting look. Before she disappeared back through the faux painting, she warned Bryn, "Don't go thinking too hard about Rangar Barendur, Bryn. Or any of the Baer brothers. You'd better keep your sights on someone like Baron Marmose. Someone civilized, whom mother and father will approve of. *Those* brothers are nothing but trouble."

5

THE ALLURE OF MAGIC...MEMORIES OF WOLVES...AN UNLIT MATCH...KINGDOMS AT ODDS

*O*nce Elysander had left her alone in the hidden passage, Bryn continued up the secret narrow stairs between the walls until she reached the floor that contained their bedrooms. She came out of the passages behind a tapestry, made her way to her bedroom, slammed the door, and groaned.

Baron Marmose wasn't an ogre. Nor was he a slug. From what her mother had told her, he had a fine estate in the kingdom of Ruma, a day's ride south of the Mirien. His land was fertile, and he raised prize-winning miniature dogs. She wouldn't mind a home filled with dogs. She liked dogs, except for big ones.

Big dogs reminded her of wolves. And wolves reminded her of Rangar.

She pressed a hand against her rib cage. She found she couldn't rouse much enthusiasm for the baron, try as she might. There were eight more days of the Low Sun Gathering. By the tenth day, he might propose. By this time the following year, she might be by his side, a ring on her finger, living in an estate full of yapping little dogs. If she squinted, she could picture herself there. But she had to squint *very* hard.

She went to her bedroom mirror, combing her fingers through her damp hair. Then, hesitantly, she pulled the sash of her robe and opened it to look at the scars. She traced a hand over the jagged lines one at a time. Would Baron Marmose care about the scars? He didn't seem the type to show disappointment, even if he felt it. A sycophant. She got the impression that Elysander could have told him that their father murdered kittens and he would smile and say there were too many cats; really, it was a public service.

She closed her robe, pulling the sash tight. Again, she thought of how she had the fortune of being able to hide her scars. Rangar couldn't hide his. Every day of his life, he had to face the world with them. What did that feel like? To be so exposed?

She flopped backward on the bed. Nan used to tell her bedtime stories, and her favorite was about an enchanted boy and girl who lived in the Outlands. Every winter, the girl turned into an eagle, and the boy turned into an otter. They were in love, but they only had three months of summer together on land.

Can magic really turn a person into an animal? Bryn had asked Nan.

No, child, it's just a fiction. Same as magic.

But magic *wasn't* fiction. Bryn had seen the Baer mage, Rangar's aunt, using her hexmarks to translate Baer words into Mir. And Rangar had made a spark appear to light his *statua* pipe. Elysander would have rolled her eyes at this and said she could summon fire just as easily—with a match. Magic was what ancient cultures worshiped centuries ago when everyone went without shoes and ate raw meat and barely understood how a book worked. Even now, most of the Outlanders were illiterate. She'd always been taught that even though magic could do small tricks—coax a flame, ease a headache—science was more powerful.

Magic was the old way. The dying way.

Bryn picked up a match, struck it on flint, and stared into the flame until a maid knocked on her door to let her know the feast of Second Night was beginning. She unenthusiastically changed into her evening dress. At the event, she sat between Elysander and Baron Marmose throughout dinner. She listened to Elysander sing the Chronicles of Saint Abisian. She didn't look once at the Baer royal clan seated on the far side of the hall. Mars had made sure they were as far apart as two families could be. If anyone else saw the scars on Rangar's face and remembered that night ten years ago, they might look at Bryn politely sipping her cider and assume that she had forgotten it entirely.

For a long time that night, though, alone in her bedroom after the feast, she tried to light the match without striking it. *Magic*. That was what felt so dangerous about the Baer princes. They were as forbidden as magic was, not to mention as mysterious and scandalous. She'd heard so many rumors and bedtime stories about their wild lands, filled with hexmarks and magic, with women who fought and fished alongside men, with vicious beasts and harsh climates.

She fell asleep and dreamed that it was ten years ago, and instead of relinquishing their claim on her, the Baer king stole her away back to their lands with them. Instead of growing up in Castle Mir, attended to by servants, she spent her days in the wild forests running with deer, swimming with otters...and she spent her nights with Rangar Barendur.

* * *

THE NEXT DAY, Bryn went in search of her mother to explain her middling feelings about Baron Marmose—better to address it now than by the eighth or ninth day, when he might propose. She found Queen Helena in the council chambers, standing around the Little Table arguing with Bryn's father and the heads of the other Eyrie families. Soldiers blocked the archway into the chamber, forbidding her from entering.

"Lady Bryn." Captain Carr bowed his head. "I'm sorry, your parents are in a meeting." Ever since he'd been garroted as a young soldier, his voice struggled to rise above a rasp.

"I only need a few minutes with my mother."

"I'm sorry. It's quite impossible."

Frustrated, Bryn stood on her tiptoes to peer over his shoulder into the council chamber. There was the duchess of Zaradona, the king and queen of the Wollin, the green-caped representatives from the forest kingdoms of Vil-Rossengard and Vil-Kevi. She spotted the Baer king, Aleth, and his eldest son, Trei, as well as their mage. Even with the presence of the other Outlands rulers, they were the wildest-looking with their heavy cloaks and untamed hair.

For Bryn, High Sun and Low Sun Gatherings were all about the nightly feasts and daytime countryside tours, but this was the *real* purpose of the gatherings: political arrangements. This was what happened outside of the parties.

Mars and two of the forest princes were arguing with one another. Bryn's heartbeat leaped. She glanced at Captain Carr, wondering if he ever thought about the black fawn from ten years ago. The war omen that had never come true—yet. After the wolf pack attack, no one had spoken of the black fawn again.

King Aleth slammed his fist on the Little Table and muttered something to Bryn's father in the Baer language. Mage Marna touched the scarified hexmarks on her forearm that had been long ago carved into her skin—the source of her magic. With a few small hand gestures, she was able to turn to Bryn's father and translate the Baer words into Mir. Her father listened to her response and scoffed.

"Like hell." He jabbed a finger in the mage's face. "Can your magic translate that, witch? *Like hell!*"

Bryn sucked in a breath. She'd never heard her father speak so disrespectfully to anyone, especially a woman. But magic had a way of making everyone in the Mirien nervous, and apparently, even kings were no different.

Captain Carr shifted to block Bryn's view. "Your parents aren't available, as you can see."

Bryn turned away, only to glance back over her shoulder. Mage Marna was tracing another hexmark on her opposite forearm, whispering something under her breath to Trei. Bryn's father, in a fit of anger, knocked all the maps off the Little Table. "Sinful! Take your magic away from me!"

Bryn turned and fled down the stairs, breathing hard. She thought of the anger on everyone's faces. So different from the evening gatherings when everyone was laughing, smiling, dancing. Was it only because wine and cider relaxed the tensions? Or were the tensions ever present, just under the surface, and Bryn had been too distracted to notice?

Judging by her father's temper, it seemed like the Eyrie kingdoms were on the verge of war. Maybe after ten years, the war omen of the black fawn was finally coming true. She had no way of knowing. No one told the youngest princess anything, but she should have tried to pay more attention to what was happening under her own nose. How could she have been so unaware?

How did I not see impending war? She berated herself as she made her way into the great hall—unoccupied now except for servants preparing for the evening feast—and out onto the same balcony where she and Rangar had spoken. She leaned on the stone railing, recalling the events from the night before. The smell of his pipe smoke. The gleam of his dark eyes in the low light. The rumble of his voice speaking a language he had learned for the sole purpose of communicating with her.

As she thought of the possibility of war, she descended to the remembrance garden, where the ashes of her Mir royal ancestors mixed with the soil amid stone markers. She sank onto a soft patch of grass and leaned against a headstone that was tucked into a hidden corner.

Why were the kingdoms at odds? What was the source of the tension? The Mirien provided winter rations and supplies to the Outlands—grain, animal feed, wine, medicines, textiles. Could the Outland kingdoms, in their barren wilderness, want even *more*? Did they lust after the Mirien's prosperity so much that they would wage war to get it?

The hinges of a nearby door groaned softly as someone eased it open. Bryn froze. The door was hidden from view behind the headstones, but she was fairly certain it was the one that led from the downstairs servants' realm into the garden. So, it was probably a Mir gardener or a servant needing a break.

But as heavy footsteps entered the remembrance garden, followed by low voices, she realized two men had joined her in her place of solitude. And to her horror, they were speaking not in Mir, but in Baer.

6

GARDEN WHISPERS...THE LITTLE TABLE...
HEXMARKS...GRAVESTONES..."EVERYONE
WITH A KNIFE"

*B*ryn pushed to her knees and peeked over the top of the tombstone, half-hidden by golden hemlock boughs. When she saw the two figures who had come into the garden, her breath stilled.

Valenden and Rangar Barendur.

She pressed her hand to her mouth to silence her gasp. They were only ten feet away. What were they doing here, away from the other dignitaries in the council chambers discussing impending war? And what if they took a few steps to their left and saw her?

They appeared to be arguing, but they kept their voices low and guarded—throaty, like two creatures growling at one another. They spoke in Baer, so naturally, their words meant nothing to her. Peeking over the stone, she saw how Valenden paced in the sunlight, jabbing a finger in Rangar's face as Rangar hung back in the shadows of the hemlocks. Always hiding his face, even when he was alone with his brother.

But even though Rangar hung back, it didn't mean he was passive. He threw harsh-sounding words at his brother in that same hushed tone. Whatever they were saying, they clearly had come here for some privacy and didn't wish to be overheard. Bryn wondered what could have them so worked up. Was it the tense discussions happening upstairs in the council chambers? Or was this unrelated—just a brotherly quarrel?

Rangar ran a hand over his face, and Bryn got a glimpse of some of the hexmarks carved into his own forearms. The cloak hid the rest of his arms and chest—for all she knew, he had hexmarks covering every inch of his body. She wondered what magic spells the marks commanded. She'd already seen him control fire. What else was he capable of?

Valenden paced close to the headstone where Bryn was hiding, and she sank down, breathing hard. If they found her eavesdropping on their conversation—never mind that she couldn't understand their words—they'd surely be displeased. The Baer princes were rumored to be so unpredictable and bellicose. She glanced at the nearby row of hemlocks, wondering if she could hide in their boughs and crawl to the door and from there slip into the servants' realm...

She was just about to lower to her belly when one word amid the brothers' conversation snagged her attention.

"Bryn."

She froze. Had she heard them correctly? She could have sworn that they spoke her name among the otherwise unintelligible Baer words. Valenden growled something low and repeated her name, this time unmistakably. Rangar answered in a grumpy tone, and they continued quarreling.

They're talking about me. Why? Was this finally when they would carry out their plan to steal her away, as they'd wanted to do ten years ago?

Eventually, they seemed to come to an agreement. Bryn dared to peek back over the headstone. Valenden took out his flask from an inside pocket. He passed it to Rangar, who threw back a sip, and Valenden did the same, as though they were sealing a pact. Then Valenden drew a curved knife from a holster at his side.

Bryn gasped.

The blade caught the sun and flashed in Bryn's eyes, making her duck back behind the tomb. She clamped a hand over her mouth, praying that they hadn't heard her. Her pulse was beating wildly. She should stay low, stay hidden. But curiosity made her peek over again.

She'd half feared that Valenden had run Rangar through, but he was only showing his brother the knife, explaining something about the blade. He sheathed it and drew an even larger rapier. Rangar grunted, replied, and drew his own knife. Bryn watched in anxious apprehension. They continued to compare weapons for the next few minutes, pulling out knives and bludgeons and small weaponry she'd never seen before and certainly didn't know the name of.

Lords and ladies, those two have arsenals hidden beneath their cloaks.

She bit the inside of her lip. Upstairs, there was talk of war. Downstairs, the disreputable, dangerous Baer royal brothers were readying their armaments. It felt impossible that it wasn't connected. Someone needed to know about this.

Lowering to her belly, she crawled behind the golden hemlocks until she reached the gardener's entrance to the castle. Praying the brothers hadn't heard her, she dashed into the door, then wound her way through the servants' rooms and upstairs to the east wing. She was pacing in Mars's bedroom when he returned from the council chamber.

His face was splotched in crimson. His jaw was tight. He stopped short when he saw Bryn. "What are you doing here, Mouse?"

She pounced on him, breathless. "The Baer brothers. The younger two. They have knives!"

Something darkened in her brother's expression. "I told you to stay away from them."

She groaned in frustration. "It wasn't like I sought them out!"

Mars sighed. "The Baer people are warriors. They practice magic. You shouldn't be anywhere near them."

But she wasn't going to let it drop. "Mars, I overheard the argument in the council chambers this afternoon, and then I saw two of the Baer princes with knives. That means something. I'm worried they're planning an attack."

Her brother rubbed the bridge of his nose. "Mouse, every guest who has come to the Low Sun Gathering has a knife hidden on them. No one comes here unarmed, not even the batty old queen from the Wollin." At the worried look on Bryn's face, he rested his hands on her shoulders. "Politics aren't your realm. Leave that to Father and Mother and me. If you want to be of use, put our guests at ease. I won't lie—tensions *are* high between the Eyrie kingdoms, as they always are during Gatherings. That's why the evening feasts are important. They're where the day's tensions ease. So eat and drink and dance. Charm some men. Entertain the other ladies. That's how you can help."

She tried not to be insulted by her brother's words, painting her as little more than a helpful distraction. She insisted, "I think they mean to do violence, Mars."

"Bryn. Stop." The small amount of patience he'd had was worn through. He thrust a finger toward his door. "And stay away from the Baer princes."

7

THE DANCE...TAPESTRIES...WHAT A WARRIOR LEARNS...WHAT A PRINCESS SUSPECTS

*E*at and drink and dance.

Bryn sulked in her golden lace gown, still smarting from Mars's words.

At first glance, the feast of Third Night looked like every other one. There was a quartet of musicians from the village, carafes of bloodred wine, ladies in gowns that ranged from green wool to glass-and-mirror sparkles. But now, tension suffocated the air. She studied every face with extra care. Wondered what she had been missing all those years when she'd been a child unaware of the true purpose of these Gatherings.

"A dance, Lady Bryn?"

She blinked at Baron Marmose, who extended a hand to her with a broad smile as if everything was normal. Perhaps everything *was*—perhaps only she had changed, not the world. She realized the musicians were playing a *velta*, and dancers were already moving in the first skipping steps.

At that moment, the three Baer brothers entered the great hall behind Baron Marmose. Unlike everyone else, they hadn't changed their clothes for the feast. They wore their same salt-stained cloaks, wool, and chainmail. Trei looked to have combed his hair, but that was more than she could say for the others.

"Lady Bryn?" Baron Mormose prompted.

She jumped back to the present. "Oh. Um, if you wish."

The baron led her in the *velta* dance. She took every chance she could as they circled to spy on the brothers. Searching for glimpses of steel blades beneath their cloaks or suspicious looks between their father and aunt: anything that might portend an attack. She glanced at Mars, sitting at the head table on the dais. He spoke low with Captain Carr, a glass of wine forgotten at his side, and their talk seemed grave until Mars suddenly laughed.

Her shoulders eased. Maybe it *was* just a feast.

The baron was asking something about when they might set up a tour of Castle Mir and if Elysander was available to chaperone again. Three days of the Gathering were already over. Word usually broke about proposals around the ninth day, sometimes even as soon as the eighth, if couples had come to an agreement early. As a princess of the Mirien, her betrothal would be a major announcement.

The *velta* ended, and she pried herself away from the baron, muttering something about needing a drink of water. She poured herself a glass and took her time looking over the crowd. The few other girls her age were focused on the men, as she should have been. In exchange, the men were focused on winning their various drinking bets. On the surface, it appeared the same as every banquet.

Still, she couldn't shake the feeling that something was wrong. She glanced at the servants stationed around the great hall. Was it her imagination, or did they look pale, too? As though they also sensed danger in the air?

She clenched her jaw. *Sorry, Mars.* She couldn't just eat and drink and dance.

When Bryn was little, she, Mars, and Elysander had loved to play hide-and-seek all over the castle. Because of this, she knew that each of the tapestries hid a shallow alcove where statues of the Saints rested. Now, she backed up until she reached the closest tapestry and slipped behind it. The alcove was dark, the voices on the other side of the tapestry muted. She went to the next tapestry, quietly slipping behind it. She moved from tapestry to tapestry until she reached the rear of the great hall. With the breeze from the crowd, she prayed no one would notice if the tapestries rippled more than usual.

She looked out from behind the last tapestry until she saw the Baer princes by one of the small, unlit fireplaces. Rangar and Valenden were speaking together in Baer. Valenden slapped Rangar's shoulder and then went to speak to King Aleth, their father, leaving Rangar alone with his back to her.

Bryn glanced toward the dais—she couldn't see Mars through the crowd, which likely meant he couldn't see her, either. So she slipped out from the alcove and tapped on Rangar's shoulder. He turned, his expression guarded. When their eyes met, his expression didn't change, though he studied her for a long time before his eyes shifted almost imperceptibly in Mars's direction.

She balled her fists for strength as she cleared her throat. "Dance with me?"

His guarded expression fell away. Pure surprise showed on his face, and he looked younger, the boy who had once followed her into the woods. He almost looked *terrified*, like he was once more facing a wolf. But then his mask came slamming back down. "Your brother made it clear on First Night that I am not to touch you."

"My brother is indisposed," she said. He seemed of two

minds, toying with the *statua* pipe in his hand. She tipped her chin upward, gazing at him through her eyelashes. "Is that a no?"

Slowly, half of his mouth curved in a boyish smile despite his best efforts to hide it. He extended a hand. The musicians played an upbeat *yulla* now, and she had a moment of worry. Would a wild prince from a wild kingdom know how to *yulla*? But he moved well enough. He was no natural dancer, but at least he didn't step on her toes.

Rangar's hand pressed against the small of her back, and she flinched. Remembering his touch on her ribs. *The scar.* He smirked as if he knew exactly what he was doing. Mars might have been too far away to observe them, but some of the other dancers had. Lady Winnie gave Bryn a shocked look, then whispered something to Lady Anelle.

"You surprise me," Rangar said quietly. "I would think you are the type to obey your brother."

"I obey reason," she replied. His hand pressed against her back moved to the base of her spine, where the scar began. She shivered. The scar had always been the most sensitive area of her skin. She felt suddenly exposed. Not even Baron Marmose knew about the wounds.

"*Reason.* Always speaking of *reason.*" He dismissed it with a growl. "Is it because of *reason* that you climbed into Baron Mormose's carriage yesterday?"

This caught her off guard. Flustered, she hissed quietly, "It is because of *reason* that I'm talking with you now. I saw you and Valenden among the tombs." She leaned in, her heart fluttering, so she could whisper into his ear, "I saw your *knives.*"

If he was shocked by her accusation, he didn't show it. If anything, he seemed amused. He took her hand and moved it close to his torso, down to his side, and slipped it beneath his bearskin cloak. She gasped, trying to tug her hand back, but he pressed her palm against his rib cage. A dagger was there, holstered under his arm, sheathed in leather.

"*That* knife?" he asked.

She jerked her hand back and said with a scowl, "If you and your family are planning any sort of violence, or if you know of any of the other families who are, you must tell me."

He looked at her oddly, and then his hand returned to the small of her back, where it was supposed to be. He glanced toward the dais where the crowd blocked them from Mars's view and then before she could react, tugged her to the side of the great hall. He moved so gracefully that she was barely aware of where he was leading her until he lifted the closest tapestry and pulled her into the hidden alcove.

She gasped. "How did you know about this space?"

"The first thing a warrior does is learn the secrets of his surroundings."

Her heart pounded. She reminded herself that if needed, she could merely step out from behind the tapestry and be safe in the crowd again.

"You speak of violence," Rangar said quietly, nodding toward the crowd on the other side of the tapestry. "Such things are not for others to hear."

"So there *is* an attack planned? By who?" She narrowed her eyes. "You wouldn't hurt anyone, would you?" At his silence, she took a step backward. He said, "It is not us you should fear."

She felt herself relax, though she was far from trusting him. "If we are connected, as you said on First Night, then tell me which of the families is planning to move against my father. How many? Who is with them?"

He stared at her for a long time and then muttered something in Baer. He paced slightly, searching for words in a language that wasn't his. "You misunderstand," he said at last.

She rested her hands on her hips. "Do you know something, or don't you? Why won't you tell me?"

He ran a hand over his face, then leaned in close. "After the party, close yourself in your room. Barricade the door."

Her toes went numb. "Tonight?"

He turned away as though he'd already said too much. She grabbed his arm, holding him back. She had no reason to believe him, except that way he looked so boldly into her eyes. Her hands slipped down his arm to his wrist, and she squeezed tight. "If it isn't the Baers planning an attack, then who? Which family? What are they planning?"

He shook his head, unwilling to say.

"My father's army is the strongest in the Eyrie," she pressed. "It would be folly for anyone to cross him."

He gave her an odd look as though trying to peer into her head and then suddenly cupped her face, surprising her. "Lock yourself in your room tonight," he ordered. "Barricade your door. Do not come out, no matter what you hear."

He unholstered the dagger at his side and pressed it into her hands, then disappeared from behind the tapestry back into the crowd.

8

BLOOD AND FLAMES PART 1...HIDDEN MESSAGES...SECRET PASSAGES...THE CHAMBER OF CHAMBERS

*B*ryn immediately excused herself from the feast, blaming an upset stomach, and went straight to the east wing, which held her family's private chambers. As she passed the guards, she muttered something about a chill in the air to give her an excuse for clutching her arms tight—in reality, to hide Rangar's knife.

As soon as she was in the safety of her bedroom, she set the knife on the foot of her bed and stepped back like it might come to life. She chewed on her thumbnail as she paced across the sheepskin rug in front of her fireplace. Every few seconds, her eyes went back to the knife. She could tell Mars. He might listen to her this time if she showed him the weapon. But he'd ask how she came to be in possession of a Baer blade, and she'd have to admit to being alone again with Rangar. *Ho,* they'd tar and feather her! What did the knife prove, anyway? It alone wasn't evidence of a plot.

Her eyes landed on her journal and quill. She snatched it up, tore out a page, and scribbled a note.

An Eyrie family plots against Castle Mir. Be cautious this night.

She tore out two more pages and copied the same note on

each—one for Mars, one for her parents, one for Captain Carr. Three chances that someone would listen. She stuffed the pages into her dress, then opened her door, peeking out. Even from this far away, the staccato sounds of a *yulla* floated up the stairs with the din of conversation. Third Night was always one of the most raucous feasts. The guards were at their positions, playing a game of riddles to pass the time. She'd have to walk past them to get to Mars's room at the end of the next hall; it would be obvious who planted the anonymous notes.

Across from her room was a series of armoires the maids used to store the family's linens. The middle one was faux. It hid the entrance to a servants' passage that connected the east wing with the laundry rooms in the lower levels and more storage on the opposite side of the wing. No one had used the passages in decades—now, the maids took the main stairs like everyone else. Bryn and Elysander and Mars used to play hide-and-seek there, learning all the castle's hidden spaces before Mars was called off to more important studies.

She held her breath as she made her way to the faux armoire. She eased open the door and climbed in. It was pitch-black inside, but too late to turn back for a lantern. Cautiously, she felt for the rear wall, brushing aside cobwebs. She felt along the wall, counting her steps as she tried to estimate how far to the next hall. The corridor reeked of dust and mildew. She heard some small creature scurry away and briefly shuddered. She counted out ten more steps before her hand brushed against a door. She closed her eyes and tried to remember the map of the passages. Beyond this door was the landing at the top of the stairs. If she climbed out here, she'd be right across from the guards. *No good. They'll see me.*

She felt against the wall, turned a corner, and counted out twenty more steps. Her hand grazed against another knob in the darkness. *The chamber of chambers*, Mars had teased. She let out a wry laugh at the memory.

The door she opened was the faux rear of the closet, where the servants kept the extra chamber pots. She opened the closet again and blinked into the light. Once more, she could hear the music from the great hall. The guards were out of sight around the corner. Mars's bedroom was just across the rug. As she crossed and knelt to slip the note beneath his door, she heard a moan from within. A bed joint creaked. Heat rose to her cheeks.

Did he have a girl in there?

Decorum required Mars to one day take a wife, but he was free to dally with anyone he chose until that day. And he chose a different girl almost every night.

She slipped the note under his door and then stepped cautiously to her mother's sitting room. More guards were posted around the corner, and no secret passages led to her parents' quarters. So the sitting room it was, a tidy collection of her mother's history books. She unfolded her note but paused. A note *already* rested on top of her mother's devotional of Saints.

It bore Baron Marmose's burgundy crest. She read it in one glance.

While Lady Bryn is a charming young woman whom any man would be pleased to call a wife, I should wonder if Lady Elysander's birth betrothal still stands...

Bryn made a disgusted sound, crumpling the note. Men! She didn't even *like* the baron—so why was her chest suddenly feeling tight? Why were her eyes prickling with tears?

She laughed to herself darkly and wiped away tears. What did it matter? If Rangar was right, there would be no Tenth Night with its starry-eyed proposals. The war omen of the black fawn, all those years ago, was finally coming true.

She set her note on top of Baron Marmose's and used the passages to return to her bedroom. Her memory of the passages was imperfect, but she recalled that they stopped well before the north wing, which held the Little Table chambers. She'd have to find another way to get a message to Captain Carr. She pulled down a history book from her shelf, closed the note inside, then strode into the hall and smiled politely at the two soldiers. "I borrowed this book from Captain Carr. He asked at the banquet if I'd return it. Please take it to him."

One of the soldiers took the book, glancing at the other one with a heavy air of impatience. He didn't leave his post.

"Immediately," Bryn ordered. She rarely gave commands, and it made the soldier clear his throat, visibly displeased, but he obeyed.

She returned to her room and raked her nails through her hair. Rangar's knife still rested on the foot of her bed. She'd never used a knife for more than buttering toast. Mam Delice's kitchen was full of knives, but cooking was a common art, not for nobles.

"Lords and ladies," she muttered. She picked up the knife by its hilt. For a small dagger, it was heavy in her palm. She unsheathed it slowly and touched a finger to the blade's edge. Worn enough to have lost its bite. Hexmarks were branded into the steel. She dared not touch them—the ways of magic were a mystery. She carefully practiced thrusting and slicing, then turned the knife around and slashed backhanded at the air. After an hour, her arm ached, and she sheathed the knife, feeling silly—this was hardly princess behavior. She went to the window.

Below, an empty carriage pulled up to the castle's front, and a gaggle of young men exited the main gate lugging heavy cases. It was the musicians, returning to Tureen. The banquet must have ended.

She cracked open her bedroom door and listened. The castle was quiet. When she looked back through the window at the guest wing, most of the lights were extinguished. If anyone was planning an attack, they were planning it in the dark.

She locked her door and tucked the key into her chemise. She heaved a shoulder against her heavy oak armoire until, inch by inch, it blocked the door. She left on her dress and shoes. It was overly precautious, perhaps, but a small voice told her to trust Rangar.

Lock yourself in your room. Barricade your door. Do not come out, no matter what you hear.

She sat down on her bed, fully dressed, knife in hand, and waited.

9

BLOOD AND FLAMES PART 2...GHOSTS IN THE MIST..."DON'T LOOK DOWN"...THE LANTERN...A BLOODY THRONE

*S*he woke up to the smell of smoke.

Bryn blinked, disoriented. She touched her dress, at first not remembering why she hadn't taken it off after the banquet. How much wine had she had? What was the hour? She heard roaring voices—was the feast still going on? She tottered to her feet, coughing against the smoke. She started for the door only to see the armoire barricade, and then everything came back in a rush.

The attack!

She pressed a hand against her mouth, coughing, and went to the window. She threw it open to gulp fresh air, but the air instantly stalled in her lungs. Below was a scene like out of a nightmare.

At first, she wasn't sure what she was seeing. Soldiers covered the front lawn—the Mir army, judging by their golden armor. They swarmed the castle entrance with battle cries. Smoke was thick over the scene, blocking her vision. The soldiers looked like ghosts in the mist, flashing gold armor and silver swords.

The smoke was billowing out of the north wing, which

housed the guests. The wind changed direction, blowing smoke into her room, and she coughed and ducked back inside. Rangar had been right. Only this was no mere attack; this was a war! With the heavy smoke outside, she couldn't see *whose* army was attacking, and there was no way to guess how long the Mir soldiers could hold them off.

More smoke poured in through the window and from beneath her door. She stumbled toward the armoire. It wasn't much good to be barricaded inside her room if the castle was on fire. She threw her shoulder against the heavy piece, coughing, and managed to move it a few inches. A clash of metal suddenly sounded outside her bedroom.

Then a woman's scream.

Bryn took a hasty step backward. Elysander's room was next door to hers. Was that her sister's scream? Saints, why hadn't she copied out another warning note for her sister? Her heart thudding hard, she dropped down to hands and knees and peered through the crack beneath the door. She could make out leather boots with gold buckles. *Mir soldiers.* A clash of metal came again—they must have been trying to hold off attackers. The traitors were already at the east wing! Had this been the traitors' plan, to come straight for the royal family wing?

Another scream rang out from further down the hall. Bryn pressed a clammy hand to her mouth. Was Elysander safe? Mars? Her parents?

Suddenly, two of the Mir soldier boots strode straight to her door. Someone rattled the doorknob hard enough to make Bryn jump. When the locked door didn't budge, the person slammed a fist against the door and then rattled the knob harder.

Bryn's lips parted on instinct. *I'm here*, she started to say. *I'm safe. I'm the one who warned Captain Carr...*

But before the first word came out, the soldier slammed something hard against the door, making the wood nearly splinter. She fell back, breathing hard. Something was wrong. If it was one of the Mirien's soldiers come to protect her, why wasn't he calling for her? Reassuring her that he was there to help?

She pushed to her feet. Smoke was pouring beneath the door. The soldier—if it was actually a Mir soldier—was slamming his shoulder against the door, trying to break it down. A second soldier joined him. Smoke stung Bryn's eyes, and she pressed a hand to her mouth to silence her coughs. She saw the shadows of their feet from beneath the door and realized that if she could look under the door to see them, they could also look under and see her.

She jumped on top of her bedcovers. Maybe if they looked under the door and didn't see any sign of her, they'd think she'd found some other warm bed after the feast, as Mars's companion had. She pulled the leather sheath off Rangar's knife and held it close to her chest. The hexmarks caught the faint light from the window, giving them an almost glowing impression. Magic might be a sin, but she'd gladly sin now if those hexmarks saved her.

The soldiers kept pounding at the door. The wood splintered, but the armoire held—thank goodness she hadn't moved it more. Bryn clutched the knife with all her strength. She forced her eyes open as wide as they would go, afraid even to blink. Her hands were trembling. Her palms were sweaty. Fear flowed through her from head to toes and back again.

The smoke came in thick blue-gray clouds now, and the attackers on the other side of the door began coughing. They made a few more attempts to break down the door, but as the smoke grew thicker, a voice from down the hall called for everyone to fall back. She heard the footsteps of at least a dozen soldiers running down the stairs.

For a few agonizing minutes, it was quiet except for her own ragged breath. She pressed her sleeve over her nose, too terrified to move until she couldn't stand the smoke another moment. She rushed to the window and sucked in as much fresh air as she could.

The front lawn was wrecked. Bodies lay prostrate in the grass. Blood was smeared on the stone drive. Some of the horses were running wild. Flames roared out of every window on the north wing and half of those in the great hall, billowing smoke into the sky.

She had to get out of the castle.

She dropped to hands and knees to look beneath the door again. There was the orange glow of flame just beyond the door. The whole hallway was on fire. She jumped up, pacing, and then threw together a bag of all she could lay her hands on. Her jewelry. Her journal. A change of clothes. What else? She couldn't think!

Coughing, she pushed open the window fully.

She had only done this once, when she was a little girl— scaling the parapets from her room to Elysander's. She'd thought her family would be impressed, but all it had resulted in was her mother nailing her window shut for five full years. Back then, she'd been a tiny thing, and it had been easy to scamper across the parapets to the next window. Now she was twice that size, her feet so much larger and her eyes watering. She clutched her bag in one hand and thrust the knife through her sash as she climbed out the window, clinging to the upper row of bricks.

The wind was vicious. Smoke obscured her vision. She clung to the row of jutted-out bricks with every ounce of her strength and walked.

Foot over foot. Don't look down.

It was the longest ten steps of her life. When her fingers at last reached the iron grating outside Elysander's window, she gasped with relief. Her fingers gripped the bars so hard she wasn't sure she'd ever have the courage to let go again. But she forced herself to climb over the grating and into the wide windowsill. She pushed against the window.

Locked!

Gritting her teeth, she fished out Rangar's knife and slammed the hilt against it until the glass shattered. She used the knife grip to clear out as much glass as she could, then threw her bag through the window and pushed herself in after it, wincing as a glass shard carved a deep scratch down her arm.

She collapsed into the room, clutching her bleeding arm, and then froze. Elysander's door was wide open. The bedsheets were in disarray. There were books strewn on the carpets. Elysander's dressing mirror was overturned and shattered. Blood streaked the carpet. Near the foot of the bed, a small puddle of blood soaked into ripped sheets, and then a line of it ran from bed to door as though someone had been dragged into the hall.

Bryn cupped a hand over her mouth like she might throw up. She scrambled to the door, heart racing, only to be met by smoke and flames. The hallway was mostly overtaken by fire. Blood and footprints stained the rugs. The tapestries had been slashed with swords. Defiled with mud. The armoires lay open, ransacked.

Had everyone in the castle fled? Was she the only one still trapped inside?

Flames snaked up the ruined tapestries. Eyes bleary, she stumbled through the smoke toward the stairs. But flames licked up that way, forcing her back. She doubled back, pressing her sleeve against her nose. The middle hallway armoire, which was the faux one, was open. She pushed past the faux shelves into the servants' passage. She sucked in a few breaths of stale air as she stumbled forward into pure darkness.

Instantly, she was lost.

She felt along the wall until she saw an orange glow ahead. As she neared, she realized it was the glow of a lantern someone had hung on a small hook. It smelled of fresh oil, which meant that someone had been here only moments ago. She wasn't the only one who remembered the old servant passages after all.

She unhooked the lantern with a frown. This was the kind of lantern only used by Mir kitchen workers. How could one of the visiting Eyrie families have gotten their hands on it? She couldn't spare the precious minutes to consider this, and she used the lantern to light her way forward through the tunnel. It had been a decade since she'd been down here with Mars. As she recalled, the tunnel went to the west wing, but she couldn't recall exactly which room it let out into. When she finally reached a door, she pushed it open, desperate, and stumbled straight into the throne room.

Taken off guard, her feet slowed as she pitched her head upward. The throne room had a cathedral ceiling with tall glass windows. Blessedly, the smoke pouring in from the rear council chambers billowed straight upward, giving her access to fresher air if she stooped low.

In the faint light of her lantern, she saw smeared footprints from the dais to the doorway. Mud? She knelt, touched a footprint, and squinted at her hand.

Blood.

She pushed to her feet and ran toward the opposite glass doors. They led to a balcony over the remembrance courtyard. She could scale down into the garden or jump if she had to...

As she ran past the thrones, her lantern swinging, she caught a glimpse of a figure, and she skidded to a stop. Fear coursed through her again, commanding her to draw Rangar's knife.

Someone was seated on her father's throne, the smoke too thick to make them out.

"Father?"

No answer.

"Who's there?"

She took a slow step forward, the knife in one hand and the lantern in the other. She realized she'd left her bag in the passages, but there was no time to go back for it. The light shone on the figure as she approached with caution. She stopped. Gasped. *They killed him on his own throne.*

Her father. The king. They'd dragged him here, slit his throat, and left him to burn with the rest of his empire.

10

THOSE WHO WISH US DEAD...BLOOD ON HIS SWORD...AN UNWELCOME TRUTH...IRON IN HIS HEART

*T*he blood from the puddle on the floor was still warm on her hands. *My father's blood,* she now realized with a sickening feeling.

His body rested on the throne like one of her childhood dolls: too stiff, not bending like a body should, with that waterfall of red washing down his chest and dripping onto the floor. His eyes were still open.

Bryn's hands started shaking badly. She stumbled backward away from the throne, tripping on her own feet. She hit the floor hard, pain blossoming in her knees, but the pain felt distant, like it was happening to someone else. She didn't remember standing again.

In one hand, she still clutched Rangar's knife. The other was bathed in blood. She had to get the blood off. *Father's blood.* She wiped it on her skirt, but it didn't come off. She wiped harder. Her breath was growing short. She doubled over, letting out little moans. It felt as though her heart was beating so irregularly that it would explode.

She opened her mouth to scream, but someone from behind clamped a hand over her lips.

Her eyes snapped open wide. Her spine went rigid. She thought her heart might beat so hard it would burst from fright, but after a few panicked breaths, her pulse calmed. Some instinct even stronger than panic took over. She squeezed the knife and jabbed it backward over her shoulder toward her attacker's eyes.

He blocked it with a single move, using her momentum to spin her around to face him.

"Rangar!" she tried to cry, muffled by his hand.

Rangar had one hand on her wrist and the other still pressed to her mouth. He'd shed his bearskin cloak and stood in breeches and chainmail, a sword at his side. She tried to pull away. He forced her wrist backward until she had to let go of the knife, which clattered to the floor. He then twisted her arm around behind her. His grip was iron. He clamped his right hand harder over her mouth and moved his left arm around her waist. She felt herself suddenly being picked up and thrown over his shoulder. Her mouth free, she bit his ear.

He cried out and dropped her to her feet. She stumbled back, eyes wide and wild.

There was blood on his ear. Blood on his sword. Was it Father's blood? Had Rangar killed her own father? The reek of smoke was everywhere. She was finding it hard to breathe. Rangar's hair had fallen halfway out of its knot; as wild as he looked, his eyes were clear. Blood dripped down his neck.

Something clattered in a distant hall, and he drew his sword, breathing hard.

She felt wild, too—ready to strike. "You killed him!" she spat.

In the faint light, his eyes flashed with surprise. "I did not."

She thrust a finger toward his sword in accusation. "There's blood on your blade!"

"It is not *I* who want your family dead." His voice was dangerously low as he wiped the blade on his trousers.

"Then who?" she pressed.

His eyes flashed again. "Do you really not know?"

"Know what?"

"It is your own people! It is the Mir people!"

She'd expected anything but this. At a loss for words, she could only press a hand to her hair, digging her nails into her scalp. "That's impossible. It's a lie."

He watched her for the space of a few breaths as though he wasn't sure her reaction was honest. "There have been stirrings of an uprising in the Mirien for years. Three years ago, peasants overturned your father's carriage. They nearly butchered him in the street, but he got away. This was the first time they were strong enough in numbers to try again. The Mir people despise your family." His face went grim. "They had the Mir army on their side. Captain Carr led the uprising."

Captain Carr? Bryn dug her nails in deeper, closing her eyes. No, it wasn't right. Impossible. She'd warned the captain with a note...

Had she warned the captain about his *own* coup?

She remembered seeing the Mir army on the front lawn, fighting at the castle entrance. And the soldiers' gold-buckled boots beneath her bedroom door. *Defending* her family, she'd assumed. The memory returned of Elysander screaming, and Bryn doubled over, feeling sick.

Rangar reached out for her. "Come here." She jerked back, stumbling a few steps away. He ordered, "Bryn, come with me."

"I'm not going anywhere with you!"

His face went dark, and he took a predatory step forward. Even without the sword in his hand, she'd never stand a chance against him. "Come."

"Get away from me. This is a child-snatching!"

He stopped, his eyes flashing impatience. "You are not a child, and I do not have my hands on you. Run away if you want, straight into the flames. Or to the masses waiting outside to slit your throat."

She gaped at him. "Are you part of this? Was this your scheme since we were children? Since you saved me from the wolves and my parents wouldn't let you take me as your slave?"

His eyes grew hard. "I ran into a burning castle tonight to find you. I fought against Mir soldiers with whom I have no quarrel. My brothers are outside. We have horses. We can get you out of the Mirien, but we must make haste. I told you, you are my responsibility."

Breathing hard, she asked, "Will you throw me over your shoulder again if I refuse?"

His impatient look said he might do just that. But then his voice softened. "It's either come with me or wait for death to find you."

"My people wouldn't hurt me."

"They will." There was so much certainty in his voice.

Bryn's heart was pounding. Her hand pressed against the scars beneath her dress. "My mother..."

Rangar slowly shook his head, and she felt herself pale.

"My brother and sister?"

"Your brother escaped with a few soldiers who remained loyal. I do not know about Lady Elysander. If she is dead, I have not heard of it. There is nothing you can do for them. But you can save yourself."

She shook her head, feeling trapped. "Mars will think you kidnapped me. Everyone will. They'll come after you with whatever's left of the loyal army."

He gave a shrug. "Let them." He held out his hand.

It wasn't stained with blood like hers. Everything that had happened within the span of the last few minutes felt like the weight of lifetimes. So many questions unanswered. Would her own people really have risen against them? Wasn't Father a good king? Mother a benevolent queen? They'd gifted their people the Saints Forest, the Mirien had prosperous fields, an army to protect them...

She thought again of the boots beneath her door. Those were Mir soldier boots. Whoever had been trying to break down her door—and whoever had succeeded in breaking down Elysander's—was from the Mirien or at least dressed like a Mir soldier.

Either way, the flames were rising.

She held out her hand and, for the second time in her short life, entrusted her survival to a boy with scars on his face and iron in his heart.

11

INTO SAINTS FOREST...SIX RIDERS, FIVE
HORSES...PROMISE OF THE OCEAN...ACHING
THIGHS...THE CLEARING

*B*ryn's kingdom was now nothing but smoke and
flame.

Rangar clasped her hand hard as he tugged her down the
castle halls. Scorching walls of flame licked out of each open
doorway. A ceiling joist cracked and collapsed behind them,
showering them with plaster. Bryn screamed. Rangar kept his
head down and pulled her along faster. She followed him in a
daze. She'd never felt so disconnected from her body—at least
not since that night ten years ago, mauled by wolves. Everything was different now. Her mother and father were dead. Her
home in flames. Her siblings missing. A stranger claimed she
belonged to him.

Were her own people really trying to kill her? What wrong
had she done to them? Rangar led her down another hallway,
urging her to run faster. She pushed aside all the questions in
her head—right now, only survival mattered. Rangar was right:
they couldn't stay in the castle. It was rapidly being eaten by
fire.

He turned down a hallway that led to the courtyard, but

Bryn tugged him back. "No. They'll have closed that passage off. This way."

He didn't question her. He turned down the hall she indicated, which was so thick with smoke they couldn't see more than a few feet in front of them. It was a lesser-used passage that led to the servants' latrines. Not a pleasant place, but Bryn knew that like all the castle latrines, the space had open archway windows for ventilation. Sure enough, as soon as they reached it, coughing, they were able to rush to the open arches and breathe in fresh air.

Rangar looked down at the ten-foot drop beneath the windows, calculating. "I'll go first. Then you." Before she could answer, he swung a leg over the window and disappeared. Gasping, she looked down to find he'd landed like a cat, crouched low on all fours. He straightened and called down to her.

She started to lift her skirts so she could climb out the window but then heard a clatter from further down the hallway and paused. Was it really wise to go with Rangar?

For all she knew, *his* people had started the fire. The Baer folk were the ones with the strange belief that she belonged to them. They'd tried to take her ten years ago and failed. And now she was going with them willingly—had she lost her mind?

But a shower of sparks erupted as a wall collapsed, and Bryn didn't think. She thrust one leg over the window, clinging to the windowsill.

"Jump!" Rangar called. "I'll catch you!"

Saints save me...

She let go.

As soon as she was about to scream, he caught her around the waist. She grunted at the impact. Her ribs ached. He set her down on the grass, where she collapsed to her knees, wanting to roll in the damp, cool grass to get rid of the awful smell of smoke. But Rangar was already pulling her to her feet.

"We must hurry. My family is waiting with horses."

She could hear the din of the Mir army on the opposite side of the castle. If Rangar was to be believed, they were searching for her with the intention of killing her just like they did her parents.

She gave Rangar a shaky nod. Together, they scrambled down the hill behind the castle, plunging into Saints Forest. Instantly, Bryn felt a measure of protection from the trees and the shade. She followed Rangar over stones and roots, feeling dizzy from smoke inhalation until they splashed into a creek, and she realized they were headed toward the river shrine.

She stopped. "Rangar, we can't. It's sacred water. We can't touch it."

He growled, "*You* can't. I share no such beliefs."

Before she could object, he threw her over his shoulder so that her feet were clear of the water and crashed through the creek bed. It didn't at all feel like keeping with the spirit of tradition, but she doubted Rangar would put her down even if she pounded and kicked him. After a few hundred yards, he came out on the other side of the river and set her on solid ground.

Through the trees, a horse snorted. Bryn jumped as a shadow emerged out of the woods. Valenden. The middle brother. With his bear cloak and shaggy hair, he looked one with nature, so different from the Mir soldiers' gleaming white-and-gold clothing. Valenden gave Bryn a long look up and down and then said something low to Rangar, who answered back curtly. Valenden waved for them to follow and led them down a short path to a glen where five horses stood, partially hidden behind a large boulder.

Bryn vaguely recognized the glen as a shrine she hadn't been to in years; its remote location made it hard to reach. But cutting through the creek had shaved hours off the usual path to reach it.

King Aleth stood from where he'd been seated on a stump. He, Mage Marna, and Trei had clearly been impatiently waiting. Once Valenden led them out of the woods, they began speaking quickly in Baer with one another.

Bryn turned to Rangar breathlessly. "Where are we going?"

"There is an old path through these woods," Rangar explained, "from before your family owned these lands. It will take us to the shore, and from there, to the Baersladen."

She gasped. "The coast?"

The ocean was a trek of at least five days. Three, if one had a carriage, which they didn't. Bryn had never seen the ocean. To hear her parents talk of it, it was a reeking place of jagged rocks and rotting seaweed. The water wasn't even drinkable. Despite it all, Bryn had dreamed of the sea.

Was she *really* going to see the ocean? *Not if I can help it*, she told herself. She'd never agreed to go with them that far.

The Baer princes began tightening the horses' saddle girths. Mage Marna climbed atop her horse, a dappled gray strong enough to carry her and her many traveling bags. The Baer king mounted his black gelding with surprising grace for such a beast of a man.

Rangar led Bryn to a chestnut gelding. She quickly counted the horses and riders and frowned. Six riders. Five horses. "Wait, you don't…"

Trei and Valenden each mounted a horse, and Rangar climbed atop his. He reached down a hand to Bryn. Her eyes widened. No princess would ever ride in a man's *lap*! No woman would, not even a scullery maid! But Rangar clasped her wrist and tugged her up with surprising strength, helping her to straddle the horse in front of him.

"Mir soldiers are right behind us," he breathed in her ear. "We must make haste."

He reached around her to gather the reins with one hand and slid his other arm around her waist to steady her. She sucked in a tight breath. Her back was flush against his chest so that she could feel every breath he took. She'd never been this close to a man before in her whole life. But Rangar didn't seem to think the arrangement odd. With a few words from the king, the riders kicked their horses into action.

Bryn wasn't a strong rider—in the Mirien, horses were for soldiers, not ladies. When she hunted for stirrups to hold her feet, she was dismayed to find the Baers rode without them. They used only a bridle and a folded pad for a saddle attached by a girth strap. Suddenly, she felt very grateful for Rangar's steady arm around her.

The path through the trees was too overgrown for the horses to gallop, but they charged forward at a canter, urged on by their riders. Bryn forgot about impropriety. She found herself clutching the horse's mane in one fist and Rangar's hand around her waist with her other. How did anyone ride like this and not fall off? The forest was a blur of branches. If she fell, surely she would crack her head open and die.

But Rangar didn't slow. His breathing against her back remained steady.

The only benefit of the terrifying ride was that it forced Bryn's attention away from the massacre at Castle Mir. She couldn't think about the blood on her hands. About her father slumped on the throne. Elysander's screams.

By the time the riders finally slowed after what must have been hours racing through the trees, dusk was falling. They had long ago left the portion of Saints Forest that was carefully tended to by the Mirien's fleet of gardeners. For miles, the forest had looked nothing like the manicured pathways around the eighteen shrines. Here, the land was wild. Ancient trees towered overhead. Bryn had never been this far into the forest.

For a few moments, the party remained silent. Bryn assumed they were listening for any signs of Mir soldiers pursuing them. King Aleth exchanged a few low words with his sister, Mage Marna. The mage closed her eyes and tilted her head to let her hair curtain her features. Her left hand traced a strange symbol in the air. Then she looked up and spoke in Baer.

"The Mir soldiers are not as far away as we would like," Rangar translated to Bryn quietly. "About two miles south, following the same stream we've been following. But they've made camp for the night, and my aunt doesn't believe they've sent out riders in our direction. We'll make camp as well, then leave early in the morning before they rise."

"How could your aunt possibly know all that?"

Rangar didn't reply, but the answer ripped over Bryn's skin like a shiver. *Magic.*

King Aleth gave an order, and the princes dismounted and began to untack their horses. Once more, Bryn realized how closely she had been pressed to Rangar for the better part of the day. Close enough that sweat had bound their clothes together. When he slid off the back of the horse and then helped her down, she felt her cheeks burning.

What would Mother say?

Then a sour feeling filled her mouth as she remembered her mother was gone. She slowly became aware of eyes boring into her, and she turned to find King Aleth watching her with a hardened look in his eyes. He spoke a few words to Rangar in their language.

"What did he say?" Bryn asked, breathless.

Rangar smoothed back some strands of her hair that had stuck to the blood splatters on her face. An unreadable look haunted his face. "My father says it is time for you to learn the truth about your family."

12

THE TRUTH...RABBIT STEW...HEXMARK
SCARS...A LETTER FROM CARR...PROOF

*R*angar added brusquely, "But before any discussions, we rest. Eat."

He removed his horse's saddle pad and unfolded it into a blanket, which he pushed into Bryn's arms. His chin jerked toward an area beneath the pines that Valenden was clearing of branches and stones.

Dozens of arguments sprang to Bryn's mind, but she was too tired to argue. After the long ride, her thighs were slack, and her bones felt like they'd clacked together for hours. She laid out the blanket at the base of a tree trunk and collapsed onto it. She wasn't sure how much longer she could stay awake. Every part of her yearned to shut down. She didn't want to think about the attack. Or her family. She craved the dark oblivion of sleep.

But she forced her eyes to remain open. For all she knew, these royals had ill intents toward her. She still wasn't sure why Rangar helped her or if he could be trusted. For years, her greatest fear had been the Baer princes coming to sweep her away in the night, and now here she was, with no knife, nothing to her name, too weak to even sit upright. The others hardly seemed tired, or if they were, they didn't show it. Speaking to one another in Baer, they unpacked and set up a quick bare-bones camp.

"Aren't you afraid the Mir soldiers will see campfire smoke?" she muttered to Rangar.

"The wind is blowing north," Rangar answered. "And beech burns clean."

Trei called something to Rangar, who responded in Baer and then turned back to Bryn. "My father and brothers and I must hunt. You, stay. We will not be long."

Bryn couldn't imagine eating anything after the things she'd witnessed that day, but she knew that if she didn't get something in her belly, she would only weaken further. Rangar drew his bow from his saddlebag and disappeared among the dark trees, where his brother and father had already vanished.

Only Mage Marna remained behind with Bryn. She began stacking gathered branches for a fire. Bryn watched in silence, her eyelids heavy. Her mouth tasted of soot. Her skin itched with her own father's blood covering it, but she was too tired to ask for water to bathe. Mage Marna finished stacking wood and then closed her eyes in a peculiar way. For a moment, she seemed to be deep in her own thoughts, and then she made a quick hand gesture in the air and muttered something aloud. The wood sparked and caught flame.

Despite her exhaustion, Bryn felt the undercurrent of thrill that always accompanied magic.

Sinful, her mother had said of magic. *Backward*, her scholars sneered. All Bryn's life, magic had been something she'd only read about in history books from a time before modern science.

"How do you do that?" Bryn whispered through cracked lips.

The mage gave a knowing smile as she blew on the spark to

grow the fire. She pulled back a thick woolen shirtsleeve to reveal dozens of hexmarks carved into her skin, long ago scarred over. She explained, "Each mark influences a different element. This one—" She indicated a hatch-shaped scar in the center of her left wrist. "—manipulates fire." Then she pointed to a circular symbol higher up on her arm. "This one influences sleep." She tapped a complicated collection of scars closer to her elbow. "This one has to do with communication. It allows me to speak Mir."

Bryn perked up at this, curious. She'd had no idea magic could be so powerful. "Could a hexmark let me speak Baer?" Not that she had any intention of actually going to the Baersladen. It was one thing to escape with Rangar's help but quite another to willingly run off to his remote kingdom. Still, it would be helpful to know what Rangar and his brothers said to one another. Who knew what they might be plotting.

"Magic is more complicated than that," the elder woman explained. "There is a reason why Rangar learned Mir through years of study instead of a hexmark. The mark for language manipulation is an advanced one. It requires ingestion of a poison as well as the actual scarification."

Bryn studied the scarified symbol near the mage's elbow. Whereas some of the other hexmarks were rough slashes, this one was far more intricate and looked to involve hundreds of smaller cuts.

"Hexmarks themselves are merely a tool," the mage continued. "If you don't know how to wield the tool, you might make a mess of whatever you set out to do. It's the same with magic. Most people in the Baersladen can cast a basic set of spells. Then there are the mages and our apprentices who make it our life's mission to master every spell, even develop new ones."

The campfire flourished under Mage Marna's capable hands. Though Bryn had been sweating when they'd dismounted, now that the sun had dropped, her damp clothes quickly grew clammy, and she welcomed the heat the fire gave off. Still, she kept her distance from it. The taste of smoke was still too thick in her mouth.

Mage Marna untied a small iron pot from the many belongings strapped to her saddle pad. She disappeared into the woods for a few minutes and returned with the pot full of water. There must have been a creek nearby, though Bryn hadn't heard water flowing. She briefly wondered if she should have tried to escape while she was alone, but she would be helpless in the forest without the Barendurs.

Mage Marna set the pot over the embers to boil, then uncorked a water flask she'd freshly filled and handed it to Bryn. "Drink." Bryn accepted the flask cautiously. She was parched, but the mage had just spoken of poison. Mage Marna chuckled. "If we wanted you dead, child, we would not have saved you."

Bryn would collapse if she didn't drink water, so she had no choice. After a deep drink of cool, fresh water, she handed back the flask and asked, "Why *did* you save me from the castle?"

"You are Rangar's Saved. It is his responsibility to protect you."

Bryn felt a flush of anxiousness the same way she had ten years ago when they'd talked of her belonging to Rangar. Again, she wondered about their foreign beliefs and what they intended to do with her. She rubbed her tired eyes. "I don't want his protection. Can't I release him from his duty?"

The flames threw orange light over the mage's harsh features as she studied Bryn. "That isn't how it works, child. The *fralen* bond between a Savior and a Saved is sacred. You could no sooner tell the god of death that your soul doesn't belong to him after you perish."

"I worship Saints, not gods," Bryn argued. Religion was just

68

as backward as magic. Far better to worship real humans who had achieved feats of strength or intelligence or generosity than made-up deities.

The mage made a small sound deep in her throat. "In the Baersladen, we tell a story to our children about a hawk and a fox. A young hawk choked on a fish and was dying, but the fox pulled the fish from its gull. Winter came, and the fox moved to a new forest, but the hawk appeared shortly after. The next year, the same thing. The two were bound. Eventually, the fox realized the hawk's soul was hers and suffered if it was far away." She adjusted the boiling water over the embers before continuing. "We believe that before we are born, our souls belong to the god of life. After we die, we belong to the god of death. The years between when we are living on this soil, our souls are our own—but if our lives are saved by another, then our souls belong to the Savior."

Bryn was fascinated by the story but also troubled. All the talk of gods and spiritual beliefs made her even more afraid she'd never convince them to let her go. "And there's no escaping this bond?"

"Of course there is. Surrender your soul to the god of death instead."

Bryn bristled. The mage was mocking her pain.

Sometime later, a soft footfall behind her made Bryn twist around. Rangar emerged from the shadows with his brothers and father behind him. She relaxed. It was remarkable how quietly they could move over the forest floor. She would have sounded like a drunken ox stumbling around.

Rangar carried a brace of rabbits over his shoulder. He passed them to Trei, who fetched a long skinning knife from his saddlebag and disappeared down the path to the creek. The makeshift camp was quiet as Rangar and Valenden rubbed down the horses and led them to the creek to drink. Mage

Marna skirted the clearing, gathering edible plants. Trei returned with the skinned rabbits, and soon the campsite filled with the savory smell of rabbit stew. In the Mirien, such a meal was considered peasant food. It would never be served in the royal hall. But Bryn's stomach grumbled, aching to be filled.

Besides, she thought, *I'm not a princess anymore.*

Her body began to shake as the events of the past few days caught up to her. The horseback ride had been frantic enough to distract her, but now, in the quiet calm of the forest, there was no escaping reality. She briefly closed her eyes and pictured her father's body on the throne.

Letting out a small sob, she placed a hand to her chest and said, "Excuse me. I need...a moment."

Though Rangar's eyes scanned her warily, he nodded. "Do not wander far."

She stumbled a few feet into the forest, close enough that she could still see them all through the trees and they could see her, but where she could press her back against a wide pine and feel alone for a moment. Now that reality was crashing in, she found it was harder to breathe.

Father is dead. Mother is dead.

She buried her face in her hands to hide the sounds of her sobs. The last thing she wanted was to break down in front of the Barendur family, but her grief was so great that she couldn't stuff it down any longer. She thought of her mother's beautiful face, dusted with rust, and could almost feel the warmth of her mother's arms around her. It filled her with pain to think of her mother's final moments. Turned on by her own people. Feeling the life slip out of her.

I'm so sorry, Mama, she thought.

She remained pressed against the tree, sobbing into her hands, until every last ounce of strength had seeped out of her. Then she hugged her own arms around her chest and whispered a silent blessing to her parents' spirits. Once she had calmed down and dried her tears, she picked her way back to the campsite, where thankfully, no one commented on her red-rimmed eyes.

"There, I think the stew is ready." Mage Marna dipped a tin cup into the pot. She brought it to Bryn. "Here. Eat."

Still mired in grief, Bryn blinked in surprise. Her gaze automatically turned to the king. Surely he would eat first. As though she could tell what Bryn was thinking, the mage pressed the cup into Bryn's hands in mild annoyance, softened only by her sympathy for Bryn's loss. "There is only the one cup. We all must take turns. Fill your belly so the rest of us can, too."

Bryn accepted the cup but still didn't feel right. For as long as she could remember, the Baer people and her own existed in a shaky alliance, if not outright enmity. She wasn't their ally. She might even be their prisoner...the truth was, she wasn't entirely sure of where she stood. But they were all clearly waiting on her, so she drank down the stew, surprised to find the wild herbs gave it a spicy kick, and passed back the cup. The mage filled it again and gave it to Rangar. After he had eaten and passed the cup to Valenden, he came and sat by her.

Bryn said to him, "In Mir, the king and queen would eat first."

Rangar's lips curved in a sneer as though he would expect nothing less. "A good leader ensures the well-being of his lowliest subjects before his own. My father would sooner starve than take the food from someone else's mouth."

The implication behind Rangar's words was impossible for Bryn to ignore. He was clearly stating that in the Baersladen, rulers sacrificed for their people, whereas in the Mirien, Bryn's parents had siphoned off so much wealth from their subjects that their own people turned on them.

King Aleth finally took the cup and ate. Once he was finished eating, he focused directly on Bryn, acknowledging her for the first time since the long ride through the forest. He said something in a hard tone that she didn't understand.

Rangar translated, "He wants to know if you truly did not know about your family's crimes."

Bryn's spine went rigid. Even though every muscle in her body was exhausted, she felt a flush of outrage at the accusation. "For all I know, you're making everything up about the attack," she snapped. "It could be a trick to make me come with you willingly. What proof do you have that the attack was my own people uprising?"

Rangar exchanged a few words with his family. Valenden rolled his eyes when he heard Bryn's assertion. The Baer king spoke more measuredly, and Rangar faced Bryn again and translated, "My father says that our messengers intercepted correspondence between Captain Carr and Lady Enis, a royal member of the forest kingdom Vil-Rossengard. Carr outlined the unrest amid the Mir populace and promised Lady Enis spoils of war if the forest folk fought with them, but the lady declined."

Bryn's heart walloped like she'd been kicked by a horse. "You have the actual letter? In Carr's own handwriting?"

"Yes, at Barendur Hold."

She watched Rangar and his father steadily for any signs they might be lying. She would have to wait until they arrived in the Baersladen to see the actual proof, but she wasn't sure if they were bluffing.

"My parents would have told Mars if there was unrest," she insisted.

Rangar translated to his father, who grunted and answered back a string of guttural remarks. Rangar put them into Mir for Bryn. "My father says that your brother has always known about the injustice simmering in his country. All the kingdoms of the Eyrie were aware of the Mir tyranny and the discontent among your people. It was no secret. You seem to be the only one who didn't know."

Bryn shook her head forcefully. "You're slandering my dead parents."

Rangar said, "Your parents dictated which crops to grow and then took the full harvest. They taxed their subjects to the poor house. They stationed soldiers in every village."

"To *protect* the villagers," Bryn said.

"From whom? The Mirien does not have the greatest relationship with the other kingdoms, it's true, but none were at the point of war. Your parents posted soldiers to intimidate their *own* people—"

"Stop!" Bryn clapped her hands over her ears. Her chest felt tight. Was she on trial? She suddenly realized that yes, she *was* very much on trial. The Baer royal family had risked their lives so that Rangar could save her, but that didn't mean that they trusted her. The way they kept throwing her cold looks felt like they believed *she* was just as guilty as the rest of her family.

"Bryn Lindane," Mage Marna chastised as though she was a child. "You must harden yourself if you are to survive in the Baersladen."

"Who said I would go as far as the Baersladen?" Bryn asked.

When only silence met her question, her cheeks grew warm. That was it, wasn't it? They really intended to steal her away. To make her a wild thing like themselves, dressing in furs and eating raw meat. They'd never let go of the belief that her soul belonged to Rangar. Did they think she would be his servant? His slave? Would they laugh at the princess reduced to polishing his boots?

The silence stretched as the Barendurs began preparing for bed. Mage Marna began putting away the cookware. Trei went to lead the horses to the creek again. Bryn was so lost in her troubled thoughts that she didn't realize Valenden was standing in front of her until his shadow fell on her. She looked up at him, dazed, wondering what fresh accusation he'd hurl.

Instead, he tossed her an apple.

She caught it on instinct, stared at the red peel set against the red of her father's dried blood still covering her hands. She'd expected more cruelty, not kindness, and she burst into tears as everything hit her at once.

Valenden's face fell. He muttered something in Baer that sounded along the lines of *"that's what I get for trying to be generous."*

"A bath," Mage Marna said in Mir to Bryn with more sympathy. "A bath will do you good, child. Wash off that blood. Rangar will show you the way to the creek."

Bryn wasn't going to argue with that. A bath *would* make her feel better. Rangar helped Bryn to her feet. Her legs were still shaky from the ride and from the mental exhaustion of everything she'd seen and learned. Her eyes met Rangar's dark, hooded ones, and she shivered.

Who exactly was this prince with scars that matched her own?

She feared the answer. Feared he might be some cold-hearted rogue, but even more so, feared that he might not be lying at all. Which would be worse than anything else.

Silently, he led her into the dark woods, and she had no choice but to go with him.

13

THE KNIFE AND THE BATH...A STEAMING STREAM...A BLADE GIVEN AND TAKEN BACK... A RISKY DECISION

*B*ryn followed Rangar over a small rise to a meandering forest creek, where a sandy pool made for a possible bathing area. But as soon as she toed off one boot and stuck a bare foot in the water, she cried out, "It's freezing!"

Rangar blinked as though he didn't see the problem. "Yes. And?"

Bryn hadn't pointed out the water's temperature to complain. In fact, she loved a plunge in cold water in the summertime. But given that night was falling, and she was already shivering, it was unwise to plunge in the water. "I'll get hypothermia if I bathe in there."

Rangar appraised her from a distance with a pensive air. "My brothers say you are soft—all of you in the Mirien. In the Baersladen, our waters are much colder. It is good for the heart. For the blood."

Bryn rested her hands on her hips. She'd never felt more wrung out in her life and was getting tired of being insulted so often by these smirking brothers. She scowled and looked away. "I guess I'm soft, then."

Rangar came forward and touched her chin, turning her

face to look at him. "I like how you are, Lady Bryn. My brothers only fear how you will fare in the Baersladen after being accustomed to luxury."

She hugged her arms against the chill coming off the stream and said quietly, "I'm not *quite* as delicate as you think."

Her body was bruised from hours on a horse, her muscles completely unused to the strain. Her lungs still burned from breathing in so much smoke. And there was that deep bruise in her heart whenever she thought of her father slumped on the throne... And yet, she felt a core of strength within her.

"I know that." His voice was soft as his hand slipped along her jaw, his thumb lingering there before letting his hand fall. He took a step back and closed his eyes as Mage Marna had done earlier at the campfire. With his eyes closed, he traced a symbol in the air and spoke some foreign words. Bryn watched closely, studying his movements. She hadn't noticed before how practiced the gestures were, almost as though Rangar was well trained in playing a musical instrument.

It only looks simple because he's mastered it, she realized. A ripple of thrill gathered at the base of her spine. The water in the stream's deep pool began to glow slightly, and then steam came off it. *He warmed water with no fire. With only magic.*

Magic might be sinful, but Saints, was it riveting to watch. Rangar finally opened his eyes, and Bryn noticed a heaviness to his lids as though the effort had taken a toll on him. He jerked his chin toward the water. "It is a large pool, and my spell won't last but a few minutes. Do not dally."

She hesitated. Was he going to stand there and watch? Surely not even a savage would watch a naked woman bathing. She felt suddenly vulnerable, in part still struck by the show of magic. She thought magic was used for trivialities like lighting tobacco pipes and erasing freckles—could it really *boil* an entire frigid stream?

"You're shaking," Rangar observed.

Bryn hugged her arms over her bloodstained dress. It was true. She couldn't stop her hands from trembling.

Rangar's brows pinched together as realization crossed his face. "You are afraid of me. Of my magic."

Bryn looked sharply away. "No, I'm not." But her heart was pounding in her chest with the same intensity it did when she was in the woods alone, overcome with the sensation she was being watched. If he could manipulate a stream, what else could he do? Her entire world had shifted over the past day, and now she was supposed to accept that reality could be so dramatically altered as well? Besides, this man who was practically a stranger had the wild belief that he owned her soul. He was even planning on taking her back with him to his wildlands like a stolen lamb.

Rangar took a step forward as though to prove his point, and Bryn scrambled backward on instinct. She was afraid he would only smirk, but instead, unsmiling, he tugged loose one of the knives sheathed at his side. The blade glinted in the dappled moonlight.

Bryn stumbled backward another step, but he grabbed her wrist. Before she could scream, he pressed the blade's hilt into her palm. "Take this. It will make you feel safe."

She frowned down at the knife in her hand. It was the second time he'd given her a blade. She'd lost the first one in Castle Mir's throne room when she'd seen her father's body. She started to object but immediately thought better of it. She had no weapons. No way to defend herself. She was with a band of savages and still wasn't certain if she'd been kidnapped or rescued.

She closed her fist around the knife. "Aren't you afraid I'll use it on you?"

This time, he *did* smirk. "No."

"I could stab this through your heart this very moment." She tilted the blade so the point was poised just an inch from his chest.

A mocking glow filled in his eyes. "Try it."

It wasn't what she had expected him to say, and she wasn't certain how to answer. Before she could speak, he smoothly grabbed her wrist, twisted her arm behind her back, and had taken the blade back from her in the same amount of time it would have taken her just to unsheathe it.

He released her almost as soon as he'd caught her. Gasping, she spun back around to face him. "Hey!"

Rangar grinned in a way that gave him a rare boyish look. "I do not fear you using a blade against me, Bryn, because I could take it from you in an instant. But you should have one nonetheless." He extended the hilt back to her.

She snatched it and slid the blade into the sheath. Her eyes drifted to the steaming bathwater, and he grunted. "I will wait for you at the clearing."

Her body eased in relief. He disappeared through the trees. Bryn waited until she could hear the rise and fall of his voice back at the campfire in conversation with his family. Not that she suspected he would have tried to sneak back and spy on her bathing naked, but, well, his people's beliefs were so foreign. She didn't know *what* to think. When Mage Marna had told her the story about the fox and the hawk—the Saved and the Savior—the *fralen* bond hadn't sounded nearly as scandalous as her family had made it out to be since she was a child.

A life saved is a soul owned.

That phrase had haunted her every night since she was eight years old. Fearing that the three Baer brothers—the Three Bears, as she'd thought of them in their bearskin cloaks —would come to steal her away in the night. Now here she was, and her greatest fear had come true. The "Bear" princes *had* come and taken her in the dead of night.

And it was the only reason she was still alive.

She painstakingly unbuttoned her bodice and peeled off the dress's thin layers down to her waist. She needed help to unfasten her skirt, and she didn't dare ask Rangar or even Mage Marna for assistance, so she soaked a strip of fabric torn from her underskirt in the steaming water and ran it over her arms and chest to wash away her father's blood and the blood seeping from the cut on her arm. She ran the cloth over the scar running along her bare ribs and paused.

She glanced back at the knife she'd left on the riverbank.

Rangar had saved her life twice now. He'd given her his blade. Part of her wanted to trust him, but another part of her resisted. She remembered what he'd said to her in the throne room after the seige: *It's your own people.*

She shivered and, looking up, realized night was falling fast. The water Rangar had warmed was cooling quickly. She hurried to finish her bath and then, wincing, pulled back on her bloodstained blouse. She would have done almost anything for clean clothes, but the bag she had packed was left somewhere in the castle tunnels along with her jewelry and everything valuable she owned. She was entirely at the mercy of the Barendur family.

Did she trust them?

For eighteen years, she'd grown up with distant but doting parents. With a brother and sister she adored, whom she'd played hide-and-seek with throughout the castle. With maids and cooks who slipped her treats on her birthday. Try as she might, she couldn't make herself believe her parents were the monsters the Baer princes insisted they were. Something had certainly gone very wrong back at Castle Mir, but she didn't believe that it was exactly as Rangar claimed.

There could be another explanation.

She shivered in the dark forest. What options did she have? She barely knew Rangar. And much of what she did know didn't work in his favor: that he believed she belonged to him body, soul, mind. Just because he hadn't attacked her yet didn't mean he wouldn't. It could be that as soon as they arrived at Barendur Hold, he would force her to scrub his sheets and then bed her on those same linens every night, her will be damned.

She owed a debt to Rangar, it was true. Perhaps even more than one. And Valenden had shown her some kindness, and Trei certainly had a noble countenance. But when she'd fled the castle with Rangar, she'd never agreed to go with them to the Baersladen. And she had a terrible feeling that Rangar would never let her return to her home.

As quietly as she could, heart pounding, she walked over the soft moss of the stream bank. Was it a mistake to run away from the Baer royal family—or a mistake to stay with them?

Mage Marna had said that the Mir soldiers had made camp two miles down along this same stream. Those directions seemed easy enough to follow, even for someone with no experience in the wild. If she could find the soldiers, she could eavesdrop on their conversations and determine if what Rangar said was, in fact, the truth. And if necessary, she could show herself to the soldiers and return to the Mirien with them.

Once she could no longer hear the Barendurs talking around their campfire, she started to move faster down the stream bank. She made much more noise moving through the forest than Rangar and his brothers did, but she was comforted that the flowing water masked most of her sound. As soon as she felt that she was out of range of their hearing, she started running.

Clutching Rangar's knife, she made her escape.

14

SOLDIERS OF MIR...THE RIVERBANK...A
CORRAL FOR HORSES...BODIES IN THE
NIGHT

*a*s Bryn ran through the forest, she again wondered if she was making a terrible mistake.

Something gnawed at her. Things truly hadn't seemed right during the siege. The boots she'd seen beneath her bedroom door were unmistakably the golden boots of Mir soldiers—the same soldiers she was now racing *toward,* hoping that she could trust them and that if needed, they would shelter her and defend her if Rangar tried to steal her away again.

Her mind raced as she tried to think of other explanations: It could have been enemy soldiers disguised as Mir ones. Or maybe a few disloyal Mir soldiers had turned against her family, but surely not the *entire* Mir army.

How could she trust the word of a savage prince against a lifetime of experience?

Mars would not have lied to me. And Elysander is too much of a gossip to keep something like that secret.

As she hiked along the dark streambank, Bryn racked her mind, thinking back on all the snippets of conversation from cabinet meetings she'd overheard. Lords and ladies, why hadn't she paid more attention? Maybe Rangar was right that she'd been too sheltered. In any case, it was too late to change that. But she felt fierce anger at herself that she'd spent her life wandering in gardens and reading books and leaving politics to her parents and Mars. She was still a princess of Mir, even if she was the overlooked third child. It should have been her duty.

Had she failed her people?

The vegetation along the riverbank was becoming thick and overgrown. Bryn tried climbing over twisting brambles that hugged the shore but couldn't get more than a few feet in any direction. Eventually, she splashed back into the shallow stream. It was the only path open enough to traverse. Her boots weren't watertight, but she didn't intend to be in the frigid water for long. Besides, with her boots on, it was much easier to skirt along the shore.

A branch snapped nearby. She stopped and held her breath to listen.

What else is in this forest?

Her scars began to tingle as she thought about the wolf attack that had brought her and Rangar together a decade before. It was why she still had a fear of large dogs, even the floppy-eared, friendly ones that hung around the palace stables.

Besides, there were other things to fear in the woods besides wolves: Bears. Foxes. Snakes.

Her worries began to get the best of her. She started to jog through the water, losing track of time. How far had she run? A mile? Surely more than a mile. What if Mage Marna had been wrong and the Mir soldiers *weren't* camped by this same river? There was no telling how accurate the mage's magic was or even if her spell worked at all. For all Bryn knew, the old woman could have been making it up.

She pushed on, trying not to panic.

Rangar was lying.

My parents weren't tyrants.

Our people wouldn't turn on us.

As she splashed along the riverbank, she repeated these words to herself, trying to force herself to believe them. The alternative was all too terrifying. Not just that her own subjects had indeed tried to kill her and her family, but that she would have no alternative but to go with Rangar. For as fascinated as she'd been by stories from the Baersladen, she didn't want to *live* there. The savagery of the place would eat her up, as Rangar said. Sleeping on the floors with animals. Eating raw meat. Magic everywhere, like a sickness.

And something else whispered at her, too. Like some invisible tether, she was undeniably connected to Rangar. The further she went from him, the more her feet seemed to want to turn around and return to him.

She was just about to collapse in tears, afraid she was lost, when she heard voices ahead. She went still.

The river flowed steadily around her ankles. Her toes had long since gone numb. In the light of the moon, she could see figures not far ahead filling canteens at the river.

"…oat cakes hard as rock…" one of them said.

She pressed a hand to her mouth to stop herself from gasping. They were speaking Mir! She must have found the soldiers! She forced herself to remain perfectly still until they had finished collecting water and left to rejoin their camp. Then she tiptoed out of the stream onto the bank and crept inland in a low crouch.

She'd rarely felt this terrified in her life. Could she trust these soldiers? Had they come to rescue her—or to drag her back to the gallows? What if these weren't Mir soldiers at all, but whoever had laid siege to Castle Mir in disguise? She smelled camp smoke and glimpsed flames between the trees.

Whoever they were, their fires smoked considerably more than the one Mage Marna built. They didn't bother to speak in hushed tones, either.

Bryn crept close enough to hear their horses' snorting and chomp of munching grain. She followed the sound and came out in a small clearing where they had tied the horses. The animals had been stripped of their livery; she couldn't tell if they were Mir horses or not. So she made her way behind the horses, using them as a screen to hide behind. She could just peek under their bellies and through their legs.

From her vantage point, she glimpsed the backs of a few men's heads. There were probably a dozen soldiers in all, though they had taken off their helmets, so all she saw were shaggy, sweat-stained heads and beards. She moved slightly closer to listen.

"...castle will burn until dawn..." one was saying. "Nothing to do but let it burn itself out. Anything salvageable will have to wait."

"...pass the tankard..."

"Where's Alain?"

"Gone to take a piss."

There was no doubt they were Mir soldiers. Hidden behind the horses, Bryn listened for several minutes. Their conversation revealed nothing about having betrayed their rulers, and Bryn began to feel more hopeful. She was considering coming out from her hiding place and announcing herself when a shaggy-haired man said, "...already have a grave waiting for her. Carr wants them all buried in the paupers' plot."

"...should burn them and spit on the ashes," one muttered.

"Nah, Carr wants the worms to eat them. Wants everyone to be able to curse the ground they're buried in."

Bryn froze. The hair on her arms began to rise. She

remained where she was behind the horses' swishing tails. She squeezed her eyes closed.

No, no, no.

"Think Carr will care if we have our fun with her first?" one said.

"Doubt it," answered another. "You've heard him talk about the sister. How much he'd enjoy holding her face down in the mattress and have his way until she begged for more."

Terror froze Bryn in place. *I can't be hearing right.* Captain Carr? He would never speak of Elysander—or any woman— like that! Surely they were talking of someone else...

"Wonder if they've found Lady Elysander," one of them mused. "Shame if she got away. She's the prettier of the two. Plenty of fun to be had with her before the gallows. Ah, well. Lady Bryn will beg for it just as loud."

Bryn closed her eyes. She felt a wave of revulsion roll through her. There was no denying the truth now. These soldiers—these traitors!—were speaking plainly enough.

Rangar was right.

She felt hot tears well in her eyes. It was all she could do not to scream. These soldiers had watched her grow up! They were supposed to protect her! And they had turned on her, slaughtered her family, and were threatening her even now...

I've got to get away. Back to Rangar.

The certainty hit her like a falling boulder. Her tears dried immediately as the gravity of the danger she was in swallowed her. What a fool she was to have left Rangar! The Baer king and his sons might be half-wild, but at least they weren't blackguards.

She forced herself to move. She had to get as far away from the Mir soldiers as she could. She was so afraid that she could barely breathe, but she crawled backward on hands and knees into the tall grass in the direction of the river, hoping the water would hide the sounds of her movement.

She knocked into a branch that brushed up against one of the horses' hindquarters. The horse snickered, spooked. Bryn froze again.

The soldiers went quiet. Fear hammered into her. If they came to investigate, they'd find her there, but if she ran, they would hear her for sure...

A calloused hand suddenly pressed against her mouth.

She tried to scream, but the hand gripped her harder as an urgent voice whispered, "Quiet. Move backward. Slowly."

Rangar!

How was he here? Had he followed her? She might have collapsed in relief if she wasn't so terrified. She gave a silent nod. Rangar didn't take his hand away from her mouth. Inch by inch, he led her slowly on hands and knees backward into the forest.

"...go see what spooked the horse..." one of the soldiers said.

Bryn's body went stiff. But Rangar didn't panic. Swiftly, he pulled her into a shallow depression behind a bush and pressed her to the ground, laying his own body on top of hers for protection. He wore his bearskin cloak, which at night blended in with the forest floor seamlessly.

"Shh," Rangar whispered low.

She held her breath.

Their faces were only inches apart. Her body was pressed flush against her. His wide chest against hers. His hips overtop of hers. Their feet tangled together. They'd spent all that time pressed together on his horse, but this was far more intimate. Bryn had never dreamed of having every inch of her body touching a man's. Even fully dressed and out of necessity for their safety, it felt scandalous. She could feel each angle and curve of his body. He weighed substantially more than she'd expected.

For a few moments, they remained hidden behind the bushes. Bryn put aside her modesty and buried her face in Rangar's shoulder, thankful for the safety of his arms. She heard one of the soldiers poke loudly around the corral area, but then he spit on the ground. "Probably just a fox," he said.

Once the soldier had returned to the campfire and they heard sounds of the tankard being passing around again, Rangar slowly lifted himself off her. Bryn's modesty came rushing back as she remembered the feel of his muscles against hers. How much his hair had smelled of woodsmoke. How well their bodies had seemed to fit together.

His eyes fell over her as though he was remembering it, too.

He helped her stand and motioned for her to quietly follow him through the woods. They walked for half a mile before he finally stopped and said quietly, "We are safe here. Far enough away that they will not overhear us. We should rest."

Bryn collapsed against a tree trunk, breathing hard. Rangar passed her a flask of water, and she drank it greedily. Tears she'd been holding back started rolling down her face, and she swiped them away with her sleeve. "You followed me?"

In the moonlight, his look was unmistakable. Of course he had followed her. He said evenly, "I heard you the moment you left the river."

"Why didn't you stop me?"

"I am not your jailor. Your soul is mine, but your will is your own. Still, the *fralen* bond prevents me from letting you come to harm."

Was it really just about the bond? A sense of responsibility? Did it have nothing to do with how his body had hardened while pressed on top of her?

She wasn't sure she was ready to think too far down those

lines, so she looked at the ground as her cheeks warmed. "I didn't want to believe you. You must understand that before tonight, I'd never given a thought to what kind of rulers my parents were. I understand now how foolish that was, but I can't take my ignorance back." She hugged her arms tightly. "You were right. The things those soldiers were saying…some of them who have guarded the castle my entire life…"

She started sobbing quietly.

Rangar wrapped an arm around her back and drew her into the protective lee of his body. Her body remembered all too well the feeling of his weight on her as they hid from the soldier. The way he tended to stoop to hide his scarred face made him often appear smaller than he was; she'd forgotten how large and solid he was until he'd been on top of her.

"I don't want to leave my home," she whispered into his chest. "I don't want to go to a place I've never been before."

"You do not have a choice." His words were spoken matter-of-factly. There was no threat, no command, just the simple truth that they both knew: she had no place to go other than with him.

He reached a hand up to gently tease the burrs from her hair. His fingers stroking her head felt oddly welcome. She closed her eyes. It wasn't long before she thought back to the Mir soldiers and Captain Carr. Anger formed a red-hot knot in her center. *Those traitors.* The vulgar way they talked about assaulting her and Elysander before stringing them up on the gallows made her stomach turn.

Had her whole life been a lie?

It was a nasty, harsh truth to swallow, but it was better than the ignorance she'd known before. She vowed to never again keep her eyes closed to the pain and suffering around her. With a start, she realized she'd been just as blind to honor.

This scarred prince fishing the burrs from her hair, letting her cry into his shoulder, had done nothing but keep a protective watch over her. His ways were rough, but that didn't mean they weren't honorable. For too long, she had mistaken the Mirien's higher learning and refined culture for rectitude. But even a scholar could be a bastard—just as a wild prince could be noble.

She thought of the Baer king waiting to eat last though he must have been starving. She thought of Rangar's magic warming the water, more powerful than anything she'd been led to believe magic could do.

I've been wrong about so many things.

"Rangar." She wiped her tears away and pulled back, meeting his eyes in the moonlight. "Take me to the Baersladen with you."

15

A JOURNEY OF FIVE DAYS...APPLES AND
STEW...A JOKE TAKEN TOO FAR...BROTHERS
ALWAYS...AT LAST, THE SEA

*T*he trek to Barendur Hold was five days long, and Bryn's legs were already aching after the first. She didn't think she could possibly ride another minute, yet when Rangar mounted his horse in the morning and extended his hand down to help her climb up, she took it.

This was her new life. No longer a pampered princess. Now just a girl going to a wild kingdom with a wild prince. *I had better toughen up fast.*

Once she was slightly more accustomed to riding, Rangar no longer held her with one arm around her waist. Part of her felt proud that she didn't need the assistance, but another part of her found that she'd grown quite comfortable with his arm holding her close.

When Rangar rode, he sat straight, not slouching as he did when he walked, and his chest was rigid and powerful. He hadn't bathed in days, and he smelled strongly of woodsmoke and sweat and horsehair, a distinctly masculine aroma she'd been unfamiliar with until now. Her brother, Mars, sweated plenty during his sword practice, but otherwise, he and Elysander and everyone in Castle Mir had dusted themselves with lavender-scented powder. In contrast, the Baers didn't try to deny or tame nature. They didn't manicure paths through forests. Didn't domesticate deer as exotic pets for the palace gardens. They simply lived among the forest and sky and rivers —not above the natural world, but part of it.

Halfway through the second day, they made camp again, this time in the shelter of a dried-out creek bed. Mage Marna filled her iron pot from her canteen but didn't set the water boiling right away. Instead, she closed her eyes in the meditative way that meant she was preparing to cast a spell. She traced a symbol in the air, spoke a spell, and then peered studiously into the pot of water. The men stood tensely a few feet away, waiting. At last, Mage Marna said something in Baer. Whatever she said caused the men to visibly relax.

Rangar translated to Bryn, "My aunt's scry spell reports that most of the Mir soldiers in pursuit have turned back. Only two still follow our trail. And they have not yet crested the previous rise."

This eased Bryn's fears, too. She still couldn't shake the memory of hearing those soldiers speak so brutishly about slaughtering her family and the vile things they were planning to do with her.

After a short rest, they mounted again and continued the ride. The tree cover gradually thinned as the land became rockier and mountainous. Hilly forest paths soon gave way to proper mountains, where the horses had to follow one another in a single-file line up rocky outcroppings. The higher they climbed, the shorter the trees became, stunted by the wind and lack of rich soil.

Bryn couldn't take her eyes off the scenery. Around every bend and over every rise, a spectacular new vista spread out before them. The Mirien was famous for its flat, loamy soil that was ideal for agriculture. She'd always heard the Outlands spoken of dismissively. If land wasn't good for growing crops or raising livestock, then it was a wasteland. All her life, she had never quite understood why anyone would live there, especially not by choice.

This, too, was another lie.

It was *obvious* why people would love the Outlands, even if it made for a difficult life. The crisp air that carried notes of wildflowers. The peaceful quiet only broken by birdcall. The view of sky and mountains as far as one could see. When they made camp on the third night in a glen near the top of a cliff, Bryn didn't immediately collapse and go to sleep as she had before. Instead, she took the currycomb from Rangar's saddlebag and began rubbing down his horse.

He looked at her, amused. "You are not a servant, Lady Bryn. You do not need to brush down the horses."

"I want to be of use. I can do more than cry on a blanket."

From across their camp, Valenden called out something she didn't understand. Rangar grinned and translated, "He says to take extra care with his mare. She bites."

Bryn threw Val an exasperated look. "I don't blame her. She can't like that her master is drunk half the day." Val might not have understood Bryn's words, but her tone must have been clear. He winked at her devilishly.

"Take care around my brothers," Rangar warned in a low voice. "They understand more Mir than they let on. Their pride won't let them admit it."

Bryn glanced back at Val, who was eating an apple, paying her no mind. She dutifully moved on to Val's mare after Rangar's and then Trei's. The horses were caked in dried mud from forging streams and dusty paths. Clumps of mud fell off, and soon dust and horsehair covered her from head to toe, but she didn't mind. She was starting to like the smell of horses.

"Good girl," she said softly to Rangar's mare. When Val's

tried to nip her, she gave it a firm smack on the nose, and it didn't try again.

She was exhausted by the time she accepted the hardtack and strips of roast rabbit that Mage Marna offered. Once they'd eaten and everyone had settled down to rest, Bryn wandered to the edge of their camp, looking out over the rocky outcropping at the view. Dusk had fallen, and the stars were beginning to appear overhead. The rolling mountains were a midnight-black blanket tossed haphazardly over the earth.

She heard a *crunch* of someone chewing something and looked behind her to find Valenden still eating his apple, admiring the view, too. She glanced back at camp, ten paces away. Rangar was close if she needed him, though he wasn't looking in their direction.

Valenden said something in Baer and motioned to the view.

Bryn folded her arms and asked suspiciously, "Do you really not understand Mir?"

Valenden blinked at her, looking perfectly baffled. But she detected a ripple of mischief in his eyes. He took another bite of his apple.

"What if I told you that I think you're a drunk and a cad?" she tested.

The insult didn't faze him, and he only blinked at her again, feigning ignorance. She studied him closely. It would take something more clever to get him to break his act.

She shifted her stance and traced her hand over the bark of a tree behind her. "Oh, good. So you really can't understand me. Finally, I can confess that ever since I first laid eyes on you, I've wanted nothing more than for you to push me up against a tree and kiss me senseless."

His face remained carefully stoic. He took another bite of apple and then shrugged, saying a few words in Baer that sounded along the lines of *no idea what you're saying.*

She narrowed her eyes. He was toying with her. She got the distinct feeling he had understood every word she'd said—or at least enough to get the gist.

King Aleth called to Valenden. He took a final bite and wiped the back of his mouth with his sleeve. Then, without warning, he suddenly stepped close to her. Bryn's eyes flashed in surprise. In the next instant, he had her up against the tree, one hand on the bark behind her, the other pressed to the side of her waist.

"*You cad!*" she cried. "I knew it! I knew you could understand me!" His eyes dropped to her lips, and she gaped. "Val, I wasn't serious—"

He leaned in as though for a passionate embrace, and she closed her eyes and cringed. She had to stop him. What a fool she'd been to tease him! But just when she thought he would press his lips to hers, he merely licked the tip of her nose and then let her go, laughing darkly as he chucked the apple over the side of the outcropping.

Breath heavy, Bryn pressed her back against the tree, trying to center her thoughts. "Val, you...!"

He was still chuckling to himself as he rejoined the others. Bryn's eyes immediately went to Rangar, but he was mending some torn stitching in his saddle pad.

Good.

There was no telling what Rangar would do if he had seen her and Valenden in an embrace, even if it was just a ruse. She didn't know Rangar well, but she'd already picked up on his simmering, brooding temper. He thought that Bryn belonged to him; she doubted he would be pleased to see his brother's hands on her. She returned to their camp and sat by the fire, throwing Valenden a cold, accusatory look. He only grinned as he passed a flask to Trei.

That night, Bryn shivered beneath the bear cloak Mage

Marna had lent her. The further north they traveled and the higher in altitude, the more the temperature dropped. The wind was thin and biting. Even if she had been able to bring her clothes from Castle Mir, the thin silk garments wouldn't have been much use. Her skirt was already tattered at the hem. Her white blouse was now a permanent shade of gray and still stained with her father's blood. She found herself eying Mage Marna's heavy wool dress in envy.

In the morning, when she settled into her place in front of Rangar on his horse, he said in her ear, "By this evening, we will arrive at Barendur Hold."

She could think of nothing but the stories she'd been told as a child. That Barendur Hold was a dark, unforgiving place. That even the royal family slept on the floor. That men took whatever woman they wanted, and sometimes, women did the same with men.

She felt Rangar's breath close behind her and shivered.

The horses began a steep descent down from the outcropping. On one side of the trail, a sheer cliff gave way to nothing. Bryn squeezed her eyes closed, twisting her fingers in the mare's mane to steady herself.

"Open your eyes," Rangar ordered from behind her. She shook her head tightly. "Open your eyes, Bryn." His voice was softer this time.

When she did peek open one eye, at first she wasn't certain what she was looking at. Had they traveled so high that the sky filled the entire earth? Then she recognized a faint horizon line cutting through the wall of blue; the bottom half of the sky was a darker shade, bleeding into patches of green.

"That's the ocean, isn't it?" she whispered.

She'd learned about oceans from geography books. She knew they were made of salt water and held hundreds of kinds of fish and larger sea beasts. She knew about waves and tides and how they were influenced by the phases of the moon.

But she didn't *know* the ocean.

Before this moment, she didn't know how the sunlight played on the shifting waters. She didn't know how the distant sound of crashing waves was akin to her own breath coming and going. She didn't know that the salt air on the wind smelled of briny fish.

After a brief moment to admire the view, the rest of the Baer party continued riding down the cliff. The Baersladen was a coastal land; Rangar and his brothers had grown up in this wild, wet seaside place. To them, the crashing waves must feel like a homecoming.

Bryn barely took her eyes off the vast sea for even a second, hungry to devour the awe-inspiring blue eternity until they reached the bottom of the cliff, where the view was once more hidden from sight. The land here was rockier. Hardy grasses and shrubs clung to the rocky soil. The horses had to avoid boggy marshes that would have sucked their hooves in deep.

Now Bryn understood why people in the Mirien spoke with disdain about the Outlands: this was no place for fields of swaying grain. She was surprised *anything* could grow in the cold, briny soil. There was a beauty to the land, but it was wild and raw.

Trei led them onto a well-trodden path marked by a pile of rocks that was the first sign of civilization that Bryn had seen for days. A rock wall, ancient and most of it toppled over, bordered the path at one point. She saw signs of a well and the old rock foundation of a barn. Then they spied an old man digging peat on the moors and lifted a hand in greeting.

He waved back and returned to work.

Bryn felt the creep of anxiousness run along her neck.

These were foreign lands. Foreign people. Would they embrace her? Shun her? Accuse her of being a tyrant like her parents?

A few scraggly farmsteads appeared as they moved closer to the coast. Windswept ponies and shaggy cattle blinked lazily at them while eating grass. Then Bryn heard the loud peel of a bell. When they crested the next rise, she looked down over her new home.

"Barendur Hold," Rangar said, though he needn't have explained. The structure in front of them could be no other.

It was recognizable as a castle, though it bore little else in common with Castle Mir. Whereas Castle Mir was made of dove-gray limestone and birchwood and rose from the fields like an elegant awakening fawn, Barendur Hold was a crouching, mangy wolf. Its dark gray stone walls were rough-hewn and heavy. It was built on an outcropping so that the sea battered the easternmost portion. Instead of Castle Mir's many towers, this had only one large structure rising like a monolith.

Scattered around the Hold was a meager village much smaller than any town in the Mirien, with thatched roof cottages and fenced yards for livestock. A few wooden buildings clustered around stone jetties that stretched out to sea, where small wooden vessels were tethered in the water. On the shore, fishermen stretched out their nets and brought in fresh hauls. To the west, the forest pressed in.

Bryn's courage faltered. The land was beautiful, but the castle was not. Nothing here spoke of comfort. Nothing whispered of joy. It was going to be hard to find lightness amid such a dreary place. Suddenly, the pain and loneliness of the past few days returned to her.

Her parents were dead.

Her siblings were missing.

Her home was in ashes.

Rangar slid off his mare and then held out a hand to help

her down. His velvet eyes met hers. There was so much raw emotion there. Love for this land. Relief to be home. And something else, a ripple of excitement she'd rarely seen in the brooding prince.

"Come," he said cryptically. "There is something I want to show you before we reach your new home."

16

BARENDUR HOLD...MAIDEN ROSES...PIG SLOP
AND PRINCES...THROUGH THE GATES...A
NAUGHTY GOAT

*T*he other riders dismounted to walk their horses the rest of the way into the village. Ever since the bell had rung to announce their return, commonfolk were rushing out of their homes and gathering on their side of the road to welcome home their king, mage, and princes.

But Rangar motioned for Bryn to follow him away from the crowd, back toward the forest.

There was nothing here but an old stone wall and a patch of rocky pasture. The view of the ocean was beautiful but no better than it had been from any point on the road. Bryn couldn't imagine what he could possibly want to show her.

Rangar crouched down and pointed at the meadow. "There."

It took moment for Bryn to scan through the scrubby grass to see what he meant. Growing amid the tough Baer grasses were maiden roses. She started. *Maiden roses, here?*

In the Mirien, maiden roses covered the royal gardens in bursts of flamboyant pinks. Not true roses, they were actually a type of lily that grew on delicate stalks and bloomed for only a day.

"Maiden roses?" she asked. "How? The climate isn't right."

Maiden roses were a low-country plant. They thrived on sunlight and warmth. And they were finicky. She'd heard the castle gardeners grumbling about how hard it was to keep them from disease.

"They are not native to the Baersladen," Rangar explained. "Twenty years ago, a warrior brought their seeds back from the Mirien after traveling there for a High Sun Gathering. He meant them as a present for his wife. At first, it seemed the seeds would not germinate, so the wife threw them out here by the road. Several years later, people began to notice the white petals amid the grass. The flowers had survived but changed to adapt to our land."

They were different from the maiden roses she'd seen back home, it was true. Much lighter, almost white in color, instead of showy pink. And these weren't nicely bunched but instead woodsy and leggy, growing more like wildflowers.

"You aren't the only one to leave your home," Rangar said quietly. "You, too, will find your own way to thrive here."

Bryn plucked a blossom and tucked it into Rangar's horse's mane. It did warm her soul to see a small piece of home here. Something small but familiar. Still, it was overwhelming to think of being so far from everything she'd known. Her worries were only abated when commotion at the castle caught her attention.

King Aleth and his elder two sons had made it to the castle gates, and someone was shrieking to see them approach. Bryn shielded her eyes from the sun to see. A woman perhaps ten years older than Bryn came racing out of the castle and ran across the path toward the riders.

Suddenly, Trei broke from the group and ran toward the woman. He scooped her in his arms, spinning her around.

"Is that Trei's wife?" Bryn asked in surprise. She hadn't heard that the eldest prince was married.

"They are not wed," Rangar explained. "But it seems imminent. Saraj is a huntswoman. She oversees the falconry house. They have courted since Trei was my age."

The woman, Saraj, had a strange kind of beauty. She was nearly as tall as Trei and unusually thin, with a rope of black hair that extended below her hips. They embraced shamelessly, right out in the open. Bryn flushed to watch them kiss with a kind of passion that people in the Mirien reserved for private, dark corners. She'd never seen her parents embrace like that. She'd *heard* Mars display equal passion with the women he frequented, but always behind closed doors.

The Baer king, Valenden, and Mage Marna began embracing the servants, farmers, and fishermen who came up to them. Bryn watched like she was dreaming. *A king hugging a fisherman fresh off the boat, still reeking of fish guts? Unheard of!*

As she and Rangar entered the village square—if the bare patch of ground could be called that—many people called his name, waving. Though they didn't attempt to embrace the brooding youngest prince, they clearly adored him. Bryn slid him a glance. "Is anyone going to come dashing out to kiss you passionately?" She put a teasing edge into her words—obviously, Rangar had no woman. It was *Bryn* he was obsessed with.

But Rangar raised an eyebrow and said, "I would be disappointed if she didn't."

Bryn's mood fell like a stone in water. *Wait.* Rangar had a girl? A lover? Why had he never mentioned anyone to Bryn?

As soon as the questions tumbled over one another in her mind, she wondered why the idea shook her so much. Until a few days ago, Rangar had been her enemy. A savage who wanted to steal her away and make her his own. She didn't appreciate his possessive claim, but the idea that his heart might belong to another woman made her feel surprisingly alarmed.

Why? He is only a means to safety.

But that wasn't true, and she knew it. Since she'd been eight years old, Rangar had meant something to her. Not to mention the ten years of dreaming about him ever since. In particular, she'd known he was special on the night he came back into her life, on the balcony overlooking the remembrance garden when he had touched her scars through her dress and confessed that he'd never forgotten about her.

Though she didn't believe in the *fralen* bond, the connection between them was undeniable. It was like a string just under her skin, binding her to him.

A grin broke out on his usual moody face as a hound came charging out of the castle. He dropped his sack and knelt on one knee. The dog bounded up to him, whining and wagging her tail fiercely, licking his face with dog kisses.

"I missed you, too, Lady," he laughed.

Once Bryn realized his fantasy lover was merely his favorite hound, she found herself smiling, too. Rangar usually wasn't one to joke unless it was to mock her. She liked to see him like this, laughing and scratching the dog's back as it pawed around him.

When she looked up, she was surprised to find how large the gathered crowd around had become. Hundreds of people pressed in to greet Rangar and his family. She wrapped Mage Marna's borrowed cloak tighter around her shoulders. Was she trying to hide her tattered Mir clothing? A part of her felt guilty that she felt ashamed of her home, but another part of her was still coming to terms with the fact that her parents were known to everyone but her for having been tyrants.

She suddenly wanted nothing more than to be home. Back

in her bedroom. Surrounded by her familiar things. Her books, her own bed, her view out the window. Only the faces of strangers looked at her now. This place smelled so different—not like lavender, but like fish.

A gray-haired woman in an apron with a pronounced limp said several warm words to Rangar in Baer and then looked curiously a few times at Bryn. Bryn felt the push of tears in her eyes but told herself she wouldn't cry. Not if they yelled at her. Not if they threw things at her. She would stand strong no matter what.

But after Rangar spoke with the woman, she limped forward and unexpectedly pulled Bryn into an embrace. Bryn immediately bristled. But this was no assault. The woman had the warm comfort of a grandmother, and she patted Bryn on the back and said something that Bryn didn't understand but had the steady rhythm of words of welcome.

After the gray-haired woman embraced her, several others came forward to take her hand and give her words that sounded encouraging. Their smiles were certainly friendly enough. Shockingly, Bryn felt *accepted* by the crowd, the same as if she was Rangar or Valenden or Trei. Now tears threatened at her eyes but for a different reason.

No one shamed her for having tyrants for parents. No one called her weak or unworthy. Once they understood she was Rangar's Saved, they welcomed her as one of them.

She was still getting used to the idea of shaking hands with fishermen and farmers, hating that she had ever been told it was wrong to be friendly to such people, when the frightened whinny of a horse and the sudden, sharp call of an old man made the happy crowd pause.

A cart had lost its wheel at the far end of town square. As the crowd stepped back from the cart, Bryn saw that it had been carrying pigs. Their squeals filled the square. Their messy slop was leaking out onto the muddy road. The old man driving the cart had fallen and now lay in the street, moaning, trapped under a strut.

Trei rushed forward to help, with Saraj just a step behind him. Though the mud was a foot thick and covered in pig feces, the prince and the huntswoman didn't bat an eye. They threw their shoulders under the broken cart and heaved with all their strength. A few fishermen rushed in to help the old man scramble out from under the cart. Pigs squealed frantically until Trei was able to steady the cart with the help of a few other men.

Bryn watched the scene unfold in utter fascination. She thought of her own brother. Mars was Trei's age and was also the eldest child. Mars had been physically trained for combat, but in his twenty-three years, Bryn had never once seen him step in pig slop to help a poor old man. Or do *anything* to personally help one of their subjects. And yet Trei had rushed to help without thinking: an heir who didn't hesitate to cover himself with filth if necessary.

This was true leadership, Bryn realized. *This* was what the Mirien lacked and why her people had rebelled. She hadn't understood before.

The sun sank over the horizon while the brothers continued to help with the broken cart. A chill filled the air as night fell. Bonfires were lit around the square. People laughed and poked fun at Trei's muddy clothes, but he only laughed back, one arm slung around Saraj's waist affectionately.

Rangar appeared at her side. "Come," he commanded. "Night falls. We must get you a meal and a place to rest."

Bryn stared up at the imposing castle they called Barendur Hold. There was a drawbridge over a moat that was filled with seawater at high tide and deadly jagged rocks at low tide.

Beyond was an iron gate, raised now, that opened into a central hall.

The first thing she noticed was the unmistakable stink of animals. Pressing a hand to her nose, she looked around at the hall. It was one enormous room filled with long wooden tables and benches at one side; the other side's floor was covered in straw. Farmers were bringing in their cows and sheep for the night.

"You really do sleep with your animals!" she exclaimed.

Rangar gave her an odd look. "The animals are safest within the castle walls at night. There are dangerous predators in the forest."

"I know, but…" The words died on her lips. She didn't think it would suit her interests to talk about how Mir servants tittered under their breath rumors about how dirty the Baersladen was…

Two fires roared at either end of the great hall. Bryn frowned when she saw servants rolling out pallets on the floor over top of the straw. "And you…you want me to sleep here?" It was one thing to sleep on a bearskin cloak or a saddle blanket in the woods. But after five days, Bryn's body screamed for the comfort of a feather mattress.

Rangar motioned to a slightly elevated dais flanking one of the fireplaces. "Those with royal blood sleep there. You may, as well."

It wasn't much of an improvement. Servants were unrolling pallets onto the floor of the dais, presumably for the royal family. Most of the commonfolk in the great hall didn't even bother with pallets or pillows. They simply wrapped their cloaks around themselves and leaned into one another's warmth right on the stone floor and straw.

Red flushed up Bryn's face. She was supposed to sleep like this?

Rangar gave a command to a servant, who unrolled a pallet by the fireplace and brought out a pillow and wool blanket. He motioned to the makeshift bed. "You will sleep here."

Bryn could only stare at the thin pallet on the floor. There had to be thirty other people settling down to sleep in the great hall and twice as many animals. Sheep were bleating. A wayward goat came and curled up on her blanket.

Yet, after the five-day trek, she was exhausted through and through. All she wanted was something to fill her belly and a place to rest her head. At least tonight, unlike the previous few nights, she had a roof.

She lay down in her filthy dress. Closed her eyes.

This is my new life, she told herself.

She grabbed the blanket and fought the goat for the pillow.

17

SECRET THOUGHTS...HONEY WINE AND MUSIC...CLEAN HAIR...TOO MUCH MEAD...A FLIRTATION

*B*ryn must have drifted off in exhaustion for an hour or so because when she woke up, the goat was curled tightly by her side and music was playing in the great hall.

Blinking awake, she sat up and nudged the goat away. Judging by the moon through the open windows high up on the wall, it had to be late evening, maybe nine o'clock. A few other people slumbered on their pallets, but most were still awake, chatting softly to one another, playing cards, listening to the music.

A quartet of musicians was positioned by the opposite fireplace. She recognized a violin but not the other instruments, which looked homemade and rudimentary. Still, the musicians were skilled. It wasn't the refined melodies of Mir musicians, but the notes plucked at her heartstrings in a pleasant way. The song wasn't too rousing—no one was dancing—but not slow enough to put her back to sleep, either.

She yawned and looked around for Rangar or his brothers but saw no sign of any of them. Rangar's saddle blanket was rolled out next to her, though, and she wasn't sure if she felt comforted or alarmed that he apparently intended to sleep by her side. It had been one thing to do so while making camp in the woods, but they weren't in the woods any longer.

A woman came by and pressed a tankard and a biscuit into her hands. It was warm, fresh baked, and Bryn blinked at her in surprise. "Thank you—" But the woman was already gone, and besides, the Mir words would probably have fallen on unfamiliar ears.

She bit into the biscuit and let out a groan of pleasure. There was a splash of honey and cream inside that melted in her mouth. The bit of food awakened her more, and she found herself hugging her knees, enjoying the music, watching the evening activity around her with a tingle of curiosity. She took a sip from the tankard and immediately sputtered.

Mead—honey wine. And *strong*.

She'd tried mead once with some of the kitchen maids in Castle Mir, but her mother had always told her a lady didn't drink anything but wine. Now, Bryn took another sip. She found the sweet taste wasn't nearly as off-putting as she'd first thought. She took another deep sip, enjoying the cool liquid on her throat.

Another woman bent down and touched her shoulder. Bryn jumped in surprise. The woman wore an apron over her wool dress and had her dark curls pulled back into a braid. A girl with a similar hairstyle stood behind her. They beckoned to Bryn and said something she didn't understand.

"I'm sorry, I don't speak Baer," Bryn said helplessly.

The women exchanged a glance with each other. The first one gently touched Bryn's rumpled clothes and then pinched her nose in an exaggerated gesture that anyone would have known meant *"you stink."*

Bryn felt a flush of shame, though the women motioned kindly for her to come with them. She looked around for Rangar, but he was still nowhere to be found. Hesitantly, she pushed the goat aside and stood to her feet, limping slightly. Her legs were still wrung out from five days atop a horse.

The women bade her follow them down a corridor that led away from the great hall. They seemed to bear her no ill will, but Bryn reassured herself that she had Rangar's knife tucked into her skirt waistband if she needed it. The corridor was lit only by a few tallow candles. Alcoves were tucked into the walls, not unlike at Castle Mir, and Bryn sucked in a sharp breath to hear the unmistakable sounds of couples together in the shadows.

Moaning. Skin slapping together. *Well, what did I expect?* she thought wryly. In a castle where everyone slept in one big room, couples had to have someplace to sneak off for a moment of intimacy...

To her relief, the two women turned a corner that led to a bath chamber. A sunken stone tub let off steam. A small fire in the corner heated more water for the bath.

The first woman mimicked taking off her clothes to show her what they expected. Bryn bit her lip. She'd never been naked in front of strangers. But her body yearned to sink into the warm bath. Fortunately, the bath chamber was empty except for the two women.

Toughen up. This is your life now.

She started to unbutton her blouse. One of the women padded the pot handles with heavy towels and poured more fresh steaming water into the basin. The other disappeared down another hallway. Bryn shed her blouse and motioned for the woman to help her undo her skirt buttons. As soon as it was done, she waved the woman away. She didn't want her to see the knife in the skirt's folds. She quickly balled up the clothes and set them on the floor.

Bryn quickly sank into the hot water and nearly cried in relief.

It was deliciously scalding. This was the first time she'd felt truly warm since she'd left Castle Mir. Though Rangar had warmed the stream water for her, it was hardly a luxurious experience. Now, the bathwater began to unwind her tight, sore muscles, and she closed her eyes and leaned her head back. She wanted nothing more than to remain in the steaming water for days. In the distance, the music coming from the great hall played a pleasant lullaby.

She jerked in alarm when one of the women touched her bare shoulder again, but it was only to hand Bryn a bar of lye soap.

The soap was harsh, nothing like Mir's perfumed soaps, but Bryn was so happy to have soap that she didn't care that it made her skin itch. She rubbed it into her hair and over every inch of her body.

"Rangar," the woman said tentatively in Mir. "Rangar...woman."

It was more Mir than Bryn spoke of Baer, so she could hardly judge the woman for her stilted words, but she shook her head quickly. "No. No, I'm not Rangar's woman. I'm his...Saved?"

She hated to use the word—to acknowledge the claim he thought he had on her. But she didn't know any other way to explain the situation.

The woman didn't seem to believe her anyway.

Soon, the younger woman returned carrying a towel and a stack of wool clothes. They helped Bryn out of the bath and dried her hair. The wool dress they'd brought her was simple enough, though it had an unfamiliar sash that they had to instruct her how to tie. The dress hung heavier on her and stiffer than she was used to, but the fabric was surprisingly soft. And most importantly, warm. The wool stockings kept her feet wonderfully cozy.

One of the women started to braid her damp hair into the same style of knots they wore, but Bryn shook her head. It was one thing to wear a Baer dress, but she wasn't ready to completely brand herself as a Baer woman—not that her shock of blonde hair would have fooled anyone anyway. The women relented, and Bryn coiled her hair in a simple twist at the base of her skull.

They pointed the direction for her to return to the great hall. After the bath, clean clothes, a biscuit in her belly, and mead making her pleasantly light-headed, she was feeling like a person again instead of the walking dead. She followed the dark corridor, again blushing at the sounds of rutting couples in the nearby alcoves, and turned toward where she thought the great hall was, but she must have been confused because she found herself stumbling straight into an alcove instead.

Valenden. He was the first person she noticed, but he wasn't alone.

There was only a single faint candle in the alcove, but the middle brother's sharp eyes were unmistakable. His chest was stripped bare to his waist. His hair was loose and tangled around his shoulders. An equally bare-chested boy around Bryn's age was trailing his lips along Valenden's jawline.

Bryn gaped. For a second, her eyes locked with Valenden's. Normally she would have sputtered an apology and rushed away, but the mead had made her a little bolder and a little slower-witted. She only stared.

Val gave her a slow wink.

She quickly turned and hurried down the main hallway. *That* was unexpected. How was she ever going to face him again? She had a cousin like that—a man who liked the company of other men. It wasn't so very scandalous, but still. Boy or girl, she would have been embarrassed to have seen Valenden half-naked with *anyone*.

When she returned, the goat was asleep on her pillow, but she flounced down next to it and focused on the musicians' melodies, trying not to wonder if Rangar was in another alcove right now, his lips on someone else.

Besides her thoughts, she found herself strangely at ease next to the roaring fire, with the soft music and chatter and heavy breathing of the goat. There was something comforting about not sleeping in a room alone. Here, there would always be someone close, help if needed. Not to mention the warmth of the bodies so close together.

She downed the rest of her tankard of mead and closed her eyes as it unwound her body and her mind. She thought again of Valenden in the alcove with that boy. Then, emboldened by the mead, half-asleep and possibly even half-drunk, she imagined it was her and Rangar instead. That he had pulled her into the candlelit darkness and was trailing his lips along her jawline. That Rangar's hands were on her waist and moving higher, inch by inch, until his palm grazed her breast through her clothing. For five long days on horseback, she had felt the length of his body against her back and, for a brief moment in the woods, pressed against her front. She realized that she badly wanted to feel it again. His rigid muscles against her soft body. She wanted him to slip his hot palm between the buttons of her blouse and graze her bare ribs. *The scars.*

Her breath started to quicken as she imagined touching her own lips to the scars on his face. What would he do? Even in a land of desolate wilderness, Rangar was particularly brooding, but she'd glimpsed the passion that he kept contained behind a charade of control. She relived the thrill of him leaning his weight against her in the woods…

The goat stepped on her thigh, and she winced, sitting up suddenly and opening her eyes. "Oof," she groaned at it. "Really?"

It turned in a circle, bleated, and cuddled next to her again. Then, she became aware of a different set of eyes watching her.

While she'd been half-asleep and fantasizing, Rangar had returned. He was now reclined on his saddle blanket, watching her curiously in the flickering firelight. The musicians had stopped playing and put away their instruments for the night. Most of the hall was asleep now. It was probably nearly midnight. Bryn flushed, feeling as though Rangar could read the secret thoughts that had been flowing through her head.

It was only then that she realized her knife had vanished. The women had taken away her old clothes, probably to burn them, and with them, the knife tucked in the skirt folds.

Seeing the frightened look on her face, Rangar leaned forward. "Do you fear me still?" he asked quietly.

Bryn swallowed. Did she?

Not in the way she once had. She didn't fear that he would harm her or steal her away for nefarious intentions. The *fralen* bond still didn't sit right with her and probably never would, but she suspected Rangar was no threat.

Still, that didn't mean she felt entirely *safe* with him—with a man who made her think wicked thoughts that the Mirien's priests would scold her for. She couldn't blame it *all* on the mead.

She swallowed hard. "No."

He smirked again like he knew her secret thoughts. "If you are cold tonight," he said in a low, tempting voice, "sleep against me. For warmth."

Her eyebrows shot up. Was this what passed for flirting in

the Baersladen? If he thought he was going to win her over that easily, he was wrong.

She raised an eyebrow. "I'd sooner cuddle with the goat."

The smirk tugged harder at the corner of his mouth, and he laughed and lay down on his own pallet.

18

*I*n the morning, Bryn woke to find Rangar's smirk from the night before had transformed to a frown. Worse, it was now aimed squarely at her.

She sat up in a rush, having forgotten where she was from the mead clouding her thoughts. Light pierced the room's high open windows. She squinted around the great hall as the commonfolk and farmers roused themselves, brushed the wrinkles from their clothes, and rolled up their sleeping pallets, then began to herd the bleating livestock back outside.

She had a vague memory of Rangar and her scooting dangerously close to each other in the long cold hours of night until they were barely a breath apart, wanting each other's warmth but not daring to touch skin to skin. She hadn't been bold enough to act out her secret thoughts, not even with a tankard of mead in her belly, and she was terrified of what would happen if Rangar touched her like that boy had touched Valenden in the private alcove. Would she slap him—or pull him closer?

"Why are you frowning at me like that?" she asked.

"I'm wondering if I prefer you as a blonde or a brunette," Rangar said with an appraising look.

With a frown of her own, Bryn touched her hair, confused. Black dust came off on her fingertips. Her fair curls had somehow blackened overnight. *The ashes*, she realized. She looked at the nearby fireplace and realized that sometime during the midnight cold, she had partially rolled into the hearth and was now covered in black ashes.

At least I didn't catch fire.

She pushed to her feet, brushing ashes off the wool dress the women had given her after her bath. She reknotted her tarnished hair at her nape.

Watching her steadily, Rangar said, "I have affairs to attend to now that I've returned. They are not suitable for you to accompany me. I want you to remain here, in the great hall."

"All day?" she protested. "I'll go mad stuck inside." Besides, the ocean was just outside the door. An entire world she knew nothing about. Boats. Fishermen. She wanted to see, touch, and learn everything.

"Do you still have the knife I gave you?" he asked.

She felt a flush of guilt that she'd lost it. "Why? Am I in danger?"

"Not from the Baer people. But there are still two Mir soldiers in pursuit. They will likely follow you here."

"I'll watch my back," she said tightly.

He didn't seem inclined to believe her, but he reluctantly nodded, perhaps convinced the rest of the town would keep an eye on her, and left.

Bryn watched as the castle population began their day. Baskets of biscuits were passed around as well as clay pitchers of fresh milk and small, wild strawberries. She filled her belly enthusiastically, feeling slightly guilty for taking more than her share. But how was one supposed to know exactly what one's share was when everyone shared everything freely?

When she returned to the dais beside the hearth, she found that her pallet and blanket had disappeared, rolled up and taken away by some castle servant and stored who-knows-where.

She wandered the hall until she spotted the black-eared goat that had bedded down on her pillow the night before. *The closest thing I have to a friend*, she thought wryly. A girl barely in puberty was herding Bryn's goat and the others out of the hold gates and across the footbridge. She gave Bryn a shy smile, so Bryn followed.

The goatherd girl led the herd beyond the moat into the village square. It was a misty morning, the fog hanging low and heavy. But that didn't seem to stop the fishermen, who were in the midst of preparing their ships for launch.

Bryn peeled away from the goatherd girl and wandered over to the stone causeway, watching the ships. She'd never seen any vessel larger than a paddleboat before. These massive ships looked like ancient things, hundreds of years old, repaired time and time again. She watched as a young fisherman laid out a badly tangled net; how could anyone possibly undo all the knots? Yet to her surprise, he didn't even try. Once the net was flat, he took several steps backward, then closed his eyes and traced a symbol in the air. Slowly, a gust of wind rolled over the net, seeming to loosen the knots on their own until the fisherman was able to easily tug them free.

Magic, Bryn realized.

When the boy saw her watching, he gave her a wave.

She wrapped her new wool cloak tighter around her. The goatherd, the fisherman...they didn't look at her like she was the daughter of tyrants. They weren't exactly what she would call sociable people—there was fierce independence in the way they went about their work and the same undercurrent of arrogant pride that Rangar and his brothers had. Their lives were difficult in such a barren land, and it showed in their spirits and their faces. Yet they were as quick to smile as to scowl.

She wandered the castle grounds all day, inspecting the meager vegetable garden, the stables, and the nearby village. It couldn't *be* more different from Castle Mir. Though Castle Mir outshone every aspect of Bardendur Hold in terms of wealth, no one here seemed to be lusting after riches. People spoke plainly. They appeared to trust one another and, more importantly, trust their rulers. She was watching a stableboy tame a skittish horse with hexmark magic when she felt eyes watching her and turned to find Mage Marna at the far end of the stable.

"You look as though you've seen a ghost, Lady Bryn." The old woman's familiar rumbling voice was a welcome comfort.

"I never knew magic was like this," Bryn confessed. "My parents thought it was backward. If they had only embraced it, our people could have been so much stronger."

"Magic is a tool of the commonfolk," Mage Marna explained. "There is a reason despots do not want it practiced. It gives the public too much power."

This darkened Bryn's mood. The mage came closer and ran a hand down Bryn's soot-darkened hair, and with a small magical gesture and a few words, the soot floated out of her locks like gnats until her hair gleamed blonde again. *Another spell.*

Bryn asked in a whisper, "Can you teach me to do magic?"

"As I said, it's a tool for the people. Accessible to everyone. There are no barriers, no restrictions. Anyone can learn. But it isn't simple."

"I'd like to speak Baer," Bryn said. "Could you give me the same translation hexmark that you have?"

Mage Marna shook her head. "That is not a beginner hexmark, as I told you before. It's highly advanced and would take you years of apprenticeship to be able to master the accompanying spell." Her expression softened. "I'll have one of my apprentices bring you a book we use to teach Baer children to read. You can start learning from that."

Frustrated, Bryn said, "Baer is one of the most challenging languages in the Eyrie. If this is my new home, I can't wait months or years to learn to speak to anyone but you or Rangar."

The mage cocked her head, narrowing her eyes as she studied Bryn. Bryn wasn't sure she liked the cryptic look there. "There could be another way."

Bryn perked up, interested.

Mage Marna stroked a thoughtful hand down her chin as she said, "It's part of my duties as head mage to invent new hexmarks for new spells. We carve hexmarks into our arms, chest, and back using a ritual called scarification, which give the caster unique abilities. But for the past few months, I've been experimenting with using hexes in other places, and on other entities. Trying to extend my own magic onto someone else, for example. I've only tried it so far on a horse, carving a hex into its hooves that matches one on my wrist to make it swifter of foot."

Bryn's eyes lit up. "You could do that? Transfer some of your translation ability onto me, like a spell by proxy?"

"Theoretically. You would be able to permanently tap into my ability to speak and understand other languages without having to learn the spell yourself. It's all very experimental, and I hesitate to try again."

Bryn felt a ripple of worry. "Why? What happened to the horse?"

Mage Marna's eyes shifted to an empty stall, and Bryn got a

bad feeling. Mage Marna said, "I'd be willing to try again, more cautiously this time. It would take me some time to prepare. But you'd have to understand the danger you could be in, Lady Bryn. Language involves the ear, so I'd have to carve hexes into your inner ear canal. There's a chance it could leave you deaf, perhaps even with brain damage, if not done correctly."

"I'm willing to take the risk. I trust your skill."

The mage raised an eyebrow. "But will *Rangar* let you take the risk?"

Bryn bristled. "It's my ear, not his."

Bryn thought she saw a flicker of a smile at the mage's mouth. The mage said, "I'll do some research on the possibility. I make no promises for now. In the meantime, your hands are too soft. You need good, tough work. Your body will need calluses and lean muscles if you're to survive in this land."

Bryn tried not to show her surprise at this. Work? She was a princess. Back home, her only job was to look pretty and study the noble sciences.

But that isn't my life anymore.

"All right," Bryn said, hoping she sounded more confident than she felt.

Mage Marna motioned for her to follow her. "This way. I have something in mind that will suit your skills."

A host of unpleasant jobs filled Bryn's head. *Cleaning latrines. Plucking chickens. Sweeping pigsties.*

They left the stable and crossed the chicken yard with its squawking fowl and ducks. Then Mage Marna opened a gate into a fenced-in, rocky pasture. This one held a mother ewe and four baby lambs.

"A woman named Elin used to be the shepherdess, but she is with child and must remain in bed for the next few weeks. Until her babe arrives, you will tend to the lambs. Feed the ewe and fill her water trough from the well in the town square.

Every day, take the lambs to the field down the path that skirts the village for grazing. Watch over them and ensure they return safely in the evenings."

It seemed a simple enough job, but Bryn had never tended to livestock before. She had no idea how to herd a lamb. But when Mage Marna passed her a curved wooden shepherd's crook, she could hardly say no. These people had saved her life. Given her a home. Food and clothing.

It's better than cleaning latrines, she reasoned with herself.

"Keep the lambs safe," Mage Marna said, "and we'll see about magic."

* * *

OVER THE NEXT FEW DAYS, Bryn became *very* well acquainted with lambs.

For example, what little devils they were. As cute as they seemed, the instant her back was turned, they would sprint off to greener pastures. They seemed to know all the weak parts of the stone walls surrounding the mountain pastures and would gleefully slip between the rocks as though they had a death wish.

As the days passed, she saw Rangar only at night. After his long absence from the village, he and his father and brothers were busy handling issues that had arisen while they were away, as well as running training exercises with the Baer army. But Rangar appeared at supper every evening, inquiring about her day, and slept by her side each night. She busied herself in the evenings after her chores were done by reading through the children's book that Mage Marna's apprentice had brought her, trying to learn some Baer words...but she found the Baer language utterly incomprehensible and unpronounceable and felt more and more inclined to attempt the experimental spell.

But she was hesitant to bring it up to Rangar, until one evening, as they ate from bowls of boiled vegetables and fish, Rangar brought it up first. "My aunt said something about an experimental spell she wants to try on you."

Bryn swallowed a thick bite of potato. She nodded slowly, not sure how best to convince him it was the best course of action. "She thinks she can extend her translation hex to me. It's important for me to speak Baer, Rangar. This won't be my home until I do. And my efforts to teach myself are abysmal. Your language makes no sense."

A muscle shifted in Rangar's jaw. "I assume she warned you of the risk."

"She did."

He studied her for a long time, then shook his head. "As your Savior, it is in my right to forbid it."

A blade of anger sliced into her. Rangar hadn't brought up the *fralen* bond in days. For the most part, he had let her go about her life as she pleased, and this stark reminder of his hold over her stung. He still believed she was his. "You wanted me to adapt like the maiden roses," she argued. "That's what I'm trying to do."

"You can learn the language without magic, as I learned Mir. From books."

"That will take months. Maybe years!"

"So be it."

Hot breath puffed out of her nose. Her hand itched to slap him. The audacity to think he could command her! "Rangar—" she started hotly.

"You are mine," he cut her off with a growl. "You forget that too easily."

"You still think me so soft?" She spat out at him, refusing to be cowed by his tone. She held up her calloused hands as proof. After days of wielding the shepherd's crook and climbing through rocky fields, her skin had toughed considerably.

The hard set to his face eased. "I told you, Lady Bryn, not everyone must be hardened. I like...soft things." His eyes had dropped to her lips.

She swallowed, suddenly very aware of the narrow distance between them. The roaring fire threw out heat that made her cheeks warm. Lingering anger made her chest heave, but just below it was a frustrating wave of desire.

Rangar leaned closer to brush his thumb over her chin to wipe away a drop of stew. "Why do you think I followed you into the woods all those years ago? It was because you *weren't* Baer. You were the opposite of a Baer child. You were fair of hair and had skin as soft as goose down. And yet you were bold enough to sneak off. You intrigued me. Everything about you, like a riddle. So you must forgive me if I am not too eager to see you change into something you're not."

His words were thoughtful enough, and it tempered her anger slightly. It was true that he had accepted her just as she was and never tried to force her to change. But what if she *wanted* to change? Even in this small way, just undergoing a ritual to speak his language?

A girl from the kitchen came by with baskets of rolls. She exchanged a few words with Rangar, laughing at something he said, her eyes gleaming. Bryn swallowed back the undeniable rush of jealousy she felt. As soon as the kitchen wench left, Bryn said quietly, "I've seen the way girls look at you. You have admirers. Haven't any of them caught your eye?"

"No." The swiftness of his answer caught her off guard.

She swallowed again. "There are many beautiful women in the Baersladen..."

"There are." As he regarded her, his eyes grew darker with want. "None of them are you."

Slowly, as though asking permission, he slipped his hand under her wool cloak and pressed it over her dress, over the location of her scars. Instinct told her to pull away. They were in a room full of people! Anyone could see him touching her if they cared to look.

But no one did.

His fingers curled around her hip, drawing her closer until her knee brushed against his. A part of her bristled. Only moments ago, he'd forbidden her from the experimental hexmark ritual. He was frustratingly stubborn—but she was too. *He can tell me "no" as much as he likes,* she told herself. *It doesn't mean I won't do it. Just that I won't tell him.*

She sat next to him, highly aware of his body so close to hers, and breathed in his scent as they listened to the lilting music and crackling fires.

I'm going to do it anyway, she thought.

19

HEXMARKS...THE TOWER...POTIONS AND HERBS...ALTAR UNDER THE MOON...AN ANGRY PRINCE

*A*fter Bryn had been in the Baersladen for several weeks, she felt as though her previous life was more of a dream than real life. Had there ever been a time when she hadn't slept wrapped in a wool blanket beside a fire with Rangar at her side? When her days weren't filled with long walks through rocky meadows accompanied by the bleats of little lambs? She'd become so used to the ever-present scent of salt on the air and the rhythmic crash of waves that she now marked the passage of hours by the tides instead of the sun's progress across the sky.

Like the maiden roses, she was finding a way to thrive in her new environment.

And yet, as much as she enjoyed lying in the meadow with her hair down and free, able to kick off her shoes and wade in cold mountain streams whenever she liked while lambs scampered around her, in the quiet stretches of afternoon, her thoughts often turned back to her family. The memory of her father's body slumped on his throne would be forever branded into her brain. It was somehow both better and worse that she didn't know how her mother had died. The rumor was that

Mars had escaped, but there was no word from him, nor from Elysander. She had no idea where her siblings were, how they fared, or if they knew she was alive, too.

King Aleth sent soldiers to patrol the border mountains, but they never found a trace of the Mir soldiers who had supposedly been sent to apprehend her. Mage Marna had attempted more scrying spells, but they'd come back inconclusive. For all Bryn knew, Mir soldiers could be waiting around every boulder to snatch her back to the Mirien to face the same grisly fate as her parents.

The truth was, *this* was her home now. This windswept, barren, beautiful land. And *these* were her people—though how close could she get to them if she couldn't even speak their tongue? The Baer language was incredibly challenging, with tones she couldn't pronounce and a completely new alphabet. The few phrases she'd managed to memorize—good day, thank you, where is Rangar?—didn't get her far. But she had a plan.

Whether Ranger allows it or not, I'm going to let Mage Marna give me the hexmark.

She waited until Rangar departed on a two-night voyage with a small team of fishers, following rumors of a nearby pod of whales that would provide lamp oil and meat for the whole village for weeks. She'd stood with the fishers' wives and husbands on the causeway and wished Rangar strong wind in his sails, and then the moment his ship disappeared on the horizon, she went in search of Mage Marna.

She found the mage in the upper tower of Barendur Hold, a room filled with herbs and animal skins and thick leather-bound books. Two apprentices around Bryn's age sat on a bench, a boy and a girl, practicing their spells under the older mage's tutelage. Despite the fact that Mage Marna's back was turned to Bryn in the doorway, the mage must have sensed her presence through either magic or keen hearing. She said without bothering to face Bryn, "I thought you might come tonight."

Bryn exchanged a glance with the teenage apprentices, who peeked up from their books curiously at the fair-haired foreign princess speaking a language they didn't know.

"You know why I'm here?" Bryn asked Mage Marna in Mir.

The mage gave a few instructions to the apprentices, then went to the worktable in the center of the room, where she picked up a small piece of antler and a mortar and pestle. She motioned vaguely in the direction of the room's single window, which faced the ocean, before beginning to grind the antler into a fine powder. "I saw Rangar's ship leaving the port. You've been watching his movements like a hawk over the last few weeks, as well as my own. I don't need magic to surmise you've been waiting for him to leave for a few days. Are you certain that you want to cross the wishes of your Savior? He made it clear he believes the ritual is too dangerous for you to undergo."

Bryn tipped her chin up. "The *fralen* bond is your belief, not mine. I don't owe Rangar any obedience."

Mage Marna didn't glance up from her work with the antler. "But now you are one of us. Living among us. Our culture is your culture."

Bryn came forward and rested her hands on the worktable across from the mage. "I am free to decide my own mind regardless of what culture I belong to."

Mage Marna paused her work to give Bryn an approving nod. "Good girl. Don't ever let yourself be cowed by a man, or by anyone at all, for that matter. I should warn you, however, that Rangar has a temper. You will likely bear his wrath when he returns, but I would do the same as you. Now, if you're sure of your decision, come with me." The mage selected a wicker basket from the room's shelves and went around collecting objects to fill it with: a corked bottle, a few clean rags, and a long, thin knife whose fire-tarnished sharp point made Bryn's stomach turn.

Mage Marna beckoned to the two apprentices studying on the bench. "Calista. Ren. You as well. Come."

Bryn followed Mage Marna and the apprentices up the tower's narrow winding stairs that were so tight, the sides of her body brushed the curving walls. Her legs ached by the time they arrived at the top. It opened onto a flat stone rooftop perched dizzyingly high over the nearby sea and forests. Unlike in Castle Mir, there was no guardrail to keep a person from falling off the roof. Bryn tiptoed as close to the edge as she dared and carefully peered down. It was a fall of a hundred feet onto the rocks below, battered by waves. Certain death.

Bryn hugged her wool cloak tighter against the cold.

A stone altar exposed to the open air and moonlight loomed nearby. On the opposite side of the castle's roof, a pair of sentinels scanned the night for any sign of intruders and maintained a fire beacon that would alert the Baersladen villages of possible danger. Now, only a small portion of the beacon was lit, which meant all was well. The sentinels gave them a curious glance but then returned to their conversation.

"Take off your clothes," Mage Marna ordered. "And lie flat on the altar."

Bryn looked in alarm between the sentinels and the teenage apprentices. It was one thing to strip naked in front of an elderly woman, but grown men? A flutter of fear began in her belly. She clenched her jaw. *I'm not in the Mirien anymore.* The Baersladen was much more informal when it came to modesty. It was common to see nursing mothers with their breasts free or youths swimming naked in the ocean. Still, it took all her courage to unbutton her wool dress, shivering, and slide out of it.

Moonlight shone on her bare limbs and chest. There were no shadows to hide behind, no screens. She quickly climbed onto the altar, trying hard not to feel self-conscious. Her whole life, she'd been told to hide her scars. Scars that had threatened her future marriage prospects. Scars that tied her to a kingdom that she'd been told was wicked and wrong—a kingdom that was now her home.

But if the apprentices were surprised to see the scars, they didn't show it. Bryn stared up at the sky overhead and felt herself shivering in fear. Was she really doing this? Accepting *magic* into her body, the thing she'd been told since childhood was a terrible sin? And at what risk?

Mage Marna motioned for the apprentices to hold her down.

Bryn felt her body start shaking harder. Her heart was pounding so hard she was surprised the whole altar didn't shake.

The female apprentice, Calista, reached for her wrists, and the other, Ren, grabbed her ankles at the foot of the table. Bryn pulled her appendages in, overcome by a wave of fear.

"It is necessary to restrain you," Mage Marna explained. "I cannot give you a draught to relieve the pain you're about to face. Your senses must not be dulled when receiving a hexmark, otherwise the magic will be muddled and unpredictable. My apprentices will hold you still so that I can carve the mark accurately."

Bryn was filled with second thoughts. She'd been warned this ritual was experimental and potentially dangerous. She didn't want to end up like the horse Mage Marna had experimented on before. She trusted Mage Marna's skill but now felt doubts about her own abilities. She hadn't been raised to be as hardened as these people. What if she couldn't take the pain? She might flinch and mess up the ritual, or pass out, or throw up the potion. Or what if magic really was as evil as her parents said? It struck her for a brief moment that she might never rise from this table again. If something went wrong, this could be her last night on earth.

What if Rangar is right that it's too dangerous?

Was it really wise to risk her hearing, even possibly her life, simply to be able to speak to the Baer people? But before her fears could spiral out of control, she reminded herself that it was about more than gaining the ability to speak a foreign tongue. It was about proving she belonged here. The Baer commonfolk had accepted her, and she owed them her life. Giving up her wrongheaded former beliefs that magic was sinful and embracing the wonders of the unknown.

This ritual is just the beginning.

One of the apprentices raised a questioning eyebrow, and Bryn relented and lay back down on the stone altar. She took a deep breath to calm her racing heart. She couldn't help how her limbs were shaking, but she could at least try to be brave.

At Mage Marna's signal, the two apprentices held her down again by her wrists and ankles at the corners of the altar. The white-haired mage dug through the wicker basket and took out the bottle. She uncorked it and let it decant for a moment in the moonlight while she recited a chant. Once the wispy steam had dissipated from the bottle, Mage Marna pressed the glass rim to Bryn's lips.

"Drink this," she commanded. "I warn you, it will hurt worse than the knife will. You may experience strange visions and begin to feel like you are dying, but I assure you, I will keep you alive. You will likely require several days' recovery if we are successful." At Bryn's slight nod, the mage tipped the bottle upward. Spicy liquid poured between Bryn's lips. It tasted vile and heavily of salt, like turgid seawater, and she gagged as it burned its way down her throat. Immediately, her stomach seized up in cramps. A moan slipped out of her mouth. On impulse, she buckled forward and tried to sit up.

Mage Marna swiftly motioned for the apprentices to keep holding her down.

Their hands became like iron vises around Bryn's wrists and ankles. Pain burst through every part of her body, even in places she didn't know one could *feel* pain: her bones, her hair. Starbursts exploded across her vision. The moon became a splotch of light in the dark sky. She wished the toxic potion made her groggy, but instead, it only intensified her awareness. She'd never felt so awake. She could taste the air. Hear every crackle of flame from the beacon fire. She was vaguely aware that her body was shaking hard but couldn't do a thing to stop it.

Mage Marna spoke a spell in her low, deep voice as she pressed one hand on Bryn's forehead, holding her head steady, and with the other touched the knife's point to Bryn's inner ear. Bryn felt the touch like a beesting. Her every instinct told her to pull away, but she forced herself to remain still. As the knife began to cut deep inside her ear, she felt herself rising from the table, looking down on herself in a terrifying vision. At once, she saw impossible things, like time and space were fracturing: *she was back in her bedroom in Castle Mir; she was facing her father's dead body; she was on a horse with Rangar; she was covered with blood that might be her own.*

She was dimly aware of the mage moving the knifepoint with well-practiced movements to make tiny cuts along her ear canal. The apprentices threw their weight on her to hold her steady. The potion made her weak, her muscles slack and shaking. She was vaguely aware of Mage Marna slicing open her own translation hexmark on her inner arm, spilling blood from it into Bryn's ear. *Extending her magic to me.* Bryn tasted the tang of blood somewhere in the back of her throat.

Finally, Mage Marna set down the knife. She took a rag to wipe off her hands and gave Bryn a grim smile. In her hazy delusions, the mage's smile continued to stretch wider and wider until it became the crescent moon itself. Then, everything went black.

* * *

WHEN BRYN WOKE, she was in a bed. *Real sheets. A feather mattress. A proper pillow with a satin case.*

It had been weeks since she'd slept anywhere but on a stiff pallet on the floor with a lumpy pillow if she was lucky, so it took her a while to come to terms with where she was. Could she possibly be home in Castle Mir? What if she'd never left, and her time in the Baersladen had been a dream? Where her recent memories should be was only a hazy shadow. All she could recall were improbable dreams about sea monsters holding knives in their tentacles as other tentacles pinned her down.

She sat up stiffly, reaching up to touch a bandage around her head. It ran from her forehead and covered her left ear. A memory began to return to her. A stone altar and apprentices, so much pain...

She clapped a hand over the bandage, remembering the sharp stab of pain.

The door to wherever she was suddenly flung open, and a familiar figure came striding in with barely contained anger. Her vision was still blurry around the edges, but the scowl twisting his face was unmistakable.

"Rangar?" she asked groggily.

He gripped the wooden top rail of the bed's footboard, his muscles set on edge. "You defied me, Bryn."

She pressed a hand to her forehead as more memories

returned, most of them frighteningly full of the most intense pain she'd ever felt in her life. "I don't quite remember—"

His hair fell over his eyes, which were simmering with anger. "I ordered you not to get the hexmark."

Everything came rushing back to her at his words. *The hexmark.* Now she remembered being on the castle rooftop while Rangar was away on a fishing voyage. She remembered the bottle of potion, the apprentices holding her down to the stone altar while Mage Marna carved into her ear and whispered spells. How many days ago had that been? How long had she been lying unconscious in this bed? She now noticed several empty bowls of broth on the bedside table, as though she'd woken and eaten over the course of several days, though she had no memory of it. She glanced at Rangar's damp clothes—he must have just returned from the whaling trip and come straight here after stepping back onto the dock.

Wherever this room is, she thought. She'd never once seen a real bed in Barendur Hold.

Carefully unwinding the bandage from her head, she asked, "Did it work?"

But Rangar was too angry to listen to her. "If she had cut just slightly too far into your ear, she could have left you permanently deaf. Or worse. If you'd jerked your head the wrong way, she could have stabbed into your brain." He shook his head. "I don't know who I'm more furious with, you or my aunt."

Bryn ignored his scolding and looked around the room, still trying to get her bearings. The stone walls were the same throughout Barendur Hold, so she assumed she was still in the castle. An open window let in sunlight and fresh air. Wooden shelves on one side of the room held stacks of clean rags and rolls of bandages; it appeared to be a sickroom. That explained the bed—it was for patients who needed more comfort than the floor.

Still ignoring the scowl on Rangar's face, she asked, "How will I know if the ritual worked and I can understand Baer?"

Rangar's scowl eased. In a low voice, he said, "What do you think we've been speaking in this whole time?"

Bryn's eyebrows rose in surprise. Was it true? She touched her fingers to her lips, realizing that the shape of her words felt different on her tongue. Not like the smooth precision of Mir; now, her tongue moved more gutturally. As a thrill ran through her veins, she whispered, "You mean I did magic?"

He grunted. "You're siphoning off my aunt's magic, using *her* translation hexmark by proxy. It was a foolish experiment, and my father never should have let her try."

But Bryn ignored his chastisement. True, the magic wasn't *hers*, but she was able to benefit from it just the same. A whole new world had opened up to her. She would be able to speak to and understand the villagers. And that was only the start. Now that she could communicate, she could learn. She could read the textbooks throughout Barendur Hold, study with the mage's other apprentices. *Maybe I could one day learn to cast my own spells. Have real magic, not just borrowed from a mage.*

Rangar stalked around the foot of the bed to move close to her with a predator's prowl. None of her newfound excitement seemed to rub off on him. He growled, "You are mine to protect, Bryn. You defied the orders of your Savior."

A bolt of annoyance shot through her as she threw back the covers. "I'm *not* yours, Rangar. I belong to no one but myself."

A muscle tightened in his jaw as his eyes raked down her body. "Be that as it may, I know what is best for you. This was a mistake. You could have died."

She swung her legs off the bed and stood up, resting her hands on her hips. "But I didn't die. And if I have to make a thousand mistakes, I will, because my life is my own." She picked up a wooden spoon from one of the broth bowls and waved it threateningly at him. "And my privacy is, too. Now, stop scowling at me and give me some space!"

He narrowed his eyes. He seemed to be warring with himself if he wanted to drag her out of the bed, throw her over his shoulder, and bend her to his will—perhaps by crushing his lips to hers—or respect her wishes.

She pulled back her arm to throw the spoon at him, letting it fly. He ducked just in time, and the dirty spoon clattered to the floor. He straightened, narrowed his eyes, and shook his head, running a slow hand down the stubble on his jaw. "You want space?" he muttered in a frighteningly low growl as he stalked out of the room. "Fine. I'll give you *space*."

20

THE LOST LAMB...FOOLISH DESIRES...THE WRONG BROTHER...NEWS FROM MIR...A PRISONER

*B*ryn and Rangar didn't speak for days. They each went about their work—her tending to the lambs in the pasture, him training as a captain with the soldiers—only sliding each other fleeting glances when their paths crossed. He no longer slept beside her at night on the dais by the hearth, but rather a few places away on the far side of Valenden and Trei: close enough that he could remain her protector if needed but at a distance. *Well, let him*, she thought. She had never *asked* for his protection. He'd saved her life more than once, but that had been *his* choice.

She wasn't sure which one of them was more stubborn.

As summer drew to an end and the mornings grew colder, the Baer people began preparing for the long, arduous harvest weeks that were to come and would require villagers and royals alike to pitch in. Though it was a grueling time, it was also a joyful one full of gratitude for the bounty that would get them through the winter. The Baersladen, like most kingdoms of the Eryie, planned to celebrate with a Harvest Gathering at the start of the season. The Mirien's Harvest Gathering had always been Bryn's favorite of the various annual celebrations that she was able to attend. She'd adored the flower crowns and the open-air dances held in the sunflower fields; it had always felt more carefree and casual than the formal events that took place within Castle Mir's walls.

But now her memory of the Mirien's Harvest Gathering was tainted. After learning about her parents' despotic rule, she realized Mir citizens were celebrating the upcoming harvest of crops they had toiled hard on all summer only to have confiscated by their rulers. Bryn hoped that the Baersladen's Harvest Gathering would be a chance to erase the past and give her new happy memories. She'd like to dance with Rangar in the sunflower fields, if he would stop being so difficult…

One morning, the weather was nice enough that she was able to take the four lambs in her care to the high mountain pastures on the hills overlooking Barendur Hold. It was a full morning's hike, and as she leaned back in the grass with the sun on her face, completely alone with her thoughts, she closed her eyes and pictured the fields below filled with music and merriment. *Everyone dressed in their finest. Ribbons and flowers in the women's hair. Maybe she would wander away from the crowd into the woods, and Rangar would be waiting for her beneath a twisting oak. He'd pull her into the shadows and press his weight against her. His lips would claim hers at last…*

A clap of thunder snapped her out of her reverie. She touched the back of her neck, which had turned pink from the sinful nature of her thoughts. She cleared her throat and peered up to evaluate the sky. Heavy clouds were rolling in off the ocean. She should get the lambs back to the Hold's barn before a storm broke.

"Come on, now." As a light rain began to fall, she used her crook to round up her charges. She found two of the lambs resting on a warm rock and another eating flowers. But try as she could, she couldn't find the fourth lamb.

"Ho, little fellow!" she called. "Where have you run off to?" The high mountain pasture was mostly surrounded by a rock wall, but it was many acres in size, and the lambs knew where they could squeeze through gaps or climb over lower portions. She rested her hands on her hips, looking over the three lambs. The missing one was the big male lamb who was always getting himself into trouble. But he'd never completely run off before.

More thunder cracked overhead. *Lords and ladies*, she cursed to herself. *We're going to get drenched.* It was a hike of over an hour down the mountain, and the sooner they started the journey, the better. She used her staff to herd the three lambs as she scanned the rolling fields for a glimpse of the missing one's white fur.

"Little lamb!" she called. The sprinkling of rain began to fall heavier. "Ho, little lamb! Where have you gone, you devil? You're quite the blackguard, aren't you?"

As she followed the path around a bend, she was startled to hear the unexpected crunch of someone eating an apple nearby. She froze, thinking she had been completely alone and feeling a flush of embarrassment for calling a lamb bad names. She heard the unmistakable crunch again and then a voice say, "I didn't think princesses used foul language."

As she finished rounding the bend, she found Valenden leaning against a rocky outcropping, shiny red apple in hand, smirk on his face.

She rested her hands on her hips. "Don't you have work to do?"

The truth was, she had no idea how the middle brother filled his days. While Trei was often busy with King Aleth dealing with various issues around the kingdom, and Rangar was training the army or helping the huntsmen, Valenden had a strange way of vanishing whenever there was work to be done. Bryn suspected he often disappeared to the bottom of a flask.

Valenden shrugged off her question. "Some might argue my job is to keep up morale. You know, keep everyone in happy spirits with my dashing good looks."

Bryn rolled her eyes. "You know, now that I *can* speak to you, I'm not sure I want to."

This earned her a laugh from Valenden, which she took a small amount of pride in. With another smirk, he said, "I rather liked pretending I didn't know what you were saying."

"Ah! So do you admit you do understand some Mir."

He shrugged, though the teasing sparkle in his eye reminded her of how weeks ago, on the journey to the Baersladen, he had feigned ignorance of her provocative words but then pinned her against a tree and jokingly licked her nose. Raising an eyebrow, he said, "I'm glad you went through with the ritual to speak Baer. Not only so I can now tease you directly to your face, but because it's been such a delight to see my brother so distraught over it."

She felt warm all over again. The rain was falling harder now, and Bryn pulled up her wool cloak's hood, in part to hide the pink spreading up her neck. "It wasn't my desire to go against Rangar's wishes. I'm just not nearly as obedient as he wishes I was."

"Oh, I know." Val's eyes flashed again, this time a little darker. He tossed his apple to the lambs and leaned a little closer.

She cleared her throat and readjusted her hood. "How is your *friend*? The boy I saw you with in the alcove?"

Valenden scratched an indifferent hand over his chin. "Oh, I can't even recall whom you saw me with. Ander or Jonah? After dark, the mead dulls my senses."

"I have a cousin like you," she said hesitantly. "A man who

prefers the company of men."

Valenden let his hand fall away from his chin as he gave her a curious look. "I don't *prefer* the company of men. I like beautiful women just as much as beautiful men. I've had both in my bed, and I can assure you that it isn't about the shape of their bodies but rather what they do with them."

If it had been anyone else to say something so bold, Bryn would have gasped at the impropriety. But it was Valenden, whose reputation throughout the kingdom was less than exemplary. Even now, midday, he smelled of mead. Grinning, he asked her, "And how's your love life, Bryn Lindane of the Mirien? Don't you miss the shape of my brother's body pressed up next to you at night?"

She gaped at the insinuation. "It's just for warmth!"

Now it was Valenden's turn to roll his eyes. "Don't be daft, Princess. Rangar's completely in love with you. You think if his Saved was an old man, he'd try to curl up next to him every night for *warmth?*"

She blinked hard a few times, then forced out the words "Excuse me?"

Valenden waved a dismissive hand in the air. "Rangar's always been in love with you. Well, since he's been old enough to love. Let's see, I'd say it's been since the Harvest Moon Gathering three years ago."

Bryn realized her mouth was still hanging open. There was no way what Val was saying was true, was there? Surely he was just taunting her again or trying to stir up drama between her and Rangar. She thought back to the Mirien's Harvest Moon Gathering from then, when she was fifteen years old. She recalled it well because that was the festival where Elysander's betrothed, Duke Phillipe Dryden of Dresel, had come and presented Elysander with the ruby necklace she so cherished.

Bryn shook her head. "I remember that Gathering. None of

you were there. I certainly would have remembered if you were, but the last time I saw any of your family was when I was eight years old."

A hint of mischief danced in Valenden's eyes. In a low voice, he said, "Just because you didn't see us didn't mean we weren't there."

She cocked her head, frowning at him. Thunder clapped again, and she picked up her shepherd's crook and adjusted her wool hood. "You're playing with me, Val, and I don't enjoy it. Anyway, I have a lamb to find before the storm hits."

She started to push past Valenden to continue on the trail, but Valenden grabbed her arm, stopping her. "It's true, I swear it. Naturally, Father forbade us from attending any events in the Mirien, so we snuck there in disguise. At the time, we were visiting the forest kingdoms of Vil-Kevi and Vil-Rossengard, which were only a half-day ride away. We told our father we were going to hunt boar with the forest princes. Instead, we rode to the Mirien and disguised ourselves as Mir peasants. Rangar saw you in the crowd and was lovesick the whole night. You dropped a button—he took it. Kept it sewn into his cloak for years. Ho, how we teased him mercilessly for it. The Baer people aren't known for romantic overtures. If we want something, we take it. We don't pine away years with buttons in our pockets."

Bryn narrowed her eyes, aware of the darkening clouds overhead. "I don't believe you."

He shrugged. "Believe it or not, it's still true. It happens all the time with *fralen* bonds. One person feels protective over the other, feels a particularly deep connection—well, it isn't much of a stretch to take that bond into the bedroom." His eyes took on a taunting twinkle. "Some even say it makes the intimacy that much more enjoyable."

She hugged her arms tightly against the falling rain. "Rangar's never said a word to me like that."

"Of course he hasn't. Rangar is a fool. He's probably never even kissed you." He cocked his head, curious. "Or has he?"

That underlying darkness was visible in Valenden's eyes again. Bryn felt a tremor of apprehension—was Val jealous, or was it something more? Was this a ploy to torture his brother?

"Don't be silly," she said quietly. "He hasn't kissed me."

Valenden's lips drew back in a grim smile as his eyes trailed down the length of her body. Matching her low tone, he said, "I've half a mind to kiss you myself and see if he's right to be so enamored with you."

She threw him an uncertain look. "You wouldn't dare."

"Wouldn't I?" For a moment, their eyes locked. Valenden was nothing if not handsome. Those sharp cheekbones, the dark eyelashes, the slicked-back shock of black hair. The silence was stretching too long. Her heart began to pulse. *Val's only joking*, she told herself. *He's never serious about anything.* And the smirk on his face supported her thoughts, but then something shifted in his eyes, deepened somehow, and he reached a hand toward her hair beneath her hood.

"Bryn…" he said softly, and the mocking tone was gone.

She shied away at the last minute, ducking her head under his arm and taking a few steps down the path away from the rocky outcropping. She hugged her arms anxiously, rubbing her hands over her biceps. "The lamb…" she stuttered. "I have to find him…"

Valenden kept his gaze on her for another few breaths and then swallowed, and his face shifted back. He gave another tight, mocking smile as though nothing had happened. "Well, if you change your mind…" he said in a singsong, lighthearted joke.

She looked up at the dark sky and wondered if she'd hurt his pride. Not many girls would turn down the rakish middle prince. But Valenden didn't seem particularly prideful—not like Rangar. Valenden had made it abundantly clear that he'd dally with anything that moved. Not even the trees were safe from his lust when the wind was swaying.

"Good luck with your lamb," he whispered to her as he sauntered down the hill, pulling out another apple from his pocket.

"Val…" she started, thinking that they should discuss that awkward moment between them, but he threw a careless hand over his shoulder without bothering to turn around.

"My brother is right," he called back toward her as he headed down the mountain back toward Barendur Hold. "You're trouble, Bryn Lindane."

THE STORM CAME FAST, and Bryn had no choice but to bring the three lambs back to the village. She assured herself that she'd hike back up to the mountain pasture as soon as the rain stopped to search again for the lost lamb. She comforted herself with the knowledge that these were not helpless creatures; Baer sheep were tough, half-wild things that could survive in the pastures for weeks on their own if they had to. There was plenty of forage, mountain streams for water, and places where a lamb could find shelter.

As soon as she secured the three lambs in their pen, she was surprised to find Trei in the main section of the barn, and even more surprised when he indicated that he'd been waiting for her. Her feet slowed, uncertain. The eldest Barendur brother always gave her a kind smile when their paths crossed, though that happened rarely. He was usually in high demand attending to issues in his kingdom or else hunting with Saraj and her falcons.

"Bryn. May I speak with you a moment?"

"Is everything all right?" Bryn asked. It struck her that she'd already had one strange interaction with a Barendur brother that day; she didn't particularly fancy another.

But Trei was nothing like Valenden—the last thing he would do would be to tease her about Rangar or worse, suggest he might kiss her himself. Trei's handsome face remained calm and formal as he said, "We have news from the Mirien. My father would like to speak to you in the council chambers."

A pang of worry stabbed Bryn's chest. She was still grieving the death of her parents and the loss of her home. What if something had happened to Elysander or Mars? Or if the entire kingdom of the Mirien had fallen apart without a benevolent leader to fill her parents' void?

She forced herself to be brave and not jump to terrible conclusions as she followed Trei into the Hold's great hall and through the maze of rear corridors. They climbed a flight of stairs, and Trei nodded to a guard stationed outside a closed room, who opened the heavy wooden door for them.

The council chamber at Barendur Hold was far different than the one at Castle Mir; it was lit by only a few candles, casting everything in shadows. Racks of ancient books, scrolls, and maps lined the wall. Around a circular table made of heavy, dark wood, King Aleth, Mage Marna, two white-bearded army captains, and Rangar sat, waiting for her.

Rangar met her eyes but said nothing. She stepped in hesitantly, pushing back her hood from her hair. She realized she must look like a complete mess: boots caked in mud, soaked through with rain, smelling of a barnyard. But if the royal family thought less of her for it, they didn't say so.

"Lady Bryn," the Baer king said, giving her a solemn nod. "Thank you for joining us." He motioned to an empty chair at the table. "Sit."

The heavy feeling of the room was beginning to seep into her bones and exacerbate her fears. She felt like time was moving too fast as she sank into the chair. One of the soldiers had several pieces of correspondence unfolded on the table in front of him, but the writing was too far away for her to read.

"Your sister is alive," King Aleth reported.

It took Bryn a moment to fully comprehend the words. She had been so prepared for bad news that as soon as she processed what he said, she burst into relieved tears. "Elysander? She's safe?"

King Aleth looked to the elder of the two soldiers, who nodded and indicated the correspondence. The soldier explained, "Lady Elysander was able to escape the siege on Castle Mir with the help of the Hytooth family in the Wollin. After hiding out with them for some weeks, she married her betrothed in Dresel and is under the protection of the duke's house. Now that she has relinquished any claim to the Mirien throne, it is unlikely that agitators will seek her out."

It was better news than Bryn could have ever hoped for. *Elysander escaped and is safe.* Her new husband, Duke Dryden, would ensure her safety.

"Can I write to her?" Bryn said, growing excited by the prospect.

King Aleth nodded. "If you wish, though correspondence can take months."

Bryn gripped the edge of the table, nodding fast. "I'd like to."

The good news made her heart soar. She'd been so worried about her sister, and not knowing what had happened to her had been almost impossible to live with. For weeks, she'd had nightmares about the night of the siege, where she'd found Elysander's empty room with bloodstains all over the rugs. *But it's all right. She's alive.*

Still, despite the good news, a heavy feeling hung over the

table with the weight of a cannonball, and Bryn felt the hair rise on her arms. She glanced at Rangar to find that he wasn't smiling.

"There is more news," the king added in a graver tone and took a deep breath. "Your brother, Mars, also lives."

Bryn pressed a hand to her chest, relieved but confused by the tension that hung in the air. "That's wonderful—"

King Aleth raised a hand to cut her off. "Let me explain. A small but strong faction of the Mirien's army remained loyal to your family. After a bloody battle that lasted several days, Mars was able to retake control of the kingdom from the usurper, Captain Carr, and the populace that rose up against your family."

Bryn blinked in surprise. "So Mars is..."

"King of the Mirien," King Aleth finished for her. "Or at least, he will be soon. The coronation has been delayed, given that the vast majority of his subjects still want to see his head on a spike. The commonfolk are not convinced he will rule any more justly than your parents. Unrest in the Mirien is just as strong as it has ever been, if not worse. Prince Mars's loyal soldiers and hired mercenaries are maintaining his control for now, but it might not last."

Bryn swallowed down a frightened lump in her throat. "They must give Mars a chance. He could prove himself a much more benevolent ruler than our parents."

The room fell into an uneasy silence. After a few seconds ticked by, Trei cleared his throat. "Unfortunately," he said, "from all indications we've observed thus far, Mars is doubling down on his absolute power."

Bryn wanted to deny it. She wanted to defend her brother and shout that they were mistaken. But the truth was, Mars had been trained since birth to follow in her parents' footsteps. Just because she loved her brother, and because he was a good older sibling to her, didn't mean that he wasn't just as ruthless as their parents.

A shiver ran through her, and she once more remembered she was covered in mud and soaked through. She whispered, "I wish there was something I could do. As kind as you've all been to take me in, the Mirien is still my home. Those are my people."

"There is nothing you can do from here," Mage Marna said softly. "Especially since the majority of your people believe you are as guilty as the rest of your family."

Rangar leaned forward, tenting his hands on the table. "Let them believe what they will," he said. It was the first he'd spoken at the meeting. "You can't go back." He paused before adding, "It's too dangerous."

Bryn felt relief at this, but it was mixed with uncertainty. Even with her brother on the throne, she had seen the rage in her people's faces. She felt in her gut that the commonfolk wouldn't believe that she hadn't been aware of her parents' crimes.

"How do you know all of this?" she asked, turning to King Aleth.

"Straight from the mouth of one of the usurpers." The Baer king motioned to the guards posted at the door. They disappeared and, in another moment, dragged in a shackled prisoner. Bryn immediately recognized him as one of the Mir soldiers whom she had spied on in the forest: the shaggy-haired one who had planned on raping her and stringing her up on the gallows.

Rage flamed over her face, making her hands coil into fists.

"It is your call, Lady Bryn," Mage Marna said evenly. "We have gained all the information we require from this prisoner, so he is no longer useful to us. What shall we do with him? If you call for his death, then death he shall receive."

21

THE FALCON HUNTRESS...A CRUEL CHOICE...
RUMORS IN THE VILLAGE...A BORROWED
GOWN

*B*ryn had no wish to be a tyrant like her parents. Cruelty was not the path she wanted to walk through the world. But she also knew that this Mir soldier could not be allowed to live. Regardless of whatever vile things he had planned to do to her, he couldn't be released back to the Mirien for the sake of all of their safety. He would tell Mars whatever Mars wanted to hear, probably that the vicious Baer royal family truly had abducted Bryn and was mistreating her terribly.

He was too dangerous to let live, so there was really no choice. She took a deep breath. "Kill him."

There was no malice or vengeance behind her words. If anything, she felt a terrible well of regret. She'd never want to be responsible for any person's death. But she'd seen true leadership since arriving in the Baersladen and learned that being a good leader sometimes meant helping an old man out from under a fallen wagon; sometimes it meant slaughtering a rare and beautiful whale for its bounty. And sometimes, it meant *this*.

Rangar stood, pushed back his chair and crossed the room,

drew his knife.

"Wait," the prisoner pleaded, facing King Aleth. "Lady Bryn is nothing. You're going to listen to *her?*"

Before the prisoner could plead a few more desperate words, Rangar slit the man's throat. The prisoner fell to the ground, gargling his own blood, and then slowly stopped moving until he was nothing but a husk on the ground. Bryn pressed a hand to her mouth, her eyes round and wide.

It had happened so swiftly. A man was dead because of her!

While she was still gaping at the dead body, Trei gave her a sympathetic look. "You made the right call, Lady Bryn, though I know it was not easy."

The Baer guards stationed at the door dragged the corpse out by the man's feet, leaving a smear of blood along the stone floor. Bryn sank back into her chair, shaking, her eyes fixed to that crimson stain.

So this is what it means to rule. Is Mars making the same hard choices?

King Aleth came around the table and laid a heavy hand on her shoulder. It was the first time he had ever touched her, and she looked up in surprise. The king of the Baersladen had always kept his distance, and she had secretly wondered if he trusted her or perhaps even suspected that she had been fully aware of the crimes her family had committed. To her amazement, he looked down on her with a father's stern but kind countenance, as though she were his own daughter.

"Go, then, girl," he commanded, jerked his chin toward the door. "You've done well today. The Harvest Gathering will soon be here and will make for happier times. Prepare yourself for the festivities. It will take your mind off this soldier."

She was more than grateful to push out of her chair and leave the council chambers. Her heart was thrashing around strangely in her chest. Her mind felt dazed, like she couldn't quite make sense of the blood smear on the floor and the knife still in Rangar's hand. She glanced over her shoulder, but Rangar was busy talking to Trei and didn't spare her a glance.

The following day, she tried to occupy her mind by searching the hills for the lamb who'd run away the day before. She left the other lambs in their pen and borrowed breeches from a farm boy so she could move more freely over the rocky hills. But no matter how hard she looked, she found nothing. Her throat went hoarse from calling for him, but he'd never answered with a bleat.

Finding nothing is better than finding a dead lamb, she reassured herself, though it was a small comfort. Her spirits were heavier than they'd been in a long time when she finally hiked back down from the high pastures, having failed to find the lamb again. She took her time in the barn grooming the other lambs with a currycomb and feeding their mother plenty of hay, as her mind kept drifting back to Rangar. She hated this feeling of distance between them. It felt wrong, like a boat and a dock that could never quite meet because of stormy waves.

"I'll find your little one," she promised the ewe as she stroked her head. For some reason, finding the missing lamb felt of grave importance, even though she knew livestock often went missing, and the village would not mourn one lamb. But it mattered to her. She'd taken a life from the world when she'd ordered the Mir soldier slain—or rather, Rangar had, at her command—the least she could do was save one other life.

"I can help you look," a voice said.

Bryn looked up from the pile of straw she was sitting in to find Saraj, Trei's lover and the head falconer, leaning on the barnyard fence. The huntswoman wore a deep green gown with slits down the sides that allowed her to move as freely as any man in trousers. Her bow was stowed on her back. A young falcon rested on a leather cuff on her forearm.

Saraj smiled. "We haven't properly met yet. I'm Saraj. I couldn't help but overhear that a lamb has gone missing. My falcons are skilled hunters—they can find almost anything. Tomorrow, we can go out and search."

Bryn fought her way out of the deep straw and brushed off her skirt, coming over to the fence. "That's so kind of you, but tomorrow is the start of the Harvest Gathering. Won't you have other responsibilities?"

Saraj shrugged. "It doesn't start until the evening. We can look for your lamb in the morning."

Bryn felt a rush of gratitude, not just for the offer of help, but for the friendly words. Though no one in the Baersladen had been unkind to her, they were a reticent people who were slow to open up to strangers. Ever since she'd fought with Rangar—and now had a strained relationship with Valenden after their strange exchange on the mountain—she was short on friends. "I'd like that very much." She pointed to the falcon, curious. "Who is this?"

"Ah. Zephyr," Saraj said proudly. "She's a juvenile falcon. They require constant companionship at her age, or they won't be tame. I like the birds, but I'll tell you one thing, it puts a damper on romance when a falcon can't be more than three feet apart from me."

Bryn laughed. From everything she had seen, she instantly liked this tall, fierce woman. "Thank you. Truly. I'm worried about the lamb out at night with the predators in the mountains."

"We'll find him," Saraj assured her, then glanced down at Bryn's breeches. "I hope you aren't planning on wearing those to the Gathering."

"I have a wool dress that the bathhouse attendants gave me. I was going to wear that. I imagine the dress I was wearing when I arrived has been shredded for scrap fabric by now. Mir gowns aren't made for this climate, anyway." She felt a little wistful thinking back on her old life, though even in a memory, it felt flimsy and unsubstantial.

Saraj nodded. "I think you'll find Harvest Gatherings in the Outlands to be very different than in your homeland. Our crops are small but important. Corn for the animals. Potatoes, apples, and gourds to last the winter. Wheat for flour. We try to set aside a portion of wild game and fish for smoking. In the winter, the fish tend to migrate to warmer waters."

"Winter must be hard here." Bryn glanced up at the sky, wondering about snow and roads being closed off. She hadn't given much thought to what it would be like to pass a long, frigid winter in Barendur Hold, which was already filled with chilly drafts in late summer.

"It is," Saraj said bluntly, not dancing around the truth. "Very hard. Which is why the start of the harvest is a time for celebration. Do you drink cider? I hope you do." She laughed throatily. "The whole town is drunk the night of the Gathering."

Bryn grinned, trying not to be too scandalized. Back home, she'd never be allowed to attend a party like that, mixing with commonfolk. She meant it when she said, "That sounds like a merry time."

Saraj rested one foot on the lower fence rail and leaned onto the upper one. She slid Bryn a sly look. "The Harvest Gathering is also when many couples declare their intention to marry."

Bryn felt a ripple of heat spread across her cheeks. "Oh?" She tried to feign indifference. "Will you and Trei make any announcements?"

Saraj shook her head as she straightened and dusted some errant straw off her dress. "Not this year. If I were to marry Trei, I'd become a future queen. I'd have to give up my work with the falcons, and I'm not ready to trade in my breeches just yet. Besides, King Aleth is in good health, so there is no hurry for Trei to marry and provide any heirs." She cleared her throat. "Actually, I was thinking of you and Rangar."

Now, Bryn not only felt warm, but positively on fire. She kept thinking of how Valenden had teased her that Rangar had been in love with her for years, ever since sneaking back in the Mirien and watching her from afar. Was it true? Or was that just Valenden being an ass as usual?

"There's nothing like that between Rangar and me," Bryn muttered, unable to look the falconer in the eye. She had a feeling that her pink cheeks were betraying the fluttering emotions in her heart, emotions that had been stirred and kindled since she'd arrived in the Baersladen.

Saraj scoffed loud enough to rouse the lambs from the slumber they'd fallen into. "If you truly wanted people to believe that, then you shouldn't have spent so many nights sleeping beneath the same blanket." She dropped her voice. "The whole village was talking about it."

Bryn bit her lip. She and Rangar hadn't shared a blanket for a while, but they certainly had at the beginning of her time in the Baersladen. "Were they really?"

Saraj stroked her falcon with one finger as she explained, "The three princes are well-loved by the Baer people. You can imagine that in a small kingdom like this, half of all gossip revolves around the unmarried brothers at the prime of their lives and who will end up with their hands."

"Well, they surely don't wonder that about Trei," Bryn offered, hoping to deflect the attention.

"No," Saraj admitted. "When it comes to Trei and me, the gossip revolves around *when* we'll marry, and what I'll wear, and if I'll have a falcon on my arm during the ceremony."

Bryn gave a soft laugh and then asked, "What about Valenden? Doesn't he have a sweetheart?"

Now it was Saraj's turn to laugh. "Valenden has too many sweethearts, but none of them are still his sweetheart come the dawn, if you get what I mean. Plenty of women—and men for that matter—have tried to claim his heart." She sighed, shaking her head regretfully. "Val is a good man. Val's problem is *Val*. He won't let himself be happy."

Bryn hesitated before asking, "And Rangar? Has there never been a woman in his life?"

Saraj leaned pensively on the fence as she continued to stroke the back of her falcon's head. "One of my apprentices, Aya, fancies him. But if there has been something between them, then he's kept it secret. Plenty of girls pine for him, that's for certain. His scars don't bother Baer women; in fact, most consider him to be the most handsome of the brothers. But he's so brooding. Even before the wolf attack, he was a sullen boy. Afterward, he turned inward even more. If you'll forgive me saying so, for the last several years, the villagers have speculated that he's in love with a Mir princess and doesn't have eyes for anyone else."

Bryn swallowed down a lump, feeling suddenly very self-conscious. In a whisper, she said, "He's said nothing outright to me along those lines. Made no advances."

Saraj rolled her eyes. "Well, that's Rangar for you. Courageous as a bear except when it comes to matters of the heart."

Bryn toyed with the end of her braid. "Everyone speaks of love, but in Rangar's case, I think he merely feels protective of me. It's the *fralen* bond. That's all."

Saraj gave her another sly look. "Did you know I am also bound to a *fralen* bond?"

"What? Truly?" It was the first Bryn had heard of another person involved in a *fralen* bond.

Saraj nodded and settled back against the fence as she launched into the story. "When I was eight years old, I rescued my best friend from drowning in the bay. She and I have been as close as sisters ever since. I watch out for her every day. But I'm not in *love* with her. The *fralen* bond doesn't stand in the way of my relationship with Trei in the slightest." Through the gaps in the fence slats, Saraj prodded Bryn teasingly in the ribs. "Don't take the village gossip too personally. It's just that Rangar is much beloved in these lands, but he's so brooding, so tortured by his own dark thoughts, that everyone just wants to see him happy. When he came back from the High Sun Gathering with you atop his mare, well...it seemed inevitable."

Bryn didn't know what to say. She hadn't been aware that the entire village—probably the entire kingdom—had been speculating about a romance between her and Rangar. She couldn't deny the strong connection they had. It was, after all, literally carved into both of their bodies. The scars that began at his face and finished beneath her ribs. For so many years, she had dreamed of her "Bear" prince and his wild land...

But she banished those thoughts by running her hands over her face. Sighing, she confessed, "Well, Rangar currently refuses to speak to me ever since I let Mage Marna give me the hexmark to speak Baer. Everyone else might adore him, but I think he's a controlling bore."

She had meant for the harsh words to dispel the gossip about them, but to her surprise, Saraj merely burst out laughing. "Ho, I'll not deny that about Rangar. He certainly can be an oaf. If you ask me, what he needs is a woman who will stand up to him and put him in his place." Saraj gave Bryn a satisfied smile, and Bryn realized she had walked straight into the huntress's trap, practically having to admit they were right for each other.

Saraj prodded Bryn again through the fence. "Look, I've

seen your wool dress, and while it's fine for traipsing through the mountains and tending to livestock, it simply won't do for the Harvest Gathering. You need a gown that will catch Rangar's eye and shake him out of his stubbornness." As soon as Bryn tried to object, Saraj raised a hand to silence her. "No, no, you've objected enough. You can deny your attraction to him all you want, but it won't make anyone believe it. So tonight, after supper, I want you to meet me at the docks. I'll take you to the village tailor. You can borrow one of my old dresses, and we'll alter it to fit."

Bryn wasn't sure what to say to such a kind offer. Even though she'd been close to Elysander and some of the other high-born daughters of the Mirien, she'd never had a companion like this, who she could laugh with and tease one another and trade clothes. And she'd only just come to know Saraj.

She touched the hexmark on her ear that, according to her own culture, forever branded her as a sinner. If anyone in the Mirien saw the mark, they'd shun her. But the mark—the magic—let her speak to Saraj. She didn't *feel* like a sinner.

"I'd love to try on dresses," Bryn confessed. "And I *am* looking forward to the Harvest Gathering, but I promise, there's nothing between Rangar and me other than the *fralen* bond, which I don't even believe in. That a person's soul could belong to someone else."

Saraj rolled her eyes good-naturedly. "You're as lost as that lamb, Bryn."

22

A GOWN TO TURN HEADS...FESTIVAL
PREPARATIONS...SAUSAGE...STRIPPED BARE...
A CELEBRATORY DRINK

*T*hat night, Bryn met Saraj at the docks, and Saraj led her to her small home. Bryn was shocked to learn that Saraj lived alone in a one-room stone cottage overlooking the sea with a small barn a few paces away for her falcons. In the Mirien, no women of Bryn's or Saraj's age lived independently. Bryn couldn't recall any specific edicts that forbade it, but regardless, if a woman had attempted to live alone instead of with sisters or other young women, she would have been assailed with suspicious looks, perhaps even shunned. Wisdom and learning were valued among Mir women—not independence.

The shutters of Saraj's cottage windows were open, letting in a cool breeze and the gentle, rhythmic sounds of waves. The single room was overlooked by a loft that served as a bedroom with a ladder leading up to it, and below was a hearth with an iron cooking pot and a small dining table and chairs. A cozy fire ate through wood now, keeping the room comfortably warm despite the open window.

Saraj threw open the largest wooden trunk Bryn had ever seen and practically climbed into it.

"What do you think of this one?" Saraj tossed out a forest-green-colored gown that Bryn narrowly caught before it landed in the fire. "I wore it to a Gathering when I was about your age."

Bryn held the wool gown to the light, admiring the rich color. Lords and ladies, how she had missed such simple feminine joys as trying on dresses. As much as she'd come to value the harsh life of caring for livestock and sleeping on the floor, this was utter bliss.

"Oh! And this one." Saraj tossed out another. "It was a gift from King Aleth when I was named head falconer. I'm ashamed to say I've never worn it. The fabric is too delicate for hunting, and I have little occasion to wear fine dresses."

The gown was a soft mauve color made of velvet and lace. Red and pink were not common colors one saw in the Baersladen. The seaside kingdom itself was all grays and moody blue and dark mountain greens, and most clothing dyes reflected those shades. Nor was it common to see any fabric other than leather or wool. Baer clothing was much bulkier than the gauzy summertime dresses that Bryn had worn for most of her life.

While she missed the lightness of her old gowns, they'd been suited for the warm Mir climate. Here, she was grateful for the wool and leather and thick underskirts that kept away drafts. Furthermore, her delicate Mir dresses would be ruined if so much as a spot of berry jam fell on them, but these tough Baer gowns could be dragged through mud, slept in for days on end, stomped on by goats, and only need a washing to be good as new.

Bryn laid out the two dresses on Saraj's dining table.

"They're both lovely," she said, admiring the dresses, and a thought flashed in her head. *Which would Rangar prefer?*

With her fair hair, Bryn already stood out among the Baer

women, so she considered that perhaps she should wear the green wool one to try to blend in. Then again, Rangar had told her time and time again that he liked her unusual looks…

The mauve gown would certainly draw his eye, she thought. Immediately, she chastised herself for the idea. What did she care which dress Rangar would prefer? *Rangar* wasn't going to wear the dress. Her hand drifted to her ear, brushing over the still-healing scars there from the hexmark ritual. The source of this chasm between them.

As though Saraj could read her thoughts, she said, "You'll look beautiful in either, Bryn. Rangar won't be able to take his eyes off you. Saints, you could wear a potato sack and he would still devour you with his gaze like a starving puppy."

"I wasn't thinking of Rangar," Bryn protested weakly, dropping her hand from the healing hexmark on her ear.

Saraj rolled her eyes, not fooled in the slightest. "I'm starting to think you're as stubborn as he is."

"*That* is impossible," Bryn muttered.

Saraj laughed out loud. "So then, come. Be honest now that it's just you and me and the moon. Are you in love with him?"

Bryn's eyes widened to hear someone speaking of intimate feelings so openly. Such talk was only ever whispered about in the Mirien. She bit her lip while she considered the question. It was undeniable that she owed Rangar her life, a fact that connected them whether through the *fralen* bond or just simple gratitude. And yes, those cold nights pressed together for warmth in the great hall made her skin yearn for his touch… but *love*?

Love wasn't a luxury she'd ever been allowed. Her mother had been betrothed for political purposes, as had Elysander and all royal women in the Mirien. Bryn would have been engaged to Baron Marmose under the same pretenses if the uprising hadn't happened during the High Sun Gathering.

Now, however, no one was forcing her to marry anyone. There was no talk of political alliances. No betrothals. She was free to marry for love if she wished—or remain unmarried, like Saraj, dallying with whomever she chose. It was a heady, revolutionary idea. *Free to love.*

A knock came at the door. "Come in!" Saraj called happily.

An older woman with deep wrinkles and thick gray hair woven into a crown braid entered, carrying a wicker basket over one arm.

"Ah, Helna," Saraj said, beaming, as she climbed out of the massive trunk. "You're a saint for finding the time to come help. I know you're busy as a bee tending to everyone's clothes before the festival. Bryn, this is Helna, the finest seamstress in the village."

Bryn gave a small curtsey, at which the older woman just cackled. "None of that, Princess. Just strip yourself bare, and let's get you fitted. Now, which dress are you to wear?"

Bryn blanched at the thought of stripping naked again. It wasn't that long ago that she'd been with her mother being fitted for a gown for the First Night's ball. Her mother had been so careful not to let anyone see the scars that marred Bryn's torso, fearing it would make her less desirable for a suitor. *No prince wants an imperfect princess*, her mother had said.

Now, Bryn felt a rush of anger that she had let herself feel ashamed for the scars. It was either the scars or death on that night ten years before, and the scars were a badge of survival. She had faced wolves and lived. But try as she might, she couldn't direct her anger at her mother. Her mother had been caught in the same oppressive system that Bryn would have been if Rangar hadn't taken her away from her old life. Besides, her mother was in the grave now, far beyond anger's reach.

"The mauve one," Bryn said quietly.

The seamstress jabbed a finger at her breeches. "Off."

Bryn slowly unfastened her belt and slid out of the wool breeches, then started on the buttons of her blouse, her fingers shaking. She'd stripped naked in the bathhouse, of course, and once on the rooftop in front of Mage Marna and the apprentices, but at least then it had been under the cover of night. "Can I leave on my underclothes?"

The old seamstress looked at her as though she'd grown an extra nose. "Saraj has twelve inches in height on you, girl. You think I can eyeball a hem like that? Silly thing, take off every stitch from head to toe. Don't be shy, now. I've seen every woman and girl in the village naked. Most of the men, too."

Bryn finished taking off her clothes, busying her hands in front of her ribs, moving her loose hair there, trying to hide the scars. But Helna batted away her hands and stretched out a length of measuring string across her chest. Her wrinkled hands pressed against Bryn's ribs as she took her measurements, her fingers gliding over the scars perfunctorily.

When the seamstress turned away to pick up the mauve dress, Bryn said, "The scars...I'm sorry."

"For what?" The seamstress seemed genuinely confused. "It's just skin. Here, see if you can get the dress on as it is, without me having to undo the seams."

She held out the dress for Bryn. Bryn fought to get it over her head and tugged it down with the help of both Saraj and the seamstress. Saraj was a sapling of a woman, tall and impossibly thin, and though Bryn was of slight build, she felt squeezed like a sausage.

Helna made some markings on the dress in chalk, muttering to herself, "Can't take out that hem much more—not enough fabric. Don't worry, I'll put a ribbon there. Now, don't even try to get back out of the dress—I'll cut you out instead. Have to open the seams anyway. I'll have it for you tomorrow afternoon before the opening bonfire of the gathering."

With a skilled hand, the old woman sliced through the dress, bundled up the fabric, and stuffed it into her basket. She gave Bryn a wink. "Don't you fret, Princess. A certain prince won't be able to look away."

Bryn bit her lip as she tugged back on her breeches—Saraj had been right, the whole kingdom was obsessed over her and Rangar's relationship. Everyone wanted to know if they'd end up together. *Very good question*, Bryn thought to herself. If she was being honest, she was eager to know the answer herself.

* * *

THE FOLLOWING DAY, Saraj roused Bryn early, and they hiked to the high hills to search for the lost lamb with Zephyr. They checked every stream and mountain cave for any sign of the missing lamb, disappointed to find no tracks in the mud, and reluctantly had to give up for the day and return to the village. Bryn was shocked to find the village had completely transformed itself over the course of the morning. Giant poles topped with garlands surrounded the village square, and hay bales were stacked as seating. The villagers had rigged up homespun decorations with colorful gourds, corn stalks, and men and women made of straw. On the nearby beach, logs had been stacked in preparation for the bonfire that would be lit at sundown to begin the festivities.

Once Bryn asked how she might be of help, she was swept into Barendur Hold's kitchen and given a knife and a stack of carrots. Back home, she never would be expected to chop vegetables with the kitchen servants, but after a few hours, she found she enjoyed the bustle of the kitchen, the bawdy songs the cooks sang aloud, the smell of roasted meats, and the mead that was passed around freely. She found herself grinning and even joining in some of the songs' choruses. Somehow, she realized, she'd found a home in this wild place.

After Bryn was finally released from her duties, she cleaned up quickly in the bathhouse and slid back into her old wool dress. She hadn't seen any sign of the brothers all day. Wherever Trei, Valenden, and Rangar were, they weren't among the crowd putting the finishing touches on the decorations by tying ribbons to tree branches. There was no sign of King Aleth or Mage Marna, either, and Bryn couldn't help but glance at the high windows of Barendur Hold with an eerie premonition. Only days ago, she'd been told her brother intended to take the Mir crown by force and wage war on any who opposed them. What if the Baersladen rejected his claim? It would mean war. Her loyalties would be caught between her beloved brother and her adopted new homeland.

These moody thoughts interrupted her good spirits for the remainder of the afternoon until dusk began, when Saraj found her, clutching a bundle beneath her arm.

"Bryn!" Saraj was already dressed for the festivities in a golden gown with a flower crown made of small white blossoms atop her head. "Helna gave me this. Said she stayed up all night finishing it, and something about it being suited specifically just for you. Do you want to change clothes in my cottage?"

Grateful, Bryn followed Saraj to her little cottage on the hill and tore open the package. She stared at the tailored dress, wide-eyed. The seamstress had completely transformed the gown with satin ribbons in a woven, knotted pattern that Bryn recognized as a stylized version of the Mir emblem. It must have taken hours to stitch the intricate alterations. As much as she wanted to believe the older woman had done this for her, she knew that she'd yet to become a beloved resident of the

Baersladen. No, Helna hadn't done this for Bryn but for *Rangar*. The cherished prince that everyone wanted to see happy and in love.

The entire town really was trying to push them together…

Still, Bryn was hardly in a position to turn down the gorgeous dress. She slid into it, marveling at the fine hand stitching that rivaled the advanced sewing contraptions the tailors used in the Mirien. The fabric hugged her body in just the right places. Though Saraj didn't have a mirror, Bryn was able to catch her reflection in the back of a pewter plate. Helna had lowered the neckline to an almost scandalous level and raised the sleeves from wrist-length to elbow-length.

"You look beautiful," Saraj said as she looked over Bryn in the dress but then frowned. "Except, if you don't mind me saying so, your hair is a complete rat's nest."

Bryn gaped, but she had to admit Saraj was right. She hadn't had a chance to wash or comb her hair in days and had hoped it looked appealingly windswept. But apparently, she'd been lying to herself. She let Saraj comb out her hair and wind it into curls with an iron rod heated in the fireplace. Through the window, they watched the sun dip below the horizon. There was a sudden cheer in the distance as the bonfire was lit on the beach and the musicians began to play.

Bryn tried to stand to look out the window, but Saraj pushed her back down with a firm hand. "Not so fast. The celebration is only getting started. It will go on all night, and they won't miss us for a few more minutes. Here. A little something I save for special occasions."

She dug a small green glass bottle out of the massive trunk and held it out to Bryn. Bryn took it hesitantly. There was no label on the bottle, and she shuddered at the memory of imbibing Mage Marna's vile potion. She uncorked the bottle and recoiled at the sharp smell of alcohol.

Saraj laughed at her reaction. "Go on, it won't kill you. It's pine liquor. They distill it in the forest kingdom of Vil-Kevi. Two sips and the room will start spinning."

"In that case, I'll stick with one." Bryn took a small sip, gagging at the sharp taste, but before she could lower the bottle, Saraj tipped it up, pouring more into her mouth. Bryn sputtered while Saraj only chuckled.

"You devil!" Bryn cried, wiping her mouth.

"Guilty." Saraj took a long drink from the bottle herself, then winked and thrust her arm through Bryn's. "Come on, then, Princess. Let the festivities begin."

23

THE HARVEST GATHERING...A BONFIRE...
PASSED AMID 3 BROTHERS...BLINDMAN'S
DANCE...AWAY FROM THE CROWD

*A*s Bryn and Saraj made their way over the sea dunes to the beach, Bryn gasped at the sight of the festival bonfire. It nearly took up the entire width of the beach from water to dunes, built at low tide so that as the tide slowly came in over the course of the night, the flames would be doused by morning.

Now, however, the flames rose twenty feet high, sending sparks dancing up toward the stars. Out at sea, anchored rowboats held lit tallow candles and lanterns, looking like bobbing stars floating on the sea's surface. A trio of musicians played a rousing jig as villagers dressed in golds and sage greens danced in each other's arms. There were no formal *velta* dances here, only clasped arms, dizzying spins, laughing couples.

The pine liquor Saraj had given Bryn was starting to work its magic, unknotting Bryn's worries except for one: Where was Rangar? Wasn't he coming? It didn't have to do with her brother Mars's seizure of the Mir throne, did it?

"Trei!" Saraj unlaced her arm from Bryn's when she spotted the eldest prince drinking from a jug with several fishers on the far side of the bonfire. Saraj raced over the sand and launched herself into his arms, planting a sloppy kiss on his cheek.

Trei grinned at her, obviously deeply in love. "There you are, my beautiful lady. You do realize that I'm crazy about you, don't you?"

Saraj tugged the jug out of his hands with a mischievous spark in her eye. "Well, *I'm* crazy about this cider...and I suppose you aren't so bad yourself."

Bryn stood to the side, hesitant to intrude, until Trei motioned her over. "Princess! Come. Dance with Baer's finest fishers, won't you? Yager here might look quiet, but he'll give you a whirl as you've never had."

One of the younger fishers, a lad around Bryn's age, grinned sheepishly and offered her his hand. Bryn hesitated before slipping her hand into his calloused one, and suddenly, he spun her in a circle with surprising strength, lifting her clean off her feet. After her initial shock wore off, she laughed and laughed.

Cider and mead flowed steadily throughout the night. Everywhere Bryn turned, someone was either pushing a jug of liquor into her hand or else snatching the jug away and leading her in a dance. She twirled around the bonfire with farmers and hunters, messengers and cooks. The village children ran through the crowd with flowers in their hair, waving ribbons on sticks, playing little pranks on the grown-ups.

But where was Rangar?

As the liquor started to go to her head, Bryn found herself at one point dancing with Trei, surprised by how tall he was and how solid his shoulders were, and then in the next instant was passed to Valenden. Where had the middle brother even come from? Apparently, the middle prince had bled into the crowd sometime during the evening when Bryn hadn't been paying attention.

Valenden's hair looked like it had been tamed earlier in the night but was now a mess around his face, as usual. A devilish spark lit up his eyes as he grabbed Bryn around the waist, throwing her over his shoulder and spinning her amid the crowd as she laughed and pounded on his back, until he finally tossed her down in a pile of sand, then flicked his finger over the tip of her nose.

"Val, you devil!" She was about to jokingly chastise him when, across the fire, her eyes caught on a group of soldiers swapping stories along with a jug of mead. Her eyes fell on the dark-haired prince in their midst.

Rangar.

He was here at last. He'd come to the Gathering. He stood amid the soldiers casually, every plane and curve of his face looking princely in the firelight—even the scars—dressed in a black shirt with the sleeves rolled back to show the hexmarks on his forearms.

Bryn pressed a hand over her own still-healing hexmark on her ear, shivering slightly. Rangar's eyes suddenly met hers across the flames. He didn't try to hide the fact that he was staring at her with an intensity that bordered on obsessive. She smoothed a hand down her rose-colored gown, suddenly feeling very exposed in the low-cut neckline. The couples dancing near her threw her sly looks, and her cheeks reddened.

Did everyone suspect that tonight Rangar might declare himself to her? Was the whole village in on this setup?

"The Blindman's Dance!" one of the fishers announced, and everyone cheered and began to gather around the bonfire. Bryn looked around in confusion, uncertain of what to do, until Saraj appeared by her side with a black satin strip of fabric in hand.

"It's a game," Saraj explained, grinning a little goofily from all the liquor she'd drunk. "All single dancers must be blindfolded, and those of us who already have sweethearts guide you to find other blindfolded dance partners."

Before Bryn could object, Saraj tied the fabric over her eyes. Bryn could only see a small portion through the gap at the bottom of the blindfold, which revealed only sand and shoes. She stretched out her arms hesitantly in front of her. "What if I fall into the fire?"

"Trei and I will keep an eye on you," Saraj assured her.

The music began. Bryn felt Saraj's hands on her back guiding her gently through the crowd. Fingers brushed against her from other blindfolded dancers, but Saraj quickly steered her away from all of them. At last, Saraj gave her a sharp prod, and Bryn found herself stumbling into someone's arms.

"Enjoy the dance," Saraj whispered huskily before disappearing.

Bryn heard Trei's voice close by whisper to her mysterious dance partner, "Don't be an ass, brother."

Of course, it's Rangar.

It didn't take much deduction to unravel Saraj and Trei's plot to have them dance together in the Blindman's Dance. Bryn drew in a breath—if she was being honest, she'd hoped this was where she would end up. Rangar's broad hand gripped her shoulder and ran down along her silk sleeve to her bare arm. He had to know it was her. For a moment, she wondered if he would push her away and find someone else to dance with.

But then another blindfolded couple bumped into them, laughing, and she nearly tripped. Rangar immediately grabbed her around the waist, pulling her close to keep her steady. The moment their bodies were flush, a bolt of lightning coursed through her. Rangar's hand tightened around her back as though he felt it, too.

His hand trailed down to her forearm. "Bryn..." he started.

"Shh," she breathed. "Aren't we supposed to be strangers?"

She heard his snort. "Trust me, even if I can't see you, my body knows exactly who you are."

She swallowed down a gasp, but she couldn't deny that her body felt it, too. They began to move in a slow dance as Bryn slipped her arms around his shoulders. Without her sight, her other senses flared to life. She could smell bonfire smoke on Rangar's hair and skin, a trace of sweet cider on his lips. Beneath it all was the earthy scent of a horse—he must have been riding earlier that day. Instantly, she was transported back to their voyage to the Baersladen, their bodies so close together on his mare, his breath at the back of her neck.

"I'm tired of fighting," she whispered. "Of ignoring one another. I admit that while it was my choice to get the hexmark, I shouldn't have gone through with it without telling you."

Rangar's strong fingers stroked the small of her back, pressing her a tiny bit closer. She wished she could see—what was the expression on his face? Was he still furious with her?

"Rangar?" she asked softly. "Did you hear what I said? Can we stop fighting?"

He grunted. "Thank the Saints, yes." He leaned toward her, and his lips brushed her ear as he whispered, "Because I haven't been able to take my eyes off you in this dress all night. Are you trying to torture me?"

She felt a delicious smile playing at her lips. "Not me. The seamstress. And the entire village, I think. You have no idea how many people have been hinting rather strongly that we need to make up with one another."

"Don't I?" he replied. "It's all I hear. Everywhere I go, people ask when I'll stop growling around like some wild animal and apologize to you." Through the gap at the bottom of her blindfold, Bryn watched his boots guiding her along the beach away from the danger of the fire. Even without sight, he knew this land by heart.

"I understand that you feel protective of me, but if there's one thing your people have taught me, it's that a woman can and should be independent."

Bryn feared he might object again and they'd launch into another argument, but he only said begrudgingly, "I accept that. It was wrong of me to give you an order. Your will is your own."

His hands dipped lower on her hips. Blindfolded, Bryn felt a surprising freedom. As though it was only the two of them, in the dark, where any sins could be committed without consequence. She had to remind herself that most of the villagers *weren't* blindfolded and were probably watching them dance right now and placing bets on if the brooding youngest royal brother would finally propose to his Mir princess.

Rangar's face was so close to hers that his rough cheek brushed against her smooth one. If he only turned his head slightly, his lips would graze her cheekbone. She felt herself wrapping her arms tighter around his shoulders as they swayed to the rhythm of the music and the crashing waves.

The Harvest Gathering is when many couples declare their intention to marry, Saraj had said. Bryn couldn't seem to get the words out of her head. Heart pounding, she asked, "Do you think Trei will propose to Saraj tonight?"

"Not tonight," Rangar replied.

"Why not?"

"Once Saraj becomes engaged to a prince, she'd have to give up her falcons. And I think she loves them more than anyone, even Trei."

"So won't they *ever* marry?"

She felt him shrug. "Marriage is not as important to us as it is to your people." He spun her slowly, moving further from the fire. The night's chill licked at her back, but Rangar kept her warm.

"But what if they have children? They'd be illegitimate."

"Trei would never deny an inheritance to any child of his. He would accept them as the Baersladen heir, and Saraj could go on with her falcons. Besides..." Bryn felt his energy shift, grow slightly nervous. "I think the villagers have given up hope for a grand royal wedding from the eldest prince."

"Oh. From the *eldest*," she repeated.

He grunted the affirmative, and Bryn's cheeks warmed even more. Thank goodness Rangar was blindfolded and didn't see how his words affected her. It was clear that the village had set their sights on a royal wedding, but if it didn't involve Trei or Valenden, that left only one brother.

Bryn suddenly realized that the sound of the crackling bonfire and the crowd was surprisingly distant. Through the narrow gap in the blindfold, she saw seagrass and realized that Rangar had guided them further down the beach, to the edge of the dune. She reached up to take off her blindfold, but he grabbed her hand, stopping her.

"Where are we?" she breathed.

"Away from the crowd. From...watching eyes."

Her heart began to gallop. The tide licked at the hem of her dress, pushing her toward him with every wave. He ran a hand down her cheek from blindfold to chin and muttered, "I've wanted to do this for as long as I can remember."

He cupped her jaw in his hands. Time seemed to slow. Bryn's heart was a wild stallion charging down the beach. *He's going to kiss me.* After so many agonizing nights sleeping next to one another, filled with accidental touches and simmering glances, it was finally happening. She felt her lips part, ready. He could be stubborn and infuriating and possessive, but she couldn't deny how her body responded to him. Besides, he could also be noble and kind. She'd never met such a complex person full of contradictions, a knot she was very anxious to unravel.

Still blindfolded, she tipped her chin up to meet his lips as her heartbeat kicked up even faster. But a second before their lips touched, someone shouted, "Ho, Rangar! Get your ass over here!"

The romantic moment between them shattered.

Rangar drew back slightly, clearly reluctant to part ways with her. His hands brushed along her jaw, fingers curling into her skin as though he wanted desperately to turn back time, to ignore the calls. But the person called again.

"Damn." She felt his motioned as he ripped off his blindfold.

Breathless, Bryn did the same. Her lips were already swollen with anticipation, craving his kiss. Her cheeks were flushed. She started to shake her head, unwilling to accept the lost kiss, the lost opportunity...

A pair of drunken fishers stood at the edge of the beach near the docks with a bottle of ale between them, waving to Rangar. They hooted and teased to find him alone with Bryn. "Your princess can wait!" they called. "It's time for you to crown the Wheat Maiden!"

Rangar's hands tightened around Bryn's waist as his familiar brooding mask descended over his face. He turned to look her in the eyes beneath the moonlight, and Bryn felt a jolt of lightning at the direct look after so being blindfolded.

Rangar bent down to whisper in her ear, "Later tonight. Don't go to bed. I'm going to split apart at the seams if we don't finish what we started."

She felt herself nodding, eyes wide. He squeezed her waist one more time before sauntering off after the fishers, cursing them black and blue, then grabbing their bottle of ale and pouring it down his throat.

24

THE WHEAT MAIDEN...AN URGENT NEED...
LOST IN THE FOREST...A TERRIBLE MISTAKE
AND A BRUISED RIB

*A*s Bryn rejoined the crowd around the bonfire, Saraj sidled up to her with a satisfied smirk on her face. "You disappeared."

Bryn rolled her eyes as she muttered, "Apparently not far enough." At Saraj's questioning look, Bryn clarified, "Rangar and I...we were about to be alone...but he got called back to hand out some award."

"Ah." Saraj nodded knowingly. "The Wheat Maiden. Yes, it's his duty every Harvest Gathering. There." Saraj pointed to a place on the beach where a handful of girls around seven or eight years old stood ankle-deep in the water, the bottoms of their gowns getting soaked, shrieking at each crashing wave. They each already wore a flower crown, but Rangar held a beautiful wreath-like crown of woven wheat stalks. He strode into the water and placed it on the head of the smallest girl, a tiny thing who'd been born with one arm. The girl gasped and jumped up and down, splashing the others, who only giggled and splashed her back.

Bryn settled onto the makeshift seating of a log away from the bonfire, watching the crowd. Rangar took turns spinning each of the little girls in the water and letting them go, tossing them into the waves. They were soaked but laughing, and soon a handful of fishers and older girls waded in, splashing one another as well.

Bryn's head spun. She was dizzy from drinking much more cider and mead than she ever had before. *I'm drunk*, she realized with a little laugh.

Her mother had told her never to drink enough alcohol to get intoxicated, insisting that a lady kept her wits about her at all times. But Bryn felt safe amid the Baer villagers. Bonded by mead and good cheer. For the first time in her life, she let herself not care about appearances. Half the villagers were drenched in seawater and sand. The other half were drunk out of their minds, dancing and singing loudly, a handful even passed out in the seagrass.

She felt a wonderful certainty that these villagers would never judge her for any improprieties. If she passed out or if she whooped and splashed in the waves...it didn't matter. No one expected princessly behavior in these lands. They had no expectations for her other than to enjoy the festivities like the rest of them.

Grinning, she stood up and rejoined the festivities. Wandering to the village square, she was invited into a game of seashells with the goatherd girl, then into a drinking game she barely understood with some young fishers. In the back of her mind, Rangar's words lingered. *Don't go to bed. I want to finish this.* The anticipation was killing her.

Tonight, he'll kiss me.

With the alcohol dulling her senses, she felt reckless and wild. Maybe she'd let Ranger do more than just take a kiss. In fact, she could already imagine his hands all over her body. His fingers tangled in her hair as he devoured her neck and lips. *He might even propose*. The idea both terrified and thrilled her. What answer would she give him?

As the tide inched closer to the bonfire, threatening to put an end to the festivities, she realized she had a very full bladder. Tipsy and stumbling, she made her way from the town square over the dunes onto the tall seagrass, hitched up her skirt, and relieved herself. A close-by rustling sound startled and confused her; were there animals near the cliffs? Then she heard a moan and realized it wasn't animals at all but rutting couples from the Gathering. Now that the party was winding down, people were pairing off, disappearing into the privacy of the night, finding even more pleasure from one another.

She stood quickly and straightened her skirts. Her cheeks burned at the same time that she felt a strange flutter in the base of her belly. Listening to moaning couples making love to one another out in the open was the most scandalous thing she could imagine, but something about it thrilled her, too. She felt herself touching her neckline, craving someone's touch, as she wandered down the beach. The path took her over the dunes and into the forest, and before she knew it, a nearby voice spoke.

"Are you lost, Princess?"

She spun to find Valenden sitting on a boulder, smoking a *statua* pipe. An empty bottle of mead rested at his feet.

"Val! Oh. No, I..." She turned in a circle, frowning at the trees, realizing she *was* lost.

Valenden smirked and stood, stalking toward her. He looked her up and down appraisingly. "Saints, Princess. You're drunk."

"I'm not!" she protested weakly.

That earned her another smirk. He took another step forward and then leaned in to whisper, "Everyone's drunk tonight. It would be a crime not to. Where's that brother of mine? Why isn't he ravishing you?" She gaped, but Valenden only laughed. "Has he still not kissed you? What a coward. A waste, I say. I told you before, in the mountains, I had half a mind to kiss you myself." His gaze dropped to her lips, and she felt that strange flutter in her belly again.

"Don't be a cad," she chastised him. "I should...get back."

But Valenden was still smirking at her, ignoring her words. "Have you *ever* been kissed?"

She swallowed, then shook her head.

He scoffed. "Shameful. At your age, you should have been sneaking off to closets with dashing young men for years." He raised a suggestive eyebrow. "Shall I teach you? For practice only, mind you. Don't you dare get any ideas in your head. I'm a cad, you said it yourself. You mustn't fall in love with me."

"Val, stop. You're being silly."

"Silly? Silly is accepting my brother's proposal and letting him stick his tongue down your throat without knowing what you're doing. I'm quite the expert, you know." He moved toward her slowly, and she found herself stepping backward until her back pressed against the tree. Her cheeks were flushed from the mead. It took her mind a moment to catch up to what was happening, what she was feeling, as he stopped an inch from her.

His eyes fixed on her lips, twinkling with mischief. "A lesson, that's all. Do you want a lesson? Otherwise, how will you know if a kiss with Rangar is any good? It doesn't mean anything more than that."

Her lips parted as though they had a mind of their own. Valenden smelled delicious, like fresh cider, and Bryn's head was so bubbly from the party and from dancing. She remembered how she'd felt while dancing with Valenden earlier in the night; Valenden was someone to have fun with, that was all. She'd never trust him for anything except a good time. But somehow, even though he was most *definitely* an ass, he had always managed to endear himself to her.

She felt herself giving a tipsy shrug as if to say "why not" at the same time that a voice in her head screamed for her to tell him no. But as soon as her head lifted in a slight nod, he was kissing her. It started off slow. He was in no hurry; there was none of Rangar's predatory urgency in his movements. It gave her the same giddy feeling as when she'd danced with Valenden, a carefree feeling of celebration. His lips were soft and knew just what to do. She felt herself melting into the tree, letting Valenden show her how a kiss was supposed to go—and he certainly was skilled. Her heart started pounding a little harder. She assured herself this kiss was just a joke, just fun on a festive night, but her pulse was flaring and her whole body started shaking, wanting the kiss, wanting it to deepen.

I shouldn't feel this way about Val...

Something shifted between them. The kiss went from being slow and instructional to suddenly deeper. Valenden gave a slight groan as he leaned his weight against her, pressing her back against the tree in a way that she didn't entirely mind. His lips moved faster, hungrier, as his hand slid down to her waist, nearly grazing the outside of her chest...

And then everything changed.

Valenden was somehow thrown off her. It happened so fast that she barely had time to understand what was going on.

Rangar was there, standing in the forest. He grabbed Valenden by the throat and slammed him back against the tree. The air rushed out of Valenden's chest, and he slumped forward, then started to speak in a rasping voice. "Brother—"

But before he got another word out, Rangar threw a punch against Val's jaw that sent him toppling backward.

Bryn pressed a frightened hand to her mouth. "Rangar, stop!"

But he was beyond the point of listening. With raw jealousy in his eyes, he grabbed his brother's shoulder and punched him again. Blood spurted from Valenden's nose. He raised his arm to shield himself against Rangar's next blow, but the damage had already been done.

Bryn hurled herself on Rangar, grabbing him by his shoulder, tugging him backward away from his brother. Rangar started to shrug her off but then stopped himself, his eyes wide and wild. His chest rose and fell raggedly. He stared at Valenden with pure fury. "Don't *ever* touch her."

Valenden clutched what was clearly a broken nose. Despite the violence Bryn had just witnessed, Valenden gave a grim smile as he spit out a stream of blood. "She asked me to, brother. What was I supposed to say, no?"

Valenden was acting like this kind of awful altercation was common between them, and for all she knew, maybe it was. It certainly seemed like the Baer people were more likely to settle their scores with their fists than with words, as they did in the Mirien.

Bryn's lips fell open. Rangar shot her an accusatory look, and she shook her head, unsure what to do or say.

"Is that true?" he growled.

"It was nothing," she protested. "It *meant* nothing, just a bit of fun."

"Fun?" Rangar growled. "You think it's fun to see my brother's hands all over you? When you damn well know I…" He bit off whatever he was going to say next.

Valenden gave a harsh cackle. "Sorry, brother, but you had your chance. You can't expect *all* of us to be Saints."

Rangar looked inclined to punch him again, but then he shook his head, muttered a curse in Baer that Bryn didn't understand even with Mage Marna's borrowed translation ability, and turned sharply and strode away into the forest.

Bryn considered chasing after him but thought better of it, given his temper and her level of drunkenness. She leaned back against a tree trunk, breathing hard. She shot an angry look in Valenden's direction. "You idiot! Why in the name of the Saints did you do that?"

Wincing, Valenden clutched his nose and started to say, "Bryn, I'm sorry…"

But before he could answer, she changed her mind and ran after Rangar.

25

A MESS OF EVERYTHING...NOT INTERESTED
IN TALK...TRUST AND DISTRUST...A BAD
MORNING

*R*angar strode between trees, breathing hard, every muscle in his body set tense. Bryn ran to catch up to him and touched his shoulder. "Wait! Talk to me."

He spun on her hard. His chest was rising and falling quickly. In the darkness between the trees, shadows hid the scars on his face but not the dangerous gleam in his eyes.

"Rangar, it meant nothing," she insisted quietly. "I just had too much cider and didn't want the night to end, and..."

And...then Rangar was kissing her.

In the dark forest, he dragged her close and kissed her as though every piece of him was a drowning man and she was air. As though her lips were the one and only thing he'd craved for years. Bryn could barely make out his face in the dark shadows, but his fervor said everything. The demanding touch of his lips stole her breath. His hand clutched her waist so hard she was afraid she'd have bruises in the morning. His other hand curled in the hair at her nape, tilting her head back so he could deepen the kiss.

Her momentary shock gave in, and she felt herself kissing

him back with just as much passion. The cider made her dizzy but also brave. She realized she'd wanted this for a very long time, too. Her curiosity had been nipping at her, tilting her toward him. Valenden was just an imitation of Rangar, a version with all the passion but none of the angry heart that had stolen her own...

"Rangar—" she started, but he interrupted her with his lips. Clearly, he wasn't interested in talk.

His skin was warm enough to burn; it smelled like woodsmoke and sea air. His fingers pressed against her side hunted over the thin fabric of her dress for the scars over her rib cage. His other hand threaded tighter through her hair, drawing her lips closer.

He moved her backward until she felt a tree trunk at her back. Hidden here in the heavy shadows of the forest, she felt free. No one could see them. She could almost pretend it wasn't happening at all; it was just like the dreams she had sometimes at night, scandalous dreams of his body against hers.

He wedged his knee between her legs, and she gasped. His lips trailed down her neck from the point of her jaw to the flat of her shoulder. His hand found the scars at her side over her dress, but his fingers moved hungrily as though wanting more. To touch her skin, not fabric. With a moan, he slipped a hand between the buttons of her dress, fighting past the chemise beneath, ripping the delicate silk fabric until he could touch her bare scars.

Skin against skin.

She gasped at his sudden touch. No man had ever touched her there, especially not with a bare hand. His palm ran over her hip, fingers tracing the scars as well as the edge of her underskirt, as his lips did the same against her neck.

She closed her eyes, breathing raggedly. The night was

bitter cold, especially this far from the bonfire, but Rangar was burning hotly enough for the both of them. Was it true, what Valenden had said? Did Rangar love her? Or was it some twisted thing between them, the *fralen* bond? She was taken back to that night in the snow ten years before, her own hot blood spilling on sacred ground, and then Rangar's blood, too.

On impulse, she touched the scars on his cheek. He pulled back sharply from her touch. She hesitated. She couldn't see his face clearly in the shadows. Didn't he want her to touch him? He was touching *her* scars, so it was only right that she touch his as well.

"Don't," he said tightly.

"I don't care about the scars," she whispered. "You know that."

"It isn't that." His voice was hard. He was breathing even harder. "I don't want you to think about that night. About the attack. You aren't indebted to me. You owe me nothing. Don't kiss me because I saved your life."

"I'm not."

"Is it just fun to you? Like with Valenden? What does it matter if it's one brother or the other when you've had some cider?"

"Of course not." Her passion spilled over into anger. It wasn't right for him to suggest she would be so petty. "You know that's not how I feel."

"I *don't* know. I have no idea how you feel. If you're repulsed by me or..." He swallowed. The unfinished sentence hung between them heavily. She could feel his question waiting there, but he wouldn't continue. He gave a harsh laugh. "Bryn, you have no idea..."

"I *want* you to kiss me, Rangar."

"And then?"

She blinked, surprised at his question. She wished she could see his expression in the darkness.

"You know what tonight brings," he said quietly, his hands tightening around her waist. "The Harvest Gathering, the Blindman's Dance, the cider making fools of everyone. It's the night to declare romantic intentions. Everyone in this damn kingdom is waiting for me to propose to the Mir princess I supposedly stole away because I was utterly besotted by her. Is that what you think? That I stole you?"

She pressed a finger to his lips. "Don't be ridiculous. I made the decision to leave Castle Mir, and I made the decision to stay here in the Baersladen, too. I think I've made it clear by now that I don't give a damn about the *fralen* bond or that you saved my life. If I'm here, it's because I *want* to be." He growled like he didn't believe her, and she shifted her posture against the tree. "Rangar, you're being an ass."

His eyes narrowed. She didn't know what else to say, and after a tense moment, he turned and left sharply.

Bryn slumped against the tree, feeling her legs weak. The heat at the base of her belly was nearly unbearable. She cursed him in her mind. *Princes!*

She closed her eyes. What had she gotten herself into? How had a romantic night turned into such a mess?

THE MORNING after the Harvest Gathering, breakfast was a sullen affair. Half the village was so hungover that the latrines were full of people being sick, and more slept in late on the great hall floor, shirking their daily duties. The kitchen maids and cooks were as exhausted as everyone else and only managed to pass out plain apples, water, and leftover stale bread.

184

Bryn had slept alone on the dais. Rangar hadn't returned to the great hall all night, and his absence hadn't gone unnoticed. Trei gave her a few piteous looks, and the villagers whispered about what had happened between her, Rangar, and Valenden. Somehow, word had gotten out about the fight between the brothers. The Baersladen was not a land of prattling people, but even here, romantic rivalries between the royal brothers were apparently gossip-worthy.

She took an apple from a nearby barrel and debated what to do. It was freezing in the great hall, but the hearths at both ends were surrounded by people all craving warmth, and the last thing she wanted was to sidle up to the villagers and receive an interrogation about what had happened the night before. Still, what option did she have? She'd turn to ice otherwise. She took a seat at the end of a long bench near the hearth, away from the crowd, and bit into her apple.

Saraj, freshly bathed and dressed in her huntswoman clothes, strode into the hall and, after gathering her own breakfast, took a seat next to Bryn. She slid her a knowing look. "So, Princess, did you enjoy yourself last night?"

Bryn swallowed down a thick bite of apple. "Um, I don't remember much."

That was only partially true. Memories from the night before were foggy, but she recalled clearly enough how it all ended. *The kiss with Valenden. Rangar catching them. Throwing a punch at his brother. And then that angry, passionate kiss in the forest before he stomped off.*

"I couldn't keep track of who you were spending more time with, Rangar or Val." Saraj's words had a questioning edge to them. "At one point, all three of you disappeared, and then Val came stumbling back with a bruised rib, a broken nose, and a scowl. He wouldn't say a word about what had happened, but everyone guessed."

Bryn bristled. "Does the whole village know?"

"Rumors have been spreading faster than the morning frost." The huntswoman lowered her voice. "I thought you and Rangar made up. The last I saw, at the Blindman's Dance, you were getting cozy…"

Bryn swallowed, hesitant to add more fuel to the rumors, but she trusted that Saraj wasn't just needling her for gossip. "Valenden kissed me," she admitted reluctantly. "It was stupid. Just a joke. You know how Val is."

That wasn't the entire truth, and Bryn knew it. Maybe the kiss had *started* as a joke, but Bryn couldn't lie to herself forever. The kiss had, at some point, suddenly *stopped* being a joke—and the feelings hadn't just been on Valenden's side. He was gorgeous in that rakish, smirking way of his, and Bryn had been so tipsy and swept up in the festivities…

But ultimately, it had meant nothing. She sighed deeply. "Rangar saw it happen and, well, you can guess how he took it given the state of Val this morning."

Saraj took a bite of her apple and shook her head in regret. "All that plotting wasted. Trei and I had been trying to figure out for weeks how to get you two to forgive each other and realize you're dying to tear each other's clothes off. I suppose we're right back at the starting point now. I take it there wasn't a proposal?"

"No, and there won't be." Bryn thought of the fury on Rangar's face. He was too wild, too coarse. The same things that drew her to him were the same things that pushed her away. Now, in the light of day, she second-guessed everything she'd felt about him.

Had it been right to flee Castle Mir? Of course, if she hadn't, she'd likely be dead along with her parents. But maybe she could have begged sanctuary with the forest kingdoms or even Baron Marmose in Ruma… But the thought of that awful baron made her shiver. Rangar might be an oaf, but he wasn't a weasel who was more interested in her sister.

"Where did Val go?" Bryn asked quietly, glancing toward the door. "I think I owe him an apology for nearly getting him killed."

Saraj raised her eyebrows. "I thought you said Val kissed you, not the other way around? That would suggest that you're blameless."

Bryn felt a guilty flush spread over her cheeks—she didn't want to get into a detailed explanation of what she'd done and felt the night before. She still wasn't even certain she recalled it all clearly. Head aching, she stood up, tossed her apple core in the fire, and then realized just how filthy and sea-soaked the hem of her dress was, not to mention her hair, which reeked of bonfire smoke.

"Lords and ladies, I need a bath," Bryn said.

"Good luck," Saraj said, throwing her own apple core into the fire, too. "The bathhouse has a line all the way around the side of the castle. You'd have better luck jumping in the river."

Bryn sighed, hating the sticky, sandy feeling that coated her skin, like a representation of her shame and guilt.

Saraj gave her a sympathetic look and said, "Try the mage's quarters."

"They have their own bath?"

"No, silly, they don't need one. They have spells. You look pathetic enough that Mage Marna might just take pity on you and cast you clean."

Bryn sighed as she picked at the soiled gown Saraj had lent her, feeling guilty for so much. "Thanks, Saraj. I'm so sorry I messed up everything. You've been so kind to me. I know you just want to see the Barendur brothers happy."

Saraj tilted her head, frowning slightly. "Who said anything about Trei and Val and Rangar? The villagers want to see *you* happy, Bryn."

Bryn's eyebrows rose in surprise. "Me? But why?"

Saraj gave her a soft smile. "You're one of us now, of course."

26

MAGE WISDOM...AN UNCONVENTIONAL
BATH...A FINDING SPELL...LIBRARY BOOKS...
SOLDIERS SPARRING

*E*ver since the hexmark scarification process that had nearly killed her, Bryn had kept her distance from the area of Barendur Hold that housed the mage chambers. Even thinking about those dark rooms reeking of herbs made her body ache with painful memories.

Now, as she climbed the spiral stairs, she traced the still-tender hexmark carved into the folds of her ear. It had granted her the ability to speak Baer, to work with the villagers, communicate with them—*to be one of them*—as Saraj had said. Pain was a high, but fair, price for such a gift.

She found the two apprentices, Calista and Ren, yawning as they ground herbs with mortars and pestles. They, too, had been up all night at the Gathering like everyone else and looked like they wished they could still be in bed sleeping off a hangover. When Bryn stood in the open doorway and cleared her throat to announce herself, the apprentices gave each other a quick, knowing look. Clearly, gossip about the fight between Val and Rangar had spread even here.

"I'm looking for..." Bryn started.

"Lady Bryn." Mage Marna emerged from the back room,

drying her hands with a rag. She looked over Bryn's filthy dress and tangled hair with a raised eyebrow. "I thought we'd scared you off from the last time you were here."

Bryn's eyes went wide. "Not at all."

"I'm only teasing you, child. I saw the gleam in your eye when you spoke a language fluently you hadn't studied a day in your life. The look of someone helplessly drawn to magic. Be careful, it can become addictive." The mage flung the rag into a wicker basket in the corner, then folded her arms. "Is that why you've come? To learn another spell?"

"Actually, I was hoping for a bath?" Bryn motioned to the awful state of her dress. "I thought you might have a spell to clean the dress Saraj lent me and make me look less like something a dog found in a ditch."

The apprentices laughed softly before getting a sharp look from Mage Marna and quickly returned to their work.

Mage Marna grunted. "Follow me."

Bryn followed the older woman back to the rear workrooms. She'd never been beyond the entry room in the mage chambers and was surprised to discover a warren of smaller rooms and passageways. Glancing into them, she saw storerooms full of drying herbs, shelves of ingredients for potions, a few monastic-like cells where the apprentices must sleep, and finally, a large room with a few benches and a worktable that reminded her of the schoolroom in Castle Mir where she, Elysander, and Mars had learned their lessons.

Mage Marna looked Bryn over slowly, then traced a symbol in the air and whispered a few words. As had happened previously when she'd cleaned the soot from Bryn's hair, sand and dirt simply shook themselves off her clothes. She felt crusted salt flake off her body and fall to the ground like spilled sugar. In the next moment, she stood amid an alarmingly large pile of dirt and debris.

"There," the mage said. "That's an improvement."

Running her hands over her smooth face, soft hair, and clean gown, Bryn relaxed, though tidying herself up physically wasn't the same as tidying up the mess she'd made last night.

As though sensing her troubled thoughts, Mage Marna leaned back against the worktable. "I heard my apprentices whispering this morning. Apparently, you caused quite the stir last night between Rangar and Valenden."

Bryn knit her fingers together anxiously. "About that...I didn't mean to. It was a stupid thing—I'd drank too much cider."

To Bryn's surprise, the mage only shrugged. "You aren't bound to Rangar. Your heart is free. You have nothing to feel guilty about. You are young, and youth is meant for indiscretions."

Bryn frowned. But she *was* bound to Rangar, wasn't that the whole point? "Still, it was cruel of me," she admitted quietly. "If I'm being honest, I think I knew it would hurt him. I never would have kissed Val if I'd been in my right head, but with the cider..." She let her thoughts trail off.

The mage only smirked. "Rangar has had weeks to declare his feelings, and he's done nothing. He needed to know that he can't drag his heels forever. Besides, those two have had a rivalry their entire lives. They've fought over everything before: girls, horses, swords. Nothing will spur Rangar to action like thinking his brother might win the prize he's sought after for so long."

Bryn considered the mage's words carefully—it was a perspective she hadn't considered before. She wasn't entirely sure *why* she'd let Valenden kiss her last night. *Val's* reasoning was obvious. Even when sober, he'd kiss anything that moved, whether it was a young soldier or his brother's Saved. Pour a gallon of cider into him, and he was an utterly impossible ball of lust.

Yes, she felt certain the kiss hadn't meant anything to Valenden. If it hadn't been for the bruises and broken nose he'd woken to, he probably wouldn't have even remembered their dalliance. Besides, there was something about Valenden that made her feel oddly safe. Maybe it was because his emotions were only skin-deep: lust and laughter, nothing more. Not like brooding Rangar, who was nothing *but* deep emotions.

To her surprise, Mage Marna stood up and ran a tender hand down Bryn's now-clean curls. It wasn't often that the mage, or anyone in the Baersladen, had shown affection. "A hunter came to me yesterday to get a dram of potion before the Gathering. He'd been hunting foxes up in the high meadows. He said he saw small hoof prints in the mud north of the valley where the maiden roses grow."

Bryn gasped. "The missing lamb?"

The mage smiled kindly. "Apparently your little lost sheep is still alive and gorging itself on gorse up there in the mountains."

It was the best news Bryn had gotten in days and a welcome distraction from the mess she'd made of things the night before. She started for the door, excited. "Thank you. I've got to go look for it—"

"Wait, child. That valley is vast. It could still take you days to find the creature. I had something else in mind." Bryn paused at the door, turning and raising an eyebrow. The mage continued. "One of the first lessons my apprentices learn is a finding spell. It's relatively simple and requires only a small hexmark, a single needle prick. Most of the villagers throughout the kingdom have mastered it. It's normally used to locate small objects one has misplaced—you must have a personal connection with whatever it is you seek. But I believe it might work for your lamb."

"A finding spell?" Bryn said. "That would be incredible."

"Then come on the night of the next full moon after the castle has gone to sleep. Your lamb will be fine for a few more nights. Find me here, and I'll teach you the spell."

"I will. Thank you." Bryn felt herself grinning widely as she left the mage chambers and wandered down one of the long hallways of the Hold. She wasn't sure which excited her more, the prospect of finding the lost lamb or learning magic. The experimental procedure Mage Marna had done on her to allow her to speak was incredible, but the magic wasn't coming from Bryn but rather the mage.

Now, Bryn was *actually* going to learn to do magic herself.

Her mind spun with the possibilities of all the spells she'd like to master. The ones she had seen the villagers performing so effortlessly: starting a fire without flint, untangling knots, commanding breezes, even simple communication with animals.

She had just realized she was completely lost in a hallway she'd never been down before when she heard a voice call from an open doorway, "Miss me already?"

The open doorway led to a small bedroom with a pallet on the floor, a stack of books, and a lantern. Valenden rested on the pallet, reading a book. Bryn paused in the doorway, her gaze finding the bruises on his face, the bandage around his bare chest.

"What are you doing here?" she asked.

"I could ask you the same thing," he said. "*I'm* recovering from a brutal attack, so it makes sense that I'm in the mending ward." He made a big show of looking her over from where he was reclined on the pallet. "What about you? Any broken bones? Or was it just your heart I broke last night?"

She rolled her eyes but inwardly felt immense relief that they were back to their usual banter. The kiss had shocked her with its unexpectedly passionate turn, but ultimately, Val was only a friend, and she was grateful that the events of the previous day hadn't seemed to change that. She needed all the friends she could get in this new land.

She sauntered into his mending room and glanced down at the book he was reading but didn't recognize the alphabet.

"It's an old language," Valenden explained. "An ancient text on philosophy."

"You don't seem the philosopher type, Val."

He closed the book with a bored sigh and tossed it at the foot of the bed. "I'm not. But this is all they have up here." He leaned forward, hair falling in his face, as his eyes gleamed. "Do me a favor? Fetch me something more interesting to read? You owe it to me, you know, after driving my brother to beat me black and blue."

"Barendur Hold has a library?"

"Of course. Do you think we're complete heathens? It requires a key to enter; ask my father. He'll give it to you."

She balked. "I can't ask King Aleth to unlock a door for me."

"Why not?"

"He's the king! He has a nation to run!"

"Well, your other option is to ask Rangar. He also has a key."

A sullen moodiness fell over her at the mention of Rangar's name, and Valenden read it on her face and laughed. "Is he really angry with you because of one little kiss?"

She picked nervously at her fingernails. "I haven't even seen him all morning."

"I'm sure he's out sulking. Don't worry, he'll get over it. It isn't the first time I've found myself intertwined with a girl he's fancied."

Her heart faltered for a beat. "I thought he had no sweethearts."

Valenden gave her a knowing smirk. "Bryn, he's a grown man. He might not have had a sweetheart, but there have been girls he's…" He cleared his throat, thinking better of what he was going to say. "Let's just say Rangar is no blushing virgin. Not by a long stretch."

Bryn felt her own cheeks warming, blushing just like he described, and Valenden's eyes lit up.

"Ah! And you are, aren't you! Saints, I was only joking. Is it true? Are you a virgin? It must be a Mir thing. Seems like an awful choice to me."

Her eyes flashed, annoyed. "If you're going to mock me, I'm leaving."

"Wait, wait. I won't tease you anymore. In honesty, Bryn, I owe you an apology for last night. It wasn't my intention to get between my brother and you. I'm just a cad who can't keep his hands to himself when a beautiful creature is in front of me." His eyes lost their normal mocking luster. "Forgive me?"

She softened. "It was my fault, too. But it's important that you know that I don't ever want that to happen again."

He feigned indifference, though there was still a smolder to his eyes. "Hmm. Perhaps, but may I remind you that Rangar has no claim on you. No ring on your finger. No pledge to be married one day. Until then, I make no promises. Wear a dress like you were last night and pour mead down my throat and, well, you might find yourself in trouble again."

She rolled her eyes at his words but inside felt slightly less certain about her resolve. *No more putting myself in situations where I might be tempted by Val…*

"I'll see what I can do about that book," she promised. She went looking for King Aleth to borrow his library key, still feeling like she couldn't possibly get up the courage to disturb the king for something so insignificant, and eventually found him overseeing army training in the courtyard. She hovered at the edge of the courtyard, nervous.

To her surprise, Rangar was also in the courtyard, shirtless as he sparred with one of the soldiers. For a second, in the midst of his battle, his eyes caught on Bryn standing at the side of the courtyard. A flash of both anger and desire rippled over him, giving his opponent a rare opening to strike, but a second before the soldier tapped Rangar's shoulder with the broad side of his sword, Rangar spun, drawing his own sword and tapping it on the man's thigh.

"Lady Bryn?" King Aleth had spotted her hanging back in the shadows and turned to her, his dark eyes unreadable. She suddenly wondered if the rumors had even spread to the king himself. What would he think of her, this foreign interloper causing rivalries between two of his sons? Ho, he probably rued the day he let Rangar talk them into rescuing her from Castle Mir. "Something you needed?"

"The library key," she said quickly, not meeting his eyes. "It's for...Valenden."

Some of the soldiers nearby overheard her say the middle brother's name and let out a low, teasing whistle. Had Rangar heard? The last thing he'd want to think about was Bryn on an errand for Valenden. She glanced at him for a second as she took the key from the king, but he had already turned away, sword raised, sweat glistening on his bare back.

She swallowed hard and tried to think about anything other than last night's kiss, but of course, it kept returning to her mind, again and again.

27

CORNERED BY WENCHES...WOODEN SPOONS...PLACING BETS...A TRUCE MESSENGER ARRIVES

*I*n the days following the Harvest Gathering, the entire village was consumed with harvesting and preparing the various crops for winter storage. After her duties tending to the lambs in the barn, Bryn spent most of her time in the kitchen storerooms with the scullery workers, packing harvested gourds in straw to keep them dry throughout the colder months. While she was knee-deep in onions in the cold-storage pantry, three of the kitchen girls cornered her.

"Is it true?" the stoutest girl said, whose hair was braided and pinned around the crown of her head. She waved a wooden spoon vaguely threateningly in the air. "Did Rangar give Valenden that broken nose on the night of the Harvest Gathering?"

Bryn silenced a groan. She had hoped that Valenden would have the good sense to hide away in the mending rooms until the worst of his bruises healed so that the whole castle wouldn't be immediately drawn into speculation. But Valenden wasn't one to languish for long. He'd probably gotten bored and gone searching for trouble after a single day on bed rest.

"We heard they were fighting over *you*," the smallest maid

said, also wielding a wooden spoon. The three girls practically glowered. She had no idea what these girls wanted with her.

Bryn's heart hastened with fear. All her life, growing up in Castle Mir, she'd had little contact with servants and practically none at all with commoners outside of the royal grounds. Castle Mir even had the hidden passageways within the walls to create two worlds: one for the royal family and favored members of the court and the other for the working class. Bryn had never given much thought to the arrangement—it had simply been the way things were. The few times she'd tried to talk or play with a servant girl, her mother had scolded her. So as she'd grown up, she'd looked to her older brother and sister as her models for how to interact with the world, and she did what they did—pretend the servants didn't exist.

She felt a deep burn of shame at how wrong she had been to go along with the unfair arrangement in Castle Mir. She couldn't excuse the wrongness of her actions even at her young age—she still should have known better. No person deserved to be ignored, especially not the very people that kept her fed and cared for. They deserved her gratitude. And the very least, to be looked in the eye.

Here, in Barendur Hold, there was still a division between royal family members and servants, but everything felt far less rigid. More like people simply fulfilling their roles and thinking of the good of the community. The three princes wouldn't hesitate to jump on a fisher's rig to fill the spot of an injured crew member; likewise, the servants didn't hold the royal family in such exalted reverence. The primary pastime in the Baersladen seemed to be teasing the brothers, dancing with them, laughing when one fell off a horse.

Bryn's eyes went anxiously between the three scullery maids who had trapped her in the storeroom. Did they hate her? Scorn her? Were they jealous of her trysts with the princes? After all, it had been made very clear to Bryn that Rangar was a favorite among the castle's women...

But this was Bryn's home now, and these were her neighbors, and she owed them honesty. "It is true," she admitted.

She braced herself for the worst they might do to her: beat her with those wooden spoons, berate her as a harlot, vow to never speak to her again. The girls shared a cryptic look amongst themselves—and then suddenly burst into laughter. They laughed so hard that they had to lean against the door-jamb to keep from falling. Tears of mirth ran down their faces.

Bryn frowned, confused. "You aren't angry with me?"

The smallest of the girls wiped the tears from her eyes and gave Bryn the strangest look. "Why in Saints' name would we be angry at you? You've given the whole town something to talk about!"

A girl with pigtails down to her waist spun on the first one. "And this means *I* win the bet." She prodded the stout girl with her wooden spoon, who reluctantly took off a pretty wooden bracelet and handed it over to the pigtail girl.

Bryn felt her shoulders relax partway. "Where I come from, interfering in the affairs of princes wouldn't be taken so lightly. I'd probably be banished."

The girls shook their heads in disbelief. "Is that truly how it is in the Mirien? Why, it's just a few bruises and a broken nose. Noses heal. Saints, they're young men. What else are they to do but get in trouble?"

Still snickering at the idea of Rangar's fist in Valenden's nose, two of the scullery maids left to continue their chores, but the stout girl remained. She drew a pear out of her apron and tossed it to Bryn, who had to dive forward to catch it. "Here. You look pale." She chuckled to herself, shaking her head. "Ho, how I wish I'd seen the look on Prince Rangar's face when he saw Val's hands on you."

For the remainder of the afternoon, Bryn replayed the interaction with the kitchen maids in her head. If Bryn's indiscretion with Valenden had happened in Castle Mir, she would have been strongly chastised for the tryst, and all whispers of gossip immediately hushed even at knifepoint. Here, the princes' indiscretions were treated as a sport, even to place bets on.

Evening came, and Bryn watched as Rangar ate and drank across the great hall with a few of the soldiers he'd been sparring with earlier in the day. Their eyes found and caught one another a few times, causing Bryn to look away as her heartbeat soared immediately. Her mind kept turning back to watching Rangar spar earlier: bare-chested, drenched in sweat, muscles rippling.

She hadn't known until that moment that the scars marring Rangar's beautiful face continued down his neck, all the way across his chest and shoulders. Her memories from when it happened ten years ago were hazy. Right after the attack, as soon as Rangar had fought off the wolves, she'd obviously seen the claw marks across his face—she didn't know that the wolves had in fact shredded not just his face but his entire upper half.

She pressed a hand to her collar, trailing her fingers against the soft lace as she stared into the roaring fire and tried her best not to think of Rangar. But, of course, it was impossible not to.

The scars running down his chest hadn't marred his impressive physique. On the contrary, they served to highlight it. The contrast of jagged lines on smooth muscle replayed in her head repeatedly as she remembered him thrusting and parrying while sparring, grunting with the exertion. She was so caught up in her fantasies that it took her a moment to realize that Rangar, on the other side of the great hall, had stopped speaking to the soldiers and was watching her through the crowd.

She dropped her hand from her lace collar, feeling suddenly warm. The hint of a smirk crossed Rangar's face before he returned to his conversation with a soldier.

Did he guess what I was thinking about?

It was the night of the full moon, so once most of the castle's residents had bedded down that night, she crept out from her cloak-blanket. She borrowed one of the lanterns hanging on hooks around the hall and used it to light her way as she climbed the spiral tower stairs to the mage's chambers. The apprentices were still awake. One read through a heavy leather-bound book by candlelight. The other was processing herbs on a worktable near the open window, letting the moonlight shine on her mortar and pestle.

The apprentice grinding the herbs was the same one who had held Bryn's wrists down to the altar when she'd gotten that painful experimental ritual. Now, the girl dipped her chin at Bryn in silent greeting, then wiped her hands on a towel and came around to where Bryn waited.

"Mage Marna told me you were coming," Calista said. "Unfortunately, she's been called off to speak with the king."

Bryn felt both a pang of disappointment and a ripple of worry. "Has something happened?"

The girl hesitated. "A truce messenger arrived after supper."

Truce messengers were members of a loose, wandering clan that swore no allegiance to any kingdom. Their members were made up of people from as far as Ruma and the Wollin and even beyond the Outlands. Because of their neutrality, they could safely pass where others couldn't and carry messages without fear of attack.

However, the arrival of a truce messenger was never a good

sign. Their services were expensive, so they were only used in dire circumstances.

"Saints," Bryn muttered, anxious, wondering what this meant and if the truce messenger had brought any news about the Mirien. "Well, I suppose I'll come back tomorrow." She turned to go, but the apprentice stopped her.

"Wait. Don't go. Mage Marna asked me to help you instead."

28

THE FINDING SPELL...MEETING CALISTA...A
MISSING BUTTON NOW FOUND...A LETTER
FOR BRYN

"*Y*ou can carve hexmarks?" Bryn asked.

"The finding spell is something even children learn," the apprentice said with a dismissive flick of her fingers. "There is no intricate scarification process like before: just one small cut and a few words to memorize. I can lead you in learning the spell. I'm Calista, by the way."

"Bryn."

Calista unhooked a woven basket from a wall hook and went around the storeroom, gathering a few herbs from the various clay canisters and glass jars. Then she jerked her head toward Bryn. "This way."

Bryn followed Calista down the long hallway into the deeper portion of the mage chambers. She stopped when they reached the innermost room and pointed to a chair next to the open window, bathed in moonlight.

"Sit."

Bryn did as directed, shivering in the wind blowing through the open window. The chill didn't seem to affect Calista, who drew a knife from a holster hidden under her flowy robes that glinted in the moonlight.

Bryn's heart shot to her throat. Her body remembered the overwhelming pain from the experimental hex scarification in her ear, and she started breathing hard, her mouth suddenly dry.

Calista rested a reassuring hand on her shoulder. "This is a simple spell with a simple ritual. Not like before. Here, drink this. It will ease the process."

She mixed a quick potion from the herbs she had gathered and passed the tonic to Bryn, who sipped the spicy, warm liquid from a pewter cup. The liquid blossomed in her belly, unwinding her muscles, easing her fears.

"Unbutton your blouse," Calista said. Bryn did as commanded, slowly unfastening her buttons. When she had undone the upper few, Calista stayed her hand. "That's enough. Pull your shirt down over your shoulder."

Bryn slipped the loosened collar down over her left shoulder. Calista ran her finger over the curvature of her arm as though searching for a particular spot and then nodded to herself. She picked up her knife and, with a practiced flick, made a small cut in the skin.

Bryn flinched. Fortunately, other than the initial sting, the wound barely hurt. A bead of blood formed, and Calista pressed a damp cloth against it. "Press this against the mark. It will only bleed for a moment."

"That's it? That one scratch?"

"I told you, even children get the hex for the finding spell." Calista gave her another dram to drink and then, after checking the hexmark to make sure it had stopped bleeding, nodded. "Now you must learn the spell. It's in the old tongue, which your translation hex won't work on, but it isn't long. Try to repeat this: *jin jan en veera.*"

Bryn listened carefully and then tried, "*Jin jan en vara...*"

"Veera."

"Veera. *Jin jan en veera.*"

Calista grinned. "Good. Now, it's time to test out your ability." With the tip of her knife, she popped off the uppermost button on Bryn's blouse, catching it in her palm. "Close your eyes."

Bryn hesitated but did so. She heard Calista's footsteps walking around the room and the rustle of some objects. After a brief moment, Calista said, "Open them."

When Bryn did, she found Calista's hands were now empty of the button. The apprentice said, "I've hidden the button somewhere in this room. Picture the button. Try to use all your senses. Feel its smooth edge. Taste its saltiness from sweat and the sea. Once you have a strong sense of the button in your head, recite the spell."

Bryn closed her eyes and tried to imagine the button as best she could, even moving her fingers in the phantom movements of unbuttoning it. Then she said, "*Jin jan en veera.*" The strangest sensation called to her—it wasn't quite like anything she'd experienced before.

"Do you feel it?" Calista asked.

"Not exactly," Bryn said hesitantly. "It's more like a scent in the air than a feeling. Does that make sense? I can't actually smell the button, but that's the closest I can come to describing it. I feel like I could follow that sensation as though smelling out a pie you've left somewhere in the room."

Calista nodded. "That's it. A deep, intuitive sense." *Magic*, Bryn thought and marveled at the idea of magic as another sense like touch or smell. "Follow it," Calista commanded.

Bryn rose from the bench, searching the room with her eyes. But no, that wasn't right. Calista wouldn't have hidden it in plain sight. *Sight* wouldn't find the button. So instead, she followed the tug of magic like a smell, which led her toward a pile of dirty rags in a woven basket in the corner of the room.

She dropped to her knees. *I can feel it. The button.* The cut on her shoulder itched. She started going through the linens until something small and hard fell out onto the floor.

Her button!

She picked it up, incredulous. She'd done magic again! That strange pull was like nothing she'd ever felt before, a sense she'd never known. Yet, as much as she delighted in the show of magic, a kernel of anger hardened in her. Why had the Mirien forbidden magic for so long? This was such a beneficial spell, and it hurt no one; there was nothing evil or backward about it as she'd been taught. Rangar had told her once that her parents forbade magic not because it was backward but because it was too powerful; give magic to the masses, and the masses wouldn't need their rulers anymore.

Maybe Rangar was right.

Calista observed, "I thought you'd be pleased, but you look like someone's stepped in your supper."

Bryn stood, pocketing the button so she could sew it back on later. "I'm sorry. This finding spell is incredible—I can't thank you enough. I was just thinking how much magic could help the people of the Mirien. But hexes aren't viewed favorably there. They prefer science, and as beneficial as science can be, it requires high levels of education and equipment not accessible to the commonfolk."

Calista nodded as she began to pack away the herbs and supplies. "Magic is egalitarian."

"I'm learning that," Bryn said. "My parents always taught me it was evil. A sin."

Calista glanced at Bryn from the corner of her eyes as she continued her work. Then, she asked slyly, "Are you so sure your parents didn't know any magic spells themselves?"

Bryn nearly laughed. "They would never touch magic."

But Calista wasn't laughing, and Bryn hesitated. There was

so little she knew about her parents. Was there a chance that they *had* regularly engaged with magic? With mages? After all, magic would have given them a strong advantage to maintain their position...

Dwelling on the questions Calista had put in her head, she thanked the apprentice again and then left, holding a poultice against the small wound on her shoulder. Her thoughts were absorbed in the possibility that her parents had used magic secretly. Would they have really kept that information from her? Then again, Bryn was the youngest. Still practically a child. No one ever told her anything important.

She was so consumed in her thoughts that she turned the corner in the maze of hallways and ran straight into someone. "Oh!"

She took a step backward, suddenly very aware that it was well past midnight and that her shirt collar was tugged down, the uppermost button missing, fully exposing her bare shoulder. But the person she'd run into didn't seem to notice her state of semi-undress.

"Lady Bryn." Despite the late hour, Trei was dressed in his full soldier's garb and bearskin cloak.

"Trei," she said, pressing a hand to her chest. "I was just visiting the—"

He cut her off, distracted. "I'm glad I found you. My brothers and I have been searching for you."

Her eyebrows rose. "Why? Has something happened?"

He drew a small scroll from his pocket. Her lantern light reflected on the crest of the truce messengers. Bryn felt a heaviness sink into her belly. Trei said, "A letter arrived for you."

29

A LETTER FROM MARS...LATE NIGHT NEGOTIATIONS...WARNINGS...INSUFFERABLE PRINCES

"*A* letter?" Bryn asked hesitantly. "For me?"

Trei looked very solemn in the flickering light of her lantern. Bryn realized that this was perhaps the first time she had been alone with the eldest Barendur brother. Trei had always been kind to her while keeping himself at a distance, and no wonder why: he had the affairs of the entire Baer kingdom to occupy his thoughts during the day and Saraj to occupy his nights. He was a stark contrast from his two brothers: Valenden's reckless hedonism and Rangar's brooding moods. Trei was a paragon of nobility—the ideal heir to the throne.

He towered over her, and she recalled briefly dancing with him at the Harvest Gathering. She had never paid much attention to the handsome eldest prince, but now she found herself unable to stop looking for comparisons with her own brother. Mars, the eldest prince of the Mirien. In many ways, Trei and Mars were similar. Both tall and attractive with a naturally regal bearing. Trei's hair was a few shades darker than Mars's, though their haircut was the same length with almost the same curl. But more than mere appearances, it was the gleam in their eye that she recognized. Both men knew that the weight of an entire kingdom rested on their shoulders; the only difference was, how would each of them handle that responsibility?

Trei didn't hand her the letter. Instead, he tucked it back into his inner pocket and said, "My father wishes to speak with you before you read it."

"Now? But it must be past midnight."

"I'm afraid this news cannot wait until dawn."

Knitting her fingers together anxiously, Bryn nodded. "Where is Rangar?"

"In the council chambers with Valenden and our aunt."

She nodded. Trei led her down the dark halls. Few residents were awake at this late hour; they passed an elderly woman sweeping the floors with a thatch broom and a drunk man singing to himself. Bryn wanted to ask Trei for details but found her throat thick. Something about Trei intimidated her in a way that she didn't feel with his younger brothers. He was so noble that it was like a wall around him, closing himself off to anyone but Saraj.

When they reached the chambers, Mage Marna was the first to see them enter. "Ah. Lady Bryn." The family was gathered around the council table; a tray of provisions had been brought up but was largely untouched except for the bottle of mead, which someone had drained to the dregs. Bryn immediately gave Valenden a suspicious look.

Mage Marna touched the poultice that Bryn held to her shoulder. "You found Calista, I take it?"

Bryn nodded. "And a missing button."

The mage gave a solemn nod. "Good girl. You'll be able to use the spell to find your lamb—but not tonight. There are graver issues at hand."

Bryn's attention shifted to Rangar. He was leaning on the table, inclined over a map of the kingdoms of the Eyrie, but his eyes were on her, simmering in the candlelight. She felt a shiver. There was still so much unresolved between them.

Trei turned to Bryn. "So, a truce messenger arrived earlier this evening. He bore a letter for my father, one for me, and one for my brother." He nodded in Rangar's direction. "And the one addressed to you." He removed it from his pocket and handed it to her.

As she started to rip open the seal, she asked the others, "What did he have to say in his letters to you?"

Rangar ran a hand through his hair, his body tense. "He demanded that we release our ransomed captive immediately or else face the full force of the Mir army."

"*Captive?*" Bryn near choked on the word. "I assume Mars means me."

"*We* know you came here willingly," Trei said evenly. "Your brother does not."

Bryn couldn't open Mars's letter fast enough. She quickly took in the few lines of his familiar handwriting, mentally verifying that this had truly come from him, not an imposter. The letter read:

Dear Sister,

I write to you as a brother hurting as deeply as I know you are. The loss of our parents weighs heavily on my heart, and I cannot also bear the loss of you, as well. Know that I will do everything in my power to rescue you from your captors and bring you home.

Mars

She stared at the brief few lines in confusion. Did he really believe the Barendur family had abducted her?

"Prince Mars is threatening war to get you back," King Aleth said in a low voice, studying Bryn for her reaction.

"But…" Bryn shook her head, setting down the letter. "It's a misunderstanding. Mars wasn't there when I fled the Mirien with you. He didn't hear what Captain Carr and the Mir soldiers threatened to do if they got their hands on me. Please, let me write Mars a letter back and explain. Once I tell him that I came with you of my own volition and that I am perfectly safe here, even well cared for, he will certainly retract his threat."

She'd asked to write a letter before, and they had dragged their heels. Now, she didn't see that they had a choice. Bryn felt certain her logic was sound, but none of the Barendurs seemed convinced. They remained uncomfortably silent. King Aleth's face was set hard, revealing nothing.

At last, Mage Marna spoke. "This goes beyond a brother concerned for his youngest sister," she explained. "Your words will not sway him."

Bryn shook her head. "Mars is reasonable."

King Aleth raised an eyebrow. "Is he?" He paced around the table, rubbing his hands together in the cold before continuing. "We already sent a letter the day you arrived. Trei wrote to your brother to inform him of the situation and assure him that this wasn't a claim of the *fralen* bond—that it wasn't ransom or captive. That you had come freely, and we meant to keep you safe."

Bryn's eyes widened. "Did he respond?"

The king's eyes fell to the maps laid out on the table. "Not at the time, but these letters prove that he received our missive and didn't believe us. Or doesn't care."

"Your brother craves war, Bryn," Rangar said in a low growl. "And he means to get it however he has to."

Her mood darkened further. "Are you suggesting he's using me as an excuse to invade?" She held up his letter. "All I see here is concern for his family."

"Of course that's what he would write to *you*," Valenden said from across the table. "Come on, Bryn. Open your eyes. It's obvious. Mars knows that you left the Mirien willingly, but it's more convenient for him if he can claim you're a captive. It gives him an excuse to attack."

As Bryn started to object, Trei interjected in a more measured tone, "Wait. There's more. Our Baer spies have told us that the unrest in the Mirien has not stopped now that Mars has control. The Mir commoners hate still being under the hold of a Lindane royal. We've heard substantiated accounts that a handful of Mir refugees are on their way here, fleeing your brother's rule. We've agreed to take them in just as we took you in. Your brother doesn't like this. He wants his people to have no alternative but the Mirien."

"Refugees?" Bryn whispered, shocked. "Is it really that bad back home?"

"Worse," Valenden muttered, throwing back a handful of roasted nuts from the provisions.

Rangar walked around the table to stand beside her, and despite the unresolved issues between them, she felt relief to have his sturdy presence near. "Mars Lindane has doubled down on your parents' reign. He's demanding higher taxes and harvest yields in retribution for the uprising. He's punishing your people to within an inch of their lives. His soldiers are hunting down the siege's leaders. It's mostly their wives and children that are fleeing here."

Bryn let out a long, troubled breath. The Mir commonfolk tended to view the Outlands with disdain; it would take a lot for them to give up their homes and flee to such a harsh land, as she had.

"When do the Mir refugees arrive?" she asked.

King Aleth said, "In the next day or two, most likely. We've sent out riders to escort them."

"I'd like to meet with them when they arrive. Help them settle in," Bryn said.

Trei nodded, approving. "A familiar face will be welcome to them."

Bryn knit her hands harder. "And Elysander? Is there any further word from my sister?"

"She is still safe, as far as we know, with her husband in Dresel," Mage Marna reassured her. "The Dresel royal family has never been very political. They prefer to focus on their own affairs. They will not meddle in this impending war unless forced to."

It was like Eylsander to stay out of the drama. Elysander had always been more concerned with education and decorum than politics, though her parents had taught her more about politics than Bryn. Still, though Bryn was happy to think of her sister safe, she didn't understand how Elysander could know what was happening in their kingdom and not do anything about it. Didn't Elysander feel an urge to do something to help the Mir commonfolk? And what did Elysander think of Mars's taking the throne and, if rumors were to be believed, continuing their parents' harsh rule?

Bryn was determined not to be like her sister. Somehow, she would find a way to help her people, even if all she could do for now was serve as a kind face to the refugees headed to the Baersladen. "I'd like to write to my brother, regardless," she insisted. "I need to at least try to reason with him. There's a chance he'll listen to me."

None of the Barendur family members seemed to agree, but Trei relented at last. "Very well. We'll send your letter at first light. The truce messenger will be here, resting, until tomorrow."

Once the briefing had concluded, King Aleth dismissed Bryn while he, Trei, and Mage Marna continued speaking of this new threat of war.

Hanging by her side, Rangar walked her out of the chamber.

Once they were in the hallway, he asked in a low voice, "You're certain you want to confront your brother?"

"Everyone in that chamber spoke of Mars as a tyrant, but he's my brother. I know him as no one else does. Let me try to reason with him. I know the rumors aren't encouraging, but I need to know for myself. To speak with him even if only through a letter."

Rangar didn't answer right away, holding back his feelings as was so habitual for him. They walked down the dark hallway as the sounds of a woman singing a lullaby to her fussy baby filled the air with a sweet tune.

"And your shoulder?" Rangar nodded his chin toward the poultice.

Bryn hesitated. They still hadn't spoken about the incident on the night of the Harvest Gathering; neither her kiss with Valenden nor her kiss with *him*. So naturally, she'd been afraid to tell Rangar that she'd gotten another hexmark without telling him, even though he'd sworn she was free to make her own decision.

Well, here was his chance to prove that he wouldn't fly up in arms.

"The finding spell," she said tightly. "One of Mage Marna's apprentices performed the ritual."

Whatever Rangar was thinking, he kept his thoughts to himself, and in the dark hall, his face was unreadable. He merely grunted, "To find your lamb?"

She nodded. "I'll go looking for him as soon as I've had some sleep and it's light outside. I plan to hike up into the mountains with supplies for a full day."

He grunted again—at least he wasn't launching into a rage.

She cocked her head, encouraged by this seeming control of his temper. "You aren't cross that I got another hexmark?"

He raised a shoulder. "Your life is your own."

She stopped and rested her hands on her hips, turning to face him in the dark hallway. "You've changed your tune."

"Have I?"

She waved her hand in the space between them. "What happened to all of this *fralen* bond talk? That you own me? I'm yours and no one else's? Have you suddenly changed your mind on ten years of beliefs?"

A corner of his mouth hitched in a grim smirk, and something shifted in the tight set of his face. "To be honest, I think if I have any hope of kissing you again, I'd best keep my beliefs to myself."

Bryn's lips parted in surprise at the mention of the kiss, but she quickly closed her mouth again. Her heart started thumping. She was suddenly very aware that they were alone in the hallway as most of the castle slumbered. "Be honest, Rangar. Is that really what you think?"

With an intense look, he stalked toward her, making her instantly regret her words. She took a hesitant step back, but it was a narrow hall, and the stone wall pressed against her spine. He stopped a pace in front of her. "What I *really* think?" He smirked again, though his eyes trailed down her body, pausing at her lacy neckline that was unbuttoned and lowered over her shoulder to accommodate the poultice. "That's between the gods and me."

The air shifted again, crackled with a tension that made her toes curl. "So, I can get as many hexmarks as I wish, and you won't object?"

"I won't object to *you*."

She narrowed her eyes as she shook her head softly. "You Barendur brothers. All of you are such a mystery. I can never figure out what's going on in any of your heads."

"That's easy," Rangar said as he ran a hand over the stubble on his jaw. "Trei thinks about duty. Val thinks about wine."

"And you?" she prompted when he didn't finish.

He leaned closer, and her breath stilled. Was her heart even still beating? He smelled like lye soap, his wool cloak, and potent herbs. He moved close enough that his lips grazed her ear as he whispered, "What I think about is too wicked to tell a lady like yourself."

Instantly, her cheeks went on fire.

"Heathenly things," he continued in a purr. "Things that would make that blush spread from your cheeks all the way down to your toes."

Her lips parted again, speechless. She wasn't sure she'd ever be able to speak again, let alone think.

Rangar smirked as he left her there in the hallway, calling back over his shoulder, "Good luck finding your lamb."

30

FINDERS KEEPERS...A LONG HIKE...THE PULL
OF MAGIC...SPLIT THOUGHTS...BREAKING
AND ENTERING

*I*t had been a long night. After receiving the hexmark and meeting with the Baer royal family, Bryn returned to the great hall to find the goat sleeping on her pallet. She nudged it aside and curled up under her cloak, tossing and turning. She was deeply troubled by the alarming news about her brother, but she also couldn't stop thinking about the words Rangar had whispered to her before leaving. *Things that would make your blush spread from cheeks to toes.* Why was he torturing her? Furthermore, could she believe that he'd actually changed and was no longer obsessed with the idea that he owned her soul?

By the time she stretched awake, most of the castle was already up and working. The majority of pallets had been cleared away, the livestock herded back outside for grazing— even her goat sleeping companion—and she'd even missed breakfast. She scrubbed her face in the bathhouse and rebraided her hair, then wandered down to the kitchen. The stout scullery maid who had cornered her before tossed her a fruit tart with a wink.

"Thanks," Bryn said, catching it. "Could I take a few more of these? I'm going to hike to the upper hills and might not be back until dusk."

"Of course," the girl said. "We pack midday meals all the time for the fishermen and soldiers who will be gone for days. By the way, I'm Roxin."

"Bryn."

Roxin grinned. "Yeah, I know. Everybody knows who you are." She started wrapping a few tarts in a cloth napkin along with a tin cup for water and a few ripe figs. She tucked the package into a basket and passed it to Bryn. As she did, her sleeve rode up, flashing the hexmarks on her arm. Some Bryn was starting to recognize, but one circular one was utterly foreign.

Bryn motioned to it. "I can't help but notice that hexmark on your wrist. I haven't seen one like it before."

Roxin grinned proudly. "That's because I'm the only one with it. It's a unique spell that Mage Marna developed. She asked for volunteers to test it out, and I was the only one who agreed."

"What does it do?"

"Well, Mage Marna designed it as a duplication spell. Multiply one apple into two. Handy for a kitchen wench, eh? But it didn't work as she'd planned."

"What do you mean?"

Roxin picked up one of the figs from a basket. She folded it into her palm, whispered a spell, then traced the shape of the hexmark in the air. When she opened her hand, the fig looked precisely the same. Bryn frowned and said as much.

Roxin laughed. "Eat it."

Bryn accepted the fig and ate a small bite. She immediately gagged and handed it back. "It's rotten!"

Roxin shook her head as she happily bit into the fig Bryn had returned to her. "No, not rotten. Fermented. Now you know why Barendur Hold always has plenty of cider and fruit wine." She shrugged as she ate the other half of the fermented fruit, grimacing at the strong bite of alcohol. "It's still a handy spell, even if it wasn't what the mage intended."

Bryn left the kitchen and finished packing a bag with provisions, a small knife—handy for any number of possibilities—and a heavier cloak since it could become icy in the upper hills. As she made her way around the castle, she kept an eye out for Rangar, but there was no sign of him.

"Rangar isn't here," Valenden called, reading her thoughts as he leaned in a doorway. "One of the farmers needed extra hands cutting and bailing wheat."

She tipped up her chin. "I wasn't looking for Rangar."

"Sure." Val strode forward, raising his eyebrows. His nose was still bruised but looked like it would heal cleanly. "Now get away from me, wench, before you start even more rumors."

Bryn made a show of rolling her eyes, though, in truth, she was relieved they were in a public place with plenty of witnesses. She'd made a mess of things already with Valenden, and the last thing she needed was *more* rumors of them alone together in secret places.

"You know you dream of it, Val," she said slyly, feeling proud of herself for throwing back his own taunting insults.

He grinned back.

The hike to the upper mountain pastures was a painstaking one and took Bryn the better part of the morning. A narrow path led up the side of the mountain, passing over unsteady scree that threatened to collapse at any moment. The wind was so harsh that the trees were gnarled and miniature. By midday, she had reached the furthest high pasture that she'd ever taken the sheep to before, and she stopped and ate her meal and then pulled down her collar to look at the hexmark.

"Good a time as any," she said aloud.

She closed her eyes and pictured the lamb in her mind. She imagined stroking its soft fur and breathing in its barnyard scent. Its black eyes and plaintive bleat. Once she had the lamb pictured, she recited the wording of the finding spell that Calista had taught her.

As soon as the final word was out of her mouth, she felt a tiny but noticeable tug in the back of her mind. It wasn't as strong as it had been with the button, but even a faint sensation gave her hope. The lamb must be alive! If not, the finding spell wouldn't be working at all.

She painstakingly followed the pull of the magic as she traipsed over the hills. Before, in the mage quarters, following the pull of the missing button had been almost like following the scent of apple pie; but here, there was no clear message to follow in the open wild. She found herself following the pull for a few yards in one direction, then turning and climbing in the opposite. She backtracked more than once. This spell was as infuriating as Rangar!

As she tromped along, she couldn't help but think of the mess of their situation. Of course, she took the blame for a portion of their argument—she certainly shouldn't have let Valenden put his hands all over her. But it wasn't *all* her fault. Rangar was so frustratingly possessive and distant at the same time. His mind always remained a mystery. His body, on the other hand...ever since she'd seen him without his shirt on, that particular mystery had been solved. And she couldn't seem to stop imagining what it would feel like to touch his bare skin, breathe in his scent...

As the hours passed, she made progress. Finally, the pull of the finding spell led her off the main path onto a narrow deer run. Sometime around midafternoon, the pull tugged harder. Her heart began to beat faster. This was unmistakably guidance. The pull led her back down the mountain, toward the valley where the main road to town cut through. The trail she was following met up with an alpine stream, and she paused to drink from her tin cup, feeling heartened. If the lamb had passed here, it would have found the creek, too. And in all likelihood, it would have remained close to a water source. The pull of the spell led her downhill, following the stream. She was in a part of the Baersladen she hadn't visited before, most populated by sparse farmsteads. A few cottages dotted the hills, smoke rising from their chimneys. The grass was taller here, ready to be harvested and baled into straw. Enough forage to feed a lost lamb for weeks. Her hopes soared when she spotted a small farmhouse nestled in the valley and the hexmark on her shoulder began to burn. This had to be it!

She ran to the farmhouse door and knocked, but there was no answer. So she walked around back, searching for the farmer or his family, but it was empty, too. She spotted the barn and decided to peek inside to see if the lost lamb had wandered in, lured by the scent of other animals' grain.

The latch on the barn gate was stuck, so she had to lift her skirt and climb over, nearly falling into the muck on the other side. She dusted herself off and poked around the stalls, peeking through the horses' legs, calling gently for the lamb.

She was on hands and knees to peer beneath a closed stall door when she nearly collided with two feet at the far end of the barn. "Oh!"

Rangar towered over her, looking down with a perplexed frown. He was shirtless, his torso drenched in sweat, his hair pulled off his face with a twist of twine. He held a scythe in one hand.

"Rangar!" Bryn scrambled to her feet, dusting straw off her dress. "What on earth are you doing here?"

"What am *I* doing here?" He motioned to the scythe. "I was

in the fields with the others when the farmer noticed a girl in a rose-colored dress breaking into his barn."

Bryn cried, "I wasn't *breaking* in!"

"Hmm." Mischief danced in Rangar's eyes. "Well, that's yet to be determined, but in any case, I offered to capture the trespasser."

She scowled at him as she plucked straw out of her hair. "I was attempting to use the finding spell to search for the lamb. I thought he might have wandered in here looking for feed."

"I thought you lost the animal in the high pastures."

"I did, and I've been up there all morning. But the finding spell led me here for some reason. I thought perhaps the lamb had mixed in with a different flock. That this whole time it was cozy in someone else's barn."

Rangar cocked his head, curious. He stroked his chin slowly. "You say the finding spell led you here?"

"That's right. Though, I suppose I didn't do the magic correctly. It's the first time I've tried it on anything other than a button." She sighed. A smirk slowly stretched across his face, and she said defensively, "What?"

"You know how the finding spell works, don't you?"

She toyed with the ribbons on her dress. "Well, yes. Calista explained it to me. The hexmark, the spell, how you picture what you want to find."

Rangar leaned back against the barn door, grinning. "So what were you picturing while you were traipsing along up there in the wilds? A lost lamb or a dark-haired prince?"

Her jaw dropped. "Rangar, don't be ridiculous."

But he continued to grin, and the terrible truth hit her. *He's right.* She'd spent half her time thinking of Rangar, even picturing him down to every last detail: His scars, his dark eyes, his rumbling voice. She'd even thought of his smell from the night before, herbs and lye soap! She'd gone and spent so much time fantasizing about Rangar rather than focusing on the lamb, and the spell had worked exactly as it should. It had led her straight to what she'd been dwelling on: *him*.

"I wasn't thinking about you!" she lied. "I just... I haven't mastered the spell yet..."

"Let me guess," he said, flicking back his hair and retying it. "You didn't like how I left things last night. Telling you all the wicked things I imagined doing with you, then leaving you to stew."

She scoffed. "You seem to think awful highly of yourself."

"I think we've established that *you* are the one thinking highly of me, Princess. Or at least thinking of me *often*."

It was impossible to ignore his current state of undress. The sweat had dried on his chest, but Bryn wasn't used to seeing half-naked men. Especially not Rangar, with the scars so deeply embedded in his taut muscles. She briefly remembered running her hands over those muscles over his shirt, how it had thrilled her to feel his strength. How she'd thought more often than she wanted to admit about the night in the forest when he'd lain on top of her to hide her from the Mir soldiers, his body flush against hers.

"Are you embarrassed, Princess?" he said in a low voice.

Bryn shook her head hard, though it was a blatant lie, and they both knew it. "So what if I was thinking of you? Don't taunt me, Rangar. I've had enough of being teased by you and Val. You're cruel."

She turned to go, and the smirk fell off his face. He ran to catch up with her, grabbing her wrist. "Bryn, don't go."

She kept her gaze low, not wanting him to see the mix of desire and pain on her face. She *was* embarrassed. Mortified. The truth was, she *had* been thinking about him all day. It seemed like more and more, he was all she thought about. Missing sleeping beside him. Riding together on his mare. That passionate night after the Gathering that had ended in disaster but before that had been such utter bliss…

"Forgive me," he said. Any trace of mocking had vanished from his voice. "It wasn't my intention to be cruel." She didn't answer, but she didn't pull away, either, and he continued. "The truth is, Bryn, you have no idea how it delights me to know that the spell led you to me. That you were thinking about me enough for magic to intervene."

"Rangar," she groaned, embarrassed, trying to pull away.

"I'm not trying to humiliate you." He drew her in closer, dropping his voice. "You must forgive me. The Baer way is one of dark humor. But Bryn, don't you see? This gives me hope that you think about me even a fraction of how often I think about you."

She hesitantly glanced up at him through her lashes. "Oh?"

"All day," he muttered in a growling voice. "Every day. If *I* cast a finding spell, it would lead me to follow at your feet like a dog, begging for scraps of your attention. And the fact that the spell led you to me…it's like a greasy bone with marrow for this old dog."

"I'm a greasy bone?"

He drew her closer by her wrist until they were only a breath apart. The tension was so thick in the air it was stifling. Bryn glimpsed some farmers outside the barn, bringing in bails of straw on horse-drawn wagons.

If Rangar noticed that they were about to have company, he didn't seem to care. He leaned in and grazed her jaw with his lips. "You're mouthwatering, is what you are. And I'm famished."

He tipped her chin up and lowered his lips to hers.

31

REFUGEES FROM HOME...A SLOWER BURN...A
SIMMERING KISS...AN AUDIENCE

*T*he kiss was slower than that time when Rangar had caught her with Valenden. Now, Rangar took his time molding his lips to hers. His hand went to cup her jaw as his thumb brushed over her cheek like she was a chalice he wanted to drink from deeply. She felt herself melting into his hands. The barn smelled like fresh-baled hay, but Rangar himself had a touch of pine and sweat from the hard work. His spicy scent only made her long to taste more of him.

She moaned softly against his lips. He wrapped his other hand around her waist, drawing her closer. Her body was flush against his own, reminding her of those long days together on horseback. That was when she'd felt that first awakening of feeling for him. Or had it been earlier, when she'd seen him step out of the carriage the first night of the High Sun Gathering, grown and fully a man?

She rested a hand against his bare chest and felt a flush of desire mixed with nervousness. She'd never touched a shirtless man before. A sprinkling of hair began near his neck and ran down to his navel, the sight of which made her feel things she'd never felt before. His skin wasn't soft and supple like hers.

Touching his taut muscles felt like running her hand over a sword blade or a copper cooking pot. She flushed with embarrassment and dropped her hand.

He broke the kiss, then trailed his lips along her jawline until he reached her ear. "Touch me," he whispered. "I want you to."

"It's just...I've never..."

He reached down and took her hand, pressing it against his heart, curling his large fingers around hers. The pads of her fingers grazed against the raised scars that tore through his perfect muscles. "I want to feel your touch," he groaned.

Feeling a bit bolder, she pressed her hand on his chest and trailed her other one along his shoulder, which was so massive that she could barely palm it. His arm tensed as he gripped her again around the waist. She almost squeaked at the sudden ripple of his shifting muscles.

He captured her lips again, this time more insistently. He coaxed her lips open and slid his tongue along her upper teeth, making her gasp. Her body moved on its own as though it knew what to do, even if her head didn't. Her teeth closed gently on his bottom lip, teasingly, and his chest swelled as he growled in desire.

"Gods," he breathed. "You taste like honey."

She pressed her lips to his again. The feelings coursing through her were overwhelming. She could barely think. She felt like some primal being unable to conceive of anything but desire. The pit of her stomach ached in a strange way. Her skin begged for his attention.

Rangar ran a finger along her blouse's collar, satisfying that itch. She felt her breath coming fast as he traced a line down the exposed skin at her neck, down to the top button, just beneath the base of her throat. Then, watching her with those dark eyes, he undid the upper button and replaced it with his lips.

She gasped at the feeling of a kiss on her throat as he trailed his mouth along her collarbone. Her back arched into him on its own. His hand came around to the front of her waist and grazed the edge of her breast through her blouse. Fire raced through her as she momentarily forgot to breathe.

"Rangar..." She wasn't sure what to say, only that she needed to tell him how he was making her feel. "My heart...it's racing."

In response, he ran his hands down the outside of her skirt, cupping her backside. A thrill shot through her as he lifted her to sit on the edge of the stall gate behind her. The movement forced her legs to wrap around his waist, hugging his body. Her core was flush with him, her legs shaking. He kept her steady with one hand while the other cupped her chin for another kiss.

While their lips played, she glanced over his shoulder, remembering they had an audience. The farmers were continuing their work in the yard outside the barn, pretending not to see them, though every once in a while stealing a glance their way.

Bryn curled a hand around Rangar's neck. "We have an audience," she whispered.

Rangar's eyes were dark with lust. He shook his head, not caring. "Does it matter?"

She swallowed as she glanced again at the farmers unloading the hay. Her first instinct was to hide what they were doing. Of course, a tryst like this would be kept behind closed doors in the Mirien. She knew her brother dallied with plenty of women but never in public. But the Baersladen was different. How many times had she heard couples moaning in the castle alcoves or forest glens? Besides, their relationship was hardly a secret in Barendur Hold. The kitchen maids were even placing bets on it!

"I guess it doesn't," she said, surprising herself.

"Good." His hand hardened around her back. "I don't care who sees. Everyone in this damn kingdom, from the fishers to my own brothers, have teased me mercilessly for years about the Mir princess who has my heart, and frankly, I don't mind proving them right."

He growled as he pulled her back into the kiss. Her hands went around his neck, running over the smooth skin of his upper back. For a brief moment, she let herself imagine what it would feel like to touch all of him. No clothes. Fully undressed. The both of them pressed together like this, skin to skin. Her pulse flared to life as her legs curled tighter around his waist.

"Rangar!" one of the farmers called from the farmyard. "Wagon's leaving!"

"By the gods," Rangar muttered, his chest heaving. He pulled away from the kiss reluctantly, his loose hair falling over his face. "We should stop. Ride with them back to the castle."

She nodded a little too fast, still so breathless that she couldn't quite think. But then she stopped nodding. She didn't want the kiss to end. She wanted him to kiss her other collarbone. To brush his hand harder against her breasts. Even to lift her skirt...

She gasped at her own scandalous thought. "Yes, of course. You're right."

He stepped away, much to her dismay, and helped her off the stall gate. She smoothed her skirt with shaking hands.

He started to do up her dress button that he had undone. "Tomorrow, you can try again to find your lamb." The hint of a smirk touched his lips. "This time, try not to think about me as much. If you can manage."

She narrowed her eyes at his teasing. He grinned and led

her to where the farmers were all finishing the final loading. Rangar picked up his shirt from a fence post and slid it back on, hiding the scars—except for the ones on his face, which could never be hidden. Bryn realized that she had hardly even noticed them in days. Rangar was simply Rangar. The scars made him no less beautiful.

The farmers gave her polite nods, though she caught more than a few of them casting Rangar winks. Ho, now the rumors would *really* fly. A drunken kiss in the forest on the night of the Harvest Gathering was one thing, but to kiss in the middle of the day, in front of an audience, practically announced their intentions.

Rangar jumped on the wagon's back and held down a hand to help Bryn up beside him. The other farmers climbed on, and the driver signaled to the horses. "Show me the mark," Rangar said.

She pulled down her collar enough to show him the small incision that Calista had made. He grunted quietly. "She did well. The finding spell will work, of that I am certain."

"Thank you," she said quietly. "I'm anxious to try again. I worry about that little lamb all alone up there somewhere."

As they rode the bumpy path back to the village, Bryn once more admired the view of windswept hills and distant ocean. There was something so life-giving about this land. The ever-present wind. The taste of salt in the air. She always felt awakened here, ready for anything.

As the shape of Barendur Hold appeared on the horizon, Rangar pointed to a cluster of horses outside the gates. They weren't the usual massive, wild-maned Baer horses. These were nimble and small—Mir horses.

Bryn felt a rush of apprehension. "Soldiers from the Mirien?"

Rangar rested a calming hand on her knee. "No. Those

aren't the kind of horses the Mir army uses. They're commoner horses. I'd wager they belong to the refugees we heard were making their way here."

Bryn had something else to occupy her mind now as they finished the ride into the village. As the wagon rolled to a stop in the town center, she jumped down, followed by Rangar. "I'd like to speak with the refugees," she said.

He hesitated. "Are you certain that's wise? I know we discussed it before, but Mir commoners rose against your family and murdered your parents." His dark eyes searched hers. "They might not be pleased to see you."

"They're still my people," she insisted. "And now that I've learned *why* they planned the uprising, I can hardly fault them for it. I owe them an apology for the way my parents ran the kingdom and any form of restitution I can offer them, even if only an introduction to a foreign land."

He looked doubtful. "I need to clean up. Then, I'll inquire if these refugees wish to meet with you. If there's any chance they may try to harm you, I forbid it."

She was not fond of his controlling nature, but in this instance, she happened to agree with him and nodded.

"If they are open to a meeting," he said, "I'll send a messenger to find you."

As they parted, she noticed more than a few villagers glancing in their direction. As she suspected, word had already spread about their flagrant tryst in the barn. Heat warmed her cheeks, but she also felt the tug of a smile on her face as she remembered the heady sensation of being in his arms.

She returned to the barn and fed the rest of the lambs, then, once she was certain they were bedded down for the evening, splashed water on her own face and changed into a fresh blouse. She was headed into the kitchen to see if the scullery maids needed help in the pantry when a young boy caught up to her.

"Lady Bryn," he said. "Prince Rangar wishes you to meet him in the courtyard."

"Thank you," Bryn said, wishing she had a coin to slip him in thanks, but before she had even reached into her dress pocket, he had scampered away.

She took a deep breath as she made her way to the courtyard. Surely this was about the refugees. What if they refused to meet with her? Still considered her a tyrant like her parents? She could hardly fault them. She wasn't sure she could forgive herself, either.

She stepped into the courtyard, wringing her hands, surprised to find all three royal brothers with their backs to her. Their bearskin cloaks obscured most of her view. But when they heard her footsteps, Val and Rangar both turned, and she caught a glimpse of about a dozen people they were speaking to, all of them dressed in the soft whites and gray of the Mirien.

Then, she gasped as she spotted a familiar face amid the crowd and nearly burst out with tears.

32

FAMILIAR FACES...THE TRUTH FROM HOME...
A DIFFERENT BROTHER THAN THE ONE
I KNEW

"*M*am Delice!"

Bryn found herself hurling toward the familiar face in the crowd of refugees. Mam Delice had been Castle Mir's head chef for as long as Bryn had been alive. The elderly woman was the only person who'd consistently remembered Bryn's birthdays, including her own parents. Over the years, the cook had slipped her honey cakes and winter berries and been a comforting ear when Bryn needed to talk.

The woman cracked a wide smile when Bryn slammed into her, wrapping her arms around her thin frame. "Heard a rumor you were hiding away in these wild parts, girl," Mam Delice said. "How I hoped it was true."

Bryn squeezed the elderly woman with all her strength. She hadn't realized until then how much she missed seeing a familiar face. A small piece of home. Ever since she had fled Castle Mir, all she'd heard were horror stories about her parents and their reign of terror. Her whole life had been turned upside down. And yet, though she was safe here, she was an outsider in the Baersladen. As much as she admired the people and had grown to love the windswept land, it wasn't the home she had always known.

Mam Delice's dyed black hair showed gray signs at her scalp. Women in the Mirien, from servant to queen alike, abhorred gray hair, but the long and harrowing trek into the Outlands must have been hard on the cook. Besides, it wasn't as though hair dye was available in the wilderness.

"I missed you so much," Bryn said as her voice broke.

"Aye, girl. I missed you, too."

The tender moment was broken when Bryn shifted her gaze to the other refugees. She recognized a girl who she'd often seen carrying laundry around the castle and a boy she recognized from the stable. However, the other dozen people were unfamiliar to her. Farmers or servants or soldiers, she couldn't be sure. Though one thing was certain, they didn't look at her with nearly as much warmth as Mam Delice had. In fact, Bryn had the distinct feeling that if Mam Delice hadn't vouched for her, the other refugees either would have refused to meet with her or, worse, tried to put her head on a stake.

Bryn pulled away from the cook, steeling herself. She glanced over her shoulder at Rangar, Valenden, and Trei and then faced the refugees with as much courage as she could muster.

"I'm sure you've had a difficult journey," she said to the band of refugees. "I've made that same trek myself, though I had the benefit of guides who knew the way. If you've come here seeking a haven and sustenance, the Baer people will provide, as they have for me. I have been fortunate to have spent the past few weeks here among these hardy folk. Their culture may be different, but I assure you they are honorable."

The refugees watched her with an unreadable expression that wasn't exactly what she'd call warm. She cleared her throat, glanced at Rangar, and started again. "I can only imagine what you must think of me. I don't know what rumors are going around the Mirien and the Outlands about my situation here. I know that my brother believes the Baer princes took me hostage; I assure you, it was the opposite." She glanced again at Rangar, who nodded for her to continue.

She went on. "Prince Rangar informed me of my parents' crimes on the eve of the uprising. I went with him willingly to escape the siege. Since then, I have learned more details of their cruel reign, and it saddens me and leaves me ashamed that I did nothing to stop it. I assure you, I only ever wished the best for the Mir people. I didn't concern myself with politics, and that was my failing. But I am now committed to righting my family's wrongs, in whatever form that will take. The best I can do now is to welcome you to the Baersladen and pledge to help you during this difficult time in whatever manner I can."

She looked to the Baer princes. Trei nodded solemnly.

When none of the refugees quite seemed to know what to say to this, Valenden smacked his hands together and said, "Right. We've all grown quite fond of Lady Bryn, so as long as you don't murder her in her sleep, we'll get along perfectly well."

"Val!" she admonished. She'd tried to present herself as a royal with retributions to make, yes, but still someone honorable.

"What did I say?" He shrugged in defense.

She rolled her eyes.

Mam Delice stepped forward, taking Bryn's hand and giving it a comforting pat. "You were just a wee thing," she said loud enough for the others to hear. "Trapped without knowing it. You don't have a cruel bone in your body, my lady. Whatever sins you inherited from your family, I've no doubt you'll make amends for them threefold."

Bryn smiled at the woman, almost moved to tears at this

show of kindness. Then, she asked hesitantly, "How do things stand in the Mirien?"

The gentle smile on Mam Delice's face fell. The other refugees glanced between one another, their faces souring. It was clear that it had been a grueling, arduous trek from the Mirien into the Baersladen. Bryn remembered it well, and she had had strong horses, knowledgeable guides, even a mage. These people hadn't even had a map to guide their way. They must be hungry and exhausted, and her heart went out to them.

"Well, that's a sad story," Mam Delice admitted. "A sad story indeed."

"Your brother's even worse than the king and queen," one of the refugee men snapped. Mam Delice grimaced but didn't contradict him.

"Is it true?" Bryn demanded. "Is Mars a tyrant?"

"A small group of farmers led the uprising," Mam Delice explained, skirting around the question. "They thought they had Captain Carr and most of the Mir army on their side, and indeed the army did overtake the castle, but then Captain Carr broke from the uprising's leaders. He and your brother, Prince Mars, came to an alliance at the last moment. Prince Mars could regain control of the Mirien, but only barely. The army enforces his leadership with excessive violence. Anyone known or even suspected to have been involved in the uprising is hunted down and hung." She motioned to the small crowd. "We left as soon as we could. It isn't safe anymore, even less than it ever was."

Bryn bit her lip, fighting anger. She turned away. Rangar touched her arm gently. "Bryn."

She shook her head hard. "I know my brother. He isn't cruel. I don't know why he does such awful things."

"He's a powerful young man forced into a corner," Mam

Delice offered. "I never saw cruelty from your brother, either, my lady, but one never knows what one will do until pressed. And I'm afraid Prince Mars, in his desperation and uncertainty, has chosen the path of violence."

The other refugees muttered less charitable words to describe her brother, and Bryn had to walk away, breathing hard. Rangar followed her, waiting patiently as she paced, trying to still her racing heart. Val soon joined them, looking serious for once, no jokes on his lips. Trei's face was as regal as ever, masking whatever genuine emotion he felt.

"I want to meet with him in person," Bryn said at last to the princes.

Rangar scowled. "Mars? Your brother? Impossible."

"Rangar is right," Trei agreed. "There's no way such a meeting is feasible. We have no way of getting you safely back into the Mirien, and Prince Mars would never agree to come here to the Outlands when he only maintains control under a tight fist. In his absence, it would be easy for another uprising to occur."

Bryn chewed on the inside of her lip, thinking. "I know Mars as well as you know each other," she said, looking between the three princes of the Baersladen. "If one of you was accused of tyranny, wouldn't you defend that one? Or at the very least, speak with him? Learn if it's true? And if it is, try to sway them toward a more peaceful course?"

The three princes were silent. They glanced between one another, and finally, Valenden gave a small shrug that suggested what Bryn said might be right.

Rangar sighed. "Let her meet with him, but I want to be there."

Trei still didn't look entirely convinced, but he lifted his head and said, "Very well. But not here, and not in the Mirien, either. We'll send a message to one of the lieges of the forest kingdoms and request that they host a parlay." Trei turned to her. "Will that satisfy you, my lady?"

She nodded.

Trei and Val turned away to discuss the details of how they would arrange such a dangerous meeting and ensure everyone's safety. Left alone with Rangar, Bryn ran her hands up and down her arms, shivering against the cold.

"Take my cloak." Rangar swept off his bearskin cloak, placing it over her shoulders. It was heavy enough to nearly smother her, but she felt sheltered from the wind and chill. He suddenly palmed her cheek, running his thumb over the apple of her cheek, and reassured her in a low voice, "I will make sure you can speak with your brother. But after this, Bryn, you must be satisfied with what you hear. No more second-guessing. Take him at his word, yes?"

She nodded. "I will. I promise."

He gave a small grunt, glanced at the refugees, and then left. Some of the castle maids came with blankets and sleeping pallets for the refugees. But before they led them into the great hall, Mam Delice paused and turned back to Bryn.

"From what I see, the rumors are true," she said in a secretive voice.

"What rumors?" Bryn asked blankly.

The cook gave a small, teasing grin. "That youngest prince. The scarred one. The boy who saved you from those wolves all those years ago. He's your sweetheart, eh? It's true?"

Bryn's cheeks turned bright pink.

The cook laughed. "Back home, half the people say he stole you away. The other half said you begged to go with him. That you were lovesick for that broken boy."

"Neither is true," Bryn said. "Like all rumors, they're an exaggeration. He didn't steal me. I came of my own will." She paused. "But in the weeks I've been here, well..." She cracked a small smile, thinking of their kiss earlier in the barn. "I've certainly come to admire him."

Mam Delice patted her hand. "I'm glad for you, my lady. I am. Saints help any girl in love, especially with a broken boy like that, but I can see you've found a place for yourself here. You were always our lost little princess. Wandering the halls alone. Never had a true friend. I'm glad you have someone now."

"He isn't broken," Bryn insisted as she fell into the old woman's arms again. "He's many things, but not that."

33

THE COLDEST NIGHT...REFLECTIONS AT SEA...A WET NOSE AND WARM FUR...BACON IN THE MORNING

*T*he Mir refugees struggled to settle into life in the Baersladen. Though the Baer people were welcoming, "welcoming" looked different to the Baer people as the Mir ones. The Baer were not a gentle, polite folk. They shared their blankets and their dinner rolls, their mead and their fire, but they also kept themselves at a distance.

The Mir travelers also kept to themselves, haunted by what they'd endured in the Mirien uprising and on the long trek to the Baersladen. With the exception of Mam Delice, who was accustomed to making herself useful, the refugees didn't offer to help with castle upkeep or village duties, instead remaining huddled by the castle's hearth or staring at the sea.

Bryn tried her best to introduce the refugees to the villagers she had made friends with. Saraj led several of the younger Mir people on a tour of the Outlands with her falcon but returned saying they showed little interest, too overwhelmed by the loss of their home. Bryn raked her thoughts, trying to find ways for them to settle into their new surroundings, but unlike the maiden roses, they didn't seem inclined to adapt.

The simple truth was, the Baersladen *wasn't* their home.

They longed to return to the Mirien, but return to what? What was left?

When Bryn wasn't helping the refugees, she continued to search the hills for the lost lamb with the finding spell, but with no luck. One time, the spell led her to a bush of winter berries because her stomach was grumbling. Another day, she ended up in the high hills where frost dusted the grass after she'd had a dream of snow.

But she didn't give up. Day after day, she departed the village at dawn with a satchel full of simple provisions and hiked until her muscles were sore and her lungs burned. She recited the words that Calista had taught her and gradually began to take control over the finding spell's pulling sensation. One day, the spell led her further into the hills than she had ever gone before. After passing through a forest of gnarled trees, she came out on a bluff overlooking the ocean. She sat down on a flat boulder for a bite to eat, looking out over the water.

The rhythm of the waves reminded her of the musicians' music the previous night in the great hall. As everyone had passed around warm apple cider and prepared to go to bed, she'd let herself get carried away by the soft music. Before she'd known it, Rangar sat down beside her. His silent, strong presence. He'd wrapped a blanket around them both as they listened to the melodies. She'd leaned her head into his chest, breathing in his scent of woodsmoke and the forest mixed with sea. He'd gently run his fingers through her hair, and a sharp pang struck her heart. *It felt so right.*

Now, on the bluff, she let her thoughts turn back to that feeling. At the time, she hadn't wanted to fully admit what she had felt in her heart. She and Rangar had enjoyed a few more dalliances since that kiss in the barn, and everyone in town was convinced it was only a matter of time until the prince proposed marriage to his princess. Bryn hadn't been so certain. Rangar had said nothing to her of marriage—he seemed far more interested in bruising her lips with his own and leaving her breathless—but something had shifted last night when he'd silently stroked her hair to the soft music.

She always thought she would fall in love in a fit of passion, but now she had to admit that it had happened in that quiet, simple moment. She couldn't deny it any longer. Her heart wanted what it wanted.

I love him.

Rangar believed that her soul belonged to him because he had saved her life as a child, but he was wrong. It didn't have anything to do with that night ten years ago. The wolf attack had brought them together, but she didn't believe in fate as he did. Still, her soul *was* bound to his.

She'd fallen for him not because of a twist of fate but because of what she'd seen ever since that night. A man as devoted to his kingdom as he was to her. Who would help a farmer or a fisher as easily as sip fine wine from a golden chalice. Who loved his homeland and his family. Who had broken his body and face for her, and instead of hating her for it, had sought her out again and again. And of course, there were their passionate embraces…

Yet, the *fralen* bond still bothered her. Even though Rangar had made it clear that she was free to make her own choices and live her own life, he still believed her soul was his. It nagged at her like a thorn in the back of her mind. If it weren't for this one small thing—which wasn't a small thing at all— she'd happily fall into his arms for as long as he'd have her. She could easily imagine a future where their kisses turned even more passionate. Where he took her virginity. Where they built a life together, even growing old together.

She leaned back on the sun-warmed boulder and sighed. *I*

need to stop thinking about Rangar Barendur. That line of thinking would only lead her through the finding spell straight back to him instead of the whole reason she'd been hiking through the hills for days.

She closed her eyes and pictured the lamb as best she could. This time, however, she decided to clear her head first. Every thought that fell into her stream of consciousness she pictured as a bubble of soap bursting into nothingness. After a while, there was nothing in her mind but the fluid stream. Thoughtlessness. Out of that calm space, she pictured the lamb. Imagined brushing its coat. Smelling its scent. Listening to its soft bleats.

But apparently her mind-clearing exercise worked a little too well, because before she knew it, she'd fallen asleep. When she stirred awake, blinking slowly up at the sky, she found the sun was almost setting. Still half-asleep, she imagined she heard a lamb bleating and wondered if she was remembering a dream.

Then, a wet nose pressed into her cheek. She shrieked.

She sat up fast enough to nearly fall off the boulder onto the hill's coarse grass. The lamb scrambled backward, spooked by her flailing.

Bryn had to stare at the creature for the space of several breaths to believe it was real and not a dream conjured to life. The poor thing was filthy. What had once been white fur was now badly matted and had turned various shades of brown, making it look more like a mangy stray dog than a lamb. But its eyes were clear and black, its nose and tongue pink. It was thin but not sickly.

"You troublemaker!" Bryn swept the lamb up in her arms, bursting into sobs. The frightened creature struggled for a few seconds but then relaxed and began to nose her pocket. She tugged out the remains of an apple tart, and the lamb gulped it down happily while she threaded a rope around his neck so he couldn't sneak away again.

She watched him eat in shock. *She'd done it.* At last, the finding spell worked.

However, her joy dimmed as she realized how far the sun was setting over the horizon. Night would fall soon. She'd been stupid to fall asleep on the boulder, and now there was no way she'd be able to find her way in the dark back down the mountain with the lamb. It was a trek of many hours, and besides, the deer runs and narrow paths she'd taken would be all but invisible at night.

She pulled the shivering, exhausted lamb close and wrapped her cloak around the both of them.

Thank the saints for Baer wool. It would be a cold, harsh night, but at least they wouldn't freeze. She lay down with the lamb curled next to her. The little animal was asleep in seconds, and Bryn wasn't far behind, dreaming of soft fur like clouds.

* * *

WHEN BRYN STIRRED awake in the morning, the most delicious aroma hung in the air. Was she still dreaming? It smelled like bacon and sweet cider.

A dream, she thought. *There's no bacon in the wilderness!*

She yawned and stretched, immediately feeling for the rope that she'd tied around her wrist, attached to the lamb. She felt all the way to the rope's end but began to panic as the end came away in her hand with no lamb attached.

She scrambled to her feet, twisting in a circle. "No, no, no!" That troublesome lamb had escaped again!

"Don't fret," a deep voice said nearby. "The little devil is safe."

She whirled to find Rangar a few paces away, sitting on a

level plane of rock, leaning over a campfire with bacon roasting on a stick.

Her eyes went wide. "What in the world are you doing here?"

Rangar pointed a way down the hill. "I tied up the lamb down there, where there is more forage. He was bleating and hungry, and where he was, there was mostly only rock."

Bryn pushed to her feet and stumbled over the uneven terrain to see the small clearing where Rangar had tied the lamb; sure enough, the animal was happily munching on coarse mountain grasses. She pressed a hand to her head as she looked down at the bacon sizzling on a stick. Her stomach growled.

"You followed me?" she asked, not sure how she felt about that. He raised a shoulder dismissively. She stomped forward, hugging her arms tightly, glowering at him. "Have you followed me *every* time I hiked into the hills?"

"Not *every* time." When she continued to glower at him, he prodded the fire with a stick and then admitted, "Sometimes, when I was needed elsewhere, I sent a village boy. Val followed you once, though I threatened to cut off his hand if he so much as touched you."

She frowned sharply. Yes, she recalled the time Val followed her into the mountains, though she hadn't known Rangar had been behind it. Another instance of Rangar's obsessive need to protect her. Just as he had followed her when she'd escaped their camp and gone to eavesdrop on the Mir soldiers. But she also found she didn't have the will to be angry at him. Rangar would never change. This was who he was—an obsessive prince who couldn't let her get into her own trouble. Besides, she was thoroughly exhausted, freezing to the bone, and his bacon smelled divine.

She sank onto a log opposite the fire, holding out her hands to the flames.

That fire does feel good.

Rangar gave her a devilish grin across the flames as her stomach growled audibly. "You found your lamb. Well done."

She smiled to herself with genuine pride, though she laughed, "Now I can accomplish what every six-year-old in the kingdom can."

Rangar chuckled. "We learn that spell at five, actually." She rolled her eyes. He checked the pot of hot cider and handed her a tin cup. "I'm proud of you. A Mir princess using magic."

She sipped the cider gratefully. "I would have been fine, you know, if you hadn't followed me. I could have stayed out here all night on my own."

"You did," he pointed out. "I didn't come near you."

"But you had breakfast waiting for me."

He took a sizzling piece of bacon and ate it in one bite, then wiped his mouth. "This? I'm afraid you're mistaken. This is for me, Princess, not you. Though I'm willing to share." He gave her another teasing look. "For a price."

Her stomach grumbled again. "Oh?" she asked suspiciously. "What price?"

He raised an eyebrow and moved closer. "One I don't think you'll mind parting with."

34

THE ULTIMATE QUESTION...A VERY NICE
WAY TO START THE DAY...BACON AND
CIDER...BUTTONS

*R*angar cupped her chin, moving his lips toward
hers.

Bryn's heart leaped. *He's going to kiss me.* It didn't matter
how many times they'd embraced; she felt certain she would
always feel this giddy rush of nerves. As soon as Rangar's lips
touched hers, she moaned. He tasted like bacon and sweet
cider. Desire mixed with her hunger, and she found herself
leaning so far into the kiss that she nearly collapsed onto his
chest.

He laughed huskily and picked her up, sitting her in his lap.
His hands threaded through her hair. She expected that he
would kiss her again, but instead, he passed her a slice of
bacon, and she pounced on it, the hot oil nearly burning her
fingers. She ate it in one bite, letting the juices run down her
chin. She immediately reached for more.

After they'd finished breakfast, and she'd checked on the
lamb to find him happily curled in the lee of a rock, she helped
Rangar pack up the supplies. Once they were finished, he laid
out his bearskin cloak and sat on it, grabbing her around the
waist and pulling her back down into his lap.

"Oh!"

"I liked you in this position before." He nuzzled her neck from behind her. "It was hard to let you sleep all night, watching you shiver, wishing I could keep you warm."

Her heart began to gallop as she recalled her thoughts from the afternoon before. *I'm in love with him.* She had imagined life with him here, spending their days making the most of this harsh land and their nights wrapped in one another's arms.

She leaned back into his chest as he wrapped his arms around her. "I'm worried for the others from the Mirien," she admitted. "They don't seem to have adjusted as I have."

He placed a delicate kiss on her shoulder. "I told you that you would. Like the maiden roses."

She let out a deep breath. "Ever since Mam Delice and the others from the Mirien arrived, I've been thinking about my old life. I've fallen into such a comfortable routine here, but the disturbing news about Mars and the state of my home..." She shook her head. "I have to find a way to help my people."

"Trei is working to establish the parlay with your brother."

"I know. I'm hopeful."

He paused to brush her hair back off her shoulder, turning her chin to face him. "And what if, when you see your brother, you're reminded of all you left behind? What if he tells you what you want to hear: that with your guidance, he'll change tactics? Will you return to the Mirien in that case?"

She saw the apprehension in Rangar's features. He wasn't trying to hide it. It was one of the things she admired about him and everyone in the Baersladen, how direct they were.

"I don't want to lose you," he said softly while tucking a strand of her hair behind her ear. He pressed his forehead to hers.

She closed her eyes and breathed in his scent. There was something invigorating about being in the wilderness, high above the world with the sea stretching out below. Besides, she still felt the thrill of finding the lamb with actual magic.

"I want to help my people and guide my brother," she said, "but the Mirien isn't my home anymore. My place is here. Barendur Hold. The ocean and the hills." She swallowed. "With you."

His hand found her jaw, tilting her head back to look him in the eyes. Simmering desire reflected in his gaze.

This time, she was the one who initiated the kiss, placing a tentative touch on his lips with her own. But at first contact, he took control and deepened the kiss. His tongue played over her parted lips, demanding entrance. He shifted her on his lap, his hands circling her waist, one thumb running up to graze the underside of her breast.

She gasped, and he kissed her harder. This embrace felt different than the times before. When they had kissed in the forest after the Harvest Gathering, his touch had been tense, spurred by jealousy and impatience. The kiss in the barn had been a sort of declaration to the witnesses watching. And they had found each other since then in dark hallways, and each time had made her heart race. But here, she felt removed from the world. No one knew where they were. No one was nearby to overhear or judge them or spread rumors through the village. They could do whatever they wanted.

Our secret.

Rangar seemed to feel this too or else sense the shift in her. The kiss drifted into more dangerous territory than the ones before, with both of them knowing they wouldn't be interrupted. Bryn had felt this deep well of passion filling for a long time. It had started with their first kiss. Then, each embrace had gotten more urgent, their bodies demanding more from one another.

Now, Rangar slid his hand up to cup the outside of her

breast over her blouse, and she arched her back into his hand. He squeezed her a little roughly, and she gasped aloud.

If Val was to be believed, Rangar had bedded girls before. Bryn had no experience at all, but she was more than happy to let her body respond to him on its own.

He kissed her so feverishly that they tumbled backward, her back falling against the thick bearskin cloak as he pressed himself on top of her, never breaking the kiss. His hand was hard on the back of her neck, guiding her chin up so he could trail his lips along her jawline. She could feel his pulse throbbing in his wrists, his breath as shallow as her own. Her hair fanned out on the cloak, the gray morning sky broken with clouds overhead.

"This is your home," he whispered along her neck. "You do belong here. With me."

She felt herself nodding. It felt right. Though Castle Mir was where she'd grown up, it was only her home in name. She had loved her parents and her siblings, but she'd never had the opportunity to connect with the kingdom, always locked away behind castle walls, told to read books and educate herself instead of learning about the world itself like this, in nature, experiencing things for herself.

Experiencing *Rangar*.

His hands went to the buttons of her blouse. He raised a questioning eyebrow, and she nodded. He unbuttoned her shirt and untucked it from her skirt, leaving her chest covered only by her cotton chemise, the one thing she'd kept from the Mirien. It was delicate and trimmed in lace, unlike the practical wool undergarments the Baer women wore. As soon as Rangar saw it, his eyes darkened.

"Gods," he muttered.

The upper edges of her scars were visible at the chemise's

low neckline. His eyes fell on them but without revulsion. He'd never be repulsed by the scars they shared.

He slipped one thin strap off her shoulder and replaced it with his lips, kissing lower on her chest until his lips grazed the thin fabric covering her pink nipple. Another inch, and his lips would touch the sensitive tip of her breast. She arched her back, lips parted, unprepared for the intense sensations coursing through her body. An urgent ache had begun between her legs. She shifted her hips, but nothing eased the pressure.

Noticing her squirming beneath him, Rangar reached back to pull off her ankle-high boots. He tossed them off roughly and then ran a hand up over one of her wool stockings to where it ended just above her knee. Her pulse flared when his thumb grazed the bare skin of her thigh.

Her body bucked. Her movements only drove him wilder. His eyes were nearly black now, pupils dilated with desire. He pushed her skirt further up until he could grip her bare thigh hard with his long fingers.

She twisted her hands in the fur of the bearskin cloak, desperate for something to hold on to. She felt such intense pressure at the base of her belly that she feared she would rip apart. His big hand on her thigh made her yearn for him to touch her more, lower, deeper, *everywhere*.

He broke their kiss and ducked his head to where his hand gripped her midthigh. She gasped as he replaced his palm with his lips, trailing his mouth from her knee toward her hips. Her hips rocked upward to meet his caress, urging him on.

If her mother, Saints rest her soul, knew what she was doing with this Baer boy...

Bryn hadn't ever imagined the things they were doing. Having a man touch her in such intimate places. Her body was experiencing hundreds of new sensations. She dug her nails into Rangar's hair with one hand, feeling his movements as he kissed the sensitive inside of her thigh. He was moving closer to that secret place between her legs covered only by her thin undergarments—not much of a barrier. Rangar could easily rip away the fabric with a single finger or even his teeth and leave her completely bare, exposed to him... But he stopped when he reached her upper thigh and sat up on his knees, breathing hard, looking down at her with an unreadable expression.

She couldn't imagine what was going through his mind. Why did he stop? Didn't he feel this magical sensation, too? This delicious pain?

"Bryn." He was breathing hard. "You have no idea how much I want you. How much I've always wanted you."

She pushed up to her elbows, reaching out a hand to grab his shirt. "Don't stop, Rangar. I can't bear it."

He let out a groan as he fell back against her, kissing her, pressing her into the cloak so hard she nearly couldn't breathe. He ground his hips against her, and she gasped. His body was rigid, ready. She didn't know much about male anatomy, but she'd seen farm animals mating and had overheard enough from her sister and brother to get the idea of what that stiff part was between his legs and what was supposed to happen with it.

He pressed her hand against his pants, breathing into her ear, "You feel how much I want you?"

Her eyes went wide.

Was he planning to bed her? She knew he would stop if she asked, but did she want him to? What they were doing was already scandalous back home; if her parents had discovered this, she'd be shamed and lose all her marriage prospects. Virginity was prized among Mir women, princesses in particular. Elysander had hardly let her betrothed hold her hand on the occasions he'd visited.

But the Baersladen didn't hold virginity in any exalted position for women or men. Saraj had told her how she and Trei made love whenever they wanted, though they weren't married. Saraj didn't even *want* to marry Trei yet, knowing what she'd have to give up to become the future queen. She was content to maintain their relationship outside of the bonds of marriage, and not even the king seemed to care. So maybe Bryn could have the same. Could do whatever she liked with her body.

She tentatively rubbed her hand over the bulge in his pants, and he closed his eyes and groaned. He dug his hips into her palm as a drip of sweat ran down his face. Then, he curled a fist around her wrist, pressing it up over her head as he ground against her enough to make her gasp.

"You're mine, Bryn Lindane," he growled into her ear. "You belong to me. You always have."

Her body was so overwhelmed with desire that she barely processed his words. *That possessiveness again...* But in the throes of passion, desire eclipsed anything else.

One hand still pinning her wrist overhead on the cloak, Rangar's other hand went back to her skirt, sliding up over her leg until he reached her bare thigh. His finger grazed her core outside of her thin undergarments, and she moaned and tossed her head back.

For a second, he seemed to war with himself. His hand under her skirt, her blouse unbuttoned halfway down her chest. He looked over her writhing body with parted lips like he wanted to devour every piece of her.

Then he let her wrist go and sat back, breathing hard. He shook his head. "We should stop. We *have* to stop."

She leaned up in alarm. "What? Why?"

His eyes were still heavy with lust, but he ran a hand over his sweaty face, then combed back his wild hair. The morning light caught the scars running from his forehead to jaw, from the tip of his neck to disappear beneath his shirt, where she knew they continued down to his hip.

"I don't want to take you like this. On a dirty cloak. Rocks at your back. You deserve to be bedded on clean sheets by a man who doesn't reek of bacon and smoke."

"I like how you smell," she said breathlessly.

He shook his head, looking up at the sky as he took a few deep breaths to calm himself. "No. We should wait until our marriage night."

She sat up higher, brow furrowed. *"Marriage?"*

35

STEAM AND SECRETS...A QUESTIONABLE PROPOSAL...AN UNDENIABLE BOND...A WARM BATHHOUSE

*M*arrying Rangar had always been a possibility in the back of Bryn's mind. It was hard not to be when the Mir refugees and everyone in the Baersladen had whispered speculation about the youngest prince making her his bride. But the concept of marriage had always felt abstract, like when she had been a little girl, and Elysander's betrothal was so distant in the future as to be meaningless.

Rangar nodded solemnly as he gazed down at her on the bearskin cloak. "We in the Baersladen are not as concerned about marriage before lovemaking as your people are, but I want a ring on your finger before I bed you."

She closed her eyes. Her body shuddered from unspent desire. Her skin hadn't yet gotten the message, still craving his touch. She took a few deep breaths and said, "You've never spoken about marriage."

He stared down at her as though her words were a technicality. "I'm speaking of it now."

She sat up fully, scooting backward on the cloak. The sun was rising higher and burning off the morning fog. The lamb bleated from the nearby grassy patch. The bright light of day suddenly made her feel far too exposed. She started buttoning up her shirt.

"You speak of marriage like it's a certainty," she said.

He pushed to his feet, straightening his clothes as he towered over her. "Isn't it?"

"It most certainly isn't!" She glowered up at him. "Things might happen differently here, but they aren't *that* different. Even in this savage place, I believe a man still *asks* a woman for her hand."

Rangar shamelessly adjusted himself in his pants, making her blush. Then, once he had put himself somewhat back in order, he raised an eyebrow. "You want a proposal? Something proper, something Mir? Flowers and gemstones?"

"Well, *yes*," she countered, feeling rankled that he would make her feel guilty for something that many girls would want. "But more than that, I want my feelings to be considered. You act as though you know I'll say yes when I've never given you any indication of what my answer would be."

He ran a hand over his chin, eyes settled on the small triangle of skin still exposed at her neck. "Haven't you given me an answer, though?" he said in a seductive voice.

She glowered again as she finished buttoning the last button. "Letting you ravish me isn't the same as accepting a proposal."

He crouched down, tipping her chin up. "You're mine, Bryn. I don't need to ask. I know what your answer will be."

Angry, she smacked his hand away. "See? There it is again. You won't let go of what happened ten years ago. The *fralen* bond. You say I have free will and that you won't command me to do anything, and yet here you are speaking of soul ownership."

He frowned. "This truly troubles you."

"Of course it does!"

He sighed, raking his nails back over his scalp, mussing his curls even more. "I do not wish to control you. I've tried to explain before. The *fralen* bond does not make me your master. You do not need to obey me..." His eyes flashed. "Though I admit, I might wish that at times. But yes, ten years ago, I saved your life, which bound us. It's something my people have believed for hundreds of years, tied up in hexes and magic. I can no sooner shed my responsibility toward you than I can my own skin."

"Yet you assume you can force me to marry you?"

"No, not force." He looked truly troubled now. "I would never force such a thing—I don't have the authority nor the inclination to do so, and the Baer people would never allow a woman to be forced into any marriage." He sighed. "I assumed we were as good as betrothed already, ever since I brought you here. Not because of the *fralen* bond or a sense of ownership. Because of..." He searched for the words, finally lowering his voice as he looked her in the eyes. "Because of how I felt. And how I thought you felt in return."

His words softened her somewhat. It took the edge off her anger, but it was still hard for her to set aside his possessive beliefs. It was clear that he would never let go of the idea that their souls were bound together; he as protector and she in need of his saving. It was an idea she didn't care for at all, and it sat between them like some rotten apple, ugly and stinking.

"I do feel...the same way," she admitted quietly.

He dropped to his knees before her, taking her hand. "Then what holds you back? Marry me, Bryn Lindane. I'll give you flowers. I'll buy you jewels. I'll stand on a table in the great hall and propose to you in front of the entire kingdom. Whatever you wish, I'll do." He intertwined his fingers in hers, searching her eyes.

She bit her lip. "I don't know, Rangar."

Alarm flashed in his eyes. It looked as though it had never occurred to him that she wouldn't accept a proposal, and now panic ringed his eyes in red.

He pressed her hand against his chest, where she felt his heart pounding. "You've heard the rumors. The broken young prince helplessly in love with a Mir princess he'd only laid eyes on twice. When I saved you, we were both just children. But I couldn't get my mind off you. Then, when my brothers and I snuck back into the Mirien three years ago..." His throat tightened with raw emotion. "I was lovesick. It happened at once, instantly. Like being blinded looking at the sun. I saw you dancing and knew there would never be another woman for me. I'd never seen anyone more beautiful. Your fair hair, so unusual. The way you smiled, so light-hearted. I'd come from a land of storms and wind, and you were a ray of sun. I coveted it more than anything." He moved forward, still holding her hand over his heart. "I've been in love with you for years, Bryn. My heart, my soul, my body. Every piece of me is yours, as you are mine."

His words shook her deeply. Everyone in the kingdom seemed to know that Rangar lusted after the blonde foreign princess, but he had never spoken to her like this, so raw about his feelings.

"But you don't mean that," she whispered. "You don't *really* believe I own you in the same way you think you own me. And that imbalance troubles me."

His eyes simmering with a strange look, he clutched her hand harder as though he feared she would slip away. "What if you did?"

"What are you talking about?"

"What if we were even?" She'd never seen such intensity on his face.

She shook her head. "Rangar, you can't change what

happened. As much as I wish you would forget about the bond, I know you can't. You just said as much."

"That isn't what I meant."

She didn't like the look in his eye. But as much as she pressed, he wouldn't say any more about whatever was going through his head. He finished packing up their campsite and doused the fire with dirt while she untied the lamb.

"Come on, troublemaker," she chided the creature. "Time for you to come home."

The hike down from the mountain was heavy with anxious silence. Rangar had retreated into his brooding silence with a scowl on his face, hunched over to let his hair hide his scars. Bryn wasn't sure what to say to make him feel better. He shouldn't have assumed their marriage was a certainty. The least he could have done was *ask* her before assuming.

She hated not knowing where they stood. The truth was, she had already made her decision the day before, looking out over the ocean, that she wanted to remain here with him. She'd do what she could to help the Mir people and negotiate with Mars, but this was her home now. *Rangar* was her home. Whether they were married or not didn't feel so pressing to her; they were committed to one another. Meant for one another. But how could she fully accept him as long as he believed he *owned her soul?*

When they reached the village, a goatherd boy came running up, jumping up and down to see the lost lamb alive. The workers in the livestock yard rushed over to congratulate Bryn on using the spell successfully, teasing her good-naturedly about the one time the spell had led her to Rangar. Rangar hung back, and by the time Bryn managed to extract herself from the crowd congratulating her, he was gone.

* * *

Over the next few days, Rangar made himself scarce. More unsettling news was pouring in from messengers about the rising tension between the Mirien, the lesser southern kingdoms, and the northern Outlands. It was rumored that Ruma had pledged allegiance to Mars as the rightful ruler of the Mirien, which in turn aggravated the rulers of the Wollin, who supported the Mirien commoners' uprising. Rangar spent long hours in the council chambers with his family and dignitaries from the other kingdoms.

After days full of troubling news from the Mirien, Bryn managed to corner Rangar as he was headed to the bathhouse after a long day of training with the Baer army. "Rangar, wait."

He looked her up and down, then motioned to the doorway she was blocking. Steam rose from the cracked door. "That's the men's bathhouse, you know. Stand there too long and you'll get a glimpse of more skin than you might be comfortable with. I saw the old fishmonger go in there a few minutes ago."

The fishmonger was a heavyset, ancient man covered in thick gray hair. Bryn shuddered at the thought of seeing him nude but didn't back down.

"You've been avoiding me," she accused.

His face betrayed nothing. "We're on the eve of war. I've had other concerns on my mind."

But she wouldn't back down, and he sighed and grabbed her hand, leading her to an alcove outside the bathhouse. "Fine. I'm here now, reeking, sweaty, and in desperate need of a wash. Tell me what you need to say."

She hesitated, feeling suddenly at a loss for words. They hadn't yet spoken about their conversation on the mountain. Had it been a genuine proposal? Everything was a mess between them, but she pushed that aside. "I want to know what's happening in the Mirien."

He scratched the back of his head as his eyes scanned the

hallway, looking for anyone who might be within earshot. Then he lowered his voice. "We received a response from your brother this morning. He's willing to meet in Vil-Kevi for a parlay."

She sucked in an anxious breath. "When?"

"Shh." He glanced down the halls again and then dragged her into the bathhouse, where the thick billows of steam hid them from any watching eyes. She could hear the sounds of men speaking in further interior rooms, but Rangar led her to the empty laundry room and pulled a cloth curtain shut.

"When will we have the rendezvous?" she asked in a whisper.

"Three days from now. The rulers of Vil-Kevi have granted us permission to meet in an abandoned guesthouse deep in the forest that's no longer used. It's a trek of a day or a day and a half, depending on the weather."

Bryn nodded, feeling a wash of nerves. In three days, she'd see her brother. So many warring emotions filled her. This was a political parlay, not a family reunion. She didn't know if the rumors about Mars's iron rule were true or not. Still, she felt a rush of longing to see her big brother again. To know he was safe. To get straight answers out of him.

Rangar brushed the sweat out of his eyes as he said quietly, "There's one more thing."

36

INTO THE FOREST...A POSSIBLE SPY...
READYING THE HORSES...A LONG RIDE...A
MAGIC LESSON

"There's something else," Rangar repeated, the steam from the bathhouse obscuring his features. "Valenden has been speaking more with the Mir refugees—"

"By speaking with, you mean drinking with," she said wryly.

Rangar shrugged. "It's the same to him. Anyway, he suspects one or two of the refugees aren't true refugees at all but spies sent by your brother or Captain Carr."

Bryn drew in a breath. "Surely not Mam Delice."

Rangar ran an uncertain hand over his chin. "I don't know which ones he suspects, but I agree, an elderly cook who adores you is not likely a spy. Anyway, take care of what you say and where you say it. There could be enemy ears anywhere." A cloud of steam from the bathhouse floated into the laundry room, rising around them. Bryn felt sweat break out on her forehead.

"I don't want you to be alone," Rangar continued. "Stay in public spaces, or if you must go somewhere private, make certain I or one of my brothers is with you. I trust even Valenden more than I do the refugees. He might not keep his hands to himself, but he certainly would never harm you. Which is more than I could say for the spies."

"But if they work for my brother, they wouldn't hurt me, either." Alarm laced her voice.

Rangar looked grave. "I wouldn't think so, but we can't be sure of anything. They may try to capture you and take you back to Castle Mir, justifying it under the false belief that we are keeping you here against your will. Or perhaps..." Dark thoughts passed over his face, and he stopped.

Bryn prodded him. "Or perhaps what?"

"Nothing. Forget I said it."

He started to go, but she grabbed his arm. "Rangar, wait. What were you going to say?"

Hesitantly, he dropped his voice. "There is a distant chance that your brother may indeed wish you harm. If the crown prince's sister is murdered while supposedly imprisoned by the savage Outlanders, your brother would have every justification to attack us."

She stared at him in shock, feeling like she'd just been slapped in the face.

He quickly ran a reassuring hand over her shoulder. "I'm certain that isn't the case. It was only something my aunt brought up as a distant possibility in one of our council meetings."

"My brother would never harm me," she said gravely.

"I know, Bryn."

She expected him to insist that he would be there to protect her no matter the danger. Her Savior. After all, he'd spent the last several weeks secretly stalking her in the mountains to make sure she was safe. But he held his tongue, and she wondered if it harkened back to their discussion on the mountain about her discomfort with the *fralen* bond and his obsessive protectiveness.

Maybe he's trying to give me space. To respect what I said.

"We'll leave for the parlay at dawn on the day after tomorrow," he said.

"Who is coming?" she asked, knitting her fingers together.

"My aunt, Val, and myself. My father and Trei will remain here. They want to keep an eye on the refugees, and besides, it's no time to leave a throne empty."

She nodded, her mind already filling with worries. For the remainder of the day and the next, she couldn't help but constantly look over her shoulder, worried she was being followed. She stuck to the great hall, or the barn, or the village square, all of which were always crowded with people. She fed the lambs and left them in the livestock yard instead of taking them up into the hills to graze, afraid of being alone in the wilderness.

On the day of the trek, Rangar woke her at dawn, but she was already awake. She hadn't slept all night, which didn't bode well for her mood on the voyage. When they dressed and went out into the courtyard, she found that a stable worker had readied four horses.

Mage Marna and Val were loading their meager belongings for the trek into the saddlebags. When Bryn approached, the mage rested a hand on her shoulder. "I heard about your lamb. Well done." The older woman brushed the spot on Bryn's shoulder where she knew the small hexmark was cut into her skin. "When we return, perhaps it will be time to learn the next spell."

Bryn gave a weak smile, still feeling too troubled to be excited by the prospect of more magic. She needed to pack flagons of water into her horse's bag but was hesitant to get close to the animal. In the Mirien, only peasant women rode horses, and the enormous beast frightened her. "Whoa, there. Easy, girl."

Valenden came around the other side of her horse, leaning easily on the saddle pad. The horse didn't flinch under his presence. "Girl? Saints, Bryn, this is clearly a male horse." He grinned rakishly, wiggling his eyebrows. "Shall I give you a lesson in male anatomy?"

She gave him a sharp look. "I see your nose has healed."

"Are you disappointed?" He dropped his voice playfully. "I hear you're partial to broken faces." His eyes flickered to Rangar, who was speaking to the soldiers who would be accompanying them.

She gasped in indignation. But before she could chastise Valenden, the horse snorted, and she shrieked and backed away from it, nearly dropping a water flagon.

"Were you hoping for only three horses?" Valenden glanced again at his brother. "Looking forward to riding in my brother's lap again?"

"Val, please," she said, rolling her eyes.

He laughed good-naturedly this time. "Don't worry; this is the gelding we all learned to ride on when we were boys. He's a sturdy, dependable old horse. You'll ride tethered to Rangar's mare, so all you need to do is hold on and not fall off. You'll be fine."

"Thanks, I suppose."

"If you *do* fall, I'll try my best not to trample you."

She rolled her eyes again.

As they finished preparations for the journey, Bryn heard someone calling her name. She spotted Saraj hurrying across the courtyard with her falcon, Zephyr, perched on her arm. She handed Bryn a small package wrapped in cloth and twine.

"Honey cakes," Saraj said. "As much as I'd like to take credit for them, Mam Delice made them for your journey and asked me to give them to you before you left."

Bryn pressed the still-warm bundle to her chest, breathing in the delicious scent. "Please thank her for me."

Saraj nodded but then hesitated, glancing at the soldiers mounting their horses. Her voice lowered. "Bryn, are you sure this trip is wise? To meet with your brother?"

"Mars won't harm me."

"That isn't what I meant. I don't fear him hurting you, not with Valenden and Rangar and Mage Marna there—*she's* more formidable than any soldier. What I meant was, what if you don't like what Mars has to say?"

Bryn had been troubled by the same possibility. She stowed the honey cakes in her saddlebag to buy herself some time to think and then sighed. "I need to know, whatever the outcome."

Saraj seemed like there was more she wanted to say, but instead, she pulled Bryn into an embrace. "Be well. We will be anxiously awaiting your return. Trei sends his best wishes as well for a safe journey."

Bryn squeezed Saraj's hand and then felt Rangar come up behind them.

"Ready?" he asked.

She took a deep breath and nodded. He formed a stirrup with his hands and helped her mount the horse rather ungracefully. Bryn managed to scoot onto the gelding and arrange her skirts on either side of the saddle pad. She held on to the reins tightly.

Maybe I do *want to be riding in Rangar's lap again*, she thought fleetingly.

Rangar adjusted her feet in the stirrups and patted her leg. "Lightning will follow my mare, have no fear."

"*Lightning?*" She practically choked on the name of the horse, which Valenden had assured her was a slow old beast.

Valenden, sitting on his own steed not far away, had overheard the exchange and grinned at her. "Don't worry; we named him that in irony."

Saraj waved to them as they set off down the road. Bryn clutched the horse's mane tightly for the first few steps, not used to the swaying movement. But by the time they reached the farms on the outskirts of the village, she was more used to the movement and relaxed slightly.

It felt different to be leaving the Baersladen on this same road than it had to arrive. Weeks ago, she had arrived clinging to Rangar, not sure if she was a captive or if he'd rescued her, her brooding prince just as much a mystery as his windswept kingdom. They passed the copse of maiden roses where he'd assured her that she would find her way in this new land, and she was happy to see them still blooming.

They rode into the hills until the ocean disappeared behind them. Then, up the craggy mountain passes that were so terrifyingly narrow that Bryn had to squeeze her eyes shut and trust in Lightning's steady footing on the scree, then back down even more precarious paths. Dusk fell as they entered the thick of the forest where the trees grew straight and towering.

Mage Marna raised her fist, signaling for them to stop. "We'll make camp here for the night," she said. "We should be at the rendezvous point by midday tomorrow."

Valenden and Rangar dismounted, and the soldiers began clearing an area for a fire and felling lumber to burn. Rangar came over to help Bryn down. She slid off the horse, wincing as she nearly collapsed into his arms.

"I can't tell you how badly I ache between my legs," she muttered.

Valenden, overhearing, immediately opened his mouth to say something rude, but Rangar lifted a finger. "Don't, Val. Just don't."

Valenden groaned at the idea of having to keep his dirty thoughts to himself.

"I can rub down the horses," Bryn offered, wincing at her sore leg muscles.

Rangar shook his head. "You should rest. If you show up tomorrow carrying yourself like that, looking like I've spent the night ravishing you, your brother will run me through before I can get a word out."

She unrolled her saddle pad and sat down by the fire, which one of the soldiers was coaxing to life with a muttered hex spell. She watched in fascination. What was the next spell Mage Marna would teach her? She touched her shoulder, where beneath her clothes the skin was marred now by the small incision of the finding hex.

She'd have to hide the hexmark from Mars, which would be easy enough. The one on her ear would be harder to hide, but she could style her hair around it and hope for the best. She didn't want to imagine what her brother would do if he thought the Baer people had marred his sister with their "sinful" magic.

Once the horses were settled, Valenden dropped onto the blanket beside her. He drew a flask out of his pocket. "This will help with sore muscles."

"Medicine?" she asked skeptically.

He took a long drink before passing it to her. "Not exactly."

She winced as she threw back what she assumed was cider or mead, gagging at the sharp taste. She sputtered, wiping her mouth, and exclaimed, "Saints! What is *that?*"

"Mushroom liquor," he said with a laugh. "Strong, isn't it? The forest kingdoms make it."

"Too much of that and I fear I'll be dancing naked in the trees."

"Hmm. Interesting." He took another long drink, giving her

a wink. When Rangar joined them, Valenden offered him the flask, and he easily threw back a sip.

"Are you certain it isn't poison?" Bryn said, not entirely joking.

Rangar passed the flask back to Valenden. "Concerned about poison, are you?"

She shrugged. "It's one of the first things Mir princesses learn, to be wary of suspicious food and drink."

Rangar leaned back on the blanket. "Baer princes as well. But we learn not to fear what we consume, rather, how to rescue our bodies if we *have* unknowingly imbibed something dangerous." His eyes danced with mischief. "Would you like to learn another spell?"

She sat up ramrod straight. "What, now? Here? Shouldn't your aunt be the one teaching me?"

Rangar exchanged a cryptic look with Valenden. "This one isn't exactly sanctioned. It would be our little secret."

Val nodded solemnly, motioning to lock his lips with an imaginary key.

Bryn glanced over her shoulder. There was no sign of Mage Marna. She was probably deep in the forest, foraging herbs or mushrooms. Bryn leaned toward the two brothers. "Tell me more about this hex."

37

A PLACE OF MIRTH...A SPELL FOR POISON...
OR MAYBE A TRICK...THE ANCIENT
GUESTHOUSE...A RIDER

*R*angar explained to Bryn in a low voice, "Earlier, you joked about the mushroom liquor being poison. It isn't, but what if it was? How would you counteract it?"

"I don't know," she answered. "With an antidote, I suppose."

"That's an option *if* you have the correct antidote on hand. Not if you're out in the wilderness, alone, without supplies."

"So then how?" she asked, curious about how this hex could rescue a body from poison it had already ingested.

Val pantomimed sticking a finger in his mouth and gagging.

"*Vomiting?*" Bryn gasped. "You want to teach me a spell to make me *vomit?*" She stood up, rolling her eyes. "You two are only taunting me again, as you love to do."

But Rangar held her by her wrist, not letting her leave. "It's a purge spell," he explained. "And it isn't a joke. Anyone can make themselves vomit by sticking something down their throat, but that will only help if they've eaten something rotten. Not for most poisons, which move too quickly into the bloodstream. In that case, you need magic to purge toxic substances from the body."

Bryn wrinkled her nose, still not interested. "If it's the same to you, I'd rather learn to ignite a spark with a hex."

"It *isn't* the same to me," Rangar said evenly. "What I mean is, not all spells can be learned by a novice. This is one of the easier ones."

Bryn was inclined to turn down the offer but then reconsidered. Magic was magic, after all. Spells were spells. If this was something every Baer royal child learned to do to protect themselves, then she might as well learn it, too. Though she was starting to suspect Rangar and Val had been sipping on mushroom liquor longer than they'd let on and were already drunk.

"Fine," she relented.

Rangar drew his knife. She flinched at the gleam of firelight on the metal blade, even though she'd known this would be necessary. *All hexes demand blood.* Hesitantly, she rolled up her shirtsleeve.

"I'll carve the mark on the side of your wrist. Here. See?" He showed her the small cross mark on his own wrist, and Valenden did the same.

"Go ahead." Bryn grimaced, bracing herself for the pain.

Rangar touched the blade to a specific point on the side of her wrist, making a quick, nearly painless set of cuts, which he immediately bound with a strip of linen torn from one of the napkins that their food had been wrapped in. He glanced over her shoulder at the forest, probably making sure Mage Marna hadn't returned from foraging, and said, "The spell is only two words: *En videl.* Recite it as you trace the mark in the air at about heart level, starting from the bottom and moving upward."

She held out her hand, trying to match the exact shape that he'd carved into her arm. He adjusted her hand a little lower, then nodded. "Try it again."

"*En videl,*" she said.

Immediately, her stomach cramped. Her eyes went wide as she gripped her belly and leaned over, ready to heave. The burning liquor raced back up her throat as she coughed it out into the grass.

Val burst out laughing.

She wiped her mouth, narrowing her eyes. "I knew it! You just wanted to torment me, didn't you?"

The middle brother waved his hands in a weak attempt to deny it, but he wasn't a very good actor.

Rangar took her hand and closed his own over it, meeting her eyes with a more serious look. "If that *had* been poison," he explained, "you would have felt it vacating from your blood-stream. Everywhere, even out of your pores. It would have been a lot more unpleasant than just vomiting. But at least you'd be alive."

"Thanks, I think," she muttered, wiping her mouth. "How about some regular cider now to wash away the taste?"

Valenden called to the soldiers, who brought over a dram of fermented apple cider. She took a deep drink to get the taste out of her mouth. Rangar placed his hand on her knee, and she instantly flushed with warmth.

He leaned in close. "The next spell I teach you," he assured her, "will be less messy. I promise."

She shifted closer, enjoying the warmth of his touch. "Don't take offense at this, but I think I'll stick to lessons from your aunt."

He chuckled darkly. "Fair enough."

By the time Mage Marna returned with gathered herbs, Bryn was already yawning. She lay down and let herself drift off while listening to the sounds of soldiers and princes swapping stories late into the night.

Tomorrow, she would see her brother.

Tomorrow, she would get answers.

* * *

By the time Bryn woke in the morning, the soldiers had already disassembled the campsite. She sat up in surprise, finding herself on a saddle pad in a clearing that looked completely untouched. They'd hidden any trace of the campfire or the logs they'd used as seating and even sprinkled fresh dirt over the horses' tracks. Hiding all signs they'd been there.

It was a stark reminder of the dangers they faced.

After they mounted the horses, the traveling party appeared far less jovial than they'd been the day before. Instead, everyone appeared on edge, even Valenden, who rarely seemed serious about anything. The forest grew thicker as they progressed. Plants Bryn had never seen fought for any scrap of sunlight.

For most of the morning, they followed a path that was fairly well trod, though they passed no other travelers. But after a few hours, Mage Marna directed them onto a narrower path that wound between the trees. Bryn suspected that magic was required to navigate this particular path, because the trail sometimes disappeared entirely, yet Mage Marna continued forward confidently. They led the horses scrambling up a steep stream bank more than once. She'd never been in a forest like this one, where the trees were wider than most houses and rose so high she could barely see the tops. Every once in a while, she saw evidence that people had once lived here: a stone water-wheel lying on its side, long ago mossed over. A broken ladder led into what must have once been a lookout in the trees.

Mage Marna stopped her horse in a section of the forest that looked to Bryn's eyes just like every other stretch. The mage lifted her hand for the others to pause and be silent. She studied the woods for a moment, then touched a hexmark and whispered something that Bryn didn't hear. Then she looked back at them over her shoulder. "This is it. The big tree ahead. There, with the burn marks."

To Bryn's surprise, one of the largest trees wasn't a tree at all. It was a structure built to resemble a tree, shingled in bark, with divots and holes to serve as windows. Bryn felt her jaw fall open at the incredible architectural feat. She'd never seen anything like it, made to mimic nature so seamlessly.

"This was a famous guesthouse once," Rangar said from his horse beside her. "From long before even my parents were born, when there used to be a proper road traversing through this section of Vil-Kevi. Half a decade ago, the guesthouse caught fire and has been rotting here ever since, completely abandoned. The road was rerouted not long after due to banditry."

Soon, three figures materialized from between the trees and came toward them. Bryn sucked in a breath, searching for Mars's familiar outline, but these people moved much more gracefully than her brother ever had. It was two men and a woman, dressed in cloaks the same mottled browns and greens as the trees, making them almost completely camouflaged until they were directly in front of them.

Mage Marna nodded her head in greeting. "Lady Enis."

The woman touched a hexmark on her own arm before saying in Baer, "Welcome." Her dark eyes scanned the riders. "You are the first to arrive. We expect the riders from the Mirien to be here within the hour. Out scouts will alert us when they near."

Satisfied with the safety, Mage Marna signaled to the others, who dismounted.

Lady Enis motioned to the abandoned guesthouse. "The

structure is no longer sound. I do not advise entering. My associates will help you make camp out in the open instead."

"We are grateful," Mage Marna said with a formal nod.

As the two servants from Vil-Kevi began helping unload the supplies, Bryn shook out her aching legs, looking around the eerie abandoned structure curiously. "The forest kingdoms use magic, too?" she asked Rangar. "I never knew that."

"A little," he replied. "Not as much as the Baer people or the Wollins."

She gazed up at the towering tree-like building. "This must have been quite a structure."

"Back when the kingdoms were at peace," Rangar said, "there were many gatherings here. Weddings, feasts, competitions. It was known as a center of peace and celebration. Like everything else, that peace is long gone."

As Mage Marna spoke quietly with Lady Enis, who Rangar explained was a lesser royal in the kingdom of Vil-Kevi akin to a countess, the Baer soldiers took up their positions around the clearing. Gone was the joking and passing around flasks from the night before. Their faces were grave. Everyone was on edge.

An hour passed without any sign of Mars's approach. Bryn felt her own nerves crackling, too. There was something eerie about this forest. It was too quiet, with a strange kind of energy, almost as though the trees were somehow more cognizant than normal ones. She wished she had spent more time listening to her tutors tell her about the other kingdoms. But then again, most of what they focused on were the eligible bachelors within each royal family. Since the princes of Vil-Rossengard and Vil-Kevi were already betrothed, it had hardly come up in her schooling.

"Something feels wrong," Rangar said as the afternoon stretched on. "I'm going to speak with my aunt. Bryn, stay with

Val. And you." He jerked a finger at his brother. "Behave yourself around her, or this time I'll break your jaw in addition to your nose."

Valenden held up his hands in mock defense as Rangar strode away. Once they were alone, Valenden leaned back against a tree, smoking his *statua* pipe. "So, should we expect wedding bells soon?"

Bryn slid him a sidelong look, untrusting of his seemingly innocent topic of conversation. She muttered, "I think to be engaged, one must have a ring." She held up her bare hand.

Valenden chuckled darkly. "You turned him down! How delicious. What was it, the scars? His breath?"

"He didn't ask," Bryn responded in a hard voice. "At least, not exactly. Not until it was too late."

Valenden took a long smoke and groaned, "And here I was thinking the two of you were becoming less insufferable."

Bryn waved away the smoke he blew in her direction. "What about you? Any young woman or man or horse stolen your heart recently?"

The laughter in his eyes told her that he respected her joke. "I don't do commitment. I already told you that. I wasn't lying when I said I was a cad. I'm a prick, too. Look at me; I even tried to kiss my brother's sweetheart once."

She hugged her arms and started to pace, not liking this reminder of their altercation. It was still too fresh. As much as Rangar might have worked it out with his fists and Valenden had joked it off, Bryn was still very aware of that kiss in the woods with Val. *You don't ever forget your first kiss.* Especially not when it had ended in such spectacular disaster.

Valenden leaned back, puffing on his pipe, and eyed her up and down. "Your sister. She's betrothed?"

Bryn raised her eyebrows, surprised that he brought up Elysander. "Married now, I hear."

"Hmm." He considered this. "I wonder if she could be seduced away from her husband…"

Bryn gave him a light slap on the arm.

"What?" he said defensively. "We Baer princes are partial to blondes, and Rangar has made it more than clear now that *you're* unavailable."

She was about to admonish him for such talk when a shout came from the far end of the clearing. A rider materialized on horseback, his woolen cloak and the horse's brown coloring blending in seamlessly with the forest undergrowth.

The Baer soldiers were instantly at attention, weapons raised. Rangar quickly strode back to Bryn's side, resting one hand on the hilt of his sword. "Stay close to me," he commanded her.

The rider was one of the forest folk. He slid gracefully off his horse and strode up to Mage Marna and Lady Enis. They spoke quietly for a moment, far enough away to maintain privacy, and then, suddenly, all eyes turned to Bryn.

Bryn dropped her arms from where she'd had them folded over her chest. Her hands were already shaking. She balled them, feigning strength.

Mage Marna's and Lady Enis's faces were grave. The rider —likely a messenger—looked shaken.

"Lady Bryn," Mage Marna said, raising her voice across the clearing. "I'm afraid I have troubling news."

38

THE CROWN...A CURSED FAMILY...A FOREST
RIDE AT NIGHT...RETURN TO THE HOLD...
DANGER AT EVERY CORNER

*W*hen Bryn finally found the courage to cross the clearing, Mage Marna took her hand and led her into the privacy of the trees, signaling to Rangar to join them.

Bryn was shaking with an awful premonition. She watched Valenden sidle up to the messenger and the forest folk on the opposite side of the clearing, no doubt seeking gossip.

"What's happened?" Bryn asked breathlessly. It was getting late. Mars and the Mir riders should have arrived long ago.

Mage Marna glanced at Rangar with a steely look in her eye. "A messenger arrived from among the forest folk's scouts stationed along the path from here to the Mirien. It happened last night, apparently, but it took this long for the message to make it to us."

"*What* happened last night?" Bryn said, her breath stilled.

The mage met her gaze steadily, then glanced away. "Your brother is dead."

At first, Bryn was certain she hadn't heard right. Mage Marna's experimental translation hex must not be working. But when the mage didn't immediately correct her words, Bryn felt the strength go out of her. Her legs were already so shaky and spent from the day on horseback that now she found herself suddenly without breath, unable to move, frozen.

Rangar flared to life as she went frozen, facing his aunt gravely. "How?"

"He was murdered," the mage said evenly. "Betrayed by Captain Carr. The captain of the guard wanted the throne for himself. When he didn't get it through the uprising, he pretended to support your brother's claim to the crown. Then, he rigged some weaponry that Mars was sparring with. Replaced a dull blade with a sharp one and ran him through. Claimed it was all an accident. Or so our spies tell me."

Rangar muttered a dark curse.

Bryn still couldn't seem to pull her thoughts together. Her parents were gone. She'd put her hand in her own father's cold blood running down his breathless chest. Heard her mother's screams. The one thing that had held her sanity together was knowing that her brother and sister had survived the siege.

But now Mars was gone, too.

That only left Bryn and Elysander, who wanted nothing to do with politics, content to keep her head firmly attached to her neck by running away with her duke from Dresel.

Bryn stumbled backward, pressing her back against a tree, relieved for its support. Rangar was by her side in an instant. "We'll avenge his death," Rangar insisted. "Captain Carr won't get away with this."

Mage Marna made a small sound in the base of her throat. "It isn't our kingdom, Rangar. It isn't our murdered prince."

"It's her brother," he seethed. "She and I are as good as married..." He glanced at Bryn, a moment of hesitancy flashing there, before continuing. "It doesn't matter. We can't let this stand."

"All reports indicate that Prince Mars was a tyrant," the

mage said, holding out her hands. "We don't avenge tyrants. It's as simple as that."

The mage's words were cold, but Bryn was at least glad for the truth, even if it was harsh. She fully believed Rangar would ride to the Mirien overnight and slit Captain Carr's throat if she asked him to, but the last thing she wanted was Rangar going back to that cursed kingdom.

Mage Marna rested a gentle hand on Bryn's shoulder. Even though her words had been harsh, there was tenderness in her touch. "I am sorry for your loss."

Tears started rolling down Bryn's cheeks. Rangar pulled her into an embrace, clutching her tightly. She heard Mage Marna return to the others as they all discussed what had happened and what to do next.

Alone in the trees, Bryn wiped at her tears and asked Rangar, "And now?"

"We go home," he whispered into her ear, rubbing her arms for reassurance. "An empty throne breeds violence. Mark my words, there will be a battle tonight in the Mirien. Plenty besides Captain Carr will use this as an opportunity to attempt to take the crown. You are safest in Barendur Hold, where my brothers and I can keep watch over you. I'm afraid this isn't going to end anytime soon."

She brushed away more tears, shaking her head. "What do you mean? What does the unrest in the Mirien have to do with me? I don't live there anymore."

Rangar hesitated, and then he pulled her close and placed a kiss on her forehead. "Don't worry yourself with the details. We should hasten back to the Baersladen and inform my father and Trei. Now, I must speak with my aunt in private. Can you stay here? Rest a moment."

She nodded shakily. "Yes."

He seemed reluctant to leave her but went to speak with

Valenden and his aunt. With Lady Enis consulting, Bryn could hear their sharp voices bandied about but couldn't make out the words. They kept throwing her looks that made her shiver even more.

What was she missing? Her grief was so great that she couldn't rouse the curiosity to know what they spoke of.

At last, Rangar returned and started packing his saddlebag. "You'll ride with me this time. We can move faster that way. We need to get back as soon as possible."

"But it'll be dark soon!"

"We'll ride through the night."

She gaped at him. The danger must be extreme if they were prepared for such an arduous night ride.

It didn't take long for the Baer traveling party to pack their things and mount. Then, after a few more exchanges with Lady Enis, who promised to send messengers with any new information, they spurred the horses on.

With Lightning tethered to Rangar's mare and Bryn mounted in front of Rangar, Bryn let herself sink into his strong arms. The news of her brother's murder had exhausted her through and through. As the horses galloped through the winding forest paths as night fell, she let her mind go blank. Her heart ached for her brother. Did Elysander know? It was just the two of them now. Ever since marrying the duke, Elysander wasn't even a Lindane anymore but a Dryden.

I'm the only surviving member of my family who still has the Lindane name...

Then, like a blow to the gut, it hit her.

Rangar's hesitation. All those shifting eyes poised at her. The rush to get back to the safety of Barendur Hold.

With her brother dead and her sister married, the crown now fell to *her*.

It was a shocking revelation.

That's what had everyone so fearful. They weren't worried about bandits or uprisings in the Mirien; they now had the crown princess of an entire kingdom in their midst, with only four soldiers as guards, riding through the middle of the wilderness.

They rode at such breakneck speed, with the wind whipping her face, that she couldn't have yelled a single word to Rangar. She was left with her own confused thoughts.

I'm the crown princess. The kingdom is, by right, mine.

Never had she wished more that her parents had included her in Mars and Elysander's political education. Her siblings had been heavily trained in political theory and history. They knew all the rules of succession, whereas Bryn knew nothing. As the third child, she'd always been treated as an extra, a pet, an afterthought.

When they finally stopped to rest the horses and drink from a stream, Bryn grabbed Rangar's arm and pulled him away from the crowd. Keeping her voice low, she hissed, "It's because the crown falls to me now, isn't it? That's why everyone is in such a panic."

In the darkness, she couldn't quite make out his face. He brushed her sweaty hair off her forehead, nodding solemnly. "You've seen the lengths people have gone to for that throne. Murder. Uprising. Betrayal. It isn't just any throne, Bryn. The Mirien is the jewel of the Eyrie. The wealthiest kingdom with the most resources and the greatest army. Everyone wants it. Everyone wants *you*."

"Do you think Captain Carr has already sent soldiers after me?"

Rangar didn't answer, which was an answer in and of itself. "Back on the horse" was all he said. "We need to keep going." His voice was gruff.

With the swift speed of the horses, they reached the high

mountain pass at dawn and started down the other side, glimpsing the ocean again. From there, it wasn't long before they reached the road to Barendur Hold. A few farmers waved to them, only to hesitate when they saw the urgency of the riders. It wouldn't be long before everyone knew something was wrong, and not much longer than that before everyone knew why.

The horses were frothing by the time they reached the Hold. Servants ran out of the stables to give the animals water and walk them to calm their pulses after the long journey. Rangar dismounted and pulled Bryn down after him. Her legs still weak, she stumbled at his side.

"Come," he said, dragging her along toward the Hold. "Hurry. We need to speak to my father and Trei."

Was it really so dangerous? Already? Surely they had beat any rumors about what had happened to Mars. But then, she glimpsed two of the Mir refugees loitering by the dock and remembered that Valenden had suspected a spy in their midst.

Danger might already be in the Baersladen.

Rangar wrapped an arm around her back, glancing over his shoulder. Then, hidden by her cloak, he slipped her a small dagger. "Keep this with you at all times," he warned. "I can't be by your side in every moment, and a moment is all it might take."

He led her up the winding stairs to the council chamber, pausing to speak with a few castle workers, urging them to find King Aleth, Trei, and Saraj and summon them immediately.

In another thirty minutes, the entire Barendur family sat around the council table, along with Saraj and several of their most trusted advisors. Rangar, Valenden, and Mage Marna hadn't taken the time to change out of their riding clothes, but they were used to looking dusty; in fact, it suited them. Bryn, on the other hand, felt as rumpled as an old rag in her riding clothes, kicked and chewed on and trampled by goats.

She sank into a chair, feeling numb through and through, every muscle aching, her heart bruised, as the rulers of her adoptive kingdom debated what to do with the girl whose life they had saved more than once, who was now the greatest threat to them all.

39

A MOST DANGEROUS GIRL...UNEXPECTED
COMFORTS...MAGE ROBES...UNFAIR
SUCCESSION...BLACK LIPS

"Your parents are dead," King Aleth said to Bryn from the far side of the council table. "Your brother murdered. Your sister is married to the duke of Dresel and thus has relinquished any claim on the kingdom of the Mirien. That means you, Lady Bryn, are the rightful heir."

Bryn shook her head, still too stunned to accept the truth. "There must be another way. I don't want the Mir throne. I've never been trained in how to lead. Shouldn't it go to a cousin or an advisor? Someone who's been educated in leadership?"

"You know how bloodlines work," the king said gruffly. "As sole unmarried child of the former king and queen, all of the Mirien is yours." He hesitated. "Or rather, to be precise, the kingdom is yours in temporary guardianship."

Her eyes widened slightly. "You mean that the crown is mine until I'm married."

Like all kingdoms of the Eyrie, only a man—a king—could rule the Mirien. As much power as queens could gain, it would never equal their husbands'.

Bryn felt her gaze slice to Rangar. He had his arms folded

tightly, staring down at the table broodily. What was he thinking? He was certainly the closest thing to a husband she had, or *would* have...

She balled her fists in her skirt, trying to concentrate on what they were saying through the pain throbbing in her skull. "Does this mean I must return to the Mirien?"

King Aleth remained stony-faced. "Not unless you wish to be murdered like your brother."

"So, what?" she countered. "Even if I had the ability to rule, I can't do it from here. From exile."

The king exchanged a look with his sons and his sister and then began to pace. "For the foreseeable future, you will remain here, in the Baersladen," he pronounced. "We will ensure your safety. As far as what steps to take next, I must consult with my advisors."

He came around and rested a heavy hand on Bryn's shoulder. He had never spoken much to her—a gruff, taciturn ruler. And his face betrayed little sympathy now, but he gave her shoulder a squeeze, and that small gesture spoke volumes. "Go," he commanded softly. "Rest. Mourn your brother."

She nodded and wiped her nose. Rangar came to her side and said quietly, "Gather your belongings and move to the mage chambers. It's the safest place in the Hold. I'll post guards by the door."

"What will you do?" she asked him.

"I must speak at greater length with my family. Saraj, will you accompany her?"

"Of course," the falconer said.

Bryn felt herself standing and moving as though someone else was in control of her body. Two guards followed her and Saraj as they made their dazed way through the hallways and up another set of stairs to the tower.

"Have no fear for your safety," Saraj assured her. "Trei will do everything in his power to protect you until the question of your inheritance is resolved."

"It doesn't sit right with me that only a man can ultimately rule the Mirien. I suppose when I was younger, I never even thought about it. But now, it's so starkly unfair."

"It is unfair," Saraj agreed. "It's the same here in our lands. Such archaic rules run deep. It's hard to change the course of thousands of years of tradition. Of course, here it's never been a concern, at least with this generation. With three brothers, it's always been understood that a man will inherit King Aleth's crown."

When they reached the mage chambers, Calista and the other apprentice studying at the main worktable stood in surprise. "Lady Bryn," Calista said. "What's happened? You look as though you've seen a ghost."

Saraj went to Calista and whispered something in her ear. The apprentice raised her eyebrows. "Gods." She gently urged Bryn to sit on the worktable bench. "We'll get you cleaned up, eh? Some strong broth in your belly. It won't take away the hurt, but it will help. Ren, go to the kitchen and ask for some broth and plain bread."

The male apprentice nodded and disappeared through the doorway.

Saraj ran her hand tenderly over Bryn's hair like a big sister. "Take heart. The Barendur family will do right by you, even if you aren't Baer yourself."

"Thank you, Saraj."

Once the falconer had left, Calista helped Bryn peel off her filthy riding clothes and cast the same cleaning spell that Mage Marna had before: softening her locks, letting the dirt and sweat shimmer and fall away from her body. She let Bryn borrow apprentice robes, which were softer and lighter than the heavy wool garments she'd been given to work in the barn with the sheep. Calista hummed softly as she combed out Bryn's hair.

"My lady!" Mam Delice appeared in the doorway along with the other apprentice, Ren, who held a small tray of food. The old cook rushed into the room. "When this one told me what happened, not even the guards could keep me away. Oh, your poor brother."

Bryn rushed into the old woman's arms. She'd been jumpy whenever she'd seen any of the Mir refugees—knowing there was a suspected spy among them—but Mam Delice was above suspicion. Bryn had never trusted anyone more.

"I can't believe he's gone," she confessed.

"I know, child. I know." The cook hugged Bryn to her ample bosom and patted her back. Bryn felt herself sobbing. All she'd heard for weeks was what a monster Mars was—and perhaps it was true—but there had been another side to him. *She'd* known it. Mam Delice had known it, too. And it cracked a wall inside her to hear another person also mourn her brother's passing.

"And now the little mouse of Castle Mir is the crown heir," Mam Delice sighed, referring to Bryn's old nickname. "I don't envy you, child. It's a heavy crown."

"Does everyone in the Hold know about the succession?"

Mam Delice nodded solemnly. "Word spread quickly."

"What do the Mir refugees think?"

Mam Delice hesitated. "Well, they were not fond of your brother. You and I knew Mars since he was a boy, saw the good in him, but I'm afraid not many others did. Most of the others I came here with were part of the uprising against your family, including Mars. So I'm afraid they aren't too upset by the news of his death, though they do fear what will happen to our homeland now. They say violence is already breaking out in the Mirien, even spilling into the Outlands."

"Do you think the refugees...they would want me to rule them?"

Mam Delice smoothed Bryn's hair down her face. "I can't say that I know, little mouse. The Mir common folk never knew much about you. I believe they assumed you were in league with your family, though I and many others who knew you have tried to spread word that wasn't the case. That you were sheltered from all of it, unaware of your family's crimes."

After another long hug, Bryn thanked the cook and retired to one of the spartan but clean apprentice bedrooms to eat and take some time to think. She soon found herself nodding off after the long journey. Exhaustion overcame her, and when she woke, the candle was out. She had no way of knowing what time it was without a window in the room.

When she eased the door open, she found it was dark in the mage chambers. A few lanterns and candles had been set out, but there was no sign of the mages and apprentices. The moon was high outside the window.

Two guards stood by the door, nodding to acknowledge her. "Lady Bryn," one said, "the prince has requested I bring you to him when you wake."

She nodded as she followed them down the halls, wondering if Rangar would have more news to report from his further talks with his family. But to her surprise, the guards led her to the castle library, where Trei was waiting for her, not Rangar.

"Trei?" she asked hesitantly.

"Ah, Lady Bryn. How are you? Did you rest?"

She rubbed her arms over the smooth mage robes and nodded. Trei, always a bit overly formal, motioned to a seat at a table in front of an open book.

"I wanted to show you this," he explained. "It's a guide to our inheritance protocol, which isn't so different from the

Mirien's. Most of the kingdoms of the Eyrie follow similar traditions with the exception of the forest kingdoms, who vote for their next ruler, and the Wollins, who select a new ruler through combat."

She sank into the chair as Trei motioned to a diagram in the book that contained so many different titles and positions that her head spun.

"You'll see here that in the case of a queen passing, power is retained by her husband, the king. If he remarries, the new queen's offspring from that marriage will fall into secondary inheritance from the first set of children. Now, if the new queen already has offspring, say in the case of a widow..."

Bryn's head ached as he explained the complicated rules of inheritance, but she came away with the gist of it. In her case, it actually *wasn't* complicated in the slightest: Everyone was dead except for her. Her father had no brothers who might make a play for the throne. Her mother had a sister who had married a commoner, absolving her of any royal claim.

Trei continued. "So Captain Carr or whoever else may be vying for the throne only has three options. They can attempt to take the throne by force as before, but that will lead to war within all the kingdoms. A much easier path would be to marry you. Whomever you marry gains complete control over the Mirien. I believe Carr will attempt that course first, and he isn't the only one. The baron of Ruma is claiming that you were betrothed during the High Sun Gathering before the siege..."

"That's a lie!" Bryn gasped. "He never proposed, and I certainly never accepted. In fact, he wrote a letter to my mother expressing interest in my *sister*."

Trei nodded calmly as though this information didn't surprise him. "I see. Well, he's clearly grasping at straws, but there is no telling which straws may work. In any case, Captain Carr is definitively the greater threat."

Bryn thought bitterly about the vile things she'd overheard the soldiers say Captain Carr would do to her and Elysander. Perhaps they had been making it up, but knowing Captain Carr, she didn't exactly doubt it. "I'd sooner die than marry that man."

"Well," Trei said gravely. "That's actually the third option."

Her eyebrows shot up. "You think he'll try to *kill* me?"

Trei nodded softly.

Bryn swallowed, forcing herself to remain calm. "What happens to the crown if I die? Who inherits it next?" She looked at the complicated diagram again, but it made little sense.

"If you die with no husband or children, it passes by blood to the next relative. That gets complicated in your family's case. Third cousins, distant great-uncles, countless people could appear with a claim, and it would be almost impossible to verify their lineage. The advisors might decide to appoint Carr or another in a temporary ruler position while it's worked out."

"And once Carr is on the seat, I'd wager he won't ever let go."

Trei nodded. "Exactly." He took the book and closed it. "I don't know if this was helpful, but I wanted you to understand the politics behind the situation."

"Thank you," she said weakly but sincerely, looking up to meet the handsome eldest prince's eyes. "It's more than anyone else has ever explained to me."

Even if my fate lies in marriage or the grave.

THE FOLLOWING DAYS WERE A RUSH. Reports flooded in about violence breaking out throughout the Eyrie as various parties attempted to assert their claim on the Mir throne. It all felt so eerily distant to Bryn, safe in Barendur Hold. Listening to reports of villages burning and skirmishes so far away. A team of Baer sentries stationed at the border of the Baersladen was attacked by unknown assailants suspected to be Baron Marmose's soldiers, bringing the violence closer to their doorstep.

Trei comforted her with informative reports, giving her as many updates as he could, advising her on the history and politics of the situation.

Valenden cornered her with rude jokes and fresh ale, trying to lift her spirits.

Rangar was at her side nearly every moment, awake or asleep. He slept outside the door to her room in the mage quarters, his sword drawn and crossed over his chest. The topic of marriage hadn't come back up between them, though she had heard plenty of whispering among the castle servants and advisors. She was now the crown princess of the richest kingdom of the Eyrie, so her future husband would be king. None of that had been a question that morning on the mountain when he'd proposed marriage to her. But now, it was an unavoidable topic, and if he wasn't going to bring it up, she figured she would have to.

She was eating alone in her room, waiting for him to finish his work for the day and find her so she could finally bring up the subject they'd been dancing around, when she heard a sword clatter outside her door.

She instantly went stiff.

It was strange—Baer soldiers were highly trained, so accidentally dropping a sword was unheard of. Besides, all soldiers except for Rangar remained stationed at the main entrance to the mage chambers, never coming this far inside.

Her mind filled with fears about spies and assassins. With shaking hands, she drew her dagger. Her heart thrashed in her chest. She didn't dare call out for help in case whoever was outside the door had nefarious purposes and was waiting for a sign she was inside.

After a grueling few moments when her pulse threatened to burst from her veins, the hallway outside remained quiet. Steeling her nerves, she cracked open the door, making sure to hold the knife at the ready.

She gasped.

Rangar was slumped facedown on the floor just outside of her room. His sword lay by his side as though he'd dropped it unintentionally.

His lips were black. He wasn't moving.

No, no, no...

Bryn screamed until her throat went hoarse.

40

A POISONOUS TRICK...NO ONE TO HELP...A
TOUCH OF MAGIC...FINALLY EVEN

"Help!" Bryn screamed, hoping to wake Calista and Ren, the other apprentices. They knew magic, so surely they'd be able to cure whatever had afflicted Rangar. She fell to her knees next to where he lay facedown on the floor, feeling for his pulse. It was there but terribly faint. It took all her strength to roll him over onto his back.

His eyes were closed. His lips had turned blueish-black. The veins on his face stood out strangely; they were dark and threaded against his pale skin. She called for help again, but there was no answer. Where were the mages and apprentices? And the soldiers who were supposed to be stationed at the door?

A creeping feeling of foreboding spread down her skin. It was never this quiet. The guards occasionally took a break when Rangar arrived to guard Bryn's door, but it felt like too much of a coincidence that they'd suddenly vanish now.

Is this a trap? Are the guards in on it?

Her own pulse staggered as a hundred fears filled her head. Had word of her succession spread so fast that the knives were already out?

"Rangar, wake up!" She shook him by the shoulders, but his head only slumped to the side. She lowered her cheek to his lips to feel for breath, then recoiled. His mouth reeked of henbane. She'd smelled it enough times in the mage storerooms and been warned repeatedly how dangerous—even fatal —it was if ingested.

She inhaled sharply as she understood what had happened.

Someone poisoned Rangar.

The realization struck her with a clap of terror. It must have been one of the Mir spies or someone who had infiltrated the Hold, trying to sow disorder. Could it be one of Baron Marmose's men? She certainly couldn't fathom any of the loyal Baer people doing this to their own beloved prince.

Then a new possibility threaded through her mind. Maybe whoever had done this to Rangar had actually meant to poison *her*, and Rangar had unknowingly ingested whatever food was meant for her instead. She raked a hand through her hair as she considered her options. What was she supposed to do? Where were the other mages?

Rangar's body started to convulse. Bryn's jaw slackened in a silent cry.

Saints, this is bad!

"Shh, shh," she whispered frantically as she tried to hold his head steady without unintentionally harming him more, but it didn't do any good. He continued to shake. Foam appeared at the corners of his mouth.

"Blast!" she cursed aloud. She didn't dare run to get help and leave him like this to possibly die alone on the floor—but what other option did she have? Her pulse was throbbing. Everything was happening so fast.

Then, with a swift inhale, she remembered what Rangar and Val had taught her in the woods in Vil-Kevi: the purge spell to use when there was no antidote to poison.

"That's it," she whispered aloud, stroking Rangar's face as he continued to tremor. "You taught me the spell. I can do it."

She pushed to her feet, pacing as she tried to think through the process. Would the spell even work on another person? As Rangar and Val had explained it to her, it was to be used by the person being poisoned—but had they actually said that specifically?

She bit her lip as she threw a glance toward the mage storerooms at the far end of the hall. There had to be a henbane antidote somewhere there, but Bryn had no idea what it looked like, and the apprentices had all eerily vanished.

So really, the hex was the only choice.

She pulled back her sleeve to examine the scar on the side of her wrist. It was a simple two-line cross mark, with one of the lines curving slightly at the end. She raked her mind to remember the wording to accompany the hex. *En vit? En vineo?*

"*En videl!*" she gasped.

She tried to still her shaking hand long enough to trace the symbol on her wrist in the air above Rangar. Whenever Mage Marna had worked a spell on her, such as the cleaning spell, she'd aimed her hand in Bryn's direction and kept her eyes fixed on her, so that was what Bryn did now with Rangar.

Once she had spoken the spell and made the hand gesture, she waited, pacing tightly, not taking her eyes off Rangar. She still had no idea if the purge spell only worked on the caster or if it would work on another person. In the forest, the brothers hadn't gone into detailed explanation. The whole incident of them teaching her the spell seemed to have been one of Val's jokes, just something to taunt her with. But now Rangar's life relied on it.

Rangar's body slowly stopped tremoring, but he didn't open his eyes. His lips remained black.

"Saints! Rangar, wake up! I don't know what else to do!" Bryn fell to her knees next to him, grabbing his shirt.

He suddenly let out a burst of coughs.

Bryn sucked in air. She felt her body shaking in relief. She cried and pressed her hands to his chest, rubbing it, trying to loosen whatever was in his lungs and get his blood flow going. "Rangar! Wake up!"

She slapped him lightly on the cheeks, trying to rouse him.

He moaned as he coughed again. The dark veins pulsing in his face appeared to ripple strangely, and then he twisted to the side, hacking up a black, reeking liquid that oozed out onto the floor. He rolled onto his back again and slowly blinked open his eyes.

His eyes were bloodshot. His lips were still twinged with black, though the color was returning to his face.

Bryn burst into grateful tears. The spell had worked!

She threw her arms around his neck, sobbing into his shoulder as he leaned over and continued to empty his stomach of the poison. At last, he wiped his mouth with his sleeve and scooted backward until he could sit up and lean against the hallway wall, breathing hard.

"Bryn?" his voice creaked.

"Rangar," she moaned between sobs. "I thought you were dead. I thought I'd lost you!" He groaned, still groggy from the near death experience, as he rubbed his chest as though it ached. She placed a hand on his cheek. "Talk to me," she urged. "Tell me you're all right."

"Did you use..." He wet his cracked lips. "The purge spell?"

She nodded frantically. "I can't believe it, but I remembered the wording. I didn't know if it would work for you, but it did. I'm so thankful."

He shut his eyes and drew in a deep breath. His face was

twisted with pain. After a few moments, he mumbled, "We're even."

She shook her head in confusion. "Even? What are you talking about? Listen, this is important. Do you know who poisoned you? Was it a Mir spy sent by Captain Carr? One of Baron Marmose's men?"

He coughed again, then leaned his head back against the wall and slowly opened his eyes. His bloodshot eyes found hers, sparking with some secret she couldn't yet figure out. The corner of his mouth tugged back in a hint of a pained smile. She scrunched up her nose, worried for him. *Has the poison gotten to his brain, made him delirious?*

"What?" she breathed.

He rasped, "You don't get it. We're *even*, Bryn. That's what you wanted. A life saved is a soul owned."

She stared at him in utter bafflement as she tried to make sense of what he was saying. Why was he talking about the *fralen* bond now? Getting to the bottom of whoever tried to kill him was far more important in the moment. Then a realization seized her system: *She'd saved his life.* That's what he meant. She was now *his* Savior, and he was now *her* Saved. After ten years, their positions were reversed.

They were even.

Her eyes widened as she began to understand what had actually happened with the poison. "Rangar..." She shook her head in disbelief. "Did you...did you poison *yourself*?"

He didn't answer immediately. He winced as he shifted his body on the floor, trying to ease the pain in his limbs.

"Rangar! Tell me!" She grabbed the shoulder of his shirt hard.

"I had to," he rasped.

She blinked, unable to believe what he was saying. She slumped back against the opposite wall, digging her fingers into her temple. "And the purge spell you taught me in the woods...that was part of it, wasn't it? It wasn't a coincidence that you got poisoned so soon after teaching me that particular spell. You've had this planned for a while."

He gave a small shrug.

She slammed her hands into his chest, making him wince. "You idiot! You could have died! You poisoned yourself just so we'd be even with the *fralen* bond? I don't *care* about that bond!"

"You do," he murmured, his eyes simmering. "You wouldn't marry me unless we were even."

She sank back on her heels, staring at him in shock. What a colossally stupid thing he'd done. What if she hadn't remembered the words? Or hadn't been able to get the hand gesture right?

Rangar coughed before adding, "It was Val's idea."

Bryn narrowed her eyes. "I bet it was. Only Valenden could come up with such an asinine plan. What if you'd died?" She raised a hand to smack him again, but he caught it with a weak hand and pressed it to his chest.

He met her eyes. "I didn't die, though."

She bit her lip, holding back tears, terrified by how close they'd come to losing him. Over *nothing*.

He said slowly, "Now I'm your Savior, and you are my Savior. You said on the mountain you couldn't marry me so long as you were bound by the *fralen* bond. Well, now we're *both* bound. Your soul belongs to me, and mine belongs to you."

She made a fist with her hand against his chest. "I hate you. This was a terrible idea." But then she sank her whole body against his chest, just relieved to feel him breathing, hear his steady heartbeat. "Come lie down in my room, you idiot," she mumbled into his shirt. "You almost died—you need some rest."

She helped him to his feet and into her small bedroom in the mage quarters, where he collapsed on her low pallet bed. She tried to press bread on him to ease his aching stomach, but he refused. He caught her in his arms, pulling her down onto the bed with him.

"You're mine, Bryn Lindane. And I'm yours. If you'll have me."

"Soulbound? Hmm. I don't know," she said wryly, still angry at his stupid stunt, but then lay down next to him, pressing her face into his shoulder, feeling the reassuring rise and fall of his breath.

Perhaps they *were* meant for each other.

THE FOLLOWING DAY, after Mage Marna had thoroughly examined Rangar and declared that he would survive—as long as she didn't kill him first for going through with such a stupid stunt—Bryn fetched some simple foods from Mam Delice in the kitchen and brought them back up to Rangar.

He grinned as he ate, though there was still a pained grimace whenever he swallowed. The henbane might be out of his system, but it had done some damage to his throat before Bryn had purged it.

"I might poison myself more often if it means you nurse me back to health," he said with a wink.

She rolled her eyes as she sat on the bed next to him, toying with the folds of her robe. "I'm not sure who I'm most angry at, you or Val. How did this awful scheme come about, anyway?"

"He owed me," Rangar said. "For trying to kiss you, and he knew it. After you found the lamb and we came back down from the mountain, he got it out of me that we'd had a disagreement over the idea of marriage. It was his idea to have you save my life so that we'd be equally soulbound by the bond."

"And you listened to him. I'm not sure I want to marry such a fool," she said, though Rangar gave her a knowing smile in response. Then, her thoughts grew more serious. "This whole marriage scheme isn't about...my brother, is it? The inheritance?"

He set down his breakfast as the smile faded from his face. He took her hand in his. "Are you asking if I poisoned myself so that I could marry you to become the future king of the Mirien?"

She tipped up her chin defensively. "I suppose I am."

His eyes darkened. "Val and I came up with this plan long before we heard about your brother's passing," he reminded her. "And besides, I have no wish to rule the Mirien. You know that."

"But if we marry, you would rule it. You'd be king."

He nodded slowly, brow pinched. "Yes, I've considered that fact since your brother's passing. It is not my desire to be king of the Mirien, but if I am, then at least the target is on my back, not yours. Everyone clamoring after the throne will come for me. You'll be safer."

"I don't want *either* of us to have a target on our backs. And I don't want you to be king just to protect me."

He pushed aside the plate of bread and rubbed his face with one hand. "It's a complicated situation. My father will work with the advisors of the other Eyrie kingdoms. You and I could rule from here—from exile—until a more permanent solution is found. If you truly wish to remain here, then we can give up the crown, but not until a suitable replacement is found. Otherwise, there will be full-out war."

She sighed deeply. She hated to think of the unrest happening back in her homeland—*her* kingdom now, *her* responsibility. But maybe Rangar was right. With the power of the Baer army and the support of other kingdoms, maybe they could all get out of this with their heads still attached and her kingdom not in flames.

"There's one more thing," Rangar said in a low voice.

He reached into his cloak pocket, taking out a ring. It was a simple twist of silver imprinted with maiden rose petal markings.

"I promised you jewelry and flowers." His voice was low, intimate. "Will you officially be my bride, Bryn Lindane?"

41

WAR AT THE DOOR STEP...A WOUNDED
WARRIOR...AN ATTENTIVE NURSE...AN
UNDENIABLE ATTRACTION

*R*angar just proposed.

It was real this time. Not just vague speculation on a mountaintop or gossip spreading through the town. He wanted her to be his wife. *His queen.*

Bryn practically pounced on him, causing the ring to clatter to the floor. But she didn't care. It had never been about the ring. She threw her arms around his neck and clung tightly to him as she breathed into the place where his neck met his shoulder.

"You promise you don't just want the throne?" she whispered.

"Never have."

"And that my soul and your soul are even?"

"Completely even."

She pulled back, seeking out his gaze. His eyes were clear now, no longer bloodshot. His luxurious brown irises reflected back her own beaming face. "Then yes, Rangar Barendur. I will marry you."

She pressed her lips to his.

He sat up fully, shoving aside the plate of bread. It clattered to the floor with a clank of tin on stone. Not breaking the kiss, he picked her up around the waist and positioned her to sit in his lap, sliding a hand around the small of her back.

Her pulse quickened its throb. He still smelled like henbane, a hint of danger. But beneath it was Rangar's usual scent: the forest and the sea. She dragged her nails over his forehead and hair, pushing the dark strands back to expose his face. *To reveal the scars.* How strange that they were bound together by flesh that had been torn and mended back together. As though he knew what she was thinking, he ran a hand over her robe along her ribs where her own matching scars lay.

He deepened the kiss by gripping the back of her neck, guiding her head back. His lips claimed hers with an intensity she'd never before felt. His teeth lightly glided over her lips, igniting her pulse.

"My betrothed," he breathed as he trailed his lips down her jawline. "You have no idea how long I've wanted to call you that." His hands dug deeper into the flesh of her waist and then gripped the folds of her robe, twisting in the fabric as though he wanted to rip the cloth right off her.

"Betrothed," she whispered back, testing out the sound of it. Though right now, she was far more interested in the sensations that his touch was stirring in her body than semantics about what they called each other.

With a growl she didn't know she had in her, she gripped his hair at his nape and pulled his own head back, dipping down to kiss his neck. His spine went rigid. He tilted his head to give her better access as his hand slid down from her waist to cup her backside.

"Saints, you feel good," he whispered into the side of her head.

Her lips reached his collar. She sat up and began to unbutton his shirt. He leaned back on the bed's pillows, eyes simmering as he watched her undress him. Her hands trembled but not from nerves. Her body was coursing with desire so hard that she wasn't sure she could contain herself.

Once she finished the last button, she smoothed her hands over his bare chest, letting her palms ripple over the uneven scars bisecting his torso. She bit her lip, thinking about the wolves that had done this. They hadn't been evil, just doing what wolves were made to do. And now she was doing what people in love were made to do.

Rangar shifted his hips to get more comfortable. Still in his lap, Bryn felt their bodies sliding against one another in a way that felt deliciously scandalous. The mage robes she wore were thinner than the heavy wool dresses she was used to, allowing her to become intimately acquainted with every edge of Rangar's hips and thighs. She felt a rush of blood pooling at her core.

His hand traced along her side from her hips up to the bottom of her breast. She arched her back into his hand as he cupped the edge of one breast, his thumb grazing over the sensitive tip beneath the thin fabric.

"Still so certain you want to wait until marriage to bed me?" she whispered.

His eyes flashed with a dangerous amount of desire, but he maintained control of himself. Giving her the hint of a smirk, he continued to tease her body with his thumb. "I don't mind the anticipation," he said in a low growl. "Though I wouldn't mind a *sample* of what's to come on our wedding night."

Her breath hitched to hear him talk about such things. Her mind filled with wicked thoughts of what that night would entail. Not a scrap of clothing between them. All of them bared, scars and all. His hands touching her most intimate places. Her lips on every part of him.

His other hand found where her robe fell to her knee and

began to slowly push the fabric back, sliding his palm over her bare thigh.

"Now that we're even," he purred dangerously, "I don't have to watch what I say. I can tell you as much as I want that you're mine. You belong to me. *Only* to me."

A flare of the old anger ran up her spine, but then she managed to tame it. "And you belong to *me* now, too."

He grinned devilishly. "I was already yours long before you saved my life, Bryn."

His hand continued to push up the hem of her robe to midthigh. His broad fingers squeezed her flesh, making her hips buck on instinct. He clenched his jaw, watching her intently as he continued to move his hand higher up her body.

"For years, I've dreamed of being with you like this." His voice was growing breathless, ragged. His index finger grazed the lace undergarment covering her hips, teasing her by running along the seam.

"Of touching you," he breathed, dipping his finger beneath the lace band.

Bryn gripped him around the neck, eyes falling closed as he continued to torment her.

"Of hearing you moan," he added, brushing his finger closer to her private territory.

She felt herself unable to speak. She was vaguely aware that she should answer him or tell him how much she'd thought about him, too, but her body was overcome. He had nearly died, which only made her that much more aware of how she couldn't ever tolerate losing him. She dug her fingers into his arms, never wanting to let go.

Her skin had never felt so alive. She was aware of every small movement he made, every breath that brushed against her face and neck. His hand under her robes brought heat to her cheeks and everywhere else on her body. He slid his thumb under her lace undergarments to join his index finger, dragging it lightly over her tight, hot center.

She cried out, digging her fingers into his shoulder muscles. "Rangar," she panted. "I don't know…"

"Do you want me to stop?" he murmured in her ear.

She shook her head violently, clinging to him harder. *Don't stop. Saints, it feels good.*

He chuckled darkly as he started to move his thumb again. Bryn bit her lip, trying to contain the overwhelming sensation spreading through her nerves. He ran his thumb up and down over her, bringing a coil of heat to her very center. But it wasn't enough. She needed more.

She pushed up on her knees and straddled his waist instead of sitting in his lap, granting him closer access to touch her.

He raised an eyebrow, impressed at her boldness. His hand reached between her legs again, spurring waves of pleasure and torment in equal parts. He leaned back to watch her face as he slowly slipped one finger into the aching chasm at her core. Her jaw parted. He moved his finger slowly, stroking her in places she didn't even know were parts people touched one another.

She briefly wondered what it would be like to touch *him* between his legs. His manly part was extremely evident, given the bulge straining at his pants. What would it feel like to wrap her hand around it? To stroke him up and down? Would he feel as mindless and wild as she was feeling right now?

"One day soon," he murmured as he stroked her deeper with his finger, "I'm going to take you entirely. Soul, mind, body. You'll be mine in every way."

Bryn could barely focus on his words. The feeling at the base of her belly was intensifying so much that it consumed every part of her. Rangar's big hand all over her most intimate places, stroking and teasing, was rapidly awakening her senses in a way that was so powerful it was almost painful. But she wouldn't have traded it for anything.

"Don't stop," she panted in his ear.

He chuckled again as he cupped her breast with his free hand. He tugged down the wide collar of her robe, freeing her breast, and ducked his head to capture her nipple in his mouth.

One finger buried inside her, his lips on her bare pink nipple, sent Bryn over the edge. She cried out as her thighs tightened around his hips. A wave of pleasure crashed down over her, drenching her from the tip of her head to her toes. Her whole body trembled in his hands as he continued to stroke her.

"That's it," he urged. He wasn't smiling now, his face serious.

She threw her head back, lips parted, as the wave spread deliciously throughout her body. Rangar palmed her breast harder. He leaned in to capture her lips with his own, breathing in her moans of pleasure.

She gave one more cry and collapsed on his bare chest, spent and shaking. Her breath was shallow. Rangar turned to the side and coughed, his whole body shaking. When she looked up, she saw his skin was pale again.

Gasping, she pulled up the collar of her dress to cover her chest and said, "You're still weak. You nearly died. We shouldn't be doing this, it's too much of a strain!"

"It's a strain, all right," he agreed, adjusting his pants over his demanding bulge. Then his mouth pulled back in another smirk. "I'm fine."

She rested her hands on his chest in concern. "No, you should rest. I don't know what came over me."

"Bryn, really. I'm fine."

She stroked the sweat-soaked skin on his temple. What had

she been thinking, rolling around and moaning in bed with him when he'd just nearly died?

Her cheeks grew warm all over again, remembering it.

She cleared her throat and climbed off his lap, shaking out her robe to settle back over her body. Then she got to hands and knees and searched around the floor until she found the ring he'd given her.

Perching back on the side of the bed, she slid it onto her finger and admired the simple elegance. "Shall we tell your family now?"

Rangar considered this while stroking her arm. "Yes, but only my family. No formal announcement, at least not yet. It might only spur your enemies to act faster if they believe you'll soon be married."

She nodded.

He ran his hand up her arm. "We'll figure everything out. I promise. Do not worry about the future. My family will protect you. My father and Trei understand politics; they'll come up with a solution."

She sighed and leaned against his chest, listening to his heartbeat. Everything in her life might be a mess, but at least this one thing was certain. *Rangar. Her future husband.*

She closed her eyes and let herself drift off to the steady rhythm of his breath.

42

CALLED OFF TO WAR...RANGAR LIKES HIS
PRIVACY...BAD NEWS FROM THE BORDER...
LEARNING TO LEAD

*S*ometime in the night, Bryn woke groggily to find Rangar pulling back on his shirt. He kissed her briefly and whispered that he had to speak to his family; not even her protests that he needed rest after almost dying convinced him to stay. She fell back into an uneasy sleep as reality tangled with dreams. She was back in his arms with his hands all over her body; in the next instant, he was on the floor with black lips and pale skin. Then they were in Castle Mir as flames rose higher, only instead of her father's body bleeding out on the throne, it was her own neck slashed.

In the morning, it was hard to shake the disturbing dreams. She dressed in fresh robes and finished the bread from the night before. When she came out into the mage chambers, Calista looked up with a sly look.

"Ah, there you are."

Bryn took a seat at the worktable opposite the apprentice. One glance at the door confirmed that the guards were back at their station. Calista followed her gaze and said, "Rangar ordered all of us to leave last night. All the apprentices, all the guards. Said we weren't to return until morning even if we heard you scream."

Calista raised her eyebrows suggestively, a touch of mirth in them.

Bryn bit her lip, considering if she should tell Calista the truth. Clearly, Calista thought that Rangar had just wanted privacy with Bryn to ravage her alone in her bedroom. And yes, that *had* happened to an extent—she blushed thinking about it—but the reason he'd ordered them away was because he'd poisoned himself and didn't want anyone but Bryn to be on hand to help for his twisted plan to become soulbound.

She decided it was best not to let the entire kingdom know their youngest prince had done something so idiotic. She pressed her hand to her robe's pocket, where she had placed the ring until their engagement was formalized, and gave Calista a small shrug. "Sometimes Rangar likes his privacy."

"I bet he does." Calista flashed Bryn a wink. Then she leaned over the table and dropped her voice. "Is it true what everyone is saying? You're the crown heir to the Mirien now?"

The smile melted off Bryn's face. "Everyone already knows?"

"Hard to keep news like that secret."

Calista reached out to squeeze Bryn's hand across the table. "I'm sorry about your brother. We have a saying here in the Baersladen to those we've lost: 'You go to sea, I'll stay on shore, but I'll join you before the whales sing of the end of days.'"

Bryn nodded her thanks, holding back the sting of tears.

One of the guards stuck his head into the workroom and said, "The king has requested your presence, my lady."

A wave of apprehension rolled over Bryn—Aleth Barendur must have come to some sort of decision about her position. She nodded. "All right."

They strode through the hallways of Barendur Hold,

passing servants who glanced at Bryn and then rushed off to whisper with their friends. A few gave her respectful nods and called her "my lady" in a more formal way than they ever had before. Bryn didn't feel comfortable with the attention at all. She'd never considered herself to be any sort of leader: she was a princess in title, but that had never meant much. Now that she was heir, everyone seemed to view her differently.

At the council chambers, Bryn had expected to find the entire family along with the Baersladen advisors, as usual, but was surprised to see only King Aleth and Rangar standing on opposite sides of the table. Rangar turned to her with a troubled expression.

She immediately sucked in a tight breath, now filled with even more apprehension. "You called for me?"

King Aleth nodded soberly as his eyes flashed to his son. "My son has informed me of your betrothal."

She glanced again at Rangar, but his expression was unreadable. Surely the king wouldn't forbid their marriage? She opened her lips to speak, but the king addressed her first, though he didn't meet her gaze.

He continued. "We've come to value your presence in this castle, and you've carried yourself with dignity and a generosity of spirit. We would be pleased to have you formally join our family."

Her shoulders eased from their tight posture. "Oh. That's great to hear."

But Rangar still wasn't smiling. Arms folded tightly across his chest, he ran a hand over his chin as though something was troubling him.

She swallowed. "But...?"

The king and his son exchanged a knowing look. There was clearly something they weren't telling her.

Rangar dropped his hands as he paced slowly in her direction. "We received a report that Mir soldiers crossed the Baersladen border yesterday. They razed the village of Casim to the ground. Burned every house. Slaughtered anyone they found, including children."

A shudder worked through her backbone. Unsteady, she stumbled toward the table, catching herself.

Rangar was by her side in an instant.

"I'm all right," she said quietly.

King Aleth added, "It's a declaration of war. Captain Carr ordered the attack; he's trying to provoke us, and unfortunately, he's succeeded. We can't let such an outrage go unpunished, nor can we allow Baer people to be in danger from the Mir army."

"Of course," she whispered.

Rangar placed a hand on the small of her back. "My father is sending half the Baer army to defend the border. The rest will remain here to protect the castle." His neck muscles constricted as he swallowed. "I'm going to the border with the squadrons."

She pulled air in sharply. "You're going to war?"

"Rangar is one of our most highly trained captains," King Aleth explained. "Trei and Valenden will remain here at the castle. Have no fear; they will ensure your safety."

"I'm not worried about *my* safety," she insisted. "I fear for Rangar. He wasn't well last night—" She glanced at him, silently asking if he'd told his father about the poisoning.

"Yes, I'm aware." The king's deep growl betrayed his disapproving feelings about his son's near death experience. "The army will wait until tomorrow to depart to give my son a bit more time to recover. But we dare not wait longer than that."

It was a small relief, but it was better than him leaving that instant.

Rangar gently touched her arm. "I have to go, Bryn. I can't

let my people be killed. But I'll be back within a few weeks, and as soon as I return, we'll be married."

Bryn glanced at the Baer king, whose stony face revealed nothing—cryptic as it ever was. "I don't like this," she whispered. "You nearly died. You can't just go off to battle."

"I must." He cupped her cheek softly.

Bryn wanted to protest and convince them otherwise, but she knew how stubborn the Baer spirit was. There was no convincing Rangar to stay behind to save his own skin when Baer villagers were being slaughtered. As they left the council chambers, fury burned in her as she thought of Captain Carr.

Murderer. Traitor. Usurper.

Rangar was gone for most of the day, preparing for his voyage. He had an entire fleet of soldiers to meet with to discuss strategy and battle plans, and she wasn't allowed to be present for any of it. She found herself pacing the castle halls, frustrated that she couldn't do more to help. She comforted herself with the thought that once Rangar was back and they were married, they would have more of an ability to intervene on behalf of the Mir and Baer commonfolk. By then, Prince Trei and King Aleth would have negotiated with the other kingdoms to gain their support.

I won't sit by and do nothing this time. While Rangar was away, she'd learn what she could about politics. She'd begin to shape herself into the leader her people deserved.

The morning of Rangar's departure came all too soon. Bryn found herself standing on the dais in the village square with Valenden on one side and Saraj on the other as they faced the squadrons of the Baer army, preparing to send them off. The soldiers wore their full armor, made of thick leather and iron rivets, with swords at their sides. At least twenty mounted riders sat atop massive Baer horses that were also fitted with armor. Rangar and one of the other army captains rode at their head.

King Aleth stood to address the army. "May the strength of the bear rest in your flesh. May the speed of the seal grace your feet. May the mountains shelter you, and may the sea greet each of you on your return."

The soldiers remained solemn and serious. Bryn shivered at the sight of them. The Mir soldiers she'd grown up seeing were skilled in battle but were much slighter people; their armor was gold-plated and shone brilliantly, their weaponry finely crafted. The Baer army, in contrast, looked like bears wielding giant slabs of sharp iron. Never had she seen such massive men and women before, such broad shoulders and powerful bodies.

The army captain pounded on his shield as he steered his horse to lead the soldiers on their march. Rangar, however, broke away from the squadron and rode to the dais. He dismounted swiftly, removed his helmet, and touched Bryn's cheek.

"I'll return to you," he said quietly. "I promise I will. A life saved is a soul owned, Bryn Lindane. I'm your Saved and Savior, as you are my Saved and Savior. We're soulbound now. Nothing, not even war, will keep us apart."

She threw her arms around him, holding back tears. And then he was back on his horse, his face hidden by his helmet as he rode to the front of the squadron.

The royal family and the gathered villagers watched until the last soldier disappeared over the hill, bound for the border.

Saraj rested her arm around Bryn's shoulders, hugging her tight. "He'll be fine," Saraj reassured her, at the same time that she reached out to squeeze Trei's hand beside her. She gave the eldest prince an adoring look. "Love is a powerful thing."

* * *

As soon as Rangar was gone, Bryn felt his absence terribly. For her safety, the king forbade her from continuing her work in the barn with the lambs and confined her to the castle grounds or the village square, always accompanied by two guards. She was beginning to feel like a bird in a gilded cage: she was safe and had every comfort she could ask for, except for one —Rangar.

But she felt for the ring in her pocket, assuring herself that they were not only engaged but soulbound; as Saraj said, love had to count for something. As the days passed with no news from the army, she busied herself in the castle library reading Trei's guides to the various kingdoms and history of the Eyrie, learning about the geography and topography of the land, studying the philosophy of past rulers.

But no matter how much she studied, it felt insufficient. She was the crown heir to a kingdom she didn't even live in and whose people would likely murder her if she ever set foot in again—how was she supposed to rule from exile even with Rangar by her side?

Somehow, she would have to return to the Mirien—to her home. And hope her own people didn't string her up on the same gallows as the rest of her family.

43

AN ENGAGEMENT...VAL AND TREI...THE KING'S OFFER...THE NEW QUEEN...RANGAR'S FURY

a week after Rangar departed to go to war, Bryn was once more summoned to the council chambers. She didn't feel as apprehensive this time upon facing King Aleth and Mage Marna. They had received a report only the day before that Rangar's squadron was safe and had suffered no casualties. And her time in the library studying governance and history had given her more confidence in her newfound position.

Besides, she thought with a mix of incredulity and hope, *Aleth Barendur is going to be my father-in-law soon.*

"Ah, Bryn." As soon as she entered the chambers, the king flicked his fingers toward the guards, dismissing them. "Come. Sit." He motioned to a wooden chair at the table.

Mage Marna and Valenden were already present. Valenden leaned casually against the window frame, gazing out at the laundry women in the courtyard below stringing up sheets to dry; from this angle, Bryn suspected he had a nice view down their shirts. She fought the urge to roll her eyes.

Mage Marna paced by the door, glancing down the hall as though looking for someone.

King Aleth explained gruffly, "We are waiting for Trei to begin."

"Has there been more news from the army?" Bryn asked.

The king scratched his nose, saying curtly, "A messenger this morning reported that they are riding south to check on the villages near Bluefin Lake. There have been no further altercations with Captain Carr's army."

Bryn nodded, relieved at the news.

Footsteps sounded in the hall, and Trei appeared in the doorway. As soon as he entered, Mage Marna closed the council door. Bryn sat up a little more at attention. They rarely closed the council door.

The king cleared his throat. "I won't mince words. Lady Bryn, you are aware of your newfound position as crown heir to the Mir throne, and I believe you have been studying the rules of succession, is that correct?" His eyes shifted to Trei.

Bryn glanced at Trei, too, who had been the one to show her the books in the library. "That's right."

She was starting to get a strange premonition that something was off. The king rarely looked her in the eye, but she'd always gotten the sense before that it was because she wasn't significant enough; now, however, she felt as though he was *intentionally* avoiding her gaze.

She twisted her hands in her lap where they couldn't see. She glanced at Valenden and raised an eyebrow in a silent question. He shrugged, as uninformed as she was.

"Then you are aware," King Aleth continued, "that as queen of the Mirien, your position is one of importance but not ultimate leadership. It will be your husband who assumes reign over the Mirien, not you."

"Yes, that's what I understand, though it seems an archaic rule."

He nodded. "The wheel of time moves slowly. Neither you nor I will change centuries of tradition in our lifetimes."

She shifted uncomfortably, throwing looks between Valenden, who appeared as bored and detached as he always did, and Trei, who patiently listened to his father, and Mage Marna, who was chewing anxiously on her lip. That didn't make Bryn feel any more reassured—hardly anything rattled Mage Marna.

Bryn blurted out, "Rangar's all right, isn't he?"

The mage lifted her chin and reassured her, "Of course. As far as we know, there is no reason to suspect he is in danger."

Bryn relaxed, but the voice in the back of her head whispering something was off didn't go away.

The king cleared his throat again. "It is in the interest of both our kingdoms for you to marry a Baer prince, so a Baer king will ultimately sit on the Mir throne. By consolidating the kingdoms under one rule, we benefit from the Mirien's fields and harvests, without which we couldn't get through our winters. And the Mirien gets strong, stable leadership."

She nodded slowly. "Yes, that's how I understand it." She and Rangar had already discussed this, and she knew that Rangar had spoken about it with his family. Though he didn't want the throne, he was willing to step up and do his duty.

She rested her palms on the table, fingers extended, still waiting to hear whatever challenging news the king was getting at. She wished he would simply speak directly. In the past few weeks, she had learned the hard way how to receive difficult news. She'd been informed of her family's death. Her kingdom's downfall. Her brother's murder. What could he possibly tell her that would be worse than what she'd already been through?

King Aleth's face was unreadable. He'd always been a gruff man but not unkind, and Bryn wasn't sure what to make of the strange silence coming from him now. He finally drew in a breath and said, "If that is what you wish, then in two days, you must marry Trei."

For a moment, time seemed to go still. Bryn had the disorienting feeling that she was still trapped in that awful dream from a few nights before when so much had gone wrong. Her palms on the table began to sweat. She blinked slowly, trying to focus.

Her eyes slid to Trei.

The eldest Baer prince's back had gone ramrod straight. Trei had been schooled in diplomacy well enough that masking his true emotions was second nature to him; even so, his shock was apparent.

"Father," Trei stammered, "you mean *Rangar*..."

"I don't," King Aleth said firmly.

Valenden shoved up from where he'd been languishing by the window and cried, "Father, what the—"

The king silenced him with a stern look. Then he turned to Trei. "Your aunt and I have discussed this at length with our advisors, and it is the only way to ensure security for both the Baersladen and the Mirien. You, Trei, are set to inherit our kingdom. Bryn will now inherit hers. This means that you will be king over both realms when you wed. They can consolidate into a single kingdom under a single ruler."

Bryn still hadn't even begun to process her shock. Trei's eyes were wide. His breathing wasn't as steady as it had been a moment ago. It was small comfort to know that he hadn't been made aware of this situation beforehand, either, but she still felt aghast. She stared at the eldest prince in a stupor.

Marry *Trei*?

"I don't..." She closed her mouth and started again. "I don't understand why that's necessary. Rangar and I are betrothed. He will become king of the Mirien. Both kingdoms will still be under joint rule between our families."

For the first time, Trei's attention riveted to Bryn. His eyes wavered with unspoken worries that matched her own. She wondered what must be going through his head. King Aleth hadn't once mentioned Saraj in all of this.

"I'm afraid that isn't possible," Mage Marna informed them. "We've been looking into all options, and this is the only way. The rulership system agreed upon five hundred years ago in the Eyrie's foundation requires that royal siblings not maintain rival monarchies. Bryn, that is why your sister was betrothed to a duke, not a prince, and why you were aligned with a baron. Neither you nor Elysander could be the queen of any kingdom since Mars was set to become king."

Bryn blinked, uncertain. She'd read something about this in the reference books, but it had been written in archaic legal language, difficult to comprehend. "This is a lot to understand."

Mage Marna said, "Do you know the legend of Wynn and Niall?"

Still dazed by everything she'd heard, Bryn said, "The children's story?"

"The story is based on real history," Mage Marna explained. "Wynn and Niall were princes and brothers who wanted to marry princesses from two different kingdoms. They both became king of their respective kingdom and…"

"…and it tore both kingdoms apart," Val interrupted hotly. "We know the story."

Trei stepped forward and said, "I know the old rules, but surely an exception can be made."

The king and the mage remained silent, which spoke volumes.

"Fairness and happiness are rare luxuries afforded to royal children," Mage Marna said.

Bryn felt like wild horses had trampled her and left her

bruised and bleeding in the mud. Starting to feel panicked, she said, "There must be another way."

King Aleth walked around the table and rested a hand on her shoulder, a small kindness that felt like a drop in the bucket compared to the ocean currently drowning her heart. "The decision is yours, Bryn. And that goes for you, too, Trei. We don't force our children into marriages here as they do in other kingdoms. That said, we have brought you into this family and will treat you as one of our own. This is the same advice I'd give you if you were my blood daughter. If you marry Rangar, you will have to give up the Mir throne, which will throw the Mirien into even greater violence and uncertainty. Your kingdom is already at the breaking point—I don't believe your people can withstand much more. The only way our advisors see a peaceful resolution is if you marry Trei and consolidate the kingdoms."

Bryn's hands started shaking as she realized they were completely earnest. This was the only way for her to save her people. No one was going to swoop in now with another option to save them all.

Bryn twisted her body toward Trei, staring at this man who she didn't love. *It can't be. I can't marry Trei. It's Rangar I love.*

"What do you think of this?" she asked, still trying to wrap her mind around any other options. "Would you truly break your betrothal?"

Trei ran a hand over his face and said in a hollow voice, "Saraj and I aren't betrothed. Not officially. Saraj wasn't ready for marriage and all that she would have to give up."

The regal mask over Trei's face was slipping, revealing anguish beneath. Bryn could only imagine the intense thoughts and fears going through his head. Whether their relationship was formal or not, he and Saraj were clearly in love and planned on a lifetime together.

Saraj was her closest friend. *She'd be heartbroken.*

But Bryn had more pressing fears. Quietly, she asked, "Does Rangar know about this...possibility?"

"Of course not," Mage Marna said quietly. "Why do you think we sent him away to the edge of the kingdom?"

Bryn hit her with a fierce look. "You sent him to *war* to get him out of the way?"

"Rangar's blood runs hot," Mage Marna said. "I don't have to tell you that. He's been possessive over you since you were eight years old and besotted with you since you were fifteen. He learned Mir just to be able to speak with you. Asked us to risk our lives to get you out of Castle Mir and shelter you here. If he was here now, hearing that the only way to save your kingdom was to marry his brother, do you think any of us would leave the room with our heads?"

Bryn wanted to argue. Heat was flushing through her body. But she couldn't find the words to contradict the mage. *It was true—every word.* Rangar was viciously possessive and had a hair-trigger temper. When Valenden had kissed Bryn the night of the Harvest Gathering, Rangar had broken his own brother's nose. His jealousy combined with sibling rivalry would be an explosive force.

"He'll find out when he returns," she cried. "You can't keep it from him forever!"

Mage Marna nodded. Though her face looked calm, her hands tapped anxiously on the table. "That's why the wedding would have to happen within two days. If you and Trei marry, it will have to be before he returns. He won't be able to stop it. And once it's done, he'll have no choice but to respect the law or be thrown in the dungeon."

Bryn's eyes shot to King Aleth. Did Rangar's father know about the nights they'd shared? The confessions Rangar had whispered against her skin? It would be a disaster if Rangar returned and found his betrothed married to his brother!

As though mirroring her thoughts, Valenden said, "Trei, Rangar will *murder* you if you go through with this."

King Aleth rested his hands on the table in a way that silenced everyone. Slowly, he said, "We've laid out the situation. Now you two must decide if you'd rather marry or plunge both kingdoms into warfare." He faced his son. "I've never held my thoughts back from you, Trei. I know this isn't what you intended, but thousands will die if this marriage doesn't happen. You would do well, as future king, to consider your people before yourself. You have a choice, but I fear it is, in effect, no choice at all."

Trei's cheeks were burning. A pained look filled his face. As much as he loved Saraj and didn't want to hurt Rangar, he was the noblest person Bryn knew. He would do whatever was necessary to ensure success for his kingdom, and if it meant a political union, so be it.

"I don't think I can," Bryn choked out. "Rangar and I…" She didn't finish, nor did she need to. Everyone in the room was well aware of their relationship. Trei and Valenden both hung back, looking as shocked as she felt, but the king and Mage Marna were older, more accustomed to such difficult situations.

King Aleth said, "Lady Bryn, these past few months, I've seen you grow from a naïve slip of a girl into a woman who puts in a hard day's work, who looks everyone in the eye, whether a king or a servant, who understands the responsibilities of her station. You've expressed regret for your parents' crimes. You've admitted your own faults. You've done what you can to make the Mir refugees feel at home here. Now, you are no longer naïve. It is up to you to decide if you want to go back to your parents' way, putting your own interests above those of your people. Or if you will sacrifice for them."

Though his words were harsh, there was no judgment in them. He was simply stating the facts: Bryn had a choice. She could either marry Rangar and let her kingdom suffer or accept Trei and have both the Mirien and the Baersladen thrive.

As the king had posed to his son, it wasn't really a choice at all.

She stared at the king. Then at Trei: the crown prince, the most judicious of all of them. It felt impossible that this prince could be her husband. The handsome eldest son, the one so many girls swooned over even though they knew he was sworn to Saraj. Bryn had always admired Trei and respected his cool head and devotion to his kingdom, but now that same devotion was going to be her downfall.

Marry Trei? And what about everything that came with that? *Bed him every night, provide him heirs...*

It would kill her. It would kill *Rangar*. She pressed a hand to her chest, feeling already like her heart was breaking.

"This is a terrible idea," Valenden observed coolly, then opened the door and stomped out of the room, slamming it behind him.

The room was deathly silent. Bryn closed her eyes, trying to steady her racing heart. When she opened them, King Aleth was watching her closely.

"I'll give the two of you time to discuss this amongst yourselves," he said, looking between Trei and Bryn. "Debate whatever you must, but we need an answer by tonight. We dare not wait more than the day after tomorrow for the wedding."

He and Mage Marna left. Bryn felt a self-conscious flush spread up her neck; she'd rarely been alone with Trei. Out of the three Barendur brothers, he was the one she knew the least. She finally found the courage to look him in the eye.

"I understand it's what is best for our kingdoms," she whispered, "but you know Rangar won't stand for this. Even if he also wants what is best for the people, his temper will blind him."

Trei paced the length of the table next to where she sat. "We've had disputes before, the three of us brothers. Even fights over women. We've always gotten over it. His temper will cool in time."

"He and I are *engaged*."

"It isn't what I want, either," Trei said, stopping his pacing. "I mean you no offense, but my heart lies with Saraj. Still, I have to do what is best for the Baersladen, as my father said."

"And what about Saraj? What will you tell her?"

A pained look flickered over his face. "Saraj will understand in time. She's always known that my duty comes first." He hesitated. "Love isn't something people like you and I can ever have. I was a fool ever to think otherwise. Maybe if we weren't the heirs, then we could marry for love. But that isn't our position."

She braced her elbows on the table, burying her face in her hands. Not that long ago, she'd accepted the fact that she'd marry Baron Marmose or whoever else her mother had picked out for her. She'd understood then that most princesses didn't marry for love. But that was before she'd known what love was.

Trei pulled out a chair and sat next to her. "Bryn, listen. If we do this, I swear to be faithful to you. I will be fair. I will be the best husband I can be to you. I'll not touch Saraj or any other woman."

She dropped her hands and gave him an incredulous look. "Of course, Trei. I know you wouldn't." She hesitated. "I wouldn't, either."

Her face flushed as that fact sank in. Never kiss Rangar again? Never whisper wicked thoughts together at night?

As though he could read her mind, he said, "I know that you prefer my brothers—both of them—to me. And I love Saraj. I think I always will. But if we must put our kingdoms over our hearts, it doesn't have to mean misery for us. You and I have always gotten along. We can start from a place of friendship, see what grows in time. Sometimes love isn't about stolen kisses in dark closets. It can grow. Perhaps it can grow between us."

Trei held out his hand, palm up, on the table. It was shaking a little.

He was significantly older than her, had spent most of his life preparing to be king. Though it was breaking his heart, he'd had many years' practice in putting the good of his people before his own, and his mind seemed made up, even if his heart was elsewhere.

Bryn didn't know what to do. What to think. When she had walked into the council chamber, she'd had no idea how life-altering the next few minutes would be. Her entire body was a knot of anguish and indecision, utterly bereft at the thought of losing Rangar.

If this was the only way to ensure the safety of both the Baersladen and the Mirien, what choice did she have? Was she really so selfish that she would place her own heart over the good of her kingdom? Her whole childhood had been spent frolicking, ignorant of the people's suffering around her. When she'd come to the Baersladen, she'd sworn never to follow in her parents' footsteps taking advantage of the people they were supposed to rule benevolently. Now, the crown was hers.

It came down to her own happiness or the good of her kingdom.

She closed her eyes, pained, knowing what she had to do.

Slowly, she placed her hand in Trei's.

Rangar was going to be heartbroken when he learned that his family had conspired behind his back to marry her to Trei. *Trei* would bed Bryn on their wedding night, not him; *Trei* would start a family with her, not him; *Trei* would rule as king by her side. And what would Rangar do as he seethed all the while, furiously watching his brother and his intended bride together every day?

He would try to tear the world apart.

Bryn swallowed hard, knowing how bad it would be when Rangar returned to Barendur Hold. But he would have to live with it, just as she would.

We're soulbound.

She felt that deep connection keenly and knew that her heart would always be with him...but her hand now belonged to someone else.

END OF BOOK ONE

CONTINUE THE ADVENTURE

Not ready for *Scarlight* to end? Continue the series right now with *Scarbound*!

THE FULL CASTLES OF THE EYRIE SERIES

Scarlight, Book One

Scarbound, Book Two

Scarcrossed, Book Three

Princes of the Outlands, a prequel novella

ALSO BY EVIE MARCEAU

Welcome to Wilde Tower, Manhattan's most private address—and home to a powerful fae court.

When Willow answers a mysterious nanny ad, she's shocked to learn the employer is the handsome and reclusive billionaire Severn Wilde—and even more surprised when he reveals himself to be a fae prince.

Willow never dreamed that the fae bedtime stories her mother told her as a child were real. Now, Severn grants Willow the fae sight, allowing her to see the hidden magical world of the Gifted Ones. But as wondrous as his realm is, the greatest risk of all might be falling for her arrogant, cold, achingly handsome employer—the one person she can't have.

KEEP IN TOUCH WITH EVIE!

Visit Evie's website at www.eviemarceau.com or connect on Facebook, Instagram, and TikTok.

Join the newsletter at www.eviemarceau.com/newsletter for a free book!

ABOUT THE AUTHOR

Evie Marceau writes fantasies to satisfy her nagging curiosity that there is more out there just beyond the veil. She is the author of romantic fantasies with a touch of darkness and hint of magic.

www.eviemarceau.com

eviemarceaubooks@gmail.com

www.eviemarceau.com/newsletter
(PS: get a free book when you join!)

Printed in Great Britain
by Amazon